DEAD CLEVER

As soon as I got close to him I could understand what Cress had meant about the smell. It wasn't just that Jason hadn't washed for a long time; his blue Oasis T-shirt was stained with vomit and his white jeans yellowly encrusted with what I assumed must be urine. As well as this, he looked as if he'd been on some kind of hike: his shoes and trousers were coated with dried mud and his T-shirt ripped slightly on one arm.

'She's dead,' he said, pronouncing the words slowly as if his tongue was too big for his mouth. 'And I couldn't do anything.'

'No one could do anything, Jason,' I said calmly. 'I'm afraid sometimes we just can't help—'

'Shut up!' he shouted, making me jump and my heart start to race. 'Please. Just, just . . . Shut. Up.'

'I'm going to fetch someone who can help.'

'I saw it,' Jason said simply, sounding almost normal. 'I saw it happen.'

'What?' I asked. 'What did you see?'

About the author

Scarlett Thomas is twenty-five and lives in Devon. She is a journalist and a writer. Her second Lily Pascale novel, *In Your Face*, is available in Hodder & Stoughton hardback.

Dead Clever

Scarlett Thomas

NEW ENGLISH LIBRARY
Hodder & Stoughton

First published in Great Britain in 1998
by Hodder and Stoughton
A division of Hodder Headline PLC
First published in paperback in 1999
by Hodder and Stoughton
A New English Library Paperback

10 9 8 7 6 5 4 3 2 1

A CIP catalogue record for this title
is available from the British Library.

ISBN 0 340 71834 X

Typeset by Hewer Text Ltd, Edinburgh
Printed and bound in Great Britain by
Clays Ltd, St Ives PLC

Hodder and Stoughton
A division of Hodder Headline PLC
338 Euston Road
London NW1 3BH

For Tom

ACKNOWLEDGEMENTS

Thank you to my parents, Francesca and Couze, for everything. Thanks also to Gordian, my brothers Hari and Sam, to Kirsty, Dinah and Tom.

EPIGRAPH

'We need the books that affect us like a disaster, that grieve us deeply, like the death of someone we loved far more than ourselves, like being banished into forests far from everyone, like suicide. A book must be the axe for the frozen sea inside us' – Franz Kafka

'Once my fancy was soothed with dreams of virtue, of fame, and of enjoyment. Once I falsely hoped to meet with beings who, pardoning my outward form, would love me for the excellent qualities which I was capable of unfolding. I was nourished with high thoughts of honour and devotion. But now . . . no misery can be found comparable to mine' – Mary Shelley, *Frankenstein*

PROLOGUE

The boy emerged from the tunnel and walked as quietly as he could across the stone until he was finally on the grass, following a man who was following a girl; trying to work out how he could stop what was going on. He couldn't see his way very well in the dark. As the path grew narrower, the lights dimmed until eventually he walked into the blackness of the forest, guided only by the voices and the faint torchlight up ahead.

The boy was jealous, really, that was all. He knew the man and the girl were having an affair. But he loved her, and tonight he was going to tell her: him or me. That was what he had planned to say: him or me. An ultimatum, yes, but a reasonable one. She had been leading him on with empty promises for too long. So he was going to do it, tonight.

CHAPTER ONE

Big City, Bright Lights

With my voice raised I spoke the words again.

'*Over*, Anthony. It's over.'

'No.'

'Yes.'

This had been going on for the last three hours. Scene: his flat, Islington, into which I had recently moved. I ran my hand through my long hair and sighed as my fingers caught in a tangled curl. The message just wasn't getting through.

'Lil, *please*,' said Anthony desperately.

'My name is not Lil.'

'You never minded before.'

'Well, I do now. My name is Lily.'

'Okay, whatever you say.' Anthony started pacing in the large spacious room, looking fraught and disbelieving, his footsteps echoing on the bare pine floorboards. I knew for a fact that no one had ever dared leave Anthony before and this was all a great shock to him but I wasn't going to let that stop me. Some things just had to be said.

In the middle of the room my half-Siamese cat, Maude, sat purring inappropriately, her small triangular face bobbing comically as she watched Anthony stomp up and down. Next to her was a Grecian urn which, when she tired of watching Anthony, she returned to sniffing furtively, trying to work out what it was and where it had come from. The urn made a good centerpiece since it was the reason for this argument, on the surface at least.

I had bought the urn this afternoon, in Covent Garden, where I had been auditioning for a part in a play which I hadn't got. I was at a loose end: still in London after finishing my degree two years ago; still trying out careers as if they were blouses in the Whistles sale. I'd taught contemporary literature at a community college while I did my MA but there weren't any career prospects in that. Looking for a career with *prospects* was my way of justifying my prolonged stay in London. Most of my family was still in Devon, where I grew up, and I couldn't help feeling a pang of nostalgia when I remembered how easy life had been there; or at least had been when I was still a child.

The audition was my first attempt at a professional part; the only other acting I had done was as part of Freak Show theatre company which was semi-professional and totally avant-garde. I had only decided to act full-time last week; I needed a lot of money and didn't mind the idea of fame – neither of which I would acquire by teaching. I was trying to fill a big gap in my life and if a change of career wouldn't do it, I had reasoned, then shopping might. The urn was an impulse buy, like most of my purchases, and had been intended to bring some character to this, *our* flat. Anthony had thought otherwise, of course. He was a minimalist, or so he claimed, which so far as I could see meant having one chair in the living room and loads of clutter in the cupboards. He objected to the urn and I objected to his objection. That was when the argument started.

I met him originally at the Stagecoach Theatre where he was working behind the bar and waiting for acting work. That was when Freak Show was running a feminist re-interpretation of *Hamlet* where Ophelia was the one that did it and knocked Hamlet off before he could find out. Anthony was very impressed that I was a 'serious' actress and we went out for a few drinks, ostensibly so I could advise him on his acting career. Eventually he did one commercial and from that moment on thought he was Robert de Niro. Our few dates, fuelled by his new-found celebrity, soon flowered into a full-blown relationship and shortly after his commercial came out, he left the Stagecoach so he could concentrate on his acting, which was unfortunate since he didn't get any more parts. I moved in at around that time, initially while I was looking for a new flat myself but inevitably for good, as a weekend became a week and the weeks became months and I stopped looking at the *To Let* section of the *Evening Standard*. That was six months ago. Now I was living with someone who just didn't do anything, which included paying the bills.

I looked at the numberless clock on the wall and worked out that it was gone seven o'clock. This meant I was certainly going to be late for work, which would have been a bigger deal had the job been any better than it was: barwork in the Underground Club. My wages were supposed to cover rent and bills but didn't scratch the surface. So it didn't matter that I wasn't going in. I had slipped so far into debt that I couldn't see any way out of it unless I got a good acting job or won the lottery. The urn had taken my last credit card to its limit and this fact, which I had been aware of but had ignored, thinking facetiously, *My money – my urn*, had been dwelt on at length by Anthony in the first two hours of the argument. Now it was getting personal.

Or less personal, depending on how you looked at it. We were breaking up, that was for sure, which made me unhappy, albeit in a rather tepid way. There had been a time when Anthony made me melt; when a little flick of his blond curls would have had me swooning like a Gothic heroine and a smile would have made me fall into his arms or his bed, whichever was the nearer. He looked like a Renaissance angel and talked like the man on the trailers at the cinema. Manly but gentle; intelligent but fun.

Or so I had thought.

As is often the case (according to magazines I read) the Anthony I moved in with was not the Anthony with whom I had enjoyed such profoundly passionate dates (for which I even painted my toenails dusky pink). The tornado in my heart whenever I saw him walk into the pub or get up in the morning had turned into something else: an irritation, a hair-prickling annoyance whenever he did *anything* but particularly the habits that had bothered me all along. Like tidying up after me (very New Man but also very distracting when I was trying to concentrate on something), complaining about my books (I had thousands and he had one) and the clutter they made in the flat, *liking* Pamela Anderson (she blonde and artificial, me brunette and natural – *you* work it out) and only shopping at Muji and Paul Smith (I preferred flea markets).

Hard though it was to admit, in the end Anthony turned out to be neither manly nor gentle, intelligent nor fun. I discovered all this in one traumatic evening about a month ago and things had been going downhill since then.

Anthony had run into the living room naked, having discovered a spider in the bath.

'Oh my God!' he'd squealed desperately, letting the pitch of his normally deep voice rise by an embarrassing amount. 'Lil, help!'

'What?'

'*Spider*. Kill it, *kill* it!'

'I'm not killing a living creature,' I said, assuming the moral high ground that applied to all animals except wasps and turning back to my book.

'Please!' he wailed. 'Get Maude to eat it.'

'She doesn't like spiders,' I said calmly, trying to ignore the sight of the man I was potentially relying on to save me from burglars or psychopaths in the middle of the night, hopping up and down like an overwrought schoolgirl. 'She likes mammals.'

'Don't be so semantic!'

'*Is* semantic an adjective?' I wondered aloud, thinking he probably meant pedantic and being unable to stop myself from teasing him. I burst into laughter at this point and went to fetch a glass to put over the spider so that I could release it.

On my return Anthony was sitting looking serious at my desk, staring at the cover of *The Name of the Rose*.

'Sometimes I wish I'd gone to university like you,' he said gruffly. 'I try to be interested in the stuff you're into but I'm just not. I hate using ten words when one will do and all that. I just hope you don't think I'm stupid.'

'No,' I said soothingly. 'Of course not.'

But once the thought was in my mind it stayed there, and however much I tried to make it go away it became apparent that Anthony and I were from different worlds. He had been to the *university of life*, as he called it, but what I knew about literature (my degree subject) and detective fiction (my MA thesis) greatly outstripped what I knew about sex, drugs and rock and roll. These things, however, were Anthony's area of expertise, along with minimalist art (interesting but not my thing) and the Stanislavski method. Sooner or later I had to face it: we just were not suited.

Then came the urn. If it went, I had decided, then so did I.

'Forget the urn,' said Anthony wearily as he turned to face me from the window where he had been standing in silence for the last ten minutes while I picked cat hair off my jumper. 'I suppose it can stay.'

'Oh, *thanks*,' I retorted. 'Is that supposed to be a favour?'

'It's ugly, Lily, can't you just accept that?'

'I like it. And, anyway, who made you the expert on *objets d'art*?'

'Can't you talk English for once?'

'That is English! Well – by adoption.'

'It'll just make everything look, well, *messy*. But then you are messy, aren't you?' said Anthony nastily, turning back to the window.

I felt tears prick my eyes as I realised this was going to be it.

'So what else don't you like about me?' I said, much more aggressively than I intended, tossing my hair and glaring at him, challenging him to insult me so I'd have a better reason to leave than the urn. 'Come on. What else?'

'Well, that, for a start,' said Anthony, gesturing at my

pose, which had now mutated into a full hands-on-hips, red-faced bodily *pout*. 'It's so fucking French. Why does every-thing have to be so difficult with you?'

'I am,' I said, 'as you put it, *fucking* French. And has it occurred to you that it's not me who's difficult – that it might just be you with all your stainless steel and *one chair*, for goodness' sake?'

'Oh, that's right. It's always my fault. Maybe if you weren't so . . .'

'So what?'

'Serious. Domineering.' He shook his head and lowered his voice. 'I don't know.'

'Serious? Domineering? Me? Oh, I see, you want some fluffy bunny who won't ever disagree with you. Like Dahlia.'

'This has nothing to do with Dahlia.'

'Except that you slept with her!'

'Yeah, but only because . . . Shit.'

'So you *did* sleep with her! I knew it. Because what? Because she likes the missionary position? Because she's blonde? I bet she's perfect for you.'

'What do you want me to say?' asked Anthony jadedly, as if I was making a fuss about nothing. 'I expect sorry won't be good enough for you.'

'No,' I said, flinging back my head defiantly. 'It won't. I think you'd better leave.'

'What?'

'Go on,' I said, forgetting it was his flat. 'Get out.'

'But it's my flat,' said Anthony, smiling.

I almost smiled too, and if I had then everything would probably have been okay. But I didn't, my pride wouldn't let me, and anyway I had to go at some point. Things just weren't working out.

Half an hour later, all the important things were packed. The only thing left to put in my car was my cat and possibly the urn, although I thought I might leave that as a souvenir.

'So where are you going to go?' asked Anthony smugly,

knowing I didn't really have anywhere much to go. I didn't have many close friends in London and although my father lived in Camden he wouldn't be back from Australia for another week. Camden would be too close anyway, considering I wanted to be a long way from here right now.

'Devon,' I said, sounding more uncertain than I'd intended.

'What?'

'Devon,' I repeated with more confidence. 'Back where I belong.'

'Yeah, right,' said Anthony. 'I hope you don't expect me to take you back when you get bored.'

'Don't hold your breath,' I said, reaching down to pick up my cat who squeaked at me, forgetting as usual that she could miaow if she tried hard enough.

Anthony's expression changed dramatically and he put his head in his hands. I wondered what he was thinking. I knew he wanted me to stay, but I suspected that might be because he would miss my credit cards and my wages if I went. He straightened up and looked at me seriously.

'Lily, why don't you stay? We could work everything out.'

'We've been through all that,' I said. 'I can't. It's over.'

'But Devon's so far away,' he pleaded.

'I know,' I said.

I picked up my cat, smiled deliciously and walked out, holding my head high. *Goodbye, Anthony*, I thought. *Goodbye, London*. I banged the door behind me and stepped into the street, feeling the first spot of an appropriate April shower fall on my cheek like a tear. I stopped for a minute and stared at my car, a dirty silver Volvo which contained everything I owned: not much, just books, tapes, clothes and my stereo. It looked like it had when I'd moved in last September, on a hot and heady day, full of optimism and plans. Now I was doing it in reverse.

I got in my car and started to drive.

★   ★   ★

I got as far as the shop on the corner of Anthony's road before realising that I should call my mother and tell her I was coming. I pulled up by the kerb and checked my change before running into the shop for some cigarettes and Coke for the journey, needing to have everything in place for the long drive and intending to call Mum after that.

I didn't spend as long as I usually would in the shop, looking at the racks of magazines, the stationery and all the musty shelves of kosher breads and meats, before walking to the counter to pay. I had always been a very enthusiastic shopper, feeling the need to inspect everything before deciding what to buy. I read an article once about how people got addicted to shopping because they craved the rush of serotonin to the brain when they made a purchase. There was something else today, though, something to explain my distraction and the tear in my eye when I said 'bye to the shopkeeper. Today I meant it. I knew I was never coming back.

I threw the cold can of Coke and fresh powder blue packet of Gauloises down on the passenger seat and grabbed my mobile phone from the dashboard. My hand was shaking and I realised I still hadn't calmed down properly yet after the argument. Operating in crisis mode involved *doing* now and *thinking* later so, without allowing myself to dwell too heavily on everything. I lit a much-needed cigarette and started pushing the small squelchy buttons on the phone. As I did so I wondered vaguely why Anthony hadn't yet called to beg me to come back. Then I saw Dahlia, who lived miles away in Camberwell, drive past and pull up outside the flat. This confused me for a minute, as I couldn't work out how she could have got there so quickly. Then it dawned on me: I was meant to be at work and she would have been here anyway, whether Anthony and I had split up or not. At that moment I realised that we really were history: this was it, it was *over*. Needing to just drive I switched off the phone, put the car into gear and accelerated out of London, eventually hitting the M4 in such a daze that I really wasn't sure how I'd got there.

CHAPTER TWO

Wild at Heart

———◦≫◦◦◦≪◦———

The motorway calmed me down. I found it both hypnotic and restful just driving down the same road at the same speed for what seemed like an age, watching night fall steadily but slowly, as the sun set in the same direction I was driving. The composition of society always seemed to be intriguingly mirrored on the motorway: drunk lorry drivers avoided; nice-looking families in estate cars given way to; and friendly warnings of rain, accidents or police speed traps provided by the muted orange pulse of hazard lights ahead. I set the radio on the local frequency and amused myself with the way the stations changed; Kiss FM, which reminded me of Anthony gradually became Berkshire Radio and then a Bristol station I'd never heard before.

As I drove I started to get a funny feeling in my stomach, like loneliness but not as unpleasant. I realised that no one had spoken to me for a few hours, that I didn't have to answer to anyone or ask their opinion. I was all on my own and, surprisingly, it felt good. I shivered inside when I realised that what I was feeling was the thrill of independence and it was exhilarating. I'd been stuck in a rut for far too long and now I was breaking free.

Just past Bristol I decided to stop to try and clear my head (I'd smoked too much) and get something to eat. I pulled into a service station and got out of the car, feeling my legs go weak and my stomach wobble at the feeling of the hard concrete, motionless beneath my feet. I looked at my watch and saw that it was almost ten o'clock. I yawned and moved slowly and creakily to the bright entrance, still hearing Anthony's voice playing in my head like an over-sampled record. Had I done the right thing, I wondered as I walked through the expansive bright hallway. And, more importantly, had I been fair? Then I remembered Dahlia and put the whole thing out of my mind. I was independent now, and free.

With these thoughts in mind I walked to the Ladies' to apply a fresh coat of the red lipstick that Anthony had always hated and to wash my hands. I hadn't even stopped to think that I was all alone until the door burst open and a girl ran in, still laughing at some joke that had been left outside in the artificial brightness of the corridor. Suddenly immersed in silence she stopped abruptly and went into one of the cubicles, from which the sound of giggling shortly came. It must have been a good joke, I thought, then dried my hands and left.

The restaurant (if you could call it that) had been eerily empty when I walked in, but now it was full of life, colour and noise. This perplexed me for a moment and I couldn't work out where so many people had come from until I saw the three massive coaches parked outside with people still spilling off them.

I queued behind an endless line of young men until I was jolted out of my thoughts by a friendly woman wielding a cake-slice behind the counter.

'Bloody students,' she said, looking at the boys she had just served, who all seemed to think they were Liam Gallagher. 'You look pale, dear, are you all right?'

'Yes,' I said, watching the affected side-burned swagger of one lad fade off to the till before turning back to the woman. 'Just a long drive, that's all.'

I ordered a black coffee and two doughnuts which I ate quickly, wanting to get out of here and back on the road as soon as possible. When I had finished, and just as the coach-party was beginning a food-fight, I stood up and hurried out, ducking a bread roll as I went. There was a newsagent just before the exit so I stopped there to buy some more Coke to keep me going for the rest of the journey, lingering by the clotted-cream fudge for longer than necessary, intrigued by the cottage scenes on the front, and the tourist ideal of the West Country, trying to remember if it really was like that.

'Excuse me,' said a man's voice from behind me, his German intonation cutting through his words and making him sound quite sinister. I turned around to find a small thin man wearing wire-rimmed glasses and carrying a well-worn rucksack from which the dog-eared edges of books and pieces of paper poked out. He looked and sounded like a prime-time mad scientist from a cold-war TV drama, but seemed harmless enough.

'Yes?' I replied.

'We're looking for *De*-von,' said a girl, walking out from behind one of the shelves. Her voice was distinctly American and made the word 'Devon' into a question, the way you would pronounce the name of a place whose existence as well as location you were questioning. I laughed and pointed at the motorway.

'You just keep going really,' I said. 'You're on the right road. Did you think you were lost?'

'She did,' said the man crisply. 'She can't read maps.'

'Aw, Hans,' said the girl. 'Stop teasing me.'

He smiled. 'We have been travelling for several weeks now. We have done Mexico, Europe . . .

'*Scot*-land.'

'Yes. We have been a long way. I am sorry to have disturbed you, we just wanted to check that we were on the right, um, track.'

'Stop apologising,' said the girl, hitting him playfully on the arm. 'It's so European.'

As a couple they looked good: neat, tidy and slightly worn around the edges, like academics on holiday. In fact, I suspected they *were* academics on holiday. They both had earnest, bookish faces and the girl's long mousy hair was pulled into a long plait down her back.

'I'm Dell,' she said. 'Are you from Devon?'

'No,' I said, playing the game I used to play on holiday as a child. 'I'm from Australia.'

'A wonderful country,' said Hans. 'We really want to go there again.'

'What's your name?' asked Dell.

'Nancy,' I said, continuing the game. It was slightly out of character for me but fun (and all part of being an actress, which I suspected I wouldn't be now but never mind), pretending to be someone else when you met strangers you were never going to see again.

'Well, Nancy,' said Hans, patting me on the arm. 'Thank you for your instructions.'

'We just keep going, right?' said Dell.

'Yes,' I said, smiling. 'Just keep going for a couple of hours and you'll get there.'

We said our goodbyes and I walked to the counter to pay for my drink. As I passed the place where Hans had stood I noticed a thin piece of paper lying on the ground. I assumed it must be his, but when I ran out of the doors after them the couple seemed to have vanished. I looked at it briefly and saw that it was a flyer; a very psychedelic-looking party invitation − lost litter from suburban streets that I hadn't seen since the end of the eighties. I took about as much notice of it now as I had done then, never having been very interested in drug culture. I winced, remembering how Anthony used to go on about 1988 and the summer of love when he'd done acid for the first time (at Glastonbury). All I remembered about 1988 was being excited about leaving my stuffy school and starting my A levels at the local sixth-form college with my best friend Eugénie. I stuck the flyer in my pocket and walked back to my car, vaguely thinking I might run into Dell and Hans again further down the motorway.

It was getting late and I imagined Mum waiting for me to get in, like she did in the old days, and me being late as usual.

Damn! I suddenly realised she wouldn't be waiting for me because I hadn't rung her. Suddenly feeling more lonely than just alone, I reached for my mobile and dialled her number, hoping she hadn't already gone to bed.

I felt the lump I thought I'd left in London develop in my throat as I listened to the distant ringing of the phone. Eventually she answered.

'Hi, Mum, it's me,' I said, trying not to sound tearful.

'Lily,' she said, sounding surprised and tired. 'Hello, darling. How are you?'

'Fine. Well, kind of.'

'Oh, you sound miserable. What on earth's the matter?'

'I didn't get the part.'

'Never mind. At least you'll be able to look for a real job now.'

'It would have been a real job!' I said, not wanting to have another row, and feeling the lump thicken in my throat.

'How's Anthony?' asked Mum through a yawn.

'Not very good.'

'Oh dear, what's wrong?'

'We've split up.'

'Oh dear.'

'Actually, Mum, I was thinking of coming for a little holiday. Can I borrow your spare room for a few weeks?'

'Of course you can. You haven't been for so long.'

'Sorry, Mum. It's hard for me, you know, because of . . .'

'I know, darling, you don't have to explain. But since you *are* coming back, you might want to know that they're looking for a new lecturer at the university to do some part-time hours and I was wondering . . .' I groaned. Mum was known for her slightly bad timing and although I knew she cared about me a lot, I wasn't in the mood for planning my future at the moment; just getting to Devon in one piece would be enough for me.

'I'll think about it,' I said. 'I'm really not sure what I'm going to do next. I need something new but . . .' I trailed off, not wanting to have this conversation (one we'd had many times before because Mum thought I should *want* to be a teacher) on the phone in the middle of a service station car park.

'You might find it's only temporary anyway,' she said. 'I think they're in a spot because the girl they did have left very abruptly.'

'I'll think about it,' I said again. 'Let's see how I feel when I get there.'

'When are you coming?'

'Is tonight all right? I'm kind of on my way now.'

'Oh, I see,' said Mum, sounding surprised. 'Well, of course. Maybe you can talk some sense into your brother. Oh! He's trying to grab the phone from me. *Get off!*'

'Mum? Are you still there?'

'Yes. *Get off*. Hello?'

'I'll see you later. Or,' I said, looking at my watch, 'probably tomorrow morning at this rate.'

'Okay. It'll be lovely to see you, darling. Your room has seemed *so* empty since you left.'

'I'm not moving back in, Mum. I'm twenty-five now.'

'Yes, of course. I'll see you tomorrow. Oh, here's your dreadful brother.'

My brother Nat was nineteen and in his first year of a degree course at the local university where Mum also worked. I was glad he was still living at home otherwise Mum would have been on her own in the middle of nowhere. After the divorce, my feckless but sweet father, Henri, moved to London to set up his own psychiatry practice. He did very well and now had an office on Harley Street and one of the reasons I never saw him was because he was constantly either curing or entertaining his multitude of celebrity clients.

'Lily?'

'Hi, Nat. I can't talk for long – I'm on the mobile. How are you?'

'Yeah, really good actually. Are you coming to stay?'

'Yep.'

'Cool.' He sounded excited. 'And are you going to work at the university?'

'I don't know yet. It depends.'

'Yeah, well, if you do you'll get to see all the investigation and everything.'

'What?'

'This girl, in the year above Beth, right?' He paused dramatically. Beth was his girlfriend and had been since they were at school together. 'She got murdered yesterday. Isn't it exciting?'

'Exciting?' It sounded dreadful.

'You know what I mean. I don't mean *exciting* exciting, it's just that nothing like that ever happens around here.'

'Thank God. What happened?' I couldn't help being curious, even though I knew I should get off the phone. My interest in detective fiction had not led to an interest in real-life crime, but once someone started a story, however real it was, I always felt compelled to know the end, the *whodunnit*, although preferably with as little detail as possible.

'Nobody knows. But there are police everywhere and there's this rumour going round that they found her body and not her head.'

'How awful,' I said, trying to stop all the hideous images invading my mind. I'd thought you only got headless corpses in films and fiction. A *real* one? The idea made me shudder involuntarily and I suddenly felt more wary than I had of driving through the night on my own. I pressed the central-locking button in my car and felt the reassuring click as all the doors locked themselves.

'I should get off the phone,' I said. 'You'll have to tell me all about it later.'

'Do you want me to wait up?' Nat asked.

'If you don't mind. I probably won't get there until gone midnight.'

'Okay. Mum will probably have gone to bed, but I'll be here.'

'Good.'

'I've got loads of things to tell you.'

'Yeah, me too.'

I switched off the phone and started the car once more, leaving London even further behind me as the alternately black and grey concrete moved beneath the car like a conveyor belt once again. I wanted to think that it would be forever, that I would never go back, but I knew that to be unrealistic. My future was probably going to be in London and Devon was going to be just a temporary thing; like a holiday. I didn't think there would be many career opportunities for someone like me in the small village where I grew up and, bad memories aside, if I remembered correctly, the pace of life was too slow there even for me.

The voice was clear and soft – the voice he loved.

'Why did you bring me here?'

'I told you, there's someone I want you to meet.' The man's voice, also recognisable, was slow and deliberate.

'I'm cold,' the girl said crossly. Then, with a touch more humour: 'This is why we usually stay inside.'

'Yes.'

'What if someone sees us?'

'They won't. We were careful, weren't we?'

'Yes, I suppose so.'

The boy shrank down into the undergrowth, sick with himself, sick with the SITUATION. Was he anything more than a despicable voyeur, he wondered. Then his thoughts were broken again by the girl's voice, sounding softer and cracked.

'Why won't you touch me anymore? Is it because of her? I knew nothing would change once she left . . .'

Silence.

The muted glare from the lights on the other side of the river caught the lens of the camera, but only just, as the small dark figure moved stealthily through the trees. The boy ducked out of the way as the camera swung around, almost catching him on film as he moved quickly behind a tree.

The dull thud caught him by surprise. He didn't know what it was, except that it was followed by a gasp and then more silence. A slight protest from the man – he hadn't been expecting it to be like this – then another thud, and then a fast scraping noise that the boy couldn't place but which indicated an almost-silent frenzy; probably sexual.

The girl was on the ground now, as always, so the boy just waited. He could go to her afterwards, he thought. With his ultimatum.

'I suppose we could just leave it here,' said the man eventually. 'I mean, they have to find it sooner or later.'

'That would make sense,' said a voice the boy didn't recognise: the dark figure, the late arrival. 'Dump this somewhere, then.'

The man took the stick and threw it in the bushes. The boy didn't know what they had used it for. There had been no noise, except for the scraping and that weird silent shuffling. The two figures moved off towards the river and the boy seized his moment. He went to the girl, wanting to ask her what she thought she was doing out here with those people, but it was too late.

She was dead, but that wasn't the worst part. What had they done to her? Sobbing and half-blind with fear and pain, he ran away, not stopping until he ran into something solid enough to dull the agony of what he had seen.

CHAPTER THREE

The Purring of a Happy Cat

Even though I only stopped once on the journey to Devon it still took me six hours to get there. My Volvo had the ability to go rather fast but I feared that any great speed would be dangerous under the circumstances. I had been meaning to put the car in a garage for a while but since I only ever remembered that while I was actually on the motorway and things started rattling, it never actually got fixed.

After I left the service station the journey passed quickly as I cut swiftly through Dorset and Somerset and into Devon, which was always like drifting into another country, another world, or at least another time zone. Tarmac gradually gave way to gravel and flat fields became hilly landscapes as London became a faraway place few people ever visited and nobody cared about very much. I always knew I had reached Devon when I started seeing signs for cheap caravan sites and when every other house seemed to be a bed and breakfast or a tacky hotel. The closer you got to the sea, the more classy the holiday accommodation became. I always wondered what went on in the rural hotels amongst the guests whose seaside holiday would always remain so near and yet so far.

Mawlish, my mum's village, was on the coast between Dartmouth and Start Point, the southernmost point in Devon. Mawlish was hard to get to at the best of times, but it was made more inaccessible than usual by the fact that

I was too late to take the ferry across the River Dart. The last boat went at about ten o'clock, so I had missed it by at least two hours: 'at least' because most of the time the ferrymen would knock off at about nine-thirty and go down the pub anyway. Since I had come through Torquay, this meant I would have to take the detour around the river and through Totnes, the 'alternative capital of the South West'.

Picking up my phone to call Nat again I wasn't surprised to see there was no signal here. Devon was either charming or annoying, depending on what you were doing at the time. My mobile phone wouldn't work because the local councils refused to have reception towers tarnishing the landscape and much as I liked that when I was having a picnic, it didn't make for a very reassuring drive through dense countryside in the middle of the night.

The roads were so dark that if you switched your lights off you would literally disappear, swallowed up by the invisibility of night. In contrast with London this was simultaneously comforting and disturbing. Was it good not having *anything at all* in my rear-view mirror (no light, no road, nothing) or just frightening? I switched the radio back on for company, but it wasn't much help since the local frequency was now giving me the low-down on the horrible death of the girl at the university.

'Police are still looking for leads in the brutal murder of a local student whose body was discovered in dense woodland on the university campus in the early hours of Wednesday morning. The nineteen-year-old student was seriously sexually assaulted in what one police officer described as "the most sickening and frenzied attack" he had ever investigated. Forensic pathologists are working around the clock, gathering tiny pieces of evidence from the body and the scene, desperately trying to find vital clues to the identity of this man before he strikes again. In a unique move by Devon and Cornwall police, criminal profilers are working alongside detectives to attempt to create a psychological profile of the killer . . .'

An interesting but near-impossible task, I thought, idly fantasising about a career in psychology. I didn't have the qualifications on paper, but then criminal profiling wasn't that different from literary criticism. Both areas involved finding hidden meaning from (often) very few clues; looking for the existence of types and themes – sequences and character motivation. Because of the interesting parallels I thought more about the story as I drove, scaring myself but not being able to help it. Who could have done something like that? Definitely a man, I decided, probably a stranger from outside the university. From the report on the radio the attack had been impersonal: frenzied meant quick and uncaring; mad. So someone had been waiting in the woods for a girl to walk past and then grabbed the first one who came along. On the basis of the news report I suspected this had probably been the case. But then apparently most murders are committed by someone the victim knows so perhaps there were details left out of the report.

I stopped myself thinking about it eventually, by then fearing every shadow I drove past. I remembered playing detective as a child; stalking strange-looking men in the woods and taking down suspicious-looking car number plates 'just in case'. That was my problem: my mind was always too active, constantly trying to work things out. If I hadn't loved literature so much – and if I could have stomached it – I would have been a good candidate for the police force. As it was I was happy to have grisly scenes served up to me in books rather than real life, and hoped that was the way it would stay.

When I reached Totnes I decided I had better use a call box in case Nat was worrying. In the current climate, I suspected that despite his brash exterior he probably would be. When I stopped Maude squeaked from her basket on the back seat and I stuck my finger through the wicker and let her nibble it a bit while I waited for two girls in long floaty skirts to finish making a call. They staggered out of the red box and I realised they must be drunk. They veered all over the road, the beads in their hair flipping around with every lurch and mistimed step. I smiled. They were probably from the local art college, stranded without a lift back. I thought again about the girl in the woods. Poor thing. Had she been out like this, drunk with a friend, in a deserted town in the middle of the night? Did she stop to think there might be danger waiting for her that night, when she walked alone in the woods? It was a fairly stupid thing to do, I decided, but not an unreasonable one. Why shouldn't women be able to walk in the dark without having to be concerned about who might spring out at them?

I entered the old phone box, surprised to note that it didn't seem to have any odour, or more specifically that it didn't smell of urine. I was about to attempt to swipe my credit card through the phone when I realised it was an old-style box that only took coins. Closer inspection revealed it took 10p or 50ps. Further proof, if any were needed, that Devon was about seven years behind the rest of the country. I looked in my pocket for the right change but all I found was a 20p and some old fluff.

I looked at my watch. It was almost one o'clock and the moon was casting malevolent-looking shadows across the junction where I had stopped. I shivered. I got spooked quite easily and just wanted to make the call and go.

'Excuse me?' I called out to the girls. They had emerged from the public toilets although I hadn't seen them go in. 'Have you got any change?'

They didn't seem able to hear me clearly. I walked over to them. As I drew closer one girl recoiled as if being approached by the devil.

'Get away from me!' she shrieked, her voice choked and broken with fear, running her fingers through her short red hair as if it were full of insects. I wondered what was wrong with her.

'She's having a bad trip,' said the other girl, a wrecked-looking blonde.

'What sort of bad trip?' I said.

'Acid. E.' The girl stared at me and then started giggling. 'She'll be all right. *I'm* all right.'

'Look,' I said, unimpressed, 'have you got a 10p piece?'

'Yeah, probably,' said the blonde girl. She handed me her purse, a shabby blue velvet thing with a daisy pattern made from small yellow and white beads.

'We're being robbed!' yelled the other girl.

'Shut up,' said her friend. 'Look in there. I can't really see properly.'

I fished a 10p out of the purse and noted there was only about 70p inside. Not enough for a taxi, even if there were any. I put my 20p in the purse and gave it back to the girl.

'How are you going to get home?' I asked.

'Dunno. She feels sick.'

I thanked her and went to the call box. I dialled Mum's number and my brother answered after two rings.

'Lily?'

'Hi, Nat. Did I wake you?'

'No, I've been waiting up. I was really worried.'

'Yeah, sorry. The bloody mobile won't work around here.'

'Where are you?'

'Totnes.'

'Oh, right.'

'I'll be about an hour.'

'Okay. I'll have the kettle on if I haven't passed out with tiredness by then.'

'Oh, Nat?'

'What?'

'There's some girl here. You know the public toilets just outside the station?'

'Yeah?'

'Well, she's done some acid or something. She's having a bad time. Would you call an ambulance for her?'

'Yeah, sure.'

'See you later.'

'Yeah, 'bye.'

I would have given the girls a lift home myself, but I didn't have space in the car. I had brought hardly anything from the flat, but my car had been quickly filled up with the important things.

Just before I pulled off into the darkness I got a Miles Davis tape out of the glove box and put it in the cassette player, having had enough of the radio with its scary true-crime stories. The rest of the journey passed without incident, and as the country roads became narrower and narrower I grew more tired but the stark notes of the trumpet kept me awake. For a while I imagined I was an escaped (but innocent, of course) convict on the run and enjoyed the feeling of safety and invisibility, hidden amongst the jumbled hedges and lopsided walls that lined these roads. When I saw the sea I imagined I was seeing freedom.

I drove into Mawlish at 1.55 and the only light on the whole village was at my mother's house.

The wife was woken by a sound she couldn't place. Was he home? She didn't know. It was a strangled sound. The sleeping pill she had taken meant she couldn't stay awake so she lapsed back into sleep.

He wept like a baby at the kitchen table. He was home. That was what she wanted. Where was she? In bed. Always in bed by ten o'clock.

He held the video in his hand. The evidence: two people in the woods, killing a girl then cutting off her head.

Nat handed me a steaming mug of coffee the moment I stepped in the door. At that hour you could see a car approaching the village about five minutes before it got there, because of the way the headlights played over the hill in the distance. This road only went to and from the village, so if you saw any lights you knew someone was coming.

There were several UFO sightings in the village before

people began to appreciate the weird things that the hill did to light. That was the thing about the countryside around here. It was almost as if it had been designed to fool you, to distort and exaggerate shapes and objects, making them into parodies of themselves.

The fog was a different thing altogether. When the fog came down you couldn't go anywhere, because all of a sudden there was nowhere to go.

'I called the ambulance,' said Nat.

'What?'

'You know, for the girl.'

'Oh, yeah. Thanks.'

'I bet she'll be gutted when it gets there.'

'Yeah, well, maybe she'll think next time. Anyway, how are you?'

'Great,' he said looking anything but.

Nat looked tired and I felt like death. We had always been close, despite the five-year age difference, and enjoyed a rapport that I doubted either of us had with anyone else. We even looked similar: our features were more or less the same and the only real difference was our colouring. Where I was dark, Nat was blond, and some quirk of nature had given him dark green eyes which looked quite imposing set against his shoulder-length hair. He was good-looking – and he knew it.

There were complications, however, and the phrase *too close for comfort* often applied to us, meaning that a good game of cards or a touching heart-to-heart could all too easily be spoilt by an argument over who'd had the last of the milk or used the last of the hot water. Since I hadn't lived at home for a few years, these problems had more or less disappeared. I seriously hoped they wouldn't resurface now I was back.

'Mum's made up your old room,' said Nat after we'd finished our coffee. 'I've got a seminar in the morning so I'd better go to bed. It's really nice to see you, Lily.'

'Yeah, you too.'

He kissed me on the cheek and turned to go upstairs to his room. As I watched him go it struck me that he had really grown up since starting university last autumn. There was a time when he would never have kissed me and I smiled when I thought of him as a teenager, moodily storming up to his room at the merest hint of anything he didn't like. Now he let out all his aggression in his songs.

I had another cup of milky coffee before bed while Maude was reunited with her mother, Sappho, my mum's two-year-old cat. Maude inherited her squeak from her mother so while the kettle boiled the kitchen was full of chirruping sounds and feverish purring. The cats went into the larder and so did I, all of us with the intention of rummaging for biscuits. I looked down and saw that Maude was on her back. Sappho had one paw on her head and was licking her passionately as if to say, *Look at you, you haven't had a good wash in ages*. Maude looked at me and appeared to be smiling. I smiled too and thought how glad I was to be home.

Then the whistling started and I remembered that it was so quiet here that an innocent kettle could be enough to wake the whole village.

I didn't even manage to get my jeans off before I fell asleep on my bed and dreamt all night about being in a station, waiting for a train that never came. I woke up to the sound of purring as usual, with Maude wrapped around the top of my head. But this morning that was all I could hear: the purring of a happy cat and the sound of birds in the distance.

CHAPTER FOUR

Into Insanity

There was no one else in the house when I got up on Thursday morning. It was nine o'clock and although I would usually sleep for another hour at least, I was made restless by the difference in my surroundings. Nevertheless, when I did get up my head felt as if it was closing in on itself. I hadn't gone to bed until about three in the end and I felt I needed at least ten hours more sleep.

I lit a cigarette and wandered through to the kitchen in my bare feet, still wearing my jeans from the night before. After putting some milk on the stove I looked around for cocoa powder so that I could have my usual milky hot chocolate and crusty bread for breakfast, a habit picked up from my father.

Some part of me still believed that mornings were for exercise; but then thoughts and plans rarely became reality (which I thought was quite a good thing, considering some of the mad ideas people had) and I usually preferred taking things easy before midday. Unfortunately for my health, I didn't need to exercise to stay fairly thin and my brain was the only part of my body that got a regular workout. When I was younger I thought I would start taking these things seriously (and give up smoking) at twenty-five. Now I was twenty-five I was happy to put those things off until I was thirty.

After breakfast I woke up and felt much better. I loved the

clean air in Devon and the sense of peace which I sat taking in quietly until I felt the need for action. I brought all my stuff in from the car and arranged it in a heap in my room. Then I sat watching TV in the living room until I heard the gravelly crunching sound of Mum's car pulling into the drive. Instinctively, I went into the kitchen and put the kettle on. Mum was one of those people who had to have a 'nice hot strong cup of tea' on arriving home, even if she had only been out for five minutes.

I heard the back door open and then her voice, its usual confident tone tinged with warmth.

'Lily?'

'Hi, Mum.' I rushed to greet her and threw my arms around her as soon as she walked in the door.

'I knew you were coming home,' she said.

'I'm only having a holiday.' Mum arched her eyebrows and I decided to change the subject. 'You look wonderful.'

'Thank you, darling. Oh, is that tea you're making? That's very thoughtful, I've been gasping for a cup.'

'Where were you?'

'Taking Nat to the station. He slept in, poor lamb.'

'Oh, sorry, that was probably my fault. The journey took longer than I thought.'

'I didn't mind. I had to go to the organic shop anyway.'

'No work today?'

'No, I'm only teaching two days a week now.'

'Oh, that's good.'

'Yes, it gives me time to get on with the novel.' Mum winked and smiled when she said that. She had been writing *the novel* for the best part of ten years. I'd thought it was exciting when she'd started it but now it seemed it would be a miracle if she ever finished.

When Mum wasn't writing the long-awaited novel, she liked to paint. Otherwise she was usually caught up in university life; teaching, marking and going to conferences. She and her colleague Sue ran the degree course in Women's Studies at the university.

'How's Sue?' I asked, putting tea bags in cups and searching around for sugar.

'She's fine. Is that tea ready yet?'

'Oh, yes. Sorry.' I finished pouring it and sat at the old oak table with Mum. She did look good, actually. She dyed her greying hair red now, which looked striking set against her green eyes. Nat had inherited her eyes while I'd got one from each parent: a blue one from Henri and a green one from Mum. It gave people something to talk about at parties, and I liked them except that they clashed. *Blue and green should never be seen.* That's what the fashion magazines said, at least.

'Have you heard?' asked Mum.

'About the murder?' I asked, knowing the answer. 'It's dreadful, isn't it?'

'It was such a shock,' she said, shaking her head. 'There should have been lights there.'

'What, in the woods?'

'No, on the path. You've never been to the university, have you?'

'No.'

'There's a path going down to the river, through the woods. The students use it as a short cut and the Student Union has been asking for lights ever since a woman student saw a flasher there a couple of years ago.'

'Don't tell me,' I said. 'Not enough in the budget?'

'You got it,' said Mum, smiling weakly. 'What an awful price to pay.'

'Sometimes the cost of not doing something is greater than doing it,' I said thoughtfully.

'Yes, but they never realise that until it's too late,' said Mum, crossly. I knew that anything like this upset her greatly. One of the reasons the family had been based in Devon for so long was the quality of life it offered, and to give Nat and me somewhere safe to grow up. I shared her feeling that it would be an awful loss if this was taken away from local people.

'Right!' said Mum, startling me out of my thoughts. 'I'm off to the chiropractor. Before I go, Lily, I had a word with Professor Valentine and he wants to talk to you about those literature teaching hours, if you're interested.'

'What exactly will it involve?' I asked suspiciously, not wanting to be landed with anything outside my area.

'I think there's some kind of contemporary unit and some genre stuff. Just your sort of thing. Oh, the Professor was talking about using the new person on first-year creative writing as well.'

'Okay, I might give him a call.'

'I think you should. Here's his number and extension.' Mum scribbled a couple of numbers on a notepad. 'If this one doesn't work then that one will. 'Bye.'

The boy only stopped once on the way back to his room. He was cold, but didn't care; hungry but he didn't care. He just didn't care about anything anymore. He surrounded himself with the pieces of paper and the personal effects that he had and just sat there, not moving, except to shake with grief and fear, for six days.

Alone again, I looked out of the window for a while. The garden was beginning to bloom and I was struck by all the vivid yellows and greens and blues in the flowerbeds and amongst the hedgerows. Beyond the garden was the sea, and for a while I just sat there watching, hypnotised by the rise and fall of the waves and the patterns they made in the forth.

One of the things I'd always hated about London was the way everything seemed to go on inside, as people took refuge from the pollution and the muggers. Accordingly, one of the things I had always missed most about Devon was being outside, in the fresh air and safety. Although that image had been chipped by the recent tragedy it wasn't shattered yet and, needing to reacquaint myself with the countryside, I decided to go walking and thinking along the coast path to the castle.

I only had to walk out of the gate at the bottom of the

garden to begin to feel the fierce thrill of being alone with nature. There was something strangely calming about the rawness of the outside world and as I walked I was able to see things in perspective once more. I was thinking about what I was going to do, although looking around at the hills and the sea, it felt like I could very easily stay in Devon forever. In fact, I almost forgot why I didn't want to come.

I remembered going on walks like this with Eugénie when we were quite young. Our parents would picnic serenely around the coast while Eugénie and I fell into holes, tore our clothes and tried to chat up men at least four times our age. Looking back now terrified me; it was a mystery how we avoided the poisonous mushrooms, paedophiles and accidents we were warned about but didn't believe in. Maybe we really had been as immune as we imagined we were, oblivious to the idea of a world without us.

Of course, when tragedies did occur we savoured the details along with everyone else, playing detective together to the undisguised chagrin of all the innocent people we hounded. Eugénie lived in the next village and our small community made as much as possible of all local human-interest stories, manufacturing juicy stories out of the most boring non-events.

The worst thing that ever happened was when a boy fell off the cliffs near the village. I never knew his name, but I remembered being shown the spot where he had fallen as we travelled past on a boat trip one summer. I was only about seven and it was the most poignant thing I'd ever seen. I had never realised before that children actually did die; that it was possible just to tumble from the top of something and never come back.

I remembered losing Eugénie one day quite near the spot where I was walking now. Our parents knew, or strongly suspected, that she was just mucking around, but I was sure she had fallen over the cliffs. By this stage falling off cliffs had become an obsession of mine and I firmly forbade anyone I knew, children or grown-ups, from going anywhere near the cliff edge. I remember shouting for her that day and later. '*Euge, Euge!*' I would call, pronouncing my nickname for her as some people say the word 'huge'.

Eventually she reappeared, laughing and smelling slightly of cigarette smoke. I tried to be cross with her, but as she led me to our new hideout I forgave her. Shortly afterwards, sitting in some mud while Eugénie looked out for intruders, I smoked my first cigarette. It was a Marlboro, I think; damp, stale and stolen from a cousin – and rough enough to make sure I never forgot it. From that moment on I was a smoker: a *grown-up*, and I never looked back.

Walking uphill hurt my legs and I couldn't believe how unfit I had become in London. I'd thought my memories might weigh me down and make my walk more difficult, but they seemed only to spur me on and give me a sense of perspective I hadn't felt for a long time.

Every so often I stopped for a moment and looked around, hypnotised by the swishing noise of waves hitting the cliffs as I turned to look at the silhouettes of cows on the horizon behind me. I gulped in the country air and thought how good it was to be back.

Of course, a few years ago I had been desperate to get away. Like all young people I'd wanted to leave my roots behind and invent a new identity for myself. But now I realised nothing could ever replace the real thing.

After about half an hour I stopped for a cigarette on a National Trust bench. As I sat down I felt something rustle in my back pocket. I stood up and pulled it out. It was the flyer from the service station, crumpled and forgotten. I never did see Hans and Dell again to return it, so I supposed they would miss the party.

I smoothed it out and examined it, interested to see what these things looked like now, since I hadn't really studied one for a few years. At first glance nothing seemed to have changed. The patterns on the paper were made of swirling psychedelic designs, including the distinctive outline of a marijuana leaf. The light orange paper was of low quality and the ink plain black. I didn't know much about printing techniques but I knew enough to realise this flyer had been cheaply produced. It seemed a long way away from the glossy sheets that used to advertise big raves in warehouses and out-of-the-way clubs.

On top of the background pattern was some text: *Beyond Reason – The Unconventions. The Acumen challenge you once again to open your minds. Gathering number three in the West Country. Please phone the number on the night for venue details.* I looked vaguely for 'the number' but there wasn't one there. I smiled as I remembered my own brief foray into rave culture, sitting around with Eugénie in some bloke's Ford Escort, listening to pirate radio and waiting to be told which number to call.

Next to the obvious references to dope was a logo that I couldn't place. I noticed the letters H and O, which I knew stood for hydrogen and oxygen, and more impenetrable symbols as well: CH_2, CH_3 and others. My basic knowledge of chemistry told me these must be compounds of carbon and hydrogen. Since carbon and hydrogen combine to form organic matter, and because of its context, I wondered whether the 'logo' was in fact the formula for some kind of drug.

I couldn't help feeling there must be more to life for all these people. I had never been interested in getting 'out of my head'; I liked the feeling of normality too much, and whatever I needed to escape from would not be expunged with chemicals.

Eugénie and I had tried Ecstasy once at a nightclub when we were both seventeen. She danced all night while I quivered in a corner, thinking I was going to melt. We were both depressed for about two weeks afterwards and vowed never to do it again. Shopping may not have made me insanely happy, but at least it didn't strip my brain away.

There was a note at the bottom of the flyer, which appeared to have been handwritten; probably as a last-minute addition. *Special talk by Freddy Future: Paradise engineering and the future of life*. The name sounded sinister; someone with a massive ego, I thought. I crumpled the sheet of orange paper in my hand and tossed it in the bin.

I looked at my watch and saw that it was almost two o'clock. I walked on towards the castle then caught a boat taxi back to the village. I had decided to call the university and see about those teaching hours since I didn't have anything to lose.

The way I saw it, I could earn some money pretty easily by talking to students about a subject I liked. My MA course had been in Contemporary Fiction, so as long as no one wanted me to teach Shakespeare, I would be happy. I had an uncomfortable memory of having to deliver classes on *The Merchant of Venice* to some students when I was teaching literature at the community college, having just finished my degree. I hadn't read the play, and neither had any of the students. We used a lot of videos in that class and still none of us came out knowing anything about the play. From that moment I vowed never to stray out of my subject area again. Everyone assumes that because you teach literature you've read every book there is but unfortunately this had never been the case with me. I was more likely to be found reading old thrillers than classics, which was precisely why I specialised in crime.

Before I knew it, I was standing in the hall at home by the phone with a cigarette in my hand and a nauseous feeling in my stomach. I would never have admitted it to anyone but I was nervous. I dialled the number with a shaking hand and waited while I was connected by the switchboard.

'Yes?' The voice on the other end of the line sounded snappy and distracted.

'Hello. May I speak to Professor Valentine, please?'

'Yes? This is Valentine. Are you a student?' I was shocked by his acerbic tone. I'd thought only box offices employed people that rude.

'This is Lily Pascale,' I said. 'I've got some experience teaching literature and I heard that you needed somebody –'

'Can you do contemporary fiction?' he barked.

'Yes. My, um, MA course was –'

'Crime and horror?'

'Yes, those are precisely my –'

'Creative writing?'

'Yes.' He seemed to be in a hurry, and I thought it would be best not to try and add any more information.

'I suppose you're aware of the situation here?' he grunted, but didn't wait for a reply. 'Bloody media everywhere, and the police. If you think you're up to it, come in tomorrow and the secretary will give you a timetable. We'll see how you do.'

'Oh.' I was shocked that it was so easy. 'Thank you.'

The line had already gone dead.

I spent the rest of the day washing and ironing, amazed I'd got the job over the phone. Even the McJobs I'd had after leaving teaching the last time had required at least an interview and frequently a *customer service* training day. (Can you walk and talk at the same time? Yes? You've got the job!) I would have thought that higher education institutions would be more careful about who they employed, especially in the light of recent events, but apparently not.

After the washing was done I arranged my room the way I wanted it and stacked my books alphabetically on the old pine bookshelf. Soon it was four o'clock and neither Nat nor Mum was home, I looked at some of my old crime and horror titles and dug out an old folder with some ancient lesson plans in it. Not for the first time I was pleased that I wasn't a minimalist and consequently never threw anything away. I wondered what course the girl in the woods had been on, and how her murder had affected the university. It was bad publicity they didn't need, and I imagined a lot of the women students would be very frightened now.

I stood by the window for a while and marvelled once again at the scenery. Nothing moved except for the birds and insects and occasionally a leaf blowing in the wind.

Squeak.

'Hello, Maude. Would you like your food now?' My little cat was pressing against my legs and I felt her soft fur bristle at the suggestion of food.

Squeak.

I looked around the larder and noticed there wasn't much cat food left. I had some 'emergency money' Anthony hadn't known about (and that I'd actually forgotten until last night) so I drove into town to the supermarket, to stock up on cat food and buy the ingredients for dinner which I had decided to make for Mum and Nat.

My father taught me how to cook when I was quite small and although I wasn't brilliant I had a few tricks up my sleeve that made anything taste nice. My French relatives and general instinct had taught me that all you needed to do was add garlic, lemon, pepper or Parmesan cheese to something bland and it became fabulous. Fish was one of my specialities, mainly because it was so easy, and as I started the car I was already dreaming of trout smothered in butter and lemon sauce.

The small local supermarket looked as if it was going to close soon and I remembered that all the shops around here still kept traditional hours. They would almost all open at nine and close at five, except on a Wednesday when most things shut at one. Not wanting to be turfed out before my purchases had been made, I hurried around and picked up the essentials without stopping to look at everything as I normally would. The range in the supermarket was limited, but being so close to the coast meant that fresh fish was always available. I picked up six juicy, metallic-looking trout and tried not to gaze for too long into their rainbow eyes.

I walked over to the wine display, knowing I would be disappointed by whatever I chose. My friends at university had called me a 'wine snob' and laughed about my clichéd French disdain for sub-standard wine. They would drink anything alcoholic but I always refused their too-sweet German or too-sour Bulgarian offerings.

I fancied a substantial full-bodied red, the wine equivalent of comfort food, but having decided on fish I reached for the only genuine-looking Muscadet on the shelf. I remembered the days when I used to be able to afford to order cases of peppery New World reds and delicate French whites. Those days would come again, I vowed to myself as I placed the green bottle in my basket. I paid and left the shop, eager to get home and start cooking.

CHAPTER FIVE

Girls' Stuff

'I'm Lily,' I said to the circle of faces around the table. They looked confused and bewildered by something. 'I'll be taking you for this unit and also your units on genre.'

'Why are we sitting like this?' asked a striking girl with a very pale face and very long straight black hair, gesturing at the circular formation I had constructed.

'Why do you think you are sitting like that?' I asked, demonstrating the simplicity of my teaching method which largely consisted of throwing any question back at the students and making them do all the work.

'It's to make us all, like, *equal*,' said an Asian boy, waving his hands in what I assumed was a mockery of my *circular* method. He sounded as if he either came from Manchester or else was a die-hard Oasis fan. I remembered the lads at the service station; he could have been one of them with his oversized windcheater and long sideburns.

'Yeah,' said another boy, a confident, good-looking lad with a scar running the length of his face. 'So we can *share* our emotions.'

I ignored them and looked down at the register in front of me on the desk. I was at the head of the 'equal' circle, knowing I would have to assert some authority to get any respect from a class like this. According to the register there were supposed to be nineteen of them but there were only ten present today. The two boys who had already spoken sat with two other lads and I could instantly tell that these were the 'troublemakers' in the group. Pleasant enough separately, no doubt, and probably quite bright but definitely of the in-your-face New Lad variety.

I had always been intrigued by the way that young degree students acted as if they were still doing their A levels. Everyone assumed that just because they were living away from home and doing a higher education course they would instantly become sensible and grown-up, but I had never found that to be the case. In my experience having a few older students in a group usually helped settle the younger ones down, but there didn't seem to be any mature students in this class.

As well as the four lads, two thin and pretty girls sat together looking bewilderingly tearful, and four others sat in a random pattern; one of them reading a book and the others looking at me expectantly. I wondered why there were so many absentees and then studied my class. They were all second-year literature students who, so far as I could tell, had not had a smooth ride at the university this year. If I understood correctly, I was the third lecturer so far on this unit. My guess was that Professor Valentine was one of the reasons for this. He was so incredibly rude.

It was Monday, my first day, and I had already had a run in with him. I had been late for our meeting before my class started at two o'clock, which wasn't my fault but certainly didn't help. I had arrived at the university car park with ten minutes to spare, but driven straight into the middle of a *Women Against Violent Crime* protest, organised, it seemed from the banners and placards, by the Student Union.

The protest blocked the road into the campus and reminded me of pictures of the miners' strike from the early-eighties. I slowed to a halt eventually at which point a woman wearing a mini-skirt and a fishnet crop-top came up to the car window and banged on it, forcing me to wind it down.

'Did you know a girl was *murdered* in there?' she asked

dramatically, sending a wave of fear and trepidation through my body. My eyes followed the movement of her arm as she flung it off to her right where I could see woods in the distance, beyond what seemed to be Halls of Residence to the left of the road. I could vaguely make out the outline of police tape and other crime-scene paraphernalia, along with at least fifty uniformed officers who were, I assumed, 'combing the area' for clues. I also noticed the distinctive blue haze of uniformed officers mingling with protesters and a solitary policeman eating a sandwich over by the Samuel Beckett Building, which was where I was trying to get to.

'Yes,' I said nervously. 'It was awf –'

'So what are you going to do about it?' demanded the woman, pointing at me through the window.

'Well, I'm certainly not going anywhere near the woods,' I said, smiling in what I hoped was a friendly way.

'Do you think this is *funny*?' she said incredulously. 'It could have been you, you know. Butchered. *Raped.* You know he sodomised her with a stick after he strangled her?'

'I'm sorry, I've got a class,' I said, putting the car into first gear and wondering how to squeeze it past the protesters. This woman was deliberately trying to get a reaction out of me but I preferred to keep my fear and disgust private and didn't want to argue with her. Her grief and anger were heartfelt, I could see that, but I didn't understand how picking a fight with me was going to solve anything. We were on the same side, I thought it was dreadful as well, but my view was that if women stopped leading normal lives then the killer had won.

'So you're not joining the strike then?' She persisted, even though I was now looking the other way. 'All the other students are striking.'

'Why?' I asked, turning back towards her, intrigued by this idea.

'To get the lights!' she said, obviously exasperated that I didn't know anything.

'I'm new,' I explained. 'And I'm staff.'

'Oh. Well, you might want to have a word with Nadia as you go past. She's organising a candlelit vigil in the woods tomorrow night for female students and *staff*.'

'I may well do that,' I said, seeing a jagged-featured, slightly intimidating-looking young woman being pointed out to me.

I would have spoken to her but didn't really see the point of candlelit vigils and wakes. After all, none of them would bring the poor girl back. I was also about to be more than ten minutes late, so I moved my car assertively past the protest, hearing a male student being attacked for being a 'potential rapist' as I passed. I parked quickly before running into the Samuel Beckett Building to meet the Professor, get my register and hurry to the class.

Professor Valentine didn't seem to be in a good mood either, but then he had probably been called a potential rapist too, I thought with a wry smile. The poor bloke probably wouldn't have known how to handle that. He was bad-tempered with me, sure, but he seemed too other-worldly and lost in the clouds to really understand what was going on. He was a small man, probably in his late-thirties or, at a push, early-forties, and was clearly annoyed that I was late. Instead of showing me to my office he just waved me down the corridor to a poky little room next to the cleaning cupboard and more or less told me to get on with it. When the key he gave me didn't work, I went back to his office.

'You'll need a masterkey in that case,' he said, sighing, examining the key he had given me and then pocketing it slowly. He walked down the hall with me and used his own key on my door.

'How do I get one of those?'

'You go and see George,' said the Professor disdainfully. 'The technician.'

'How do I get into my office in the meantime?'

He looked at me scornfully, as if he had better things to do.

'Well, you ask someone else to open it for you, of course.'
He coughed. 'Now, if there's nothing else?'

'No.'

He walked off down the hallway, looking at his watch
and muttering like a mad March hare. I felt slightly
affronted that my usually seductive feminine charms didn't
seem to have any effect on him. Not that I minded. His idea
of being young and hip (since that was the only plausible
reason I could see) seemed to consist of combining old jeans
with a short-sleeved shirt and badly knotted 'novelty' tie.
Mum had said he was a bit of a ladies' man but I couldn't see
it myself. He hadn't even smiled at me once.

My class was getting restless. I had a register but didn't know
whether to call it or not, having always found the practice a
bit school-teacherish. I didn't know what the previous
lecturer had done so I decided on a compromise.

'I'm just going to see who's here,' I said. 'Once I get to
know you I won't bother with this, but in the meantime . . .
Michelle Chambers?'

'She's on the protest,' said the black-haired girl who'd
spoken before.

'Right,' I said, slightly surprised that the strike was so far-
reaching. It was good that students were taking the issue
seriously, but after my encounter with the woman at the
gate I was certain there was a better way. I turned back to
the register and chewed my pen thoughtfully.

'Heather Chandler?'

'Here.' A blonde, freckled girl raised her hand slightly and
smiled.

'Charlotte Dante?'

'On strike,' said Heather matter-of-factly.

'Cressida Dexter?'

The girl reading the book looked up and smiled.

'*Cress*, please,' she said.

'Hey, Cress,' said the Asian boy. 'Why aren't you burning
your bra?'

'Because my classes are more important,' she said simply and went back to her book.

'Jason Davies?'

'*Mental*,' said the boy with the scar, pulling a face and making the other boys fall about laughing, their long, ungainly teenage limbs spilling on to and around the tables as they did so.

'He's away,' said Heather, glaring at the lads.

We weren't doing very well here, I thought.

'Stephanie Duncan?'

Silence.

'Stephanie Duncan?'

'She's dead,' said the black-haired girl calmly. 'Didn't anyone tell you?'

'They cut off her head with a carving knife,' sang a male voice from the group of lads.

'Shut up!' said a girl sitting on her own, her big brown eyes filling with tears.

I had to regain control but for a second was too stunned to move. How could the Professor have forgotten to warn me about something like this? So I was taking the class that the murdered girl had been in, for *three units*? God.

I got up from behind the table and paced a bit at the front of the room, wondering what to say next. I pushed my hair back from my face and noticed that my forehead had little drops of perspiration forming on it.

'What the fuck's *wrong* with you all?' said the big-eyed girl in a strangled voice, pushing back her chair and getting up so quickly that it fell over. Everyone stopped talking for a moment, watching the chair fall which it did dreamily, as if in some sleepy slow-motion sequence in a over-dramatic TV thriller. After the crash came the sobs as the girl ran out of the room, holding her bag and notebooks tightly in both hands.

I felt a pang of tenderness watching her. It produced a strange moment of clarity in which I suddenly realised that all the murder scenes in those trendy shoot-'em-up films are only ironic or funny if you've never come into contact with real, horrific death; which is maybe why they are most popular with younger audiences.

I was acting as well as thinking, and had almost reached the door to go after the girl when the loud crash ended the slow-motion moment and Heather started shouting at the boys.

'You stupid little bastards!' she hissed as the door slammed. 'Don't you know her sister was killed last year?'

'How were we supposed to know?' asked one of the lads, a scruffy blond in skate-gear, mimicking Heather's high-pitched voice and making the others dissolve into fresh giggles.

'Oh, grow *up*,' she said, pulling out some tissues for the two tearful girls, who were now crying even harder.

'Yeah, give it a rest, Eddie,' said Cress, looking more interested than disturbed by the chaos in the class.

The rest of the students broke into discussion at this point and I thought I'd better to let them get whatever it was out of their systems. From what I could make out, the two tearful girls had been friends of Stephanie's, but intriguingly, apart from the girl who'd run out, none of the others seemed to be having much of a personal reaction to her death except for basking in the horror of it. I suspected a lot of their *don't care* attitude was in fact just bravado, but found it bizarre nevertheless. Suddenly Stephanie, whoever she had been, was dehumanised; the details of her horrific end fair game for discussion and speculation, like the gruesome plot of a TV programme.

'Do you all want to talk about it?' I asked eventually, putting down my pen and leaning back against the white board, forgetting about the register. There was silence for a few seconds as everyone shuffled uncomfortably (except Cress, who didn't look as if she would be uncomfortable doing anything).

'They were all DNA-tested on Friday,' said Heather, gesturing at the boys. 'The police found some sperm or something . . .'

'We all had to have bits of hair taken and everything. In case one of us did it,' said a black lad sitting next to the boy with the scar.

'As if any of us would *want* to,' said Eddie, grimacing.

'Just ignore them,' said Cress, putting down her book and smiling at me nicely. 'I think we've all been a bit shaken up by this.'

'I can see that,' I said. 'Have you been offered counselling or anything?'

'Are you *kidding*?' said the black-haired girl. 'Everyone's been up for the last five nights having wakes and *vigils* and therapy. Most of them hardly knew her, and everyone else hated her.'

'Yeah, like them two,' said the Asian boy, pointing at the crying girls. 'They took the piss out of her all the time. They're only upset now she's dead. They're sick, man. Fucking sick.'

'Okay, settle down,' I said, hoping I sounded more assured than I felt. 'I know this is a bad time, but I need to get your names so I know who I'm talking to. And if you don't mind, I won't have any swearing in this class unless it comes directly out of a novel.'

I was good at remembering students' names and these ones stuck particularly well. The black lad was Pete, the boy with the scar was Blake and the Asian boy, now looking a bit sheepish, was Ash. The red-haired tearful girl was Justine and her blonde friend was Lucy. The black-haired girl was Kerry and the rest I thought I knew already.

I let them talk for a bit longer, interested to see what (if anything) lurked beneath their outward, censored emotions. I guessed that the boys were frightened underneath and that some of the girls were putting on a bit of a show for the cameras – real or imagined. From what I could make out, Stephanie had been quite a loner, interested in New Age healing, her studies and not much else. From what the other students were saying, it appeared that Justine and Lucy had actually bullied her quite viciously, calling her a witch and once even breaking into her room to scatter her herbs around. So I assumed that guilt and regret had taken them to the various vigils, along with genuine grief: because what the others probably didn't understand was that you can't say sorry to someone once they're dead.

'To be honest with you,' said Kerry, her clear voice cutting through all the others, 'I hated her, and I'm not going to lie just because she's dead.'

'You're sick,' said Justine.

'No, I'm not,' said Kerry reasonably. 'Of course I'm not *glad* she's dead, but I'm just being honest. Let's face it, no one liked her.'

'I didn't really know her,' said Heather wistfully. 'And I've missed my chance now.'

'She used to go into those woods all the time,' said Lucy.

'Yeah,' said Pete. 'Collecting ingredients for her *love*-potions.'

'No,' said Lucy, 'I'm not having a go at her or suggesting anything, but, well, it's a bit *creepy*. I mean, the way it turned out and everything.'

'Maybe one of her spells went wrong,' suggested Eddie.

'Oh, leave it out,' said Cress. 'She was just a bit disturbed.' She sighed and looked at her watch. 'I might as well have gone on the protest at this rate.'

'Yeah,' said Kerry. 'I'm sick of talking about this in every class.'

'Unfeeling *bitch*,' hissed Justine.

'All right,' I said. 'We'll get on now, but if any of you wants to stop, or go out for some fresh air or anything, then just feel free.'

Why were there such mixed feelings about this girl, I thought, walking over to the white board and rubbing the previous lecturer's notes from it slowly. Gradually the class settled down and by the time I turned around, they were all looking at me expectantly.

'Contemporary fiction,' I said meaningfully. '*Contemporary fiction*. What do you think then?'

'It's load of old cack,' said Ash confidently. This surprised me. I couldn't believe someone so uninterested in literature was on this course unless . . . A quick glance at the marks in the register confirmed my suspicion. Behind Cress and the missing Jason Davies, Ash was top of the class.

'Some of it's really surprisingly pornographic,' said Blake, smiling lasciviously. He looked over at Cress for approval, but although she was smiling she was busy looking at me to see what I'd do. I noticed that Kerry was looking at Blake, though, laughing too loudly, wanting him to forget about Cress and to notice that *she* found his joke funny. The dynamics of this class were very interesting, although I would have preferred to examine them under less extraordinary circumstances.

'It's a bit of a meaningless term,' said Kerry. 'I mean, contemporary just means *now*. Dickens was contemporary once.'

'Yes,' I said, looking for any other responses but just hearing silence, punctuated by dry sniffs from Justine and Lucy. 'So which of the books on this list have you already looked at?'

I looked down at the list of titles on top of my pile of papers. They all seemed somewhat unsuitable in light of recent events. *American Psycho, The Wasp Factory, Trainspotting*. I wondered who had put the list together, and what they were trying to achieve. I assumed it was Valentine, picking all the trendy titles to impress his students.

'We were just about to do *London Fields* before Isobel left,' said Heather.

'Good,' I said, breathing a sigh of relief. *London Fields* was one of my favourite contemporary novels and the only book on the list I'd actually read all the way through. 'Let's get started then.'

Most of the students seemed to have read the book, which was encouraging. I kept having to steer them away from discussions of murder, both in the book and beyond, and on to the less sensational subject of the narrative point of view, which was what I decided we should focus on. Eventually I got them quite fired up and they arranged themselves into little groups and started some interesting discussions; except for Blake and Pete, who seemed to stall on a section about underwear.

After the students had talked about the novel for a while I let them go on a break and went to grab a can of Coke from the machine in the hall. I looked at what I had written on my pad. *London Fields*, it said. *Murder*.

When they returned there was only half an hour to go so I let them report back on their discussions. At the end of the class I set them an essay question which I made up off the top of my head, but within which I had unfortunately again included the word *murder*, which elicited plenty of fresh sniffs from Justine and Lucy, and made me cringe with embarrassment. Putting one's foot in it seemed to be an the obvious occupational hazard around here just now, but then what did people expect? I didn't imagine teaching contemporary literature to a class in which a student had been murdered would be easy under any circumstances. It was my job to teach the work of authors who didn't feel that a world without murder was very interesting: lucky, lucky me.

CHAPTER SIX

Expectation

Most of the students left fairly quickly after the class and before long the room was quiet. After I'd watched the last stragglers go I sank back in my chair and took a deep breath. I really needed a cigarette. This room was making my head swim; its bright yellow walls contrasting painfully with the blue glare of the strip lights running down the centre of the ceiling. The yellow appeared to be new; streaks of fresh-looking paint coated the edges of the white skirting board at the bottom of the walls and a shelf of old-looking books, which had obviously not been cleared before the redecoration took place, were daubed with the same daffodil-coloured drips. Rubbing my eyes, I got up to wipe the white board and put the chairs and tables back where I had found them. I didn't know the protocol here but the rule at my last college was to always leave the rooms the way you found them. I wasn't sure if anyone around here would care either way at the moment, but at least I could make an attempt to be professional.

A soft knock on the door broke into my thoughts. Through the glass panel I could see the profile of a girl I didn't recognise. Before I had a chance to say anything the door slowly opened and she peeped in.

'Are you Lily?' she asked, looking at me briefly and then lowering my eyes to the floor.

'Yes,' I said. 'Come in.'

'I'm sorry to disturb you,' said the girl. She was obviously a student, although not one from my last class. She moved quickly into the room and put her heavy-looking rucksack down on one of the chairs. She looked hot, as if she had just run up the stairs, and what must usually have been sleek blonde hair was ruffled and tinged with small droplets of perspiration.

'Are you all right?' I asked.

'Yes,' said the girl. 'I just wanted a word if that's okay?'

'Fine,' I said, gesturing for her to sit down. I wondered if this was about Stephanie. 'What's your name?'

'Bronwyn,' said the girl. 'Bronwyn Young.' She sat down on one of the chairs and I grabbed my notebook and pulled up a chair next to her.

'And what can I do for you?'

'I need to change tutor groups,' she said. 'I'd like to change into yours, if that's all right?'

'Are you a first year?' I asked, feeling my head start to spin. I didn't know what the procedure was for changing groups. I knew I had a first-year tutor group, or at least I was fairly sure I did. I hadn't studied my timetable too closely yet.

'Yes,' said Bronwyn. 'My mate Zoe is in your group.'

'How do you know?' I asked. 'I'm not even sure it's been finalised yet.'

'Well, it's obvious really,' said Bronwyn. 'It's all Isobel's old tutees. They got spread around the other groups until we got a new lecturer.'

I assumed it was Isobel whom I was replacing.

'So you weren't in that group?'

'No.'

'Why do you want to move now?'

'It's a bit, um, personal,' said Bronwyn, smiling weakly. 'Can I shut the door?'

'Of course.' I said. She closed the door and sat back down.

'I'm having some personal problems,' she said. 'And I want a woman tutor.'

'Right,' I said sympathetically, making an illegible note in my book. 'I'll have to talk to the Professor.'

'I don't want to be an extra burden or anything,' Bronwyn said quickly. 'I'm ever so glad they got another woman, though. I know a lot of the others feel the same way. You just can't tell men some things, you know?'

'Yes,' I said. 'Although all staff have to be professional. I mean, you should be able to tell any of us something in confidence.'

Bronwyn sighed.

'I'm pregnant,' she said, not looking at me. She stared at the window instead but I could see there were tears forming in her pale green eyes. I felt in my pocket for a tissue, knowing there wouldn't be any there. I wanted to hug her or something but lecturers weren't meant to get that close to students. Instead I decided to be calm and rational, as I always tried to be with people in this state. It always surprised me that students were happy to tell all their secrets to a stranger, just because that stranger was a teacher, but I didn't let that show, wondering instead whether I was ready for this new therapist's role but resolving nevertheless to *cope*.

'How do you feel about that?' I asked gently.

'Dreadful,' said Bronwyn. 'Panicked, alone. I don't know. I'm only nineteen. What am I going to do?'

'Don't panic,' I said. 'That's the first thing to remember. Have you told the father?'

'No,' said Bronwyn. 'I can't. He's already going . . . Oh, God, sorry.' She started crying even more and I patted her on the arm, feeling sympathetic but knowing this was something she would have to work out for herself. I wanted to help her in a more practical way but didn't know what they did in these situations at this university. They must have some sort of counselling facility, but as yet I had no idea where it would be or how to refer a student. At the community college you weren't allowed to give students advice or talk to them about personal problems, you had to refer them straight to a counsellor.

'Okay,' I said. 'Look. I'm going to help you sort this out, but to be honest with you the best thing I can do is help you find someone you can talk to. A counsellor. Have you thought about that already?'

'No. I only found out yesterday, and I don't think they'd have time to see someone like me at the moment. All anyone seems to care about is that girl in the woods.'

'And you should tell whoever the father is,' I said. 'He might be able to support you and help you make a decision.'

'Yeah, right,' said Bronwyn sarcastically. 'I don't think so.'

'You might be surprised,' I said, unconvincingly. 'Anyway, the main thing is that you are all right, and you know what choices you've got.'

'Yes,' she said wiping her eyes. 'You know, you're the first person I've told.'

'Sometimes it helps just to get it off your chest,' I said. I wasn't surprised she had spoken to me first; I was older, professional, and prevented by my position from telling anyone else.

'Yes.'

'So when's your next tutorial?'

'Wednesday morning, if I join your group.'

'Right. Well, the best thing to do is to come along then and in the meantime I'll find out about the university's counselling service and check it's all right for you to swap to my group and everything. Okay?'

'Thanks, Lily,' said Bronwyn, getting up and wiping her eyes on her sleeve. 'I'll be okay now.'

'Just take it easy,' I said.

'Thanks.' She picked up her bag and smiled. 'See you on Wednesday, then.'

'Yes,' I said, and watched her walk out of the door.

I couldn't believe how dry my mouth felt. Talking for a long time always did that. I knew a cigarette and a coffee would soon solve the problem and I was going to be out of here as soon as possible. I finished sorting out the room and walked over to my desk at the front to get my stuff together. The tiredness was overwhelming by then and I felt like putting my head down and going to sleep.

Out of the corner of my eye I detected some movement in the deserted corridor. I braced myself for another student, wondering why they couldn't just go home and leave me alone. I waited but no one came in. I sighed and finished gathering my things.

Outside it was beginning to drizzle and the wind was blowing a cloud of transparent droplets past the window. Great, I thought. Rush-hour traffic through the city, and then slippery roads all the way home. I pulled my cardigan around me despite the heat from the industrial radiators and watched for a few moments as drizzle became rain and then rain became hail.

There was a bang in the corridor and I jumped. Surely Bronwyn couldn't still be here?

I felt a sudden wave of sickness engulf me, moving in a matter of seconds from my feet to my throat in a rush of adrenaline. There was a *murderer* around and I suddenly realised I was probably alone in the building. I looked at my watch and saw it was almost half-past five. Shaking involuntarily but trying to calm myself, I reached into my pocket for my phone – just in case. Then I remembered. I'd left it in the car.

'Hello?' said a dark-haired man standing in the doorway, smiling at me. He looked too old to be a student. I was still panicking. Was this the murderer? Was I going to die?

'Hello,' I said, feeling my knuckles turn white as I gripped my file and pressed it close to my chest.

'Fenn,' said the man, walking towards me and holding out his hand. 'Fenn Baker. You must be the new part-timer. *Lily?*'

'Yes,' I said, breathing quickly. 'And you are?'

'The other part-timer.' He smiled. 'Are you okay? You look a little bit pale.'

I laughed and put down my file to accept his handshake.

'Sorry,' I said, stepping back. 'I thought you were, well . . .'

'The murderer?'

'Um, yes,' I said, laughing. 'Sorry.'

'No, don't worry. It's perfectly understandable under the um, circumstances.'

We stood awkwardly for a moment, looking each other up and down. I found myself wondering what he saw when he looked at me, and then blushing slightly at the thought. I knew what I saw when I looked at him: a literary hero-fantasy with messy dark hair and look-right-through-you indigo blue eyes. Tom Jones; Heathcliff; Mercutio (never Romeo) rolled into one. He smiled dazzlingly then looked at the door.

'Right,' I said, responding to his cue and breaking the moment. 'I suppose I'd better get going.'

'Yes,' he said. 'Can I give you a lift somewhere?'

'No, thanks, I've got my car.'

'Okay.'

'But if you wouldn't mind walking me to my office, you could let me in,' I said, smiling. 'I haven't got a key yet.'

'Sure,' said Fenn, grinning broadly. We walked out of the classroom and into the hall. He looked at me and broke into laughter.

'What?' I asked, indignantly.

'You don't look like a lecturer.'

'Neither do you,' I retorted, slightly more flirtatiously than I'd intended. Fenn must have been about thirty but looked much younger. He wore 501s and a T-shirt, and I noticed a pair of expensive sunglasses perched on top of his head. My only criticism if forced to come up with one would be that he looked too much like the students. But that would be hypocritical; looking down at myself, I saw almost exactly the same clothes.

We reached my office and Fenn unlocked the door for me but didn't go away.

'I'll be okay now,' I said.

'You don't look okay,' he said seriously.

I touched my hair slightly self-consciously and stared down at the ground. I felt deflated after my first day; so many questions – too many surprises. Usually my active mind would be desperate to work out the significance of everything I'd seen and heard, but I feared this was all a bit too much for me. I wasn't even sure whether I could find my way out of the building by myself. Feeling like a shadow of my usual self, I looked at him and smiled weakly.

'It's been a hell of a day.'

'You poor thing,' he said gently, making me melt a bit. 'I'll walk you out and you can tell me all about it.'

'Okay,' I said, moving quickly into my office to grab my folders and my jacket.

I wondered what he was like beyond all the matinée idol meltdown stuff. With his relaxed, confident manner and deep public school accent he seemed assured and charismatic and though I doubted very much that I was getting special treatment, I found I didn't mind; Fenn seemed nice and I needed all the friends I could get in this chaotic institution.

We walked down the corridor to his office and I waited in the doorway while he got his stuff.

'You teach Victorian Literature, don't you?' I asked, remembering something I'd seen on the wall of the main office.

'Yep, mainly. I also do history of the romance, the saga – oh, and Shakespeare of course.'

'I was getting worried for a minute there that you only did girls' books.' I laughed and pulled the door shut as he walked out into the corridor. 'What does the Professor do?'

'Pre-Shakespeare mainly. Chaucer. Spenser. You know the kind of thing.'

'Boys' stuff.'

'Yes, I suppose you could see it like that,' laughed Fenn. 'Oh, and we mustn't forget his *controversial* experimental literature unit.'

'Oh, yes,' I said, giggling slightly at his dramatic intonation. 'I've heard about that. Is it really controversial?'

'Depends on your point of view, really. They had to take *Lolita* off the list after complaints a couple of years ago and some gay sex book whose title I forget. The Professor only took over the unit last year and since then the book list has been full of Burroughs, Gibson, Ballard and all that crap.'

'I like Ballard!'

'So do I, actually, but the rest of the list is unbearable, drug-fuelled nonsense. Whoever decided that writing books after midnight with a head full of heroin could ever be a good idea, even as an experiment, deserves to be shot.'

'You need discipline to write,' I agreed.

'Which is precisely why we only teach,' said Fenn, laughing.

'Speak for yourself,' I said. 'Mind you, you're probably right. I don't think I could ever come up with all those words. At university I was the only one whose essays were too short. While all the others were cutting, I was desperately adding.'

'Concise, minimalist, to-the-point.'

'Yes, that's the way I like to see it as well,' I said. 'Although lazy is probably more accurate.'

Fenn had been leaning against his door, watching me as I spoke. Now he moved away and fiddled with one of the drawing pins on the notice board outside his room. I noticed a scrappy sheet of A4 paper on which students were supposed to write requests for tutorials. Next to that was a lit of Fenn's tutees. Bronwyn Young's name was the last one on the list and I made a mental note to ask him about her request to change groups.

'So you're doing all the contemporary stuff?' commented Fenn, wrinkling his nose slightly.

'Yep. And genre.'

'Which ones?'

'Crime and horror,' I said, smiling a slightly macabre smile.

'Nasty business,' said Fenn, shaking his head. 'All those dirty words and all that violence.'

I wasn't sure if he was teasing me or not. I looked at him, expecting to see a smile or a laugh but he just looked vague, as if trying to work something out.

He put on his jacket and locked his office door, then calmly pulled a packet of Marlboro out of his coat pocket and lit one. Grinning like the school rebel he probably had been, he waved the packet at me.

'Do you want one?'

'No,' I said, trying not to look shocked. I smiled instead. 'I'll have one of my own.'

'Oh, good,' said Fenn. 'I was hoping for another smoker.'

'Actually I've been dying for one,' I said, lighting a cigarette and feeling naughty.

'And there's nothing like the taste of a cigarette in a *No Smoking* building,' said Fenn.

'No.'

We walked down the stairs to the exit doors without further ado. I half-expected Fenn to slide down the banisters or something but we walked in silence, smoking and thinking separate thoughts. When we reached the exit his smile came back.

'I forgot to ask what your favourite book was,' he said. 'The best personality gauge.'

'I'm not sure it'll work on me,' I said. 'Fiction or non?'

'Fiction,' said Fenn. 'Novel.'

'I've got lots of favourite plays,' I said. 'Novel – hmm. *London Fields*, probably, if I were forced to name a recent one. Of all time, probably a Sherlock Holmes. *The Hound of the Baskervilles*,' maybe.

'Interesting,' said Fenn.

'I wouldn't read too much into it,' I said. 'Anyway, what's yours?'

'I don't know. It's hard to pin down really.'

'That's not fair,' I said. 'Come on.'

'*The Mill on the Floss. Lolita.* Or something.'

'You like *Lolita*?'

'The writing's amazing.'

'And unpleasant,' I said.

He scratched his head and drew on the last of his cigarette.

'So,' he said, 'shall we continue this over dinner tomorrow?'

'Um,' I said, taken aback and stalling slightly. No one had asked me out to dinner for a very long time.

'I'm sure there's stuff you want to know about the department and the students,' he said, instantly justifying his invitation with an unspoken *just-good-friends* clause. 'That is, if you're not all booked up?'

'I don't think so,' I said, momentarily playing hard-to-get. 'No.'

Fenn looked at his watch.

'What time do you finish on Tuesdays?'

'I'm not sure,' I said. 'About fiveish, I think.'

'Shall I meet you in town about seven?'

'Yes, that's fine. Oh, where?'

'I'll book something and let you know,' said Fenn then disappeared into the night, leaving only a cigarette butt as proof he was ever there.

I got into my car and yawned. When I turned the key in the ignition it seemed like the most incredible effort. I felt cold and was shivering in the way you do when you are very weary. I yawned again, put the car into gear and pulled out of the car park.

I started to feel better as the roads and landscape became more familiar. As I drove I noticed things, landmarks of my youth. The bus stop where Eugénie and I used to catch the last bus home from the city at night, the youth club where we used to listen to indie bands and drink cider when we were still slightly too young, and finally, just before I steered my car out of the city, our school, the Anglo-European, standing serene and modest, looking much smaller than I remembered it being. When I was there it had seemed menacing, big and ugly. I resolved to go back and look around one day when I was less tired. It would have been too painful before, but now I thought I was ready.

I suddenly wondered if I had brought a pack of cards with me from London. I didn't play with them much anymore but I felt like brushing up on all the tricks I used to know. Eugénie's grandfather, the 'great' Jacques Sabine (the greatest magician in France, or so he'd told us when we were ten), had taught us both everything he knew about card tricks, which was a considerable amount, while we were still at prep school. Making cards reappear and disappear was the only thing I had been better at than Eugénie and I practised every night until I became brilliant. She was good too, and at the Anglo-European we would infuriate all the teachers with our sleight of hand, a talent which we for the most part abused by using it as a method of hiding notes we weren't supposed to be passing, and cigarettes we weren't supposed to be smoking.

Of course when we moved to the local sixth-form college we only needed to speak in French to ensure that nobody understood what we were doing or planning. After that we used our cards for occasional fun; as a way of showing off to all the students who learnt juggling and the various other trendy New Age circus tricks that were fashionable then. I knew thousands of card tricks by that stage (I even made up some of my own) but spent my evenings differently by then, hanging around in pubs and clubs at the weekend or painting my toenails and thinking about boys during the week.

Nevertheless, once in possession of a pack of cards, making four kings appear together or naming a card someone had thought of was as much a part of me as scratching my nose or sneezing, which incidentally were themselves great ways of distracting the audience's attention while I slipped the right cards into their predestined position. When I taught in London, I found that a good way of bringing a difficult class under control was to show them the Seven Detectives trick or some such thing. I resolved to find a pack of cards soon and see just how much I could still remember.

These thoughts kept me occupied all the way home and, surprisingly, I didn't think about my day at work at all or about the murder, the details of which I was wilfully suppressing. Meeting Fenn had been exciting, but today had made me so tired that I didn't have the strength to let my heart beat any faster than it needed to. I thought some of my tiredness was probably due to a kind of new girl syndrome. Meeting lots of new people in one day was taxing enough, but having to cope with teaching in the middle of a murder investigation as well was almost too much and it was lucky that I thrived on challenge. As I pulled into Mum's driveway I found myself reflecting on Bronwyn Young's predicament. Poor girl. I hoped she would make the right decision, although I wasn't altogether sure what that might be.

When I got in it was almost half-past seven. Mum was sitting at the kitchen table with a huge stack of marking and Nat was watching some soap opera in the living room. The dishes in the sink indicated that I'd missed having dinner with them, and although I knew there was probably something waiting for me in the fridge or the oven, I found I wasn't particularly hungry anyway.

I gave Mum a kiss on the cheek and put the kettle on for coffee.

'You look like I feel,' I said to her, smiling as she removed her reading glasses and looked up at me sleepily.

'Dissertation time,' she said, by way of explanation. 'Utter rubbish, most of them. I don't know why I bother. Listen to this.' She started reading from the manuscript in front of her. ' "It has been scientifically proven that men are bigger, stronger and even more intelligent than women which means that it is unlikely that we can do without them altogether." Can you believe that's a Women's Studies student?'

'Is that a first year?' I asked incredulously.

'No,' said Mum, making a face. '*Third* year. Should be locked up. Anyway, how was your first day?'

'So so,' I said, yawning involuntarily and feeling my eyes water as I struggled to keep them open. 'I can't believe I'm so tired.'

'It must have been a very long day for you,' she said sympathetically. 'Especially with the university the way it is at the moment.'

'It was. I don't know what I expected when I went there. I mean, I knew there would be a massive investigation but I had no idea it would affect *everything*.'

'Yes,' said Mum, lighting an ultra-light cigarette. 'The Lit students must be such in a state.'

'Mmm,' I said, choosing not to mention that Stephanie would have been in my class. 'Although a lot of students from other departments are really upset as well.'

'Did you see the protest?'

'Yes. Was it anything to do with Women's Studies?'

'No. Student Union, I think.'

'They were a bit aggressive,' I commented, remembering my experience by the gates.

'I suppose it's just their way of taking control,' said Mum. She thought for a moment and rubbed her head thoughtfully.

'It was awful last week when they found her.'

'Who found it — I mean *her*?' I asked.

'A dog walker,' said Mum. 'It was quite early in the morning, so by the time everyone came in on Wednesday the place was absolutely saturated with police. No one knew what had happened or why they were there. It was very scary.'

'Then the rumours started, I imagine?'

'Yes,' said Mum. 'Strange about the head, isn't it? I mean, finding a body with no head . . . It makes me shiver. I suppose it'll turn up but it just makes the whole thing so much more savage — as if it isn't bad enough in the first place.'

'Yes,' I said, pouring boiling water on the coffee and sitting down opposite her at the table. I gestured at her cigarette and changed the subject. 'I thought you were giving up?'

'Not anymore,' she said, laughing. 'After the menopause maybe.'

'Menopause?' I said. 'Surely you're a bit young for that, aren't you?'

'*Au contraire*. I had my first hot flush last week,' she said almost proudly. 'I cannot imagine what's going to happen next, but I'll keep you informed. HRT probably.'

'Goodness.'

'Anyway, I want to hear about the rest of your day. Did you meet Fenn?'

'Yes,' I said, smiling with embarrassment. 'He crept up on me after everyone had gone and I thought he was the murderer.'

'You silly thing. Fenn's lovely, everyone thinks so.'

I'd suspected that they might.

'Oh, I almost forgot . . .'

'What?'

'I'm going out with him for dinner tomorrow night, so I won't be back from work till late. Will you feed Maude?'

'Of course I will.' Mum grinned and her eyes sparkled. 'So tell me everything then. Do you like him? Is it a *date*?'

'I don't know yet,' I said evasively. 'I'll let you know if anything exciting happens.'

At the sound of her name Maude had appeared from somewhere, yawning and stretching at my feet. She looked at me and squeaked so I got up and fed her. Mum went back to her marking and for a while the only sounds in the house were the scratching of Mum's pencil and the sound of my cat chewing. I read the paper for a while and planned most of my class for the next day but gave in to my tiredness at about nine o' clock and slept in until midday on Tuesday.

CHAPTER SEVEN

The Opacity of Truth
and Timber

———◆———

Tuesday morning started slowly, with my creamy mug of hot chocolate and equally delicious thoughts about what I was going to wear tonight being spoiled by only one persistent problem; all my thoughts seemed to be contaminated, as they had been yesterday, by pictures of a headless corpse. I tried to put the image out of my mind and concentrated instead on my 'date', feeling my awakening body become more alive as I anticipated being wined and dined by the lovely Fenn.

I dressed quickly in jeans and a T-shirt and arrived at the university in good time. As I drove through the gates I could see the police still swarming on the edge of the woods in the distance and three police cars in the Samuel Beckett car park. I only got lost once in the building and by a process of logic and deduction arrived at room 331 just before three o'clock, due to teach horror fiction to the same second-year group as yesterday. *Stephanie's* group.

The room was empty and unlit, some closed blinds providing an illusion of early dusk which, while appropriate for the subject matter I was to be covering, was not exactly the best atmosphere for this class at the moment. I opened the blinds and arranged the desks as I had done yesterday. I wondered what the students had already covered in this unit and, not trusting them to tell me, decided to start with a few conventions to see how they got on. I didn't feel altogether comfortable with this as a subject, though. Horror was another genre largely based on death and evil. I'd thought about this last night and decided to start next week with *Frankenstein*, since then the students would be able to discuss eugenics and science rather than blood, guts and murder. I knew it would be difficult to keep them off those subjects but I would deal with that when the time came.

At one minute to three they started filing in. Cress was first, followed by Ash and Blake. The rest followed in dribs and drabs with Justine and Lucy last. There were only nine of them, so I assumed the others were still on strike and that the poor girl whose sister had been killed hadn't recovered enough to come back yet. I saw from the register that her Personal Tutor was Professor Valentine and made a note to have a word with him about her, something I supposed should strictly have been done yesterday.

Chattering and laughing, the group seemed more relaxed today and arranged themselves around the table.

'Okay,' I said, signalling the beginning of the class. 'Conventions of horror fiction.'

'Don't go into the basement,' said Blake in what I assumed must be his horror voice as I walked over to shut the door.

'One, two, Freddy's coming for you,' sang Ash happily, watching as a couple of the girls shivered.

'That's *film*,' I said. 'But horror films and horror fiction have all sorts of things in common, don't they?'

'Do we *have* to do this?' said Lucy in a whiny voice. 'I hate doing all the scary stuff.'

'Especially at the moment,' said Justine stroppily.

'I am aware of the potential problems,' I said, getting up from behind my desk and walking over to the white board. I smiled at the class. 'I'll be gentle with you.'

The horror fiction unit was new; developed, it seemed, by

my predecessor, Isobel. I wondered whether she'd been an expert or just an enthusiast and why she had been allowed to create a whole specialist unit and then leave. The university had been lucky to get me, I thought, since there were not many people out there who had ever studied horror as a distinct genre.

'So,' I said to the class, 'conventions of horror *literature*.' The class looked blank.

'Come on,' I said. '*Horror*. What does it do?'

'Scares you,' said Heather.

'Exactly,' I said. 'How does it do that?'

'Is it *atmosphere*?' asked Pete.

'Yes,' I said. 'And?'

'It's everything,' said Cress. 'Atmosphere, pace, description, dialogue. They all have to be characteristic of the genre.'

'Good,' I said. 'Let's talk about description for a moment. In a romance someone may describe a house as stately, beautiful, warm, welcoming and so on. What about in horror?'

'Derelict, cold and squalid?' suggested Cress.

'Like the house on the hill,' called Eddie. 'All turrets and stone towers and stuff.'

'Bleeding walls,' added Blake, eliciting a quiet 'ugh' from one of the girls.

I noticed a chill go through the room as a cloud passed over the sun and the dusky light returned, casting a peculiar shadow over the table as a faint rumble of thunder echoed in the distance. I shivered and crossed my arms in front of me.

'I think we've had enough of Amityville,' I said into the silence. 'What else?'

'There's always a storm,' said Kerry.

'Not in all horror fiction,' I said. 'What are storms a convention of?'

'The Gothic genre,' said Cress.

'Good,' I said, feeling another chilled blast of air go through the room as rain started to lash the window horizontally, creating even more darkness through which the tormented sound of the wind tore loudly.

'Can we have the lights on?' asked Justine.

'Are you scared?' teased Kerry, looking slightly freaked out herself.

'You know what happens in the dark,' said Blake slowly, raising his hand unseen by Lucy behind her back and leaning in towards the others.

'Yeah,' continued Ash, whispering. 'When there's no one else around . . .'

'Where no one can hear you scream . . .' continued Blake, obviously enjoying the attention that their double-act was now receiving.

'You think you're alone . . .'

'But then the door creaks open and . . .'

'He's got you!' shouted Blake, touching Lucy's back and making her scream and jump half off her seat in fright.

What happened next was confusing. Lucy's scream made Justine and Heather scream too, which made everyone else move about jerkily in their seats, as if a spider had been dropped in the area or something. Then the door really did creak open and Ash, in a momentary lapse of cool, let out a high-pitched scream which would go down in student folklore and which I suspected nobody would ever let him forget.

'Oh my God!' exclaimed Kerry.

'Shit,' said Blake. 'What's that?'

'Ahhh,' shrieked Pete camply, imitating Ash and flapping his hands in the air. 'It's . . . oh my God, it's a . . . a . . . *TV crew*. We're all going to die!'

Everybody started laughing at this point, and the tension was broken. For *them* that was. I was wondering what on earth a TV crew was doing walking into the middle of my class.

'Shhh,' I said, intrigued by the media circus coming through the door. I got up to introduce myself and direct the cameras to the correct room (they weren't meant to be here, surely?) but there was no need, because a man with a microphone swept straight in and took over.

'A class in grief,' he declared dramatically to camera, sending all the students into fresh waves of giggles. He ignored them and continued.

'This is the class in which Stephanie Duncan attended one of her last lectures at this university –'

'Cut!' declared a man in black jeans, coming out from behind what looked like a sound-man and walking over to me.

'Why are they laughing?' he demanded.

'You burst in at a rather – um – funny moment,' I said, trying to stop my own smile from becoming a laugh. 'Sorry.'

'Didn't the Professor tell you we were coming?'

'No,' I said. 'Not unless he left a note in my pigeonhole. I haven't been there yet.'

'All right,' he said quickly, turning away from me in frustration. 'All right!' he said in a louder voice to the class. 'Now,' he boomed. 'Can we have some grief, please?'

'Hang on,' I said. 'You can't *direct* them!'

'This is the news,' he said patiently. 'We are going out on air tonight. I just need some good pictures, okay?'

I surveyed my students with interest as Justine and Lucy started attempting to look morose and bereaved, while Cress tried to wipe tears of laughter from her red face. After a while the news crew departed, taking Justine, Lucy and Heather with them for further questioning and grief shots.

Left with six students from a class that was originally meant to have comprised nineteen I gave in and decided to set them an essay question so they could go. My watch said that it was half-past four (where had the time gone?) so they wouldn't be missing much.

'Okay,' I said to the remaining students. 'Assignment time.'

'Oh, *what*?' said Ash indignantly. 'There's hardly any of us here.'

'Aaah!' shrieked Blake, mimicking his earlier scream. 'Not an essay – it'll eat us alive!'

'Very funny,' said Ash, smiling.

'I want you to read *Frankenstein*,' I began. Then something else caught my attention.

'What's that noise?' asked Cress.

'Yeah, that really is weird,' said Kerry.

From somewhere down the corridor came a strange whimpering sound, like the squeaking of a rusty wheel but definitely human, and, if you strained hard enough to hear it, almost melodic.

'Could you have a look please, Kerry?' I asked.

'You're having a laugh, aren't you?' she said. 'I'm not going out there. Send one of the boys.'

'Ooooh, don't send Ash,' joked Pete, giving his mate a dig in the ribs.

'I'll go,' said Cress, letting out a sanctimoniously mature sigh.

The boy sat there for six days. He wore the same clothes; his best clothes – the ones in which he'd been going to impress her. What was that word again? Proposition. No. Ultimatum. Why didn't he get there first?

He asked himself the question over and over until he went mad. He didn't see anyone, didn't speak to anyone. He didn't eat or wash. Then, on the seventh day, he came out.

We all sat waiting while Cress stepped out into the corridor to see what was going on. I would have gone myself but I expected it was just a student messing around and didn't want to leave my class for that. I didn't imagine it was anything dangerous, although it sounded decidedly spooky.

As the sound drew closer it became clearer. It was a voice, high-pitched and more than slightly broken, singing slowly and deliberately, though I couldn't make out the words until I came closer and realised it was 'The Teddy Bears' Picnic.'

'Jason?' came Cress's muffled voice. 'What's wrong with you?'

' *"You're in for a big sur –"'*

'What's the matter with you? Where have you been?'

Silence. Then her voice again.

'I'll get help.'

The door opened slowly and Cress poked her head in.

'Lily,' she said seriously, 'I think I need you out here.'

'Okay,' I said, nodding to the rest of the class that they could go. Before I had a chance to rush out into the corridor, Cress came over and looked earnestly into my eyes.

'It's Jason,' she said. 'You know, the one that was away?'

'Yes,' I said. 'What's wrong with him?'

'I don't know,' said Cress. 'He's not drunk or anything. I thought he was and then . . . up close . . . the *smell*. Not like someone who's been drinking. Just the smell of . . .'

She let the silence hang in the air, shaking her head folornly.

'. . . *Death*. I don't mean to be overdramatic, but he's always been a bit strange. No one thought to go and see how this had affected him.'

'Don't worry,' I said. 'I'll take over from here.'

'Are you sure?'

'Yes,' said Cress. 'Are you going to take him back to his room?'

'I don't know,' I said.

'Well, if you do, ignore what it says on the students' room guide. He in 3313.'

'Three three one three?'

'Yeah, Meredith Hall. Loads of us swapped at the beginning of term and it's all a bit confusing.'

'I see.'

'The bloke he swapped with – Adam – was in another hall entirely. I wouldn't want you to get lost.'

'Thanks.'

Cress hurried out and I followed more slowly, looking for Jason. The classroom was on the third floor which was deserted by now and there was no sign of him in the main corridor up here. I walked down the hall, trying to follow the muffled singing but not being able to work out where it was now coming from.

By the time I reached the second floor the singing had moved again; off downstairs towards the main office which would now be shut, I realised, looking at my watch. I ran the last few yards around the corner at the end of the hall and then down the last flight of stairs, eventually finding the slight young boy I assumed must be Jason. He was still singing, slumped against the Professor's door.

'Hello, Jason,' I said, walking slowly towards him the way you would approach a ferocious animal.

'Who the hell are you?' he asked. 'Are you in my imagination too?'

'No,' I said. 'I'm real, and I'm going to talk to you in this classroom.'

I pointed at an empty room slightly down the hall, shivering as I realised that everywhere was empty now. If there was such a thing as a graveyard shift for teaching staff then I suspected this was it.

Jason struggled unsteadily to his feet.

'There,' I said, soothingly, and ushered him into the small room.

As soon as I got close to him I could understand what Cress had meant about the smell. It wasn't just that Jason hadn't washed for a long time; his blue Oasis T-shirt was stained with vomit and his white jeans yellow encrusted with what I assumed must be urine. As well as this he looked as if he'd been on some kind of hike: his shoes and trousers were coated with dried mud and his T-shirt ripped slightly on one arm. But it was clear that he had been good-looking once with his dark shoulder-length hair and underneath all the stains and angrily recent spots he had a kind face. This face now crumpled into tears as I helped him to a seat and half-sat on the table next to him.

'She's dead,' he said, pronouncing the words slowly as if his tongue was too big for his mouth. 'And I couldn't do anything.'

'No one could do anything, Jason,' I said calmly. 'I'm afraid that sometimes we just can't help –'

'Shut up!' he shouted, making me jump and my heart start to race. 'Please. Just, just . . . Shut. Up.'

He started to hum to himself; a different tune this time. He mumbled some words about going into the trees, but although I strained to hear him, I couldn't make out the song he was singing. I could feel myself shaking as I watched such suffering. Talking usually worked in a crisis, but I could see that he was too far gone for that. I'd heard that grief could send you mad, but I'd never seen it so poignantly before – and certainly not at first hand. I was terrified. I didn't know what he was going to do next.

'They're watching you,' he said jerkily, giving his words a sing-song eeriness.

'Who?' I said.

'*The trees* . . . Oh God!'

He raised his hands in the air and then let them fall heavily and limply down on the desk. He looked at himself and cried out.

'What fucking use am I? What is this? Who is this?' he sobbed, grabbing my arm and betraying his strength. He breathed stiffly into my ear. 'Help me.'

'I'm going to,' I said calmly, pulling away and taking a deep breath. 'I'm going to fetch someone who can help.'

'Fetch the reaper,' he said. 'No one can help me now.'

'Don't say that. You've had a shock and just need to recover.'

'I. Will. Never. Recover. From. This.'

'Well, you're going to have to try,' I said. 'Because I am going to fetch someone who –'

'I saw it,' said Jason simply, sounding almost normal. 'I saw it happen.'

'What?' I asked. 'What did you see?'

'The . . . Oh, God. GET ME SOME HELP! I haven't eaten in a week. Help me . . .'

His body started convulsing, as if he were having a seizure. Scared and out-of-my-depth, I made for the door to try and find someone. As I ran into the corridor I heard Jason laugh.

'I'm going to get you – I know who you are,' he sang. 'I saw you kill her – I know who you are!'

I ran down the corridor as fast as I could until I came to the Professor's door on which I knocked several times but received no answer. I'd seen his car in the car park earlier, but, typically, when you want an academic there are never any around.

I realised I was alone and shivered. Fenn didn't teach on Tuesdays and there was no sign of Professor Valentine anywhere around the main office next to his room. I suspected he must have been at a long meeting because a telephone message saying *Nadia called, 16.00* was still pinned to his door. I turned away from it and glanced at the notice board on the other side of the corridor. There was a selection of police leaflets all asking for information about Stephanie's murder and a poster asking for the same information, with a picture of her parents and details of a reward. Nobody had said anything about that before. According to the poster they were prepared to give fifty thousand pounds to whoever could provide information leading to the arrest of the killer. I felt sorry for them; it must be the most awful feeling in the world, I thought. Next to that was a poster with the Student Union logo advertising the candlelit vigil tonight.

I looked through the window next to the Professor's door and saw the outline of the woods, ominous and miniaturised by distance. The Samuel Beckett Building was detached from the rest of the university and stood next to the gate leading off campus and opposite the Halls of Residence by the road where I had become embroiled in the protest yesterday. Beyond the woods was the river.

In the few seconds that I watched, I could just make out two figures in the distance walking across the playing fields. I don't know what it was that struck me as strange about them. It could have been the way they kept stopping and starting, or it could have been the way in which the woman kept holding out her arms, as if to indicate something big. In any case, I didn't have time to stare out of the window. Finding no sign of any other human presence except Jason in this block, I turned towards the main door and ran for help.

The boy sat for a few moments, waiting for the girl to come back, and then he decided to go. He would find the culprit and . . . What? He didn't know. He wanted to kill; to seek revenge. He wanted to shout and scream and feel the body convulse as he kicked and punched and . . . yes, he was going to go and find him.

I ran at full speed over to the main block, hoping to find someone to help. I didn't know quite what I was looking for and as I reached the big double doors, now as deserted as the rest of the university, I began to seriously doubt that I would actually find anyone still here.

The doors were open but the corridors were empty and I only passed one person in the whole block: a white-coated science student presumably working late. When I reached the reception area my fears were confirmed. The shutter was down. There was nobody here to help.

I turned and walked slowly back to the Samuel Beckett Building, rationalising the situation in my head. Jason was in a terrible state. Could it be drugs or something? I kept hearing his words in my head. He'd said he knew who had done *it*: that he'd seen *it*. I shivered and walked back into the Samuel Beckett Building, determined to take him to hospital myself – via the police station where he could tell them exactly what he knew (which I suspected in the end would probably be nothing but fantasy).

The block was quiet and dead when I walked in and I felt quite spooked by the atmosphere. Something about it made my hair stand on end; a feeling of being watched, of not being alone. I forced myself to think about something else instead and walked over to the classroom where I'd left Jason.

It was empty.

Feeling my heart beat faster (from the surprise? the loneliness?), I ran up the stairs to the third floor and collected my things from room 331. I ran back down the stairs, looking for Jason but really just wanting to get out of there. I hoped he'd come to his senses and gone to sort himself out. It was something else to add to my list of things to discuss with the Professor, if I ever found him. I looked out of the window and saw that his car was now gone. Tomorrow then, I thought as I left.

The boy felt a dull ache as the heavy object hit him on the back of the neck.

He was swallowing something, but he didn't know what it was. Then he shut his eyes.

Somewhere in the distance a phone rang.

'We've got a problem.'

'What sort of problem?'

The man explained, as quickly as he could. Then he explained what he'd done about it.

'That won't kill him,' said the voice, laughing. 'Can't you find something else as well?'

The man scanned the room and found something perfect. He talked into the telephone some more and then it was time to go.

CHAPTER EIGHT

Aphrodisiac

I drove out of the university car park, breathing quickly and feeling hot. Was I overreacting or had I just had a really bizarre afternoon? I smoked a cigarette as I accelerated through the city and, surrounded by normality once more, started feeling better. I was going on a date with Fenn. Maybe that would take my mind off everything.

I had been intending to get changed at the university but I was far too spooked for that. Instead I resorted to one of my old tricks: petrol station toilets. Standing in the large cubicle at the rear of a garage off the ring road in only my underwear, I was reminded of a production that Freak Show once did. It was an travelling production and we had to change costumes on the way. It made me smile to remember the way the others all got tangled up with each other on the tour bus while I followed behind in my car, unflustered and blasé as usual, knowing I had a much more comfortable plan up my sleeve. All I needed to do was stop at one of the larger service stations on the main roads and there it all was: large mirror (sometimes full-size), wash basin, tissues and soap. Everything you needed for a swift change of clothes and make-up.

I opened my bag and pulled out a little black dress that never needed ironing. I pulled it down over my head and then looked in the mirror. I could see I needed more make-up, but I had never really understood all those magazine articles about how to change a daytime 'look' into a 'more dramatic' evening style. I decided to make do with another application of red lipstick and black mascara, and as a finishing touch swept my hair back into a loose chignon. I was just putting my make-up and day clothes into my bag when there was a sharp rap on the door which made me jump, proving I wasn't as blasé as I would like to think, and that this afternoon had shaken me up more than I'd thought.

'Are you all right, love?' came a voice from outside, presumably the man I'd seen behind the counter when I walked in.

'Yes, thanks,' I said, unlocking the door to the cubicle and cheering up after I saw the surprised look on the assistant's face as he registered my transformation. It made me happy that I still had the capacity to shock: to do something unexpected and slightly rebellious. Despite my best intentions, my relationship with Anthony had been dull. I liked the feeling of not knowing what was going to happen next and thrived on adventure. Our relationship had neither of those. This would have been a clear mandate for a single life had I not been such an incurable romantic.

Fenn had booked a table at The Exchange, a new restaurant on the other side of town. I was meeting him there at seven. He'd called this morning and left a message on the answerphone at home; all deep-voiced and charming, which had made me excited, and then not. It was only a friendly meal, and I'd just come out of a complicated relationship.

I wondered why Anthony still hadn't been in touch. I didn't mind, far preferring a clean break to one of the *please take me back* variety, but my pride was dented. Surely I was worth more of a fight than this?

I pulled up outside the restaurant with ten minutes to spare and applied another coat of lipstick, knowing I shouldn't be making such an effort but not wanting to be upstaged by a bloke, particularly one as attractive as Fenn. I wasn't sure yet whether or not I should drink tonight. I thought probably not – there was nowhere for me to stay overnight if I did. Mum's house was about twenty miles from the city; commutable but not very convenient when you needed to get a taxi back.

At five to seven I made my entrance. Unfortunately Fenn had not yet arrived, but I got some appreciative looks from the waiter who hurried over to take my coat.

'Thanks,' I said, shivering slightly as he hung it on a peg.

'Table for?'

'Two,' I said. 'I think my companion has already booked.'

'What name is it please?'

'Baker,' I said. 'Fenn Baker.'

The waiter hurried off and then returned with a menu. He sat me at a cosy table for two by the window and poured a glass of mineral water. I looked at my watch. It was seven o'clock exactly.

Ten minutes later there was still no sign of Fenn. I ordered another mineral water and smoked two cigarettes so quickly that my head swam and my throat hurt. My heart was beating too fast. What if he didn't come? I wondered if Fenn was just one of those people who were always late for things. I never understood people like that. Maybe they were insecure, desperate to feel needed and wanted. (*Oh! I'm so glad you made it – I thought something terrible had happened.*) Fenn hadn't struck me as the insecure type, though, and I couldn't think what might have kept him.

Just as I was about to pay for my mineral water and leave, he swept into the restaurant looking suitably flustered and winningly tousled. He grinned at me and shrugged his shoulders as he walked over to kiss me on the cheek before taking his place opposite me.

'Sorry,' he said, putting his mobile phone, his Marlboros and a Zippo lighter down on the table. 'Have you been waiting long?'

'No,' I lied. 'I've only been here a few minutes. For a while I thought you might have been and gone.'

'I wouldn't do that,' said Fenn. He pushed back his chair

slightly and crossed his legs under the table. He looked a bit flushed and I wondered if he had run to get here. 'Anyway,' he said, looking up and smiling a broad melting smile, 'how was work?'

'Oh, complicated,' I said, laughing and lighting a cigarette. Fenn lit a cigarette as well and ran a hand through his hair. He smelt slightly of an aftershave I really liked. Gucci something. 'Bizarre,' I said.

'Par for the course at the moment,' Fenn replied.

'I know,' I said. I paused and thought about my afternoon. 'I'm beginning to wonder if the Professor actually exists. I've only seen him once.'

Fenn laughed.

'I know what you mean. Never an academic around when you need one.'

'Exactly what I was thinking,' I said. 'He sent a TV crew into my class today.'

'That's nothing,' said Fenn dryly. 'In one week I had a theatre company, a radio play producer and a troupe of nude women dancers.'

'You're joking?' I said, giggling.

'No,' said Fenn. 'The Professor is notoriously bad at telling part-timers what he's organised. The first you know about it is when who or whatever it is walks into your class.'

'Why nude dancers?' I asked.

'Oh, I was covering a theatre class,' he said, as if that explained it.

'Right.'

'Anyway, you look quite ravishing. I hope you're not making an effort for me?'

'Don't flatter yourself,' I said, teasingly. 'It wasn't much of an effort anyway.' I smiled, remembering my *mise-en-scène* in the petrol station.

We both looked at our menus, trying to ignore the charged current crackling between us. I didn't know what spark had created it but the evidence was there, just as it had been yesterday. We got a buzz from each other for no apparent reason: fascinated by the smallest look or comment; getting on together effortlessly. Of course, the more we ignored the feeling, the more intense it seemed to become. *Look at me!* it kept saying *Do something about me before I explode!* All the words in the leathery menu swam into one another as I tried to concentrate on the food they were describing. The problem was they all seemed to be saying *Fenn* or *Lovely Fenn* like peculiar remnants of a dream I hadn't yet had.

I'd had a theory, when I was about fourteen, that when you met the person you were meant to be with, you would just *know*, with heart-pounding, stomach-wrenching certainty that this was the man for you. Of course I hadn't heard of lust then, or pure animal attraction, or sheer drunkenness. I blushed at myself and inwardly berated my thoughts. I didn't usually think like this and I certainly wasn't promiscuous enough to be entertaining notions of . . . I gulped and turned a page in the vast expanse of unreadable menu. I imagined Fenn would be much too complex a proposition for someone like me anyway. I had only slept with three people in my entire life.

'See anything you like?' he asked, coquettishly.

'Maybe,' I said. 'I fancy medallions of something about five pages back.' I waved the menu about. 'Why is this thing so long?'

Fenn laughed.

'Oysters,' he said. 'And cream. Yum.'

'Mmm. Medallions of lamb with fennel and rosemary.'

'Good,' he said. 'I'll order.'

A bottle of wine appeared from nowhere, and as my allocated two glasses became an over-the-limit three I started tingling with an unbridled anticipation for food and something else I couldn't quite put my finger on. Talk about work and students gradually gave way to personal stuff. I felt slightly drunk, which wasn't like me.

'So you've come from London?'

'Yes,' I said. 'And I'm not planning to go back for a very long time.'

'Aha! A mysterious past. I knew it.'

'It's not really a mystery,' I said. 'I'd just had enough.'

'If you say so,' said Fenn, his eyes twinkling in the candlelight as he lit a cigarette.

I watched the candle as its wax melted and ran like an oily worm down the side of the brass holder. Which reminded me.

'Did you hear about the vigil?' I asked.

'Which one?' said Fenn. 'There are so bloody many.'

'It's funny the way people cope, isn't it?'

'Mmm,' he said thoughtfully. 'I keep asking myself if there was anything I could have done.'

'You?'

'Haven't they told you? Apparently, apart from the murderer, I was the last person to see Stephanie alive.'

'Really? How?'

'Late tutorial.' He shook his head in disbelief. 'She always had late tutorials. It suited me – I mean, I'm always there until about eight on the days I'm in. Anyway, she came at about seven as usual and we talked for half an hour or so. I could never work out why she needed so many tutorials. She was clever. Not as clever as Jason or Cress, but bound to do well.'

'I saw Jason today,' I said.

'Did you? I thought he'd gone back up north or something. He's been off for a week.'

'I don't know where he'd been,' I said. 'But he was in a hell of a state.'

'God,' said Fenn.

'Anyway,' I said, 'you mustn't blame yourself. These things – you know, they're fairly unpreventable, I think.'

'It was such a strange evening,' he said, shaking his head. 'That block is so atmospheric at night. Full of unexplainable bangs and crashes. I remember Stephanie wanted to talk about some personal problems. She was supposed to be seeing me about her *Tempest* essay, but we spent five minutes on that and the remaining twenty-five on the meaning of her life.'

I nodded sagely as he took a sip of his wine and carried on.

'I've been over and over the whole thing, in my head and with the police. She left at half-past seven and I walked to the main office to make a phone call. I remember being unsettled by some banging, and thought I might just as well use my mobile in the car. Anyway, just at that moment the phone in the main office started ringing, or so I thought, and I felt compelled to go in and answer it. I unlocked the door and walked in but then realised it had actually been the phone in the Professor's office. I locked the office up again and was just about to leave when Stephanie came out of the shadows and seemed to be about to walk back into the building. I asked her what she thought she was doing, but she just went red and muttered something about forgetting a book. I didn't want to get stuck with her for much longer but I was worried about her so I offered her a lift – she'd been talking about some party all the students were having at a house in town – but she refused. So I went to my car and left.'

'What's wrong with that?'

'I should have insisted, I suppose.'

'Don't be ridiculous,' I said. 'Forcing lifts on young women is much more unacceptable than what you did.'

'Maybe.'

'Why didn't anyone like her?'

'She was hard to like. She didn't hide her intelligence the way some of the others do, so she ended up seeming arrogant, separatist, and as though she had a superiority complex.'

'So you didn't like her either?' I said, responding to something in his tone beyond the outward politeness.

'That's a hard question. I felt sorry for her when the others picked on her, but you know how they are. Sometimes it's hard not to find them funny.'

'I know,' I said, smiling. 'It's difficult to keep a straight face. Like when the TV crew came in, saying "class in grief," to find them all in fits over some stunt Ash had just pulled.'

'Sounds typical,' said Fenn, downing his wine and topping up our glasses.

The waiter arrived with the food, which looked gorgeous but which both of us only picked at. I looked at Fenn, watching his earnest expression as he squeezed some lemon on to an oyster. He was an odd mixture, I thought. I didn't understand why he should want to take the blame for Stephanie's death when he had obviously tried to help. He was either a true gentleman, I decided, or just an interesting man with a guilt complex. Either way I found him fascinating. I loved the detail he saw in things. Whenever I had wanted to discuss something in depth with Anthony he had insisted that I get to the point and not waste time talking about trivialities. The problem was that I saw the world as a collection of trivialities; some more important than others. The *point* of most things was usually to be found in the small details, which was why I paid attention to them. I liked what Freud said about everything being there for a reason. Ash hadn't screamed by accident today; the scream, I thought, betrayed what he actually felt about Stephanie's death – terror, just like everyone else.

The man drove for a long time with the stereo on to drown out the noise. It was taking longer than he'd imagined.

At one point the boy woke up. He felt his body boiling. He tried to breathe but it hurt. He didn't know where he was – that ringing in his ears. It was a miracle that he opened his eyes for that second, but there was no one to witness it. All he had seen was the darkness of a car boot anyway. He had wanted blue skies.

So he slipped away. Not dead, but almost.

'So what made you specialise in Victorian stuff?' I asked.

'It impresses the girls,' joked Fenn.

'Yeah, right.'

'No, seriously. When we had to specialise at university I picked all the options that had the most girls in them. I was young and slightly green and, um, *desperate*.'

'Must have been right up your street anyway then,' I said. 'All that swooning and those heaving breasts.'

'Mmm,' said Fenn, licking his lips.

'There's a word for people like you,' I said teasingly.

'Rake?' he asked, raising his eyebrows.

'No, I was thinking more of *fop*.'

'Possibly,' said Fenn. 'Rakes were the ones who broke people's hearts but fops were just pretty boys, blindly following fashion.'

'Definitely a fop then,' I said, lighting a cigarette and watching Fenn's deep blue eyes sparkle happily. As he poured my fourth glass of wine I realised I would almost certainly be staying in the city tonight and found that the idea didn't panic me as much as it might have done under other circumstances. In fact it was a warming-brandy thought, the kind that washes over you, unannounced and soothing; a surprise to savour at the end of a long day. The only question was, would I be staying with Fenn?

'You come from around here originally, don't you?' he asked, breaking into my thoughts.

'Yes,' I said. 'My mum lives in Mawlish. How did you know?'

'I know her. She helped me out with some research I was doing.'

'Mum helped you with research?' I said disbelievingly. 'What kind of research?'

'My PhD thesis: *Heroes and Heroines in Literature and Beyond*.'

'Goodness.'

'Yes, I wanted a feminist perspective. I mean, the idea of heroism has always fascinated me, and being a hero is supposed to be a positive, honourable thing. But I was doing a chapter on real-life heroism: do women really want to be swept off their feet or rescued or whatever.'

'And do they?' I asked, thinking that I wouldn't mind if the sweeper or rescuer was Fenn.

'The jury's still out,' he said, grinning. 'Theory is some-what different from practice sometimes.'

'I know,' I said. 'People forget that ideas have effects.'

'Quite. I mean, it's all very well to sit in a university pontificating about stuff; deciding how to run economies, fight wars, or treat men and women, but people forget that these ideas are then applied and often go horrifically wrong.'

'Like all those sixties ideas about not teaching children grammar and stuff?'

'Exactly.'

'When I was at school, we had to do times tables out loud and learn about clauses and sub-clauses and everything. It was a wonderful education when I look back on it although I didn't appreciate it much at the time.'

'I suppose you went to school somewhere around here too?'

'Yes, the Anglo-European.'

'I've heard of that, but I thought you had to be semi-European to go there.'

'I am semi-European,' I said, pouring more wine. Fenn gestured to the waiter to bring another bottle then looked at me intently. 'That is, semi-French.'

'You're French?'

'Half,' I said, fiddling with my lighter. I smiled. 'The best half, obviously.'

'Mother or father?'

'Father. They're divorced now.'

'Mine, too.'

The waiter came to clear everything away and to take our orders for dessert. All this wine was making me hungry; desperate for a variety of tastes and textures to keep my palate interested in something other than the constant and therefore unfulfilling Gauloises. I had never been a very big fan of sweet things, though, and regretted not eating more of my lamb. That was the problem. I was craving all these things and then not being able to swallow them, partly because I was nervous and partly because I was talking so much. Fenn, who seemed cooler than me but in a similar state, ordered chocolate cake while I plumped for *tiramisù*, which I hoped would slip down fairly easily.

I looked up and saw that the restaurant was packed now. It was odd, we were quite near the door yet I hadn't seen anyone come in. As far as I was concerned I had been alone with Fenn.

'So what are you doing here?' I asked, pushing my fork into the cool moist pudding in the bowl that had appeared in front of me. 'I mean, why are you working at the university?'

'Same reasons as you, I think. I got bored of London and all of that. This suits me down to the ground.'

I saw a flicker in Fenn's eyes, betraying some kind of unease. Then, in an instant, he was back to normal and smiling.

'Do you have family in the West Country?' I asked.

'No. I just came here for the job really.'

'It must be hard to find friends and stuff if you do that.'

'Mmm, depends. You make friends through your job, thank goodness. I got quite well with the woman you've replaced and she introduced me to a few people. Isobel's a writer, you should look her up sometime.'

'Yes, I might do,' I said, hating myself for feeling instantly jealous of this unknown woman. Was she prettier or more interesting than me?

'You must know a lot of people anyway, since you grew up around here.'

I sighed.

'Not really,' I said. 'My best friend Eugénie died when we were both eighteen, just before we were due to go to university. We were so close, I didn't really have any other friends.'

'God,' said Fenn. 'Lily, I'm so sorry.'

'No, it's okay,' I said, shaking slightly as I gulped down more wine. 'It was a long time ago.'

We sat in silence for a few minutes while I played back

that night in my head. How many thousands of times would I have to see it, I wondered, before it finally went away? It may have been a long time ago but in my thoughts and nightmares it was as clear as this moment. Clearer, in fact.

After leaving the Anglo-European, Eugénie and I started our A levels at the local sixth-form college. Within six months we were both smoking more than ever (we were allowed!), drinking and going out with our new friends. The Anglo-European had been very strict and stuffy and we were determined to make the most of our freedom. After about eighteen months of hard partying and studying we met two surfers at a party: Dale Carter and Bobby Isles. Eugénie was already going out with someone at the time, a lad from college called Ned. But I'd never had a boyfriend before and it was all very exciting when we planned our first double date.

Eugénie was what you would call devastatingly attractive. Everyone said she looked like Béatrice Dalle but I thought she was prettier than that. She did everything first, from smoking a cigarette to losing her virginity, which she did with Dale a week after they started going out. Bobby and I took it all more slowly, but six months later he was my first.

The summer after our A levels was when Eugénie and I learnt to surf and during our year off we were inseparable; Dale and Eugénie, Bobby and me. We all worked in restaurants around the city by day and spent every night partying.

I could never remember why Eugénie and Bobby were in Kirsty's car that night. It was the wrong combination really. It should have been me and Bobby or Dale and Eugénie. For ages afterwards I wished it had been me instead, because nothing was worse than losing your boyfriend and best friend in the same car accident. I'd heard that it was natural to look for someone to blame after something like that happened, but nevertheless I knew it was Kirsty's fault. She was so over the limit when they left the party that it was a miracle she wasn't dead just from the drink and the drugs she had done. But she managed to get into the car, start it – and then crash it into a tree, killing my best friend and the first boy I'd loved.

'Are you okay?' asked Fenn, breaking into my thoughts.

'Yes, I'm fine,' I said. 'I was just thinking, you know.'

'Yes.'

'So are you at work tomorrow?' I asked, changing the subject.

'Yes,' said Fenn. 'Unfortunately. Tuesday is my only day off in the week, and I usually don't even get to take that, what with students booking their bloody tutorials at such inconvenient times.'

'Poor you.'

'I know. There is one hell of an atmosphere in that place at the moment.'

We both laughed and the tension was broken. After a couple of strong espressos and some light banter, Fenn asked for the bill.

'I don't mean to be forward or give you the wrong idea or anything,' I said, 'but I really am too drunk to drive.'

'So you want to borrow my sofa?'

'If you don't mind,' I said, grateful although slightly disappointed that he hadn't assumed I meant his bed. I wasn't very accomplished at one-night stands, possibly because whenever I said 'sofa' men seemed to think that was exactly what I meant.

'Okay,' said Fenn. 'As long as you don't mind that it's not actually mine.' He smiled at the expression on my face. 'I'm cat sitting.'

'Ah,' I said. 'Maybe I should get back. I wouldn't want to impose.'

'You can't drive like that. Come on, I really don't mind. And, well . . . I'd like to carry on talking.'

'Me too,' I said, smiling. 'But I should call my mum. She still acts like I'm fifteen and she's expecting me back.'

'I expect mothers never stop worrying about their

daughters,' said Fenn nicely. 'Especially at a time like this.'

'I've left my phone in the car,' I said, feeling in my pockets for confirmation. 'Can I borrow yours?'

'Sure,' he said.

I reached over to pick it up, but as soon as I was about to dial, it started ringing.

'Oh bollocks,' said Fenn as I passed the ringing phone over to him. 'Sorry, Lily, I should have turned it off.' He pressed a button and started to speak. 'Hello? Ah, hi. No, I can't talk right now. Sorry? No, I'm in the middle of something. Now? No, I can't. What? You're *joking*.'

'Something come up?' I asked, trying to hide my disappointment.

'What?' Fenn looked distracted. 'Yes. Sorry.'

'I'll get a cab back,' I said.

'No, you can't do that. I've promised you somewhere to stay and the offer still stands. I just have to pop out for a bit, that's all.'

My pride told me I should say no but I couldn't really afford to take a cab all the way back to Mawlish. I wished I hadn't drunk so much and accepted as gracefully as I could.

I don't know what time Fenn got back that night, but I woke up in a foreign double bed the next morning, alone and almost late for work with a note by the bed saying: *I need to talk to you. Can you meet me at the Green Dragon at eight tonight? Love, Fenn.*

Feeling confused, I sat up in bed and realised I was naked and my head hurt. I could hear a whirring noise coming from under the bed but couldn't work out what it was. I dug out my dress from the corner of the room and slipped it over my head. I thought my coat would be somewhere, although I couldn't remember where. All at once my head went into a spin. Had I slept with Fenn? I certainly couldn't remember sleeping with him. In fact, I couldn't even remember seeing him after he'd dropped me off here last night. But he must have come back, or how else would the note have got there?

He must at least have seen me lying naked in bed. How embarrassing.

But had I slept with him? I'd heard stories about people forgetting things like that, but it had never happened to me. However drunk I got, I always had a fair idea of what had happened and sleeping with strangers was not usually part of my agenda. I couldn't have done, I reasoned, feeling my breathing slow and then speed up again as I thought about what it could have been like and decided I would definitely have remembered it.

I suddenly realised that I didn't know anything about Fenn. It seemed a bit suspicious, him running off like that last night and just *happening* to be cat-sitting in a house other than his own. I hoped he didn't have a wife or girlfriend stashed away somewhere; that would be even more complicated and embarrassing.

I was startled, suddenly, by something fluffy and orange emerging from under the bed. Reassuringly, it was a large ginger tomcat; the whirring sound I had heard before was his spasmodic purring which became louder as he jumped on my lap and let me stroke him. This must be the cat that was being sat, I realised with a smile. A brief inspection of the tag on his collar indicated that my first impressions had been correct. *Fluffy*, it said.

I looked at my watch and saw that it was half-past eight. My first-year tutorial was at ten but I would have to locate my car (outside the restaurant?), my knickers and my coat before then, get changed and have some sort of breakfast.

I managed to assemble all the items within about ten minutes. Luckily I still had a packet of cigarettes in my coat pocket so I lit one and drew on it eagerly, coughing slightly as I poured myself a glass of Evian from the fridge in the kitchen. I had smoked and drunk too much last night and felt quite dreadful. Fearing the return of the flat's owner I gulped the water down quickly and left. Half an hour later I was unlocking the door to my car and depositing a parking ticket in the glove box to be dealt with later. All I kept thinking was: *Never again*. A sexless but embarrassing one-night stand, with a colleague, in a stranger's house, and then a parking ticket. How irresponsible.

Somewhere beneath my anxiety was a warning thought, though: I'd had a wonderful time with Fenn. If only it hadn't been spoiled by that damn phone call.

When I reached the university I went straight to Women's Studies to see Mum, in case she had been worried about me. She was nowhere to be found so I left a message with the secretary and went for breakfast in the student bar – an experience I would not have cared to repeat.

Since I assumed that Fenn had come into work before me I went and knocked at his door before going along to take the tutorial, but there was no reply. I walked down the corridor to the Professor's office and found to my surprise that he was actually there, although he seemed to be on his way out.

'Professor Valentine?'

'Yes?' he said. 'It's Lily, isn't it? How are you getting on?'

'Okay,' I said. 'Under the circumstances.'

'Circumstances?'

'Well, yes,' I said, wondering if he was always this vague. 'The murder investigation.'

'Oh, yes,' he said. 'Well, I did warn you.'

'I know,' I said. 'But I didn't realise the students would be so affected.'

'But you're coping?'

'Well, yes, I suppose so.'

'Good.'

I'd been following Valentine down the long ground-floor corridor but he stopped now, outside a room where I assumed he must be about to take a class.

'Actually,' I said, 'there were a couple of things I wanted to ask you.'

'Fire away,' he said, smiling and gesturing for me to go into the classroom ahead of him. 'I've got five minutes.'

'You must be a very busy man,' I said, wanting to get a friendly rapport going and make up for my embarrassing lateness on Monday.

'Oh, yes,' he said. 'Silly meetings mainly. It's the bloody weekly Tuesday one that gets me. Two till five. Inconvenient, dull and pointless, but I have to be there.'

'Yes,' I said, seeing him look at his watch. 'There were only a couple of things anyway. Firstly, Bronwyn Young came to see me the other day.'

'Yes?'

'Well, she wanted to change tutor groups, from Fenn's to mine.'

'So what's the problem?'

'I just wanted to check whether that's okay?'

'You'll need to talk to young Mr Baker about that. It's a decision you should make between the two of you.'

'Right,' I said. 'Second thing: a girl in my second-year class was very upset on Monday, about the murder and everything. She ran out and I haven't seen her since. What should I do?'

'Nothing,' said the Professor, the tone of his voice, while pleasant, suggesting that I shouldn't bring such trivial problems to him. 'There are plenty of counsellors around if she needs them. Sometimes you have to let the students work it out for themselves.'

'But you're her tutor.'

'Yes, and I'm here if she needs me. Anything else?'

'Yes, sorry. It's Jason Davies. He was in a state yesterday and . . .'

I trailed off, knowing that the answer to this one would be the same as the last: let the students sort out their own problems.

'And what?'

'Nothing. I'm sure he's fine now. Sorry to have bothered you with all of this.'

'That's all right,' said Professor Valentine. 'It'll take you a while to settle in, I expect. You've just got to remember that the students bring their problems to us. We can't go looking for them otherwise we'd never get any teaching done.'

He laughed.

'So just chill out a bit and relax.'

Chill out and relax? What an odd expression for a Professor to use. I mumbled my thanks and wandered out into the corridor.

The rest of the morning went by quickly. Bronwyn didn't turn up in my tutorial group anyway, and when I went to try to see Fenn to ask if she'd gone to his, he still wasn't there. However, apart from my walking past a few policemen in the corridor, the university seemed quite normal for the first time this week. There was no mention of murder, no demanding students and, reassuringly, no fiction to engage with today. All my first-year tutees seemed interested in was getting an extension for a project they were working on and complaining about the Professor who evidently was working them too hard.

After lunch I drove home. I was pleased to have the house to myself and sat at the kitchen table for a long time, looking at the note Fenn had left and wondering why he wanted to see me so soon and what he needed to talk about. I spent the rest of the day nursing my hangover in front of the TV until it was time to get ready. I was on the news, briefly, along with my class; now edited so they didn't seem to be laughing. A close-up of Cress with tears streaming down her face featured in the report and was used, ironically, as the caption picture for the whole story.

At six o'clock I was standing in front of the mirror in the bathroom while I waited for the hot water to spill out into the white bath. I removed my bra and knickers and stuck them in the laundry basket, hoping Fenn hadn't seen them last night; both were grey, holey and slightly old. I smiled when I thought of the contrast with what I would be wearing later. I looked at my body in the mirror for a moment before I sank into the bath. I still had the same shape I had been blessed with at puberty and no amount of diets or cream cakes would ever change it. When the 'waif' look was in I had wished that I was slightly thinner, but I didn't have anything to complain about. I would have been a size ten, except my curves pushed me into a size twelve.

I eased myself into the bath and relaxed as the soft Devon water washed over me, hot, fragrant and relaxing. I reached for the soap and washed myself slowly, not missing anywhere because I was going to have some fun tonight that I intended to remember.

An hour later, dressed in blue jeans and a tight white T-shirt, I was on my way back to the city, ready to face the world again and looking forward to seeing Fenn.

CHAPTER NINE

Death's Dateless Night

The Blue Dolphin nightclub had a bad reputation in South Devon. I had only been there once, as a teenager, and even than it had been a dive. It was situated about five miles out of the city, on the ring road, and for as long as I could remember had been known as the main venue for young locals and students to hang out, drinking Snakebites and smoking spliffs. It had always been a place parents forbade their children from going to but never more so than recently, since it had been revamped as a rave club.

Jason was found outside the doors of the Blue Dolphin just before midnight on Tuesday, his dying body twisted in panic and his face frozen with pain. This image sat hauntingly on the front page of Wednesday's *Evening Echo* along with the headline 'Every Mother's Worst Nightmare' and a story on young people and Ecstasy.

I had no idea that anything had happened until I got bored waiting for Fenn in the Green Dragon on Wednesday evening. I walked out of the pub, annoyed because it was in the middle of the city and since I had been home after my class this morning, it seemed I had made the hour-long drive for nothing.

I didn't see the paper until I went into the newsagent's next to the pub for some cigarettes and a can of Coke for the journey home.

Reading the first paragraph of the story, I felt sick.

19-year-old Jason Davies was found barely alive last night outside a notorious South Devon nightclub. Initial police enquiries suggest that he had taken a high dose of the designer drug Ecstasy, which has claimed the lives of more than ten young people in the region this year alone.

I could hardly get the change out of my pocket to pay for the paper because my hands were shaking so much. I went to sit in my car and lit a cigarette to try to steady my nerves.

I fumbled around for my keys and started the engine. The article had said that Jason was in a coma, and since the only hospital in the city was St James's I assumed he must be there. On the way I stopped outside the Blue Dolphin, which appeared to be open for business regardless of the bad publicity it was now receiving. I got out of the car and stood there for a moment looking at the large white building. It had been a cinema once and if I remembered correctly, the circle seats had been left intact and provided both a viewing gallery and an intimate chill-out area for hot sweaty clubbers.

A queue was already forming outside the club's shiny pink doors and I noted with some cynicism that news of Jason's near death experience had probably made even more people turn up tonight. If there was one thing you could be sure of about teenagers it was that they loved the authenticity of real danger.

I sat there for a while just thinking until I realised I really should get to the hospital before it got too late. I took one last look at the nightclub before starting the engine. Most of the people in the queue had been admitted now and all that was left were the stragglers, blagging their way in on pretence of being on the guest list or being turned away for having the wrong footwear. I thought that was bizarre; all young people wore trainers yet they weren't allowed in most nightclubs. I looked down at my own old Converse

One Stars and smiled. That was no problem for me – clubs like this weren't my scene.

On the way to the hospital my head was full of thoughts about what had happened to Jason. Had he been on E when I saw him yesterday? That would certainly explain the state he was in, although I found it hard to believe he would have turned to a drug like that after Stephanie's death. Even stranger was the notion that he would have gone night-clubbing after I'd seen him. He'd seemed too disturbed, too ill, and I doubted whether he could have got himself into town let alone been allowed into a club in that state. But then, you never knew. Whatever he had been on could have worn off in time for him to go out that night: it must have done or how could he have got there?

I reached the hospital at about nine and parked in the visitors' car park, making sure I paid and displayed before walking into the main reception area. I associated lots of memories with this place: it was here Mum had given birth to Nat, finally, after abandoning the natural method in favour of an epidural; where we had all come after her horse-riding accident; and where Eugénie and Bobby were brought after the crash.

I walked over to the reception desk and discovered that Jason was in ward fifteen. The receptionist looked as though she was about to tell me something else but I walked off quickly, knowing only too well where I was going. Ward fifteen was the Intensive Care ward where Eugénie and Bobby spent their last, fraught hours.

I arrived at the ward to find visiting time in full swing; the whole place full of hush and machines, bleeps and tears. I scanned the beds, looking for Jason, but couldn't see him anywhere. A kindly-looking male nurse came out of nowhere and smiled sympathetically at me.

'Are you lost?' he asked.

'I don't think so,' I said. 'I'm looking for Jason Davies.'

'Are you an immediate relative?'

I remembered the mistake I'd made all those years ago

when I was visiting Bobby and Eugénie (or rather had come to get the bad news). I'd said I wasn't an immediate relative and so learned nothing of their condition for a while. This time, much as I hated lying, I knew better.

'I'm his sister,' I said, feeling my face redden slightly but hoping it didn't show. I reminded myself that up until very recently I had been an actress and lowered my head, looking worried and upset.

'Ah,' said the nurse. 'I think you'd better come with me.'

He ushered me into a small staff room at the end of the ward, between a deserted tea-trolley and the patients' toilets.

'I'm afraid Jason's dead,' he said simply. 'I'm so sorry. We did all we could.'

'Oh,' I said, feeling real panic rise inside me. 'Oh, *God*. What happened?'

'We're not sure yet,' said the nurse. 'There'll be a post-mortem.'

'Was it Ecstasy?' I asked, thinking about the newspaper story. I wondered if they'd got their facts right, but then Jason did collapse outside a nightclub. What else could it have been?

'We're not sure,' said the nurse. 'All I can say is, we're not ruling anything out at this stage.'

'That's okay,' I said, thinking hard. 'Could it have been *suicide*?'

'That's up to the coroner to decide,' said the nurse. He pulled a piece of paper out of his pocket and started fiddling with it. 'It's all a bit of a mystery,' he added gently, smiling kindly at me. I could see from his face that some pieces of this didn't add up for him, but he probably didn't think a bereaved sister would be interested in anything like that. I dabbed my eyes with the tissue he'd given me and tried not too look too interested.

'Why?' I asked, letting my voice sound numb and distant, as if, through my grief, I was having the conversation without realising it.

'I don't know, really. It must have been your elder

brother who was in earlier, asking if I thought it was murder. I wouldn't go that far, but – well, did Jason have any enemies or anything?'

'Why?' I asked thinking: *My elder brother?* and then remembering I was supposed to be Jason's sister. I shivered inside and hoped he didn't come back and discover me impersonating one of his family at this tragic time.

I shook my head and wiped my eyes again.

'He came to me for help yesterday and I didn't do very much. If anyone's responsible for this it's me,' I said, slightly over-dramatically and only half-acting.

'You're *not*,' said the nurse, sounding as unconvincing to me now as I had probably sounded to Fenn when he was talking about Stephanie. 'I wonder if you'd be able to help me with something?'

'Yes,' I said. 'What?'

'His last words. Most patients don't say anything, contrary to what you see on the films. And those who do usually say something practical: "The will is in the bureau", that sort of thing.'

'So what did Jason say?'

'Well, when they brought him in he was barely conscious. He was muttering a sentence I couldn't understand. I sat with him for a long time, hearing the odd word here and there. *Train*, especially, and the word *murders*, which I thought particularly strange.'

'Oh,' I explained. 'There was a murder. It was a girl in his class at the university. You must have heard about it – the girl in the woods?'

'Oh, yes, of course. But he definitely said *murders*. Plural.'

'Are you sure?'

'Yes. Anyway, like I say, I couldn't make out everything he was saying until just before he passed away. At that point he tried to sit up and looked me straight in the eye. Then, clear as anything I've ever heard, he said the following words: "*Train, London, murders, psycho, mirror, pendulum*". What do you make of that?'

'Well, he was in a state when I last saw him,' I said. 'How did you remember all the words?'

'I wrote them down,' said the nurse, offering me the piece of paper. 'I thought someone might make sense of them. The police weren't interested in seeing this and neither was your brother, but . . . I don't know. There's something significant about them but I'll be damned if I can work out what it might be.'

'Can I take it away?' I asked, taking the piece of paper and looking down at the words written on it.

'Yes,' he said, handing it to me. 'I'm sure it'll mean more to someone like you,' he added, smiling defeatedly.

'You take your job very seriously, don't you?' I said nicely, taking the piece of paper and folding it once. I could never resist a riddle, and although taking it seemed like the right thing to do, I instantly felt guilty. It was my own fault for pretending to be Jason's sister. I mean, how would it have looked if I'd refused?

'Oh, yes. Very.'

Ten minutes later I was starting the car, distracted by the scrap of paper on the dashboard in front of me. The little clock which it was partially covering said quarter to ten which meant I wouldn't get home until almost eleven o'clock. I pushed some stray curls back from my face and found they were damp with perspiration. I lit a cigarette and let all my thoughts about Jason fill my head one more time. I remembered his obvious paranoia and several haunting moments from our conversation yesterday, including the way he'd talked about knowing who'd killed Stephanie Duncan. Could drugs have induced that state?

I shivered, remembering how scared I had felt. Jason had been frightened too: was the cause of his fear real or imaginary? I knew I should have stayed with him but couldn't bear to ask myself whether he would still be alive now if I had. I'd been going to take him to hospital, I remembered, and then to the police (or was it the other way around?). Maybe if I'd done that he wouldn't have gone to the Blue Dolphin. These thoughts wrestled with my conscience until I decided to let it go. I had been simply a bystander yesterday, doing what I thought was the right thing at the time. Jason had got into that state without my help and the blame for what happened to him, if indeed there was any, certainly didn't rest with me.

Nevertheless, I was very intrigued by the words on the piece of paper in front of me and my mind kept drifting to them and their possible significance. What on earth was Jason trying to say? Was it some code that only one other person would understand or, as the nurse had originally thought, just nonsense? Either way, I was the only one, apart from the nurse, who had seen the words and I had a responsibility to try and work out their significance before passing the paper on to Jason's real sister, if indeed he had one, or his brother. Code-breaking fascinated me (the great Jacques Sabine had been a code-breaker in the French Resistance) and I couldn't wait to get started on this one. I felt a cold thrill shoot through me when I considered the possibility that Jason really had known who'd killed Stephanie and that the answer was on that piece of paper somewhere. It was unlikely, I thought, but exciting enough to make me resolve to work on it as soon as I got home.

I felt the insubstantial weight of my silk underwear pressing against me as I drove and suddenly remembered why I had come into the city. What had happened to Fenn? In the light of Jason's death, being stood up didn't seem like such a bad thing but it still hurt.

The city had smelt rotten tonight, with the distinctive stench of night-time pollution invoked by daytime heat. A feature of all cities I had ever been to was the rubbish which sat constantly on display on pavements in black and green bags; beery, lumpy and greasy. Finishing at the Underground Club in the early hours of every morning had kept me in regular contact with those unmistakable odours I had smelt tonight outside the Blue Dolphin and I was as glad to drive away from them now as I had been to leave London last week. The humid night unsettled me and I felt certain there would be a storm before the week was over.

I didn't feel like listening to any music so I switched on Radio 4 instead, opening the car window and letting the cool air soothe me as I gathered speed, driving out of the city and into the countryside again. I became quite engrossed in the play on the radio and it was only when I pulled into Mum's driveway that I realised I had been shivering all the way home. As I got out of the car and walked towards the door, I vaguely thought, *Where was Fenn?* and then promptly forgot about him.

I yawned and put the kettle on. The house was dark except for a dim light in the living room. The door was shut so I assumed that Nat was doing something in there. I put the *Evening Echo* down on the table and went and knocked lightly. I heard giggling and then Nat's voice.

'Come in,' he said in a bad imitation of a Transylvanian accent.

The living room looked a bit like the inside of a hall of residence. There were Coke cans and coffee cups scattered around and I could see *Dracula* was playing on the video recorder. Nat's girlfriend, Beth, raised her head from his shoulder and smiled at me.

'Hi, Lily,' she said.

'Hi, Beth.' I tried to sound cheerful, but knew I sounded tired and shaken.

'Are you all right?' asked Nat.

'Yeah. Would you like some coffee?'

'Yes, please,' said Nat. I looked at Beth.

'I'd love a cup if you're making some,' she said. 'I hear you're going to be my lecturer.'

'Oh, yes, I suppose I am.' I had forgotten about my first-year class.

'Creative writing.'

'Yes.'

'I hope you're better than Isobel.' Beth stretched like a cat and pulled her long black hair into a loose ponytail on top of her head. 'And that prat Valentine.'

'What was wrong with Isobel?' I asked.

'She was fucking Valentine, can you believe it?'

'No.' I smiled weakly, knowing I shouldn't really be having this conversation with a student. Nat laughed.

'I reckon you fancy him,' he said. Beth hit him on the arm playfully.

'I do not. He's gross. Everyone fancies Fenn anyway.'

'Do they?' I asked, surprised by my interest and, if the truth be known, my jealousy.

'Oh, yes,' said Beth. 'We've got a competition to see who can bed him first. No one's managed yet, though. He's far too *professional*.'

'Oh,' I said, pleased and disturbed at the same time.

Despite Beth's inappropriate comments I was glad there would be a friendly face in the first-year crowd tomorrow. The second years were great, but I found myself hoping the first years would be a more subdued group. I walked back into the kitchen and Nat followed me, chattering away about something.

'What's up?' he asked eventually, cutting into my thoughts. 'I've been talking to you but you haven't heard a word I've said.'

'Sorry, Nat.' I picked up the paper and pointed to the picture on the front page. 'He was my student.'

Nat quickly scanned the story and I could see from the momentary flicker of his eyes that it shocked him. I remembered his excited attitude about the murder, but I knew that he was like any other young man; like Ash, Blake and all the others. He couldn't let me see how disturbing he found all this stuff, but he felt it nevertheless.

'God. I'm sorry, Lil,' he said, clearly finding sympathy a more acceptable emotion than fear or sadness. 'If there's anything I can do . . .'

I shook my head and finished making the coffee. I handed two mugs to Nat and he took them and turned to go back into the living room. He stopped for a moment as if suspended in space and looked back at the table. He stared at the blurred picture in front of him.

'He looked like me,' he said faintly. 'He even had the same trainers.'

'Don't worry,' I said. 'I'm sure everything will turn out okay.'

I repeated those words to myself as I fell into bed although they sounded as stupid then as they had done when I'd said them to Nat. How could everything be okay when first a girl then a boy were dead?

CHAPTER TEN

The Key (You Could Say)

I didn't sleep very well that night and woke up earlier than usual at six o'clock, unable to endure my nightmares anymore. I felt physically tired but my mind was too buzzing to let my body rest. I'd spent a long time before going to sleep looking at Jason's words and trying to figure out what they meant, and gazing at the disturbing picture in the newspaper which all my nightmares had echoed. I hadn't got very far with the words (except that I thought Jason could have been referring to someone called Ben) but I'd seen something interesting in the picture that would mean trying to talk to the police today, because I was now certain that Jason had not been inside the Blue Dolphin on Tuesday night.

I got out of bed at about half-past seven after listening to the radio news for a while and looking again at the words: *Train, London, murders, psycho, mirror, pendulum,* which blurred eventually in front of my eyes and weaved, snake-like and unreadable, around the edge of my vision. Jason's death hadn't made national news but Stephanie's was still there, in at item number five behind something about Iraq and some trivial royal stories. The investigation into her death was the local lead, of course, and the police were making persistent appeals to the public to try to remember anything that might be important. I wished I knew what Jason had meant by these words and now regretted not hanging around longer on Tuesday to listen to all the stuff he was trying to say then. I stretched and opened the curtains. Outside, another beautiful day was brewing.

Maude came scurrying into my room, chirruping and squeaking with excitement. She had never been a very good hunter so I was surprised when she dropped a small dead vole by my bed. I watched as she prodded it with her paw and growled unconvincingly at it.

'Poor vole,' I said.

Squeak.

'All right,' I said, responding to the look in her eyes. 'Clever girl, I *suppose*.' I wasn't sure whether I approved of her catching poor little creatures but it was difficult to prevent her from doing it. And it was just her nature after all; instinct made her do it. Murder wasn't like that, I thought bluntly. Murder was against nature. People didn't need to kill other people in the way animals needed to kill each other. I felt sick when I thought about the reasons that humans killed each other. Hatred, obsession, financial gain. I wondered why Stephanie had died and whether her killer had gained from it.

Squeak.

I smiled at my cat and stroked her tummy as she lay on her back, purring on my pillow. She seemed to have forgotten about her vole so I used the opportunity to pick it up and throw it away, hurrying upstairs after that to get changed so I could leave early. I wanted to have some time before my ten o'clock class, to prepare and also to phone the police.

I barely managed to feed Maude and get a quick look at the paper before I was back in my car playing rush-hour-road-rage with commuters at least twice my age. Halfway to work it started to rain again thus dispelling my optimistic prediction of a beautiful day. I looked at the clock on the dashboard and saw that it wasn't even half-past eight yet. I was far too young for this, I decided.

★　　★　　★

Having reached the door to my office, I remembered I still couldn't get in. I wandered the corridors for a while, looking for other early arrivals, and finally managed to bump into Sue, Mum's colleague, in the main corridor on the third floor and asked to borrow her key.

'Didn't the Professor give you one?' she asked.

'No,' I said. 'Well, he did give me a key but it was the wrong one. He said I would have to go and see a technician or something.'

'That's dreadful,' she said, shaking her head. 'So you mean you haven't got a key at all?'

'No.'

'That bloody man.' Sue looked concerned and upset as she opened my door with her key. 'I'm not surprised he loses staff at the rate he does.'

'He is a bit, um, weird,' I said, smiling as I remembered the TV crew.

'You can say that again.'

Sue smiled back and reached into her pocket. She drew out a set of keys and waved them at me naughtily. 'Do you know what these are?'

'No.'

She pulled one of the keys off the ring and handed it to me.

'Masterkeys,' she said. 'Thank God for departing part-timers.'

'Thanks.' I looked at her gratefully. I had known Sue for a few years and liked her naughty-little-girl attitude. I'd heard her talking to Mum and got the impression she wasn't a big fan of the university, with its rigid rules and patriarchal system. She even looked anti-establishment. Her hair was dyed purple, her nose pierced, and she always seemed to be wearing tight jeans and holey jumpers. Apparently she had been one of the first Greenham Common women, although if you asked her about it she would just laugh and say something about *the cause*.

She followed me into my office but didn't sit down.

'I suppose Valentine hasn't told you about the alarm, then?'

'What alarm?'

'If you want to stay late you're supposed to have a key and the code for the alarm so you can set it on your way out.'

'Oh,' I said.

'Otherwise the caretakers chuck out at about half-five.'

'I didn't know about that,' I said, thinking I must have been lucky over the last couple of days. 'But it is only my first week here.'

'Here's a key to the alarm box,' said Sue, extracting another from her set. 'And here's the code.' She wrote a number down on a piece of paper.

'Thanks.'

'I suppose you don't know the main keypad code either?'

'What keypad code?'

Sue smiled. 'All you have to remember is this: oo clears the keypad, and then you type in the date of Christmas. So the code is 002512.'

'Thanks.'

'You'll need that to get into the media bits of this block and pretty much anywhere in the science block.'

Sue turned to go.

'And don't let the caretakers tell you that women aren't allowed to stay late, because we are. You just have to be a bit careful at the moment.'

'I know.'

'Did you hear about that poor boy?'

'Yes,' I said. 'He was one of my students.'

'It makes me so angry,' said Sue, 'that some bastard could rape a young woman in those woods and then drive a poor boy to take an overdose.'

'Yes.'

'I'm hoping to see you on one of our protests. This affects all women, you know.'

'Yes,' I said. 'I'll do my best.'

'I'll tell you another thing,' she said, turning back one more time before walking out of the door. 'I wouldn't want to be Fenn Baker this morning.'

She was gone before I had a chance to ask her what she meant.

I went to get a can of Coke from the machine down the hallway and bumped straight into two police officers, a kind-looking WPC and a small sharp-featured PC. I wondered whether I should approach them now, but it seemed there was no need because they walked straight up to me anyway.

'Are you Lily Pascale?' asked the WPC.

'Yes,' I said. 'Are you investigating the death of Jason Davies?'

'Among other things,' said the WPC, looking at her notebook.

'I was his lecturer. I found out last night.' I said. 'In fact, I wanted to have a word with you about something, if you've got time?'

The two police officers looked at each other meaningfully.

'I'm PC Williams and this is WPC Newman,' said the policeman. 'We'd like to have a word with *you* actually. Have you got a moment?'

'Yes,' I said. 'Of course. What's it about?'

'Shall we go into your office?' said WPC Newman. 'It'll be more private in there.'

We walked along to my room and I unlocked the door with my new key, hardly noticing that I was finally able to come and go as I wanted. I couldn't think why the police would want to see me. Confused and worried, I walked in and sat down at the desk. Luckily there were two other chairs in the room and I gestured for the officers to sit down.

'Okay,' said PC Williams, looking at his notebook. 'We are trying to locate a Mr Fenn Baker. We believe you are the last person who saw him in the area. Is that correct?'

'I don't know,' I said, my heart skipping several beats.

'The last time I saw him was Tuesday night. Is he all right? I wondered why he didn't turn up . . .'

'When?'

'Last night.' I looked at PC Williams. 'I was supposed to meet him but he never showed up. I was worried there might have been an accident, but then I saw the paper and found out about Jason. I was upset about that and, well, I kind of forgot about Fenn. I just thought he'd been tied up doing something.'

I blushed at my inappropriate choice of expression. I hoped one of the police officers would smile but neither of them did.

'We want to talk to you about Tuesday night, if you don't mind,' said WPC Newman. 'We need to know what your movements were. What time did you say goodbye to Mr Baker, what time did he leave you and where did he say he was going?'

'Oh,' I said vaguely, feeling my heart pump faster. 'I don't know.'

I was playing for time. What had happened to Fenn on Tuesday? It was as much of a mystery to me as it was to the police. I couldn't remember what time he had left or even if he'd come back. The only thing I was fairly sure of was that I hadn't slept with him. I wondered if we'd kissed.

'Why are you looking for him anyway?' I asked. 'Has there been an accident?'

'No,' said PC Williams. 'We just need him to help us with some enquiries.'

'What enquiries?'

'I'm afraid we can't really go into that. Suffice to say it's to do with a very serious incident indeed.'

'Not Stephanie?' I asked incredulously.

'We can't confirm that for certain,' said PC Williams, confirming it nevertheless with his eyes. 'But you can tell him if you speak to him that he's already committed two serious offences in connection with this, one of which is leaving the area without telling us where he's going.'

'So is he actually *missing*?' I asked, my voice rising in disbelief.

'We believe so,' said PC Williams. 'He hasn't turned up for work, hasn't phoned in sick and none of his friends or colleagues has seen him since Tuesday. Our enquiries so far put you at the scene of his disappearance. So I'll ask you again: when did he leave? Where did he go?'

'He left at about eleven,' I said truthfully. There seemed no reason to go into the complications that had followed. So far as I knew he never came back. Being comatose didn't make me a very reliable witness to anything on Tuesday night so I supposed I was safe. But what about the note? He must have come back to leave that.

'Did he say where he was going?' asked WPC Newman.

'No,' I said truthfully. 'He took a phone call and then left the restaurant. I assumed he was meeting a friend or something . . .'

The thoughts going through my head were muddled and jumbled but one thing was for sure: Fenn was now an even bigger suspect for Stephanie's murder and that couldn't be right. I didn't know him very well, but there was no way he would ever do anything like that. I wasn't sure why I was so certain, but I would have bet my life on it.

I didn't hear what PC Williams was saying through my thoughts and was surprised to see he and his colleague rising from their chairs.

'Thank you, Miss Pascale,' said PC Williams. 'We'll be in touch if there's anything else.'

'Is that it?' I heard myself saying.

'Unless you can remember anything else now,' said PC Williams. 'It's very important that we locate Mr Baker.'

'No,' I said. 'I can't remember anything now, but I'll let you know if I do.'

'Thank you for your time,' said PC Williams.

'Oh,' said the WPC just before they walked out of my room. 'Didn't you want to talk to us about something?'

'Oh, no,' I said. 'It wasn't anything really. Unless . . . it was about Jason.'

'Fire away.'

'In the picture in the paper he was wearing trainers,' I said, expecting them to be dazzled with my sleuth-like powers of observation.

'So?' said the WPC, looking at her colleague and sharing a half-smile with him.

'There's a dress code at the Blue Dolphin,' I said urgently. 'They wouldn't have let him in like that. So if he didn't go in there, what was he doing outside?'

'Buying drugs probably,' said PC Williams jadedly. 'Or dealing them.'

'He wouldn't have been dealing drugs, though,' I exclaimed. 'I saw him! He was too upset about Stephanie to be doing anything like that.'

'You'd be surprised what we see out there,' said WPC Newman. 'It is perfectly probable that he either didn't go in at all or else got in with his trainers on. If he was dealing drugs or knew the bouncer it would be perfectly possible for them to disregard his footwear.'

'Anyway,' said PC Williams, 'I can't see exactly what it would prove if he didn't go in.'

'I'm not sure either,' I said, feeling slightly humiliated. 'I just thought it might be important.'

'Well, if you remember any small details about your evening with Mr Baker we'd love to hear them,' said the WPC, smiling kindly at me. 'Do you know the station number?'

'Yes,' I said, feeling slightly dizzy as I watched the police officers leave.

I had just over quarter of an hour before my class started and wasn't quite sure what I was going to do with them yet, so I wandered out into the hall and down the stairs, intending to have a cigarette and plan something quickly in peace. I popped into the main office to see if there was any mail for me, thinking that for some bizarre reason Fenn may have contacted me by post. I knew it was silly, and I was hardly his closest friend, but that spark between us . . . I was sure it had meant something. And he had wanted to talk to *me* last night; maybe to confide something or tell me something was bothering him. That made me think there might be another mysterious reason for his disappearance.

No one really took any notice of me when I walked into the office. One of the secretaries was busy typing and the other was having an in-depth, arms-on-the-counter conversation with a young lecturer from theatre studies.

So, do they think he did it?

Well, he didn't turn up for the test.

Did you all have to go?

Yep, all the male lecturers from this building. I suppose they'll start on everyone else if nothing matches. That's what they did with the students.

Did it hurt?

No, they only took a bit of hair.

So did he know that he was supposed to be there?

We all got memos.

The police treat that very seriously, don't they?

Oh yes, it's an offence if you don't let them test you.

They must be talking about Fenn, I thought. Suddenly it made sense. He must have been summoned for a DNA test and forgotten to turn up. I wanted to shout at the lecturer and the secretary and tell them of course he hadn't bloody known, or he wouldn't have disappeared like that.

I looked for a pigeon-hole with my name on it but there didn't seem to be one there. I thought of asking the secretary but there wasn't time. I assumed that if I had any mail then they would have made a pigeon-hole. I sighed and walked outside, feeling sick as my brain went into hyperdrive, desperately trying to make connections that just weren't there and to ignore the unsavoury ones that were.

I calmed down slightly as I smoked. Slowly, a plan began to form in my mind. Jason had said he knew what had gone on, and had left a posthumous clue to help reveal what that was. The riddle was in my possession, as was the knowledge that Fenn was innocent. Somehow I was going to put it all together; I just didn't know how as yet. I stubbed out my cigarette and walked back to my office, feeling perplexed but determined, my brain on the verge of overload but refusing to give up.

The first-year group seemed friendlier than the second years had been; not with me particularly, but with each other. They all sat together chatting in lowered voices except for a nice-looking couple (his arm was draped around her neck) in the corner. No one seemed deliberately left out and there didn't appear to be any nasty cliques. Good.

'I'm Lily Pascale,' I said to the ten faces present. I looked at the register and found that there were two students missing: Beth and Bronwyn. I wondered why Beth wasn't present (I had a feeling I knew why Bronwyn wasn't there poor girl), but with everything else that was on my mind it was enough for me just to remain upright in front of the class. I stalled on some of the foreign names in the register (Mercedes Santos, Ricardo Lettuce and others), wondering why there were so many in this class, then took a deep breath and tried to pull myself together. I could think about everything afterwards.

As soon as I spoke all the students stopped talking and looked at me expectantly. I paused and looked back at them in slight amazement. Now *this* was what a degree class was supposed to be like, I thought (although I had to admit I was fond of the second years, however immature they were).

'Where's the Professor?' asked a sleek cat-like blonde. Her voice was like velvet: soft, clear and faintly Italian.

'He won't be taking this class anymore,' I said. 'I'm afraid you're stuck with me – which should be much more exciting.'

'I doubt *that*,' said the boy half of the couple in the corner; a scruffy lad with long mousy-blond hair. He grimaced sardonically as he spoke and I understood that this was not intended as an insult to me but some kind of sarcastic comment on the Professor's classes. I wondered, briefly, what they could have been like and then turned back to the cat-girl.

'What's your name?' I asked.

'Mercedes,' she said in her hypnotic voice. 'Don't laugh.'

'I won't,' I said. 'It's a lovely name.'

No one laughed. No one said a word. I continued.

'Mercedes, could you please start by describing yourself and the person next to you, giving their name and anything else you know about them. Since this is creative writing, you might want to mention a favourite book or writer as well.'

'Okay, I'm Mercedes. My favourite book is *Alice in Wonderland*,' she said. Gesturing at a pale, dark-haired boy to her left: 'This is Will. He's a bit shy, but he's interested in fairies.'

Again, inexplicably, no one laughed. Then her neighbour started to speak.

'I'm Will,' he said. 'I'm interested in investigating the existence of fairies in life and in literature. My favourite writer is Hans Christian Andersen.'

'That figures,' I said, smiling but noticing that none of the other students did the same. I coughed uncomfortably and nodded at him to continue. He gestured to the blond-haired sarcastic boy.

'This is Jay. He's interested in masculinity in culture, aren't you, Jay?'

He snorted and his girlfriend smiled.

'If you say so,' he said, clearly amused by Will's serious tone. 'I'm actually interested in literature. My favourite writer is Edgar Allen Poe. This is Zoe and she's interested in writing.'

'Good,' I said.

'I'm Zoe,' said the small woman by Jay's side. She seemed almost childlike and her severely cropped black hair made her skin look paler than it was. 'My favourite writer is Umberto Eco.'

'Great,' I said, feeling more cheered by these two. I couldn't quite work out what it was that I found sinister about this group. The intellectual atmosphere in the room was amazing but most of the students themselves seemed vacant and torpid. If it didn't sound so stupid, I would have guessed they were all on drugs.

Gradually I learned all their names. Of the rest of the students in the group, Lottie, Lisa and Mark gave their interest as being experimental literature; Ricardo, who asked to be called Richie, Penny, Monica and Hélène said that theirs was out-of-body experiences.

I began by setting them a deceptively simple task: to write a story in a sentence. After I'd given them ten minutes I started walking around, hearing snippets of conversation as I went.

'I wonder why we don't have the Professor anymore,' said Hélène.

'So much for being his special group,' muttered Lottie.

'I thought he was going to take us for everything,' said Mark. 'That's what he told me.'

'Did you see we've even got Fenn Baker for our conventions unit?' grumbled Lottie, chewing her pen a bit and then returning to her sentence.

'Not anymore,' cut in Jay, snickering slightly.

I felt my heart skip a beat. *Poor Fenn*, I thought. I'd noticed a little handwritten sign on his door earlier which said ALL CLASSES CANCELLED. It was poignant and distressing. Now even the students would know something was wrong.

'Did you go to any of the vigils?' asked Zoe as I walked past, looking at me expectantly with her big dark brown eyes.

'No,' I said. 'Did you?'

'I went to one,' she said. 'We knew Stephanie quite well, you see.'

'Yeah,' said Jay. 'She used to come and give talks to us, about practical literature.'

Practical literature? I thought. Bizarre.

'She was nice,' said Zoe. 'But a bit odd.'

'She was inspirational,' said Mercedes loftily. 'But I didn't want to go to any of the vigils.'

'Why not?' I asked.

'They're all too political and rough,' said Hélène, speaking with a slight French accent. 'What no one wants to accept is that maybe she wanted to go – to reach her end.'

'But not like *that*?' I said, shocked and confused. Surely these students knew that Stephanie had been brutally raped and murdered? They all looked unmoved, though, except for Jay and Zoe who squirmed in their seats.

'Right,' I said, wanting to change the subject. 'Let's see what you've done then. Lottie, do you want to go first?'

'Okay,' she said. 'A story in a sentence: "His world shrank around him as the chemical took over; star, fish, lollipop: all the usual suspects were there."'

'Yes,' I said, drawing the word out to indicate my reservations as all the other students clapped.

'Poor Jason,' breathed Penny. 'He couldn't live without her.'

'Is that about Jason?' I asked, feeling my forehead crumple in a mixture of concentration and concern.

'Not really,' said Lottie, touching her blonde Shirley Temple curls self-consciously. 'I mean, partly, but it wouldn't really be appropriate. It's how I see death, though.'

'Okay,' I said. 'My only problem is that you don't really have a story there, do you?'

The class looked blank.

'What's your definition of a story?' I asked the group.

'Something that's not true,' suggested Mercedes. 'Like a lie?'

'It can be,' I said. 'But your own life is a story, isn't it, and that's true?'

'Is it an idea?' asked Penny.

'A collection of thoughts?' asked Richie, pushing his glasses higher on his nose.

'A fantasy?' said Will softly.

'It can be all those things,' I said. 'But a story has to have a beginning, a middle and an end.'

'Common sense at last,' muttered Jay.

'That's rubbish!' said Richie.

'Excuse me?' I said, slightly taken aback by one of my students saying that a very basic principle was rubbish. He leant back in his chair and laughed, obviously pleased he'd got a reaction from me. I noticed he had strange-looking eyes behind his glasses. They were vacant and he seemed stoned; his laughter didn't stop at a natural point, it just kept going until Hélène interrupted.

'What about experimental literature?' she asked, looking at me coldly.

'Yeah, and *new forms*,' said Mark.

'They still have to have some sort of structure,' I said. 'Otherwise they become unreadable.'

The students seemed confused, and looked at each other meaningfully.

'Okay,' I said, pressing on. 'Hélène. Your sentence?'

' "Wild passion love hate death",' she said.

'What's the problem with that one?' I asked the class.

'Nothing,' said Lisa. 'It's beautiful.'

'It's not really a sentence,' said Zoe timidly.

'Exactly,' I said.

Apart from Zoe and Jay, the rest of the class came up with similar (de)constructions, providing, I thought, a good case for units like experimental literature being kept until the third year. I was disturbed that they had almost all written about death and said so, wondering whether, like the second years, they were all reacting to the murder and to Jason's well-publicised death, which the papers were calling a tragic accident but which the students seemed to have different, if slightly enigmatic, ideas about.

'Death is interesting,' said Penny defensively. 'Most books are about death if you think about it.'

'Not *about* it,' said Jay. 'They might have it in there but . . .'

'I still can't get over the fact that Jason actually did it in the end,' said Mercedes dreamily. I wondered what she meant. Had he talked about suicide before? If so I would have expected the students to be shocked, not fascinated (in public at least). But then this group seemed to shun any type of convention, including, unfortunately, all the literary ones. As I thought about Jason I found his last words going through my head like a mantra. *Train, London, murders, psycho, mirror, pendulum.* They still didn't make sense.

'All those drugs and so little effect,' said Monica, laughing nastily. 'What a silly boy.'

'Yeah,' said Richie. 'He didn't even do that right.'

'Okay,' I said, fearing that the students' tone was becoming too sanctimonious. 'So none of you dabbles in drugs then? You're all angels, are you?'

They laughed for the first time since the class had started.

'You have to take *drugs*,' said Mercedes, 'to understand art and literature.'

'Why do you think that?' I asked, surprised and slightly disturbed.

'It's where artists get their inspiration,' said Will, ignoring a derisory groan from Jay.

'Oh,' I said, bemused, wondering what to say next.

Apparently the first years were all doing a project called *Out of Body* in their experimental literature class, from which most of these bizarre ideas were coming. It sounded a bit too abstruse to me and I set them a much more useful exercise at the end of my class. By next week they would have composed a 500-word description of themselves, which they would have written while looking in a mirror, and which, I told them, had to observe the rules of English grammar.

After class I went to buy a sandwich from the staff cafeteria in the main block. As I walked my head started to fill with confusion again and I realised that the class had been good for me, even if it had been slightly bewildering and the students more than a bit bizarre. Concentrating on teaching was a good way to get your mind off other things, even if all the students wanted to talk about was death.

I ran into Jay on the third floor of the main block, just before I reached the canteen. He smiled at me and slowed down to talk to me.

'Hi,' he said. 'Sorry about the others. They're a bit of an acquired taste.'

'I'm sure they're nice, really,' I said. 'I think everyone is acting strangely at the moment.'

'It was such a shock to find out about Jason,' he said, looking at me sadly. 'I haven't known him for long, but we used to hang around together a bit recently.' He looked away, slightly embarrassed. 'I felt sorry for him. Anyway, I'm going to meet his parents later. They're coming down from Liverpool tomorrow afternoon.'

'Oh,' I said, remembering my charade at the hospital. 'I have something for Jason's brother. Would you tell him to give me a call here?'

'I would,' said Jay. 'Except that he didn't have a brother.'

'Oh, right,' I said, feeling my brain do an uncomfortable back-flip. 'My mistake. Never mind.'

'Look,' said Jay, 'you've only been here a few days, haven't you?'

'Yes,' I said, startled by the dramatic intonation of his voice. 'Why?'

'Please don't ask me to explain this,' he said, 'but you seem nice and – well, you should keep out of most things here. It's a freaky place – not just since the murder. If I'd known I would never have come here. I even had a place at Norwich.'

'So why did you come?'

'Zoe,' he said, smiling ruefully and looking a bit guilty. 'But now we both wish we hadn't. Just watch out, okay?'

'I'll bear that in mind,' I said, watching him walk off and considering his advice. What an odd thing to say, I thought.

Even stranger, though: Jason didn't have a brother. I wasn't sure what to make of that. All in all, I was left with more of a conundrum than I had faced this morning. I needed to know even more what Jason's words meant now and felt sure they would provide some clue to what he knew about the murder. *Murders* was the word that kept preoccupying me most. Had the plural *s* been a mistake or had it been deliberate? If the latter were true then who was the other victim: surely not Jason himself? And what had all the first years been implying when they'd talked about his finally attempting something? Could it have been suicide?

I was still thinking hard when I wandered into the staff canteen where I was instantly met with hostile stares – as if I were a rogue student invading the precious territory of the older members of staff. I touched my identity card self-consciously and hoped they could read the word 'staff' on it, more concerned with my riddle than with their attitudes anyway. I paid for some sandwiches and turned to leave, noticing Professor Valentine sitting alone at a corner table, reading a battered-looking copy of *The Naked Lunch*. He looked over at me and I smiled at him. I didn't mean to smile, but some reflex made me do it. He didn't smile back, though. He just looked me up and down and went back to his book. To be honest, I don't even think he recognised me.

I took my sandwiches down to my car, stopping twice on the way; once to get a can of Coke from the machine, and the second time to get Isobel's address from the office. I decided it was time I found out more about what was going on here and the best place to start seemed to be my predecessor.

CHAPTER ELEVEN

The House of Fiction

Isobel Raven's flat was somewhere around Brixham Harbour but I couldn't quite work out where. I knew that if I phoned she might give me directions herself, but I didn't want to take the risk. She might equally well tell me to get lost and I couldn't afford that. Something unusual seemed to have been going on at the university long before Stephanie was murdered and I wanted to find out what it was, particularly in light of Jay's odd comments. I was far too intimidated by Professor Valentine to ask him anything, and besides I got on better with women.

I walked around the harbour, suddenly wondering what I was doing here. Why was I acting like some kind of private investigator? It wasn't as if Fenn had asked me to do this. I was worried about what I might find out and found myself contemplating the unthinkable. Like: what would I do if I discovered evidence that linked Fenn to the crime? Did I really know him well enough to be sure he was incapable of something like that?

The thing I couldn't understand, the wild card in all my thoughts, was Jason's riddle. He must have said those things for a reason, but what could it possibly have been? I wanted to see Isobel to try and get a clearer picture of this disturbed and seemingly unpopular young man. I was resolved to somehow find out what it was he had known, and therefore what his last words had meant, but first I had to know *him*.

One of the things that none of my ex-boyfriends could understand about me was the way I liked working out puzzles and riddles, *solving* things. One of the main reasons I'd specialised in crime fiction during my MA was my constant need for the conundrum, the whodunnit, the way I always had to work out who the villain was before the end of the book.

There was something about this situation in particular that both intrigued and infuriated me. *Whodunnit?* was becoming a real question and I wished I knew the answer. It had to make sense and I couldn't resist the challenge of working it out. I also owed it to Jason to find out what had gone on, because somehow I felt I had let him down. Besides, if I left a riddle on my death-bed I'd hate everyone to ignore it. And, of course, apart from the nurse, I was the only one who knew of the riddle – because of my charade, which made it even worse – so therefore I had a responsibility to do something about it.

Of course, if I thought they would do anything other than ignore it, I would have taken it to the police. But they had already made it quite clear what they thought of trivial details. Anyway, the riddle belonged firmly in my area of expertise. I spent all my time unpicking books and poems and if anybody could get to the meaning in a series of seemingly unconnected words then it would be someone like me. I'd never thought an interest in literature would have any practical application but suddenly it did. I felt frightened and excited. I was going to do it.

I could see Jason's face now, desperate and damp with perspiration. Why hadn't I listened to him? Why had I run away? If I was honest with myself it was clear that on that day I'd run primarily from fear rather than in search of assistance. I felt a lump start to form in my throat as I realised I had ignored a cry for help. I would pay my debt to Jason, even if it had to be posthumous. I also owed it to Fenn who had to be innocent, and to the unfortunate, mysterious Stephanie who hadn't deserved what had happened to her and who, despite what the first years said, could never have wanted *that* as an end for herself.

I lit a cigarette and watched some fishermen toss their catch into a bucket. One of them looked a bit like Anthony; tall, blond and slightly freckled. I realised I missed him a bit and that surprised me. I don't think I ever really loved him, but I missed his company. Sometimes it's nice to have a warm body next to you in bed and when you're asleep it doesn't really matter whose it is. Before I let my thoughts turn back to more disturbing images of murder I threw my cigarette into the water and spoke to the fishermen.

'Excuse me,' I said politely, not wanting any trouble.

'All right, love,' said the Anthony lookalike, and I could hear some of the other men saying things like 'Way-hey' and 'Look, a bird'.

'I'm looking for Pilgrim's Close.'

'I'll be your pilgrim,' said one of the other blokes, leering at me. I smiled at him.

'Come on then,' I said. He looked blank. 'Come on,' I repeated.

All the blokes stopped fishing or throwing or leering and turned to look at their friend.

'Sorry, weren't you trying to pull me?' I asked sweetly.

'Er – I – um –'

'Go on, my son!' shouted one of the other lads. The rest of them laughed.

'Because,' I said, 'we could just do it right here if you wanted.'

'Er, no,' said the bloke, going bright red. 'It's all right.'

'Are you sure?'

'Er, yeah.'

'Good.' I said. 'Can anyone tell me where Pilgrim's Close is please?'

Eventually I got some sense out of them and headed around the harbour. Luckily for them, Pilgrim's Close was right where they'd said it would be. I found number seven and rang the bell. No one answered for a moment and I began to wonder again whether I should have called first.

I heard a seagull screeching above my head and breathed in deeply, savouring the salty wetness of the harbour air. There was something compelling about the murkiness of this town with all its vivid smells and sounds. The air was full of fish and curses and I knew that this was one of the few local areas where women walked the streets at night selling sex for money.

'Hello?' I was startled out of my thoughts by a thin, slightly tarty-looking woman who appeared at the door wearing a red satin nightdress. She looked about my age but more weathered. 'Can I help you?'

'Yes. I'm looking for Isobel Raven.'

'That's me,' she said, in a soft, broken-sounding voice. 'Do I know you?'

'I'm Lily Pascale,' I said. 'I've taken over your classes at the university.'

'Oh,' said Isobel, smiling cynically. 'You'd better come in then.'

I walked into the hallway and sniffed the air tentatively as the smell of boiled cabbage and perfume slowly enveloped me. Isobel's flat was in a small block containing about seven others and if the smell was anything to go by then none of them had been cleaned for years.

She shut the heavy front door behind her and walked to the end of the passageway. I could hardly see where I was going because there was no light and I shivered, realising that no one knew where I was. I had been very confident out in the bright sunlight but didn't feel that way now. Images of Stephanie's last moments played like flickering film footage in my head as I imagined and re-imagined the horror of her death.

Isobel held the door to her flat open for me and I walked through it, jumping slightly as I heard it slam conclusively behind me. I followed her into the front room and sat down on a wicker chair. There were three other identical chairs in the room, a glass coffee table, and over by the window a heavy wooden desk with a typewriter on it. There was no mess or clutter, no bits of paper or envelopes. Just the typewriter.

'I'll just get some proper clothes on,' Isobel said huskily, and hurried out of the room.

I walked over to the desk and looked at the typewriter. It was dusty and old, and I wondered if it was there for show. Just as I had decided that no one ever sat at the desk I looked up and noticed the view, which was striking. All at once I understood why Isobel wanted to live here. Sitting at that desk gave you a clear view out to sea, with the harbour walls just off to the left. I thought she probably did something creative here, but I couldn't imagine what.

The only clutter in the room was created by the endless shelves of books, lining every piece of wall uninterrupted by door or window frame. I walked around the room reading the titles of all the pulp fiction classics and cheap horror novels until Isobel returned. She seemed to have the same interests as me, which was an encouraging start, but although I got on better with women than I did with men, I was generally reluctant to form meaningful friendships with them. No one could replace Eugénie, or at least no one had yet.

When Isobel returned she was carrying a tea-pot and two cups on a tray. She looked much better now that she had pulled her long red hair into a ponytail, and replaced the satin nightdress with white jeans and a blue shirt. Her face looked clean and fresh, and I realised that when she'd answered the door she had still had make-up on from the day before. It was about three o'clock in the afternoon so I assumed she must have had a heavy night.

'I'm sorry to come knocking on your door like this,' I said.

'Oh, that's all right. Sorry I looked such a state, I'd just got up.'

'Don't worry,' I said, smiling. 'You should see what I look like in the mornings. It's not a pretty sight.' Isobel looked at me curiously and started pouring the tea.

'So how are you finding the university?'

'Interesting,' I said ambiguously. '*Strange*. Although I'm assuming that's because of the murder investigation.'

'I bet the place is absolutely seething,' she said. 'I'm so glad I left when I did.'

'When was that?'

'Just after Easter,' she said, wrinkling her nose. 'A couple of weeks ago, I suppose.'

'Didn't you like it?' I asked, remembering that someone had told me she'd left suddenly.

'It was all right. It must be hell there now, though. Poor Stephanie.'

'Did you know her well?' I asked, as conversationally as I could.

'Yes,' said Isobel thoughtfully. 'She was an odd girl. Very fond of Fenn.'

'What do you mean?'

'Nothing really. Just that. I'm trying to work it all out, I suppose. You work somewhere for a while, and you know all the people, and then something like this happens. You can't help but be curious, you know?'

'Yes.'

'It can't be very easy for you, coming into a community in crisis when you weren't familiar with it before.'

'No, it is a bit peculiar,' I said with a wry smile.

'So why are you here? You seem too nice to be wanting to rub my nose in the fact that you've got my job. What's the story?'

I paused for a moment while Isobel reached for a packet of B&H from the mantelpiece. She offered me one and I took it from politeness. Her comment had made me uncomfortable and I thought I'd better explain my visit.

'I just wanted to try and clear a few things up,' I said quickly. 'And there doesn't seem to be anyone else to ask.'

Isobel walked over to the bookshelf and pulled out a couple of volumes which she looked at wistfully.

'It's trash but at least it's published,' she said, not responding to what I'd said. 'I'm glad I can write full-time now.'

She held up one of the books. It was a horror novel from a series I hadn't heard of: cheaply produced but interesting-looking, with Gothic-style covers. The author seemed to be a man: Irving Rose.

'Did you write that?' I asked, noticing that Irving's initials were the same as Isobel's.

'Yep.' She smiled. 'That was why I was Charles's golden girl. For a while.'

'Charles?'

'Charles Valentine. The *Professor*. He loved the idea of having someone young and authentic to teach his creative writing classes. I think it was the first time they'd had anyone *real* there.' She took a sip from her tea and stubbed her cigarette out. 'Do you write?'

'No, not really.'

'Oh,' she said, and came and sat down on the sofa. 'Is that why you came?' she asked. 'Is Charlie after you now?'

'*After* me?'

'Yeah, you know. After your *body*.'

'Oh, no,' I said. 'Nothing like that.' I picked up my lighter and turned it over in my hand.

'You knew Fenn, didn't you?' I asked, still distracted by the news of his disappearance.

'Yes,' said Isobel. 'From work, anyway.'

She looked at me hard.

'You shouldn't get involved, you know,' she said, adopting a concerned mother tone that I would only expect to hear from my actual mother.

'Involved in what?' I said defensively. Surely I wasn't that transparent?

'My guess is you're in love with Fenn, like everyone else. He's gone missing and you want to find him.'

'You're right except for the being in love with him part,' I said, feeling the truth of Isobel's guess sting like a slap to the face. 'How do you know he's disappeared?'

'You're not the only one who's come to see me, you know. The police were round here last night.'

'Oh,' I said. 'Were you close, then? You and Fenn, I mean.'

'I suppose so. He was always a complete sweetheart,' said Isobel, smiling. She saw the look on my face and smiled even more. 'Oh, I *see*. So I was right.'

'What?'

'What's going on?' she asked, using the confide-in-me tone of soap opera and shop girls.

'Nothing,' I said. 'We're friends, that's all.'

'Ah.' Isobel coughed and looked at me hard. 'So do you have any idea where he is?'

'No,' I said reluctantly, watching a half-smile drift across her full lips as if she was pleased I didn't know as much as I wanted to.

'What did you say about him and Stephanie before?' I asked.

'I think she was infatuated with him,' said Isobel. 'Can you keep a secret?'

'Yes.'

'He was a bit worried last term. You know why he left the university in London, don't you?'

'No,' I said, remembering the way his face had changed when I had asked him about it. 'Why?'

'He doesn't talk about it much, I only found out by accident. He had to resign after a female student claimed he *abused his power*, if you know what I mean.'

'What – you mean, he slept with her?'

'Against her will, yes.'

'*Rape*?' I said incredulously, barely able to believe what I was hearing. Not Fenn, surely? If it were true, though, I could see why the police wanted to get hold of him so badly.

'Yes,' said Isobel. 'Kind of. Apparently he had marked this

student low on an essay she thought was fantastic. She went through the usual channels and had it re-marked, but the second marker agreed with Fenn. She was a bit mad, by all accounts, and confronted him in his room one day. A scuffle ensued when she attacked him and he very gently calmed her down then took her to the medical room, or so his story goes. She waited three days and then, presumably once there wasn't any physical evidence, claimed he'd actually raped her. The case was thrown out of court, since it was obvious to everyone he hadn't done it, but his reputation at the university was ruined. That's how he ended up here.'

'Goodness,' I said. 'No wonder he didn't want to talk about it.'

'He shouldn't have had late tutorials with Stephanie,' said Isobel. 'I mean, it's no wonder he's disappeared. It must have looked *so* dodgy.'

'I can see that,' I said. 'Is it normal to have tutorials that late?'

'No. I don't know why he let it go on. It was obvious she had a crush on him.'

'Why?'

'Well, why else would she hang around till all hours with him at the university?'

'I don't know,' I said, wondering if there was another explanation but not being able to identify it.

'Was Stephanie involved with anyone else?' I asked.

'It's hard to tell,' said Isobel. 'I mean, in Halls they were all kind of tangled up in each other. I don't think even they knew at any one time exactly who was having it off with whom.'

'What about Jason?' I asked. 'Was there something going on with him and Stephanie?'

'Only in his head. They were friends in the first year for a while and then she obviously tried to distance herself from him. You know that saying about when you go to university you spend three years trying to get away from the friends you made in the first two weeks? That definitely sums up what happened with them – from Stephanie's point of view at least.'

'Mmm,' I said. 'But they weren't close at all this year?'

'I doubt it. Stephanie really distanced herself from the whole second-year group after some incident that none of us got to the bottom of.'

'What was it?'

'I can't really remember. Lots of giggling and whispering. Something they didn't want their lecturers knowing about. Anyway, Stephanie started making friends in the first year after that.'

'They're a bit weird, don't you think?'

'I didn't really know them,' said Isobel. 'They were the Professor's project, really.'

'*Project*?'

'Oh, yes. He recruited them all himself last summer. I mean, you've seen what the second years are like. He thought something had gone wrong with the process so he literally hand-picked the whole year then decided to nurture them himself. He got a few foreign students to impress the financial people and ensure he could have a small group and – hey presto!'

'The second years are all right,' I said defensively. 'They're very bright, most of them. They've just got an interesting sense of humour, that's all.'

'Are you teaching the first years as well now?'

'Only creative writing. They seemed a bit put out about it.'

'I can imagine,' she said. 'I wonder why Valentine's not doing it anymore.'

'He seems very busy.'

'So how is the mad Professor?'

'I don't speak to him much,' I said. 'I've only just started this week.'

'He is *such* a wanker,' said Isobel, blowing some smoke out of her mouth, trying to appear nonchalant and not succeeding. 'You know that's why I left?'

'What do you mean?'

'Can you believe I was actually in love with him?' she said bitterly. 'I knew he was married, of course, but he said he'd leave her. It's the same old bloody story, isn't it?'

'What, you left the university because he wouldn't leave his wife?'

'No. Because he dumped me.' She laughed bitterly. 'So much for sleeping my way to the top.'

'Sorry,' I said. 'That must have been awful.'

'Yeah. He claimed he wanted to spend more time with *her*, although I knew there was someone else on the scene. He met her at my birthday party, you know, the new mistress. October the bloody sixteenth. Then it started: the gradual distance, the cancelled dates. By Easter I'd had enough. I knew who it was and what she was after and I was pretty sick of him anyway by that point. He'd changed since he started seeing me. It was like he realised he could still impress women and just went after all of them – *all the time*. I should be grateful really. I've got my whole life ahead of me, and let's face it, *he's* past it. Of course,' she added, 'he didn't think so. He acted like he was about twenty half the time.'

I smiled, remembering the way he'd told me to *chill out*. I'd thought he was a definite candidate for a mid-life crisis then and what Isobel was saying confirmed that beyond any doubt.

'So you just walked out?' I said.

'Yeah. I knew they weren't going to renew my contract at the end of the year anyway, so I just thought stuff them, and never went back after Easter.'

She poured another cup of tea, her confident poise damaged by her revelation. Poor woman. I sat there for a while, not knowing how to break the silence.

'I assume you've heard about Jason?' I said eventually.

'Yeah,' said Isobel, pulling herself together. 'Such a shame. I suppose it was suicide.'

'That's what they seem to think.'

'You don't sound too sure.'

'Apparently some bloke was in the hospital asking if it could have been murder – and saying he was Jason's brother. But Jason hasn't got a brother. What do you make of that?'

'Why would it be murder?'

'I don't know.' I didn't want to tell Isobel about the riddle, and about the way the word *murders* was haunting me. For some reason I thought it was important that no one knew I had that piece of paper, so I backtracked instead.

'He said he knew what had happened to Stephanie,' I said. 'Do you think that's possible?'

'Yeah,' she said vaguely. 'Well, anything's *possible*.'

'Do you think he might have done it?'

'I don't know,' she said. 'I wouldn't bet money on it, though. He wouldn't have had the strength really, being such a small lad.'

Isobel got up and stretched. She threw the book she had been holding on to my lap and picked up the tea-pot and mugs.

'You should read that,' she said. 'It might help with your classes or something.'

'Thanks.'

She went into the kitchen and I scanned the back of the book, smiling at the Gothic cover and the overdramatic synopsis. I let my thoughts run away with me for a while, putting together everything I knew.

Isobel came back into the room and I stood up to go.

'Thanks,' I said.

'No problem. I hope you find out what you want to know.'

'Yes,' I said. 'Oh, incidentally, is there anyone in the university called Ben?'

This was my logic. *London* and *pendulum* could mean Big Ben. My current hypothesis therefore relied on finding someone called Ben, possibly from London, and seeing where I went from there.

'I wouldn't know,' said Isobel. 'Maybe in the Science

Department or something, but not in ours. You'd need to look through the directory for that.'

I looked blank.

'The University Directory: everyone's names, positions and extension numbers. There'll be one in your office unless you've got my old room,' she explained. 'I burnt my copy.'

I heard a kettle begin to whistle in the kitchen. Isobel turned towards it, and then, clearly having another thought altogether, walked over to the mantelpiece where behind various modern art prints a photograph of two small girls stood, covered in dust and almost invisible.

'My fucking sister,' she said, laughing bitterly, waving the frame about. 'Soap opera life or what? My married lover ran off with my bloody sister.'

I couldn't think of a fitting response to this so didn't say anything. The whistle of the kettle grew louder and Isobel put the picture down and turned back to the kitchen. I got the feeling I was supposed to see myself out which I did, walking out of the living room, holding the thin paperback in my hand.

I walked down the dingy hallway and then into the fresh air which I found myself gulping in with relief. The atmosphere in the flat had become stifling and I was glad to be outside again, surrounded once more by damp concrete and cold air. There was a little garden at the front of the apartment building that looked like the local dumping ground for lads coming out of the pub.

Something orange caught my eye, an unlikely flash of colour in this bleak beer-can cemetery. It was a familiar-looking piece of paper which for some reason I felt compelled to look at. I didn't want to be caught touching someone else's rubbish but I bent my head to get a closer look, pretending to scratch my leg at the same time. It was a flyer, identical to the one that had fallen out of Hans's bag at the service station. I couldn't imagine Isobel being interested in anything like that and wasn't surprised she'd thrown it away.

I wondered what her real suspicions were about Stephanie Duncan's murderer. I had a feeling she'd been keeping details from me; as indeed I had from her. I considered going back in and putting my cards on the table and demanding that she do the same, but I got the feeling we were motivated by different things. Isobel had been pleasant to me but I didn't entirely trust her.

I walked to where my car was parked and unlocked the door. I threw Isobel's novel on the back seat and started the engine. As I drove out of Brixham I took a last deep breath and filled my lungs with the salty air. I realised that my visit had shaken me up a bit and drove slowly back to Mawlish, enjoying the sensation of the sun filtering through the windscreen and the eventual appearance of the green fields with their seasonal scatterings of lambs and daffodils.

CHAPTER TWELVE

Follow the Yellow Brick Road

I stopped at the garage just before the turnoff for Mawlish and bought a copy of the *Evening Echo*. This evening's headline asked 'Why Are There More Drug Deaths in the South West?' The main story referred to Jason's death and quoted statistics that showed that outside Greater London, the South West had lost more young people to drugs than any other area in England and Wales.

I scanned a bit more of the paper as I walked back to the car. Looking at the date on the top, I realised there was something familiar about it and then I remembered: it was Nat's birthday. It was coming up for five o'clock, so I quickly turned the car around and drove to the nearest big supermarket, in Newton Abbott. Feeling guilty, I cruised around the aisles for about half an hour before I felt I had assembled some appropriate gifts: a video, a couple of CDs and a bottle of champagne. I thanked God for the recent supermarket boom, remembering the days when you could only buy food and drink in these shops.

I bought a card as well and slipped £20 in it before I drove back home. I knew it was guilt money but Nat deserved it. I had hardly spent any time with him since I'd been back in Devon. I knew I was letting myself become obsessed with events at the university and vowed to try and tone it down a little bit.

Reflecting on the whole scene with Isobel, I concluded

that although I was actually more confused than I had been before, there was definitely 'something worth pursuing within the jumble of information I had. I was more and more inclined to believe that Jason *had* known at least something about what had happened to Stephanie, in which case my next step would be to try and get a look in his old room in the Halls of Residence, but I resolved not to think anymore about that until after Nat's birthday.

It was quarter past six when I eventually arrived home. An amazing aroma hit me as soon as I entered the kitchen. It seemed that Mum was cooking something complex. She was the real culinary genius in the family and although Henri had taught me about the uses of garlic it was always Mum I phoned when my custard was going wrong. I walked into the kitchen and found her looking flustered and covered almost entirely in cornflour.

'Hello, darling,' she said jovially. 'Have a drink.'

Mum gestured to a nice-looking bottle of Shiraz with a name I hadn't seen before: Banrock Station. Sue was sitting at the old oak kitchen table with an almost empty glass.

'Hello, Lily,' she said. 'Grab a glass.'

'Cheers,' I said, as Sue poured some wine. 'Thanks for the keys and everything.'

'Don't mention it,' she said, smiling at me warmly and looking slightly drunk. 'I like to help out.'

'Where's Nat?' I said to Mum.

'He's upstairs, I think, getting changed.'

'Right.'

'Did you hear about Fenn?'

'Yes,' I said. 'Bloody gossips.'

'Mmm,' said Sue. 'You were getting quite friendly, or so I hear.'

'*Were*,' I said. 'God knows where he is now.'

'I'm sure it's all just a misunderstanding,' said Mum soothingly.

'I'm not so sure,' said Sue, ignoring the look Mum flashed her. 'You know what everyone's saying, don't you?'

'What?' I asked, fairly sure I knew what was coming.

'Apparently he was having an affair with Stephanie.'

'No,' said Mum, incredulously. 'That doesn't sound right.'

'It isn't,' I said. 'He just had late tutorials with her, that was all.'

'That's not what I hear from one of my students,' said Sue. 'He was *seen* with her at a party at Christmas.'

Shocked and perplexed by this new and, I hoped, inaccurate piece of information, I poured myself another generous glass of wine and went into my room to wrap Nat's presents. I could hear Mum and Sue giggling together over something I couldn't quite make out in the kitchen until the phone rang and Mum went to answer it. I instantly felt my heart leap, thinking it might be Fenn, but from Mum's tone of voice I guessed it was Alwyn, Nat's father.

Nat's birth was a bit of a mystery to all of us; a family legend. From the information I had gleaned over the years it appeared that twenty years ago, when Mum and Henri were still together, she'd got sick of all his adultery and decided to teach him a lesson by going off with the first man she could find.

Alwyn was working as a DJ on Radio West Country at the time and Mum admits that he was probably the most boring man she had ever met. Nevertheless they went on a couple of dates and Nat was the result. I didn't think he minded very much; Henri always treated him like a son, so effectively he had two dads.

I sat alone for a few moments after I'd finished wrapping the presents and stared out of the window, thinking dark thoughts about everything. I checked my mobile phone, in case Fenn had phoned me on that, but the signal wasn't very strong in the village and in any case I didn't hold out much hope that he would call. I lit a cigarette and amused myself by blowing its heavy smoke on to a sliver of sunlight that was pouring in at the window. I tried not to shut my eyes, even though I was tired, because when I did all I saw was

Jason's stricken face overlaid with endless images of Stephanie: working, relaxing, chatting with friends, and then having her head sawn off in the woods. I didn't really know what she'd looked like, but in my imagination she was small and pretty, with a desperate *leave-me-alone* expression.

After a while I heard Nat's voice next door in the kitchen and got up to give him his presents.

'Happy birthday,' I said as I handed the packages over. 'Sorry it's not much.'

Luckily all the presents turned out to be things that he had wanted. He looked pleased. Beth was with him and looked over at me sheepishly.

'I missed you in class today,' I said.

'Sorry, Lily. I just couldn't . . .'

The kitchen was silent for a moment and I felt embarrassed for her.

'Don't worry about it,' I said. 'Who wants some champagne?'

We all enjoyed a fabulous meal and everyone congratulated Mum afterwards. It was a rare treat to have her cook and probably everybody encouraged her in the hope that she would do it more often. At about midnight she drove Sue to the station and Nat, Beth and I were left alone to do the washing up. Afterwards Beth made some coffee and we all went through to the living room.

'I am really sorry I missed your class, Lily,' she said. I felt bad for her because I could see how guilty she felt.

'I marked you in anyway,' I said.

'Oh, cheers,' she said, surprised.

'How do you feel now?' I asked.

'She's feeling better,' said Nat. 'Aren't you, Beth?'

'I wasn't ill,' she said, honestly. 'The Professor's given us all an extra assignment and I had to spend the day working to catch up.'

'I'll pretend I didn't hear that,' I said. 'I shall continue to assume you were desperately ill.'

'That place is enough to make anyone ill,' grumbled Nat.

'It is amazing what a day away from it can do,' said Beth. 'Although I promise I won't do it again.'

'Is it as freaky as she says over in your department?' Nat asked me.

'It is a bit bizarre,' I said. 'But then, I suppose that's only to be expected.'

'I am so glad I don't have to live in Halls,' said Beth.

'So am I,' said Nat, squeezing her arm gently.

'Don't you get on with your group?' I asked her.

'Sometimes. The thing is, that department is just so, well, druggy. And I'm not into all that.'

'Surely the other students are just as bad?'

'I don't know,' said Beth. 'There's something different about my group. It's not just a recreation for them – it's more like a religion or something.'

'Mmm,' I said, thinking.

'The rest of the class are so immature sometimes, and weird,' said Beth, echoing my impression of them. 'Me, Bronwyn, Jay and Zoe were all deferred entrants. You know, we would have been in the second year now if we hadn't taken a year off.'

'I see,' I said. That made sense. So the students who didn't seem part of the whole first-year thing were both slightly older and had not been recruited as part of the same process or *project*. I could have worked that out for myself. I knew Beth had taken a year out because she and Nat went Euro-Railing together.

'I've heard that Jay and Zoe absolutely *hate* it in Halls,' continued Beth. 'All the drug parties and death poems. It's no wonder that boy committed suicide.'

'Why do you say that?'

'They used to bully him a bit, that's all. But then, that's what they're like. Sometimes I wish I'd done science instead,' she added wistfully, looking at Nat. Since he was studying Veterinary Science over in the main block, they didn't see each other much at university.

Nat laughed.

'I'm assuming you didn't hear about the mystery of the missing Ketamine, then?' he said.

'No,' said Beth and I together.

'They tried to hush it up, but a couple of students broke into our medicines unit and made off with about a hundred tablets.'

'So the science students are just as bad then?' I said.

'No,' said Nat. 'That's the punchline. It turned out to be some of your lot.'

He laughed. Beth and I looked at one other.

'What's Ketamine?' she asked.

'It's an animal tranquilliser, but apparently if you crush it up and snort it you can have a kind of out-of-body experience. Apparently the American troops used it in Vietnam.'

'What, when they got bored of smack?' asked Beth.

'I don't know,' said Nat. 'I do know it's pretty dangerous, though.'

'Sounds like it,' I said.

'So I suppose you didn't hear about the chemistry students who got busted then?'

'No.' Beth and I looked at each other again, slightly incredulously.

'Yeah.' Nat was warming to his theme now. 'They were manufacturing Ecstasy in the labs.'

'You're joking?' I said.

'No. Apparently they were supplying the whole city for a while.'

'God,' I said.

'Why didn't we know anything about this?' asked Beth. Nat shrugged and looked distant.

'I listen,' he said coyly. 'You know, when I'm not supposed to. *Upstairs.*'

'What – so all this is, like, a secret?' asked Beth.

'I suppose so,' he said. 'Anyway, let's change the subject.'

He took a swig of his champagne and shook his head about.

'I see no one's commented on my haircut,' he said impishly.

'You haven't had a haircut!' said Beth.

'You may not be able to see it but a minute lock of my hair is in *forensics* right now.'

'What do you mean?' Beth was sounding worried. 'Why?'

'They're testing all the male students at the moment,' I said, remembering what I'd overhead this morning. 'I wouldn't worry about it.'

Beth hit Nat again with a cushion. I didn't know how she put up with his teasing. When he was in this kind of mood he was absolutely irrepressible. Of course, when everything wasn't going his way he was a complete pain.

'Have you done any band practice lately?' I asked them. Nat's band, the Immense Standing Timbers, comprised him, Beth, and her twin brother Paul. I knew that they'd done loads of gigs a few months ago, but I hadn't heard anything since.

'We're writing some new stuff,' said Beth. 'You should come and listen to us sometime, see what you think.'

'We're brilliant,' said Nat. 'I wanted to do cover versions of songs from musicals but they wouldn't let me. I bet you didn't know that *Dark Side of the Moon* is really a soundtrack for the *Wizard of Oz?*'

'Really?' I said.

'Yeah, honestly,' said Nat. 'You have to start the record in the right place and then apparently you can hear a heart beating when the Tin Man comes on and everything.' He laughed and I smiled, unable to tell whether he was winding me up or not.

'God, you're full of it tonight, aren't you?' said Beth.

'I'm in a good mood,' said Nat. 'For I am no longer a teenager.'

I laughed at that, kissed him goodnight and left them to it. It had been a long day and I was completely tired out.

CHAPTER THIRTEEN

Dust and Cobwebs

———⊰≪◦≫⊱———

I had never got on particularly well with caretakers, security guards and technicians, but on Friday morning I decided it was time to start trying. That was, if I could ever find them. It took me over half an hour to discover the location of the main caretakers' offices, which turned out to be next to the post room in the main block, and fifteen minutes to locate the post room. When I eventually arrived at the right place I found about seven men hanging around in there, drinking tea, smoking roll-ups and not doing any work in particular.

'Excuse me?' I said. No one looked at me. I cleared my throat. 'Excuse me?' I said more loudly.

I was separated from the caretakers by a small counter which had a bell on it. I rang it and as if by magic one of the men put down his mug and came over to me.

'What can I do for you, love?'

'How do I get into the Halls of Residence?'

'Have you locked yourself out, my lovely?' he said, smiling patronisingly and scratching his head.

I sighed. The main block was too big and too busy for me. I had been knocked about and bumped into countless times on my way to this remote little room and wasn't in a good mood anyway since I'd had to get out of bed too early this morning.

'I'm staff,' I said edgily. 'And I need to get into the Halls of Residence.'

'Sorry, love,' said the man, still smiling. He took a cigarette paper from his pocket and started making a roll-up. 'We don't do Halls of Residence. We can't, you see. Union and all that. Bloody nuisance. *We* can't work twenty-four hours so they hire a *private* firm to do it. Lucky bastards earn about a grand an hour after midnight. Bates Security. You want to have a word with one of them. I'll just see if –'

'It *is* actually an emergency.'

'Oooh,' said the man, chuckling. 'You don't want to be having one of those around here. You'll be lucky if you can get on to one of them blokes before dinnertime.'

'Yes, well, thanks,' I said tersely and moved away from the desk.

'Do you want me to try and radio Steve?' said the caretaker, waving an expensive-looking walkie-talkie.

'Sorry, who's Steve?' I said, thinking I must have missed something.

'I'm Steve,' came a voice from behind me. Great. I was in a budget pantomime and no one had bothered to tell me.

'Well, what do you know?' said the caretaker. 'This is exactly the bloke you need to speak to.'

'I'm always ready to help a pretty young student,' said Steve, grinning.

'I'm staff,' I repeated.

'Oh, right,' said Steve. He was a tall, stocky man, slightly balding and suntanned, oozing the kind of effortless workman's charisma that did nothing for me. 'What can we do you for?'

'I need to get into Meredith Hall,' I said. 'It's a matter of urgency.'

'A matter of urgency, eh?' Steve looked amused by this. 'Well, I was going to tell you to come back at twelve, but since it's a *matter of urgency*, we'd better go along there now.'

'Thanks,' I said, knowing I'd been humiliated but not entirely sure how.

I walked over to the Halls of Residence with Steve,

listening to him chat about his wife and some shelves she was making him put up. Once we got outside the door to Meredith Hall he jangled his keys and looked at me.

'So you're looking for a sick student?' That was the story I'd given him on the way over.

'Yes.'

'Well, I suppose it'll be all right,' said Steve, looking at my identity card which I now wore pinned to the left pocket of my jeans. 'So long as you're sure you're not going to rob the place.'

'I doubt if there's anything in there I would want,' I said, lying.

He opened the door with a show of reluctance and held it for me while I walked in. The door shut slowly behind me and I turned to watch him move slowly away, whistling and smoking a Superking as he went.

I'd checked the room allocation documents earlier that morning at the main reception. Just as Cress had said, room 3313 in Meredith Hall had belonged to Adam Moore who, according to my register, had now left. Jason's room was supposedly on the fourth floor of Talbot Hall but it was fairly certain he'd never lived there. I wondered if anyone had told the police; as the room swap was not officially noted, it was likely no one had, so if the police had searched Jason's room it was probably Adam's. I realised this meant I might be first into Jason's *actual* room, untouched since his death.

I walked up a flight of grey concrete stairs until I reached the sterile space of the third-floor lobby, which looked disarmingly like the ground-floor entrance hall and presumably just like all the other lobbies.

Each floor in the building had eight sections, and each section was arranged in the same logical order I had studied on the map of the Halls of Residence before embarking on this expedition. Within each section there was a small common room with a TV and pay phone, two kitchens and two bathrooms clustered together around a lobby area which had three corridors leading off it. One of the corridors led back to the stairwell, and the other two contained the twenty students' rooms which could be found in each section. This was sixties design at its least imaginative, and I was glad I didn't have to stay in the building very long.

Rumour had it that a few years ago there had been a spate of suicides here, which all involved students jumping off the top of these buildings. The joke was that it was because the décor was so depressing and now that I was inside I found myself finally getting it. I mean, who would want to live in something that looked like a multi-storey car park?

It was just after ten o'clock in the morning, which I had considered to be the best time for this illicit activity. Most of the students had ten o'clock lectures and those who didn't, I remembered from my own university days, would probably sleep in until well after midday. Today was also the day of the Student Union Hustings, which would keep a lot of the resident students at bay, as they campaigned and haggled around the bars and main hall. If my guesswork was right, the common rooms would be deserted now, and all day, until about half-past five when the evening's soaps began.

I was pleased to see that my theory was correct. In fact, I hadn't seen a soul since I'd entered the building. The kitchens were empty as well, save for several stacks of dirty pans, kettles and mouldy crockery. I walked into one of them and helped myself to a cupped handful or two of water, since I couldn't find a clean glass. I was slightly breathless after walking up all the stairs and resolved to try and give up smoking soon.

I took a deep breath and walked down the passageway towards Jason's room: number 3313. I guessed that there was a code at work in the room numbering here. The first 3 probably stood for third block; the second 3 for third floor. That meant that 13 was Jason's room number. Unlucky for some. I remembered when I'd worked in a hotel being intrigued that they didn't ever have a room number 13. I–

had heard that it was the same in old people's homes, with the rooms just going straight from 12 to 14 as if they had been numbered by a GCSE maths student.

I walked down the short corridor past a sign which said 'Rooms 11–20'. Interestingly, the room numbers seemed to work backwards. Room 3320 was the first one I saw and 3319 the second, and they were set next to one another on the left-hand side of the corridor. There were no student rooms on the right, just electricity and heating cupboards, and a few notice boards with posters and petitions pinned on them. I noticed more police leaflets, the posters and publicity material for the various vigils organised by the Student Union and women's groups. They gave the hallway an eerie feeling and I felt slightly spooked as I walked slowly past them.

Rooms 3316, 3317 and 3318 were set back from the hallway and formed a little cul-de-sac all by themselves. I hoped the people who lived in them were friends. Rooms 3314 and 3315 were also set together on the corridor which appeared to end at a T-junction just beyond room 14. Around to the right were rooms 3311 and 3312 which seemed cosily tucked away. Off to the left was one room on its own: room 3313, which by contrast seemed detached and lonely.

It was no wonder Jason had felt isolated here, although it was quite clear why he had swapped. I'd noted from the room allocations that Stephanie's room was on the next floor up. Very convenient for someone in love. I stopped outside Jason's room and waited, worried about what I knew I would have to do next. I looked to the left and then to the right, like they do in the films – just to check that there wasn't anyone watching – and then I took a credit card from my pocket and swiped it down through the gap between the door and its frame. To my great relief it worked and the door opened with a reassuring click. I had learnt that trick when I was a student myself, squatting with some friends above a filthy hairdresser's in a flat that hadn't come with keys.

I crept into the room and shut the door behind me, gagging instantly at the smell of body odour, urine and vomit. Even in the dark I was already sure this was Jason's room: the smell was the one that Cress had described and that I had experienced first hand on Tuesday. Suddenly realising the gravity of my actions – I could feel my heart smacking against my breastbone as adrenaline surged through me – I stood still for a moment with my back to the door, trying not to breathe too deeply and listening for footsteps in case I had been followed.

When I was a child I had adored TV programmes like the *Red Hand Gang* and the *Nancy Drew Mysteries*. All of a sudden I smiled as I realised I was living out my childhood fantasy; I was playing detective and it felt rather good.

Remembering I was standing in the dark, I switched on the light, not wanting to draw attention to myself by opening the curtains, which were shut. The appearance of the room was, at first sight, unremarkable. Clothes were strewn here and there, empty coffee mugs littered all available surfaces, and on the bedside table below the large window was a plant that desperately needed watering.

In the corner was a small sink with a mirror above it, from which much of the smell appeared to be coming. A quick look inside (with my hand covering my nose and mouth) confirmed that this had been Jason's toilet for some time. Among the other foul traces inside was a lurid liquid that must have been vomit, and shards of broken glass. Two tumblers perched unsteadily on the edge of the sink and I followed my unconscious urge to move them on to the narrow ledge underneath the mirror. The glass in the sink must be the remains of a third, I thought.

Everything else looked comparatively normal, as you would imagine a student's room to be. Books and pieces of paper were scattered everywhere, some with Jason's name on, and odd items of women's clothing lay near the bed, along with a pillow and the duvet. It seemed as if Jason had entertained a woman here recently and I wondered if it might have been Stephanie. Then I remembered what Isobel had said. If Stephanie had distanced herself from him it was unlikely, but I didn't want to rule anything out at this stage.

The bed was covered with cardboard boxes, containing clothes, records and books, jumbled up as if they had been hurriedly packed. Had Jason been intending to move out? It was possible that one of his family had already come to clear the room but that seemed unlikely since everything else seemed untouched, and the job, if someone from outside had done it, was certainly less than half-completed.

The room itself was box-like, its thin walls housing a couple of cupboards and a wardrobe. The single bed occupied most of the space and there was a small insubstantial desk provided in the far left-hand corner. Jason's desk didn't seem to have any essays-in-progress lying unfinished on it. Instead he appeared to have used it as a dressing table. Bottles of aftershave vied with one another for the space also occupied by a number of pairs of socks and boxer shorts. I picked up a sock and sniffed it tentatively. It was clean.

I opened the doors of the wardrobe. Inside were clean shirts and trousers and even a couple of ties. None of this seemed to tally with the image of the young man I had been confronted with on Tuesday. He had obviously been too distressed to change before coming over to the Samuel Beckett Building, and then going to the Blue Dolphin. Before that no one had seen him since Stephanie died. Had he sat here for all that time? The contents of the sink seemed to suggest he had. Why?

And I was still wondering why he'd gone to the Blue Dolphin. If he had intended to kill himself, why didn't he just do it here? He had said that he was going to 'get' the person who'd killed Stephanie and maybe he'd thought he'd find them at the Blue Dolphin. I decided I should pay the club a visit soon and try to find out. I thought for a minute that maybe he'd gone there to get the drugs to kill himself with, until I noticed a packet of smooth, round yellow pills in a plastic bag on the dresser next to a bottle of Aspirin and on top of a volume of Sylvia Plath's poetry, well-thumbed and old-looking, with a splash of bright yellow paint on the cover. I picked up the bag and looked at it for a second then put it down quickly, not wanting to be in possession of drugs for even that long.

I turned my back on the wardrobe and surveyed the rest of the room. Jason's CDs were stacked in a pile on the floor by a portable stereo system. I went over to look at them. Unlike his clothes, they were just what I had expected. Oasis, Blur, The Verve. I turned away and looked into the boxes, wondering what I was searching for.

I supposed what I was really looking for were clues to *the information*: the information that Jason thought he had about Stephanie's murder; the information that was condensed in the riddle but that had to have some footnote to its meaning hidden elsewhere. I needed the information that would clear Fenn's name and make sure that Stephanie's murderer was found. Intellectual property was what I was searching for, but the problem was, I didn't know what it looked like or even if it was here. For all I knew, Jason had taken it with him to his grave.

One of the smaller boxes on the bed looked slightly more interesting than the others; more personal, somehow. It contained handwritten sheets of paper and notebooks, which were the kind of things I had come here to find, so I picked it up and started looking through it. Just as I was about to take a notebook out I was startled by a noise outside the door. It was an abrasive sound, like a cat scratching to come in.

Still clutching the box, I quickly looked around the room for somewhere to hide. I couldn't go under the bed because there were more cupboards tucked away there. I considered just standing behind the door and then I saw the handle move. I panicked slightly and threw myself into the wardrobe without thinking, which was fortunate because at that moment I heard the door open and then the sound of heavy footsteps entering the small room.

I stood in the wardrobe, trembling and trying not to breathe too loudly, clutching the box to my chest. I wondered who could possibly want to come in here. Somebody up to no good, I imagined. Great. I remembered my long walk up the empty staircase and realised that I was probably virtually alone in this block with whoever the footsteps belonged to. Could it be the murderer? I felt sick. What the hell was I doing here?

I held my breath and hoped the heavy footsteps weren't going to stay long. I listened anxiously as I heard them walk across the floor, stop, cross the room and then walk right back out again. I hardly managed to breathe until the door shut and realised that whoever it was had definitely gone. I waited in the wardrobe for a few minutes, just in case, and then slowly peered out, terrified I had been tricked and there was still someone standing there waiting for me.

I stepped out of the wardrobe and lit a cigarette, needing something to calm me and stop the hard, heavy thump of my heart. Although I had an overwhelming urge to leave the room I decided I should stay for a few moments longer, to give the intruder time to get out of the building. *Out of the building*. Damn! I suddenly realised that I could probably have seen them leave if I had looked out of the window, as Jason's room looked down on the entrance to Meredith Hall.

Hoping I wasn't too late, I twitched the curtain aside slightly and, feeling like a nosy neighbour, watched for a while. Nothing happened. Outside the green and the car park were calm, and in the distance I could see some students coming out of the Samuel Beckett Building.

I looked around the room to see what had been taken. Then I realised that nothing had been taken; instead, something had been added, or more specifically changed. The plastic bag I'd seen before didn't look the same, and didn't contain the same flat yellow tablets. I picked it up and looked at it. Instead, there were several chunky brown tablets inside. How peculiar. More peculiar still was the second change. Underneath the new bag of tablets was a book that hadn't been there before. The volume of poetry had been replaced with a thicker, glossier book: a collection of stories by Irvine Welsh. How bizarre. Thinking these items must have some significance I picked them up, putting the drugs in my pocket and the book in the small cardboard box, and turned to leave.

The book was a touch of genius, the man thought. The whole thing now clearly spelt accident. Not suicide. So there had been something in the pills. Whoops! The accomplice had been clever to suggest that. Things were looking better now, and it looked as if the plan would go ahead without any more problems. It was a good thing he had managed to make the change before the police discovered the mistake with the rooms. Now he was in the clear.

Things were improving at home as well. The wife had been to the doctor finally and got some pills of her own. Hopefully that would shut her up. Instead of going on and on about how he made her depressed (the audacity of it!), she could just snap out of it. He had been at home early one night that week, after returning from a complex journey, and there she was, with them in her hand, holding them out towards him.

'I'm going to do it,' she said. 'That'll teach you.'

He'd laughed at that, having had enough of suicide plots and murders. 'Just let me know,' he'd said, 'and I'll get a bottle of champagne.'

He entered the tall building before noon and swapped the packets. If anyone asked questions this would be their answer. And the book; that was just a joke, really, one he couldn't resist.

That night the man had a dream. It was a wonderful dream of a bright future. It included a passage from a book, although he couldn't remember which one; something about designing paradise.

CHAPTER FOURTEEN

Salt

Outside the wind was picking up as the bright April morning started to turn stormy. Chilled by the cold air and also by my (mis)adventure in Meredith Hall, I wrapped my brown suede coat around me and also around the box, which I thought it best to keep hidden until I got back to my car. I still felt shaken and wanted to go home, but I was taking the detective fiction class at two o'clock so unfortunately I had to hang around.

I walked to the car park and checked my watch. It was quarter to eleven. I unlocked my car, placed the small cardboard box in the boot, and thought about what I should do next. I was feeling quite hungry, but it was too early for lunch. I was reluctant to eat around the university anyway. I felt out of place, like a new girl alone at playtime, and had the uncomfortable impression that this feeling would take a long time to go away. I felt a pang then, remembering how I had felt when Fenn befriended me.

Train, London, murders, psycho, mirror, pendulum. The words sounded familiar now, like a well-loved poem. But the closer I grew to them the further away I became from what they might mean. The words did have a connection now, created by my endless repetition of them in my head. They seemed to go together naturally and run fluidly like the meaningless rhymes I used to chant while skipping or hopping in the playground at school. I was still certain there was an answer to the riddle they posed, and refused to entertain the idea that maybe they were just the convoluted rambling of a dying boy. I was now more inclined to believe that Jason *had* seen the murder, and what was more, that *somebody* (the pretend brother?) had been aware of what he knew.

I touched my pocket and felt the unfamiliar rustle of plastic inside it. I wasn't used to being in possession of drugs and didn't like the feeling it gave me.

My heart was still beating urgently in my chest. I stood still for a moment, waiting for a sense of calm to embrace me and pull me safely back from the edge of wherever it was I had gone to, but nothing happened. I still felt like I was speeding down a hill and although part of me wanted to just stop, a bigger part never wanted to reach the end. I hadn't liked the experience in the wardrobe but now I felt it had been over too soon, like a too-fast-don't-stop fairground ride. I was momentarily and perversely hooked on adventure and almost felt like running up the stairs in the Halls shouting, 'Again, again!' I couldn't remember the name of the chemical produced in the brain by fear but recalled reading that it was similar to that produced when you are in love. Now I needed to calm down. I needed to see the sea.

If the weather was anything to go by, and it usually was, there would be massive waves building up around the coast right now. I remembered the days when I used to surf, and the feeling of absolute delight upon waking on a day like today. That feeling was almost an instinct and storms always made me want to be by the sea. I got into the car and tapped the dashboard with my fingernails. I had enough time. Before I knew what I was doing, I had started the engine and was on my way to Kestral Sands.

Kestral Sands was only about half an hour from the city and because of that it was the main surfing beach in South Devon. It was busiest at this time of year, because come summer all the surfers would pack up and head off to

Cornwall, Australia or California. This was the time when everyone practised their moves for the summer and caught up on the gossip from last year. The problem with Kestral Sands was that you could never be sure there were going to be waves to surf unless it was a very stormy day.

As I drove out of the city I heard a distant roll of thunder. I shivered inside as the raindrops hitting the against windscreen became heavier and more insistent. I thought I heard them say *Lily, Lily, Lily* and I felt my heart take up the same rhythm. In an instant the sky went totally grey, the rain became wilder and the heavens seemed visibly to cave in on themselves and glower on all the motorists and pedestrians stupid or unlucky enough to be caught in the downpour.

I shifted the Volvo into fifth gear as the road became wider and emptier. The rain still fell heavily all over the car but that didn't stop me accelerating to about seventy-five miles an hour. As I drew nearer to the coast I would have to slow down, but for the time being I found the sensation exhilarating. I hadn't felt so free since I'd left for London all those years ago.

Soon I had to take a right turn which would lead me on to a country road and then a dirt track along the edge of the cliffs. The storm seemed to be more intense in that direction, and as I took the turning I could see regular flashes of sheet lightning up ahead. It didn't seem to be an electric storm, which was good, because that meant it would still be safe to go down and look at the waves crashing on the shore. I needed to experience the raw strength of the natural world, up close and dangerous.

As the road thinned out I began to feel nervous. In the old days it was traditional for everyone to meet up at the beach on the first stormy day of April. But I hadn't been here for years. What if there was a new crowd at the beach? What if there was no one there at all? My stomach churned slightly with fear and anticipation as the car gathered speed down the hill. After a while I saw the familiar sight of two palm trees poking out of some shrubbery to the right. I indicated and turned off towards them. The road became more stony and difficult at this point and I hoped I would be able to get back okay. Ideally, you should have a Land Rover for this kind of journey or a boat. My Volvo wasn't very good in the wet.

I pulled up next to the palm trees and parked diagonally next to a Range Rover that was already there. That meant there was at least one person down on the beach. I wondered if it was someone I knew.

I got out of the car and stepped on to the muddy track. The wind immediately swept up my hair then blew it back down in front of my face so I couldn't see where I was going. I pushed it back and started the muddy walk down the track towards Kestral Sands.

It brought back so many memories of summers past that I found myself feeling quite wistful. The storm was starting to die down but I could see another one on the way, coming from around the coast, hot on the first one's trail. The air had turned sticky and heavy but when the wind blew it was still cold, so I drew my coat closer around me. I lit a cigarette and hummed to myself as I walked the few hundred yards to the steps down to the sand. These had been cut into the cliff by fishermen over a century ago and not many people knew about them. To most people, Kestral Sands was just another inaccessible Devon cove.

When I reached the cliff face, I could already see that the waves were astonishing. I climbed down the steps quickly, not wanting to miss a moment of the crashing spectacle that nature was providing for me. When I was almost at the bottom I jumped down and felt my knees buckle as my feet came into contact with the wet sand. I kicked some seaweed out of the way and started the short walk uphill over the dunes towards the sea.

I breathed in the briny air and felt some small droplets of rain fall on my cheek. I could hear the sea groaning as it gathered up sand and silt beneath the huge breakers that would soon come crashing down on the shore. As I walked on the waves came into view once more. They were spectacular from this distance, and the closer I walked the more likely it seemed that one would just sweep me up and take me away to a watery romantic grave.

The spring tide had encouraged the sea to rise higher and the storm was making it act in a particularly intimidating way. Its pull had become random and its riptides treacherous. Only a brilliant surfer would be able to stay upright in conditions like that and I wasn't surprised there weren't many takers for the first day's surfing at Kestral Sands.

And yet there was one figure out there, scaling the watery mountains. I could see the outline of a scarlet and black wetsuit against the torrid grey sky. When the lightning flashed a few moments later the figure turned to face me. It was Dale Carter, Eugénie's ex-boyfriend, in whose arms I had shivered after the car crash. We were both devastated at losing Eugénie and Bobby but, dealing with it differently, didn't see much of each other after the funerals. A couple of years after the accident he called every so often to ask me out for a drink, but it never seemed to be at a convenient time.

I watched, transfixed, for about half an hour as the storm became more powerful and then gradually passed. I felt a rush of excitement each time I saw Dale rise on to a wave, lurching, dancing and skating over the surface of the sea as if by magic. I hadn't surfed for years, but even when I was quite good I could never have done that.

The rolls of thunder seemed to have co-ordinated themselves with the rise and fall of the waves and each time one crashed on to the beach it was as if the sky was applauding its performance, whispering, *Faster, harder!* In vain, the sea and the sky collaborated to try and overpower Dale, but each time they failed. As the eye of the storm passed, I imagined the sea foaming with anger as it tried to submerge the arrogant young man on his frail board.

By the time he came out I was hypnotised. He walked over, not recognising me.

'Hello, Dale,' I said.

He pushed some wet tendrils of hair out of his face and looked at me.

'Lily?'

'Yeah. It's me.' I looked at his body, gleaming in the wetsuit. He had lost some weight since I had last seen him and grown his hair, I had recognised him as much by his technique on the waves, which hadn't changed, as by his face. He had changed, though. He looked older, wiser and calmer. 'How's it going?'

'Did you see me out there?' he asked. 'It was fucking incredible!'

'It looked a bit dangerous,' I said, smiling. 'But fun. I missed the surf in London.'

'London. You didn't need to go so far away, you know.'

'Yeah, well.'

'Did you hear about my surfing? I'm a champion now.'

'Yes, I heard. Congratulations.'

'Cheers,' he said, and lifted his hand to stroke my cheek for a moment. 'You haven't changed at all. You're still beautiful.'

'Like the storm,' I said, feeling slightly uncomfortable and loading my words with significance and irony. I'd never admitted our one minor indiscretion to Eugénie, thinking that she'd never need to know. We'd been drunk and kind of mistook each other for Bobby and Eugénie. *Kind of.* I couldn't say no then, but this time when Dale leant down to kiss me I turned my head away.

'I have to get back to work.'

'Work?' He laughed. 'What are you doing?'

'Teaching,' I said. 'At the university.'

'Oh.' He looked dejected for a moment. I remembered how he had looked all those years ago, the first time I told him I was going away.

'Sorry,' I said. 'I shouldn't have come.'

'No, it's great to see you. Does this mean you're back then?'

'I suppose so,' I said tentatively. 'Kind of.'

'I see.'

I looked down at the sand while he dried himself off.

'We must have a coffee or something,' I said brightly, feeling slightly awkward.

'When?'

'Soon,' I said, smiling. 'I'll give you a call and we can catch up.'

We both knew this would never happen, that I was just being polite, but Dale smiled anyway and waved as I wandered off across the dunes once more.

The sun had come out and a warm breeze played through my hair, drying it slightly but not much. I looked at my watch and saw that it was one o'clock. I hadn't managed to have lunch and I was going to have to hurry if I wanted to grab a sandwich before my two o'clock class.

CHAPTER FIFTEEN

Not Drowning But Waving

Half an hour later I was back at the university, standing underneath a dysfunctional hairdryer in the Ladies', wondering if I should have been nicer to Dale; whether I should have meant it about the coffee. He could have changed, I supposed, although I had seen enough of life by now to know that that never really happened. Old surfers didn't change, I remembered from a novelty mug I'd once had, they just got washed up. I had never really understood what Eugénie had seen in him at the time but smiled when I recalled her telling me, in her characteristic husky whisper that he had a 'massive one'. I laughed to myself fondly when I thought back and realised that she had only ever seen his, so how had she known?

While I was drying the last of the moisture from my hair and clothes, I was also eating a salad sandwich and keeping a close eye on my watch. Dry or not, at ten to two I was going outside for a cigarette before my class started. I didn't just need the nicotine, I needed a few minutes to get my head together; to forget the excitement of this morning and to try and work out what I was going to teach the students.

Luckily I was virtually dry when I walked out of the Ladies, because the moment I did, I walked straight into Professor Valentine, looking much happier than when I had last seen him.

'Lilith!' he boomed, in uncharacteristically jovial fashion. 'How are we today?'

'I'm fine, Professor,' I said, wondering where on earth he had got the idea I was called Lilith.

'You seem a bit damp?'

'Oh, I got caught in the rain.'

'How distressing. You were in early today, I noticed. Reading in the library, were we?'

'Yes, just planning my class,' I said. The Professor had not shown any interest in me before this so I wondered what I had done to deserve such attention now. I looked at my watch, not to check the time but to indicate that I was in a hurry.

'Planning your class,' he boomed. 'Good.'

I wanted a cigarette and preferred to keep my distance from the Professor. He was an odd man and that was all there was to it. I thought vaguely about the cruel way his relationship with Isobel had ended and couldn't work out who to feel sorrier for, Isobel, Mrs Valentine or the Professor himself, who was clearly confused as to exactly what he wanted.

Five minutes later, after a hurried cigarette, I was back in the yellow classroom looking at the bookshelf from which the Sylvia Plath book removed from Jason's room had almost certainly originated. Cress was already sitting at the table reading as usual while the others drifted slowly through the door.

'Hi, Lily,' said Heather brightly.

'Hello, miss,' mimicked Blake, smiling at me genuinely despite his teasing.

'What are we doing today, *miss*?' asked Pete.

'Detective fiction.'

They all sat down fairly quietly and I noticed that the striking students still had not returned.

'Did you see we were on the news?' I asked the class conversationally.

'Yeah,' laughed Ash. 'Well done, Cress.'

The whole class, Cress included, started laughing.

'Don't set me off again,' she said.

'They interviewed us for ages,' said Justine. 'Sorry we never came back.'

'That's all right,' I said.

'Did you hear about Jason?' asked Heather in her high breathy voice. 'Isn't it awful?'

'I wonder what happened to him,' said Kerry. 'He was such a little twerp, I can't imagine how he got himself into such a state.'

'What do you mean?' I asked, not able to help myself.

'Looking like that, doing drugs. It just wasn't his scene,' said Heather.

'Yeah,' said Kerry. 'You remember the Christmas party?' The girls nodded and the boys looked bored.

'Well,' she continued, 'I noticed then that he wouldn't even have a puff on anyone's spliff. You know, when the first years spiked that vodka?'

Everyone groaned.

'I was sick for a week,' said Blake. 'Stupid little prats!'

'If I'd known, I wouldn't have drunk so much lager,' said Eddie.

'Do you remember Stephanie actually pissing herself?' said Kerry. 'Now *that* was a classic moment.'

'All right,' I said, having heard enough of this. 'So what's your point?'

'My point is,' said Kerry, 'that for someone who never took drugs, he did an awful lot of Ecstasy.'

'He was trying to kill himself though, wasn't he?' said Ash.

'I don't think so,' said Cress seriously. 'I don't think he was trying to kill himself at all.'

'Why?' asked Heather.

'He seemed so fired up,' she said. 'You know the way he was usually so sullen and introverted? Well, on Tuesday when I saw him in the corridor he was different; he was angry, not depressed, and angry people don't kill themselves.'

'What a prat, doing it with Ecstasy,' said Kerry. 'He should have just jumped out of his window.'

'Don't be so horrible,' said Lucy.

'I'm just being practical,' she said defensively. 'I mean, why go to all the trouble of taking so much E when there was a whole range of other ways he could have done it.'

'That is quite a good point actually,' Cress said.

'I thought everyone our age knew by now that over-dosing on E doesn't kill you,' said Heather. 'I mean, we've had it rammed down our throats on TV for years.'

'But it *did* kill him,' protested Lucy.

'No, it didn't,' said Cress. 'The papers today say it was something else, although they didn't say what.'

'But none of it makes sense,' Justine put in.

'Exactly,' said Cress.

'Da da da da . . . DUM!' sang Blake, imitating suspense music from old crime and horror films.

'Okay,' I said, holding up my hands and waiting for the laughter to stop. 'Let's get on with what we're supposed to be doing. Groups of three, please, one boy in each group.'

'Oh, *what*?'

'Why?'

'Can't you *bear* to be apart?' I teased. 'It'll do you good. Unless, of course, you're scared of the girls?'

The students got into their groups and worked quietly for an hour on a story-writing exercise. While they were occupied I was thinking about everything they had said. So Jason had been neither into drugs nor suicidal? Curiouser and curiouser.

The students completed their exercise and had finished reporting back by about quarter past three but the class didn't end until four.

'Okay,' I said. 'You've all done really well. Do you want to spend the last three-quarters of an hour researching in the library?'

'We can't,' said Heather.

'It's closed because of those renovations,' said Alex.

'Oh, yes, of course,' I said. 'Well, look, it's Friday and you've done some really good work today. Why don't you go and think about detective fiction in the bar or something?'

They all seemed happy with that and trooped off merrily. I let out a deep breath and felt a huge surge of relief that the week was over. I was quite happy with the way the class had gone, though, and it was amazing what could be done with no preparation.

I drove home as quickly as I could, just catching a bit of village rush-hour at the tail end of the journey. When I walked in the door my mood dropped slightly. Nat was having an argument with Mum in the living room. It didn't happen very often, but when it did it had usually been precipitated by Alwyn. I didn't want to get involved so hung around in the kitchen, making a sandwich and a coffee and trying to find a way of adding up all the seemingly disparate pieces of information I now had.

If only I could find the connection between Jason's words. *Train* could mean that the murderer had come from outside – in which case how would Jason know about him? *London* could be the place he came from (yet another nail in Fenn's coffin if true); *murders* was pretty obvious: Jason's way of implying what he was talking about, although I still wasn't sure about the plural. *Psycho* – well, everyone knew this person was a psycho, but maybe Jason was trying to suggest he didn't have a reason for what he had done. The attack was 'frenzied' so that could be true. *Mirror*: I didn't get this one. The word following was *pendulum*, and I couldn't work out how that went with anything else at all. I remembered I hadn't followed Isobel's advice and looked for a Ben in the directory, but it was such a tenuous interpretation I couldn't see it being correct. I had a feeling that when I did solve the riddle, all the pieces would fit together beautifully, like a well-designed puzzle.

The phone rang, cutting into my thoughts, and I ran to answer it, thinking it might be Fenn.

'Hello?'

'Lily, hi.' The male voice at the end of the line paused, I assumed for effect. 'How are you?'

'Anthony,' I said, annoyed that my logic had been interrupted by this. How dare he, after almost two weeks of nothing? Had it taken him this long to miss me? Maybe Dahlia had grown bored with him, or maybe he was getting cold in bed. I felt a brief pang of regret which was interrupted by his voice again: sounding slow, deliberate and put out.

'When are you coming back?' he whined.

'Why are you phoning me now?' I asked, responding to his question with one of my own; a more reasonable one, I thought.

'I miss you, Lily.'

I waited.

'I miss you so much.'

'Look,' I said, opting for politeness, 'I'm a bit too busy to talk right now. I'm in the middle of something.'

'What?' he demanded urgently. I sighed. What was I supposed to say? 'I'm about to go out on my own into the city, looking for drug dealers and murderers?' This was the truth, but hardly something Anthony would understand.

'Nothing. I'll call you tomorrow,' I said. 'Although I really don't think we've got much more to say to each other. Give Dahlia my love,' I added, putting down the phone and going back to the kettle which was just beginning to whistle. I was looking forward to my coffee and to some peace and quiet. Mum was really raising her voice in the living room, which was never a good sign. I poured water on my coffee and reached for the bread, pushing thoughts of Anthony away and letting my mind drift back over Jason's words and the evening ahead of me. I was planning to go into the city all right, I just had to work out what it was I was looking for.

As I spread creamy West Country butter over a slice of thick wholemeal bread the phone started to ring again. I cursed to myself in French and walked briskly over to the it, picking it up swiftly and barking an unfriendly 'hello' into the receiver. Why couldn't Anthony leave me alone?

'Lily?' said a voice that wasn't Anthony's.

'Yes,' I said, trying to place it. It was a nervous, half-familiar voice and it paused for a moment before continuing.

'It's Dale.'

'Oh . . . hi,' I said, wondering where he'd got my number, and then realising that it hadn't changed since the old days. 'How's it going?'

'Good,' he said. 'Look, I was wondering about that coffee . . . How about we turn it into a proper drink?'

'Um, yeah,' I said, wondering what he was getting at and feeling a bit jaded by riddles right now. 'Whatever.'

'Good,' he said, with a touch of cockiness in his voice I hadn't heard before. 'Nine o' clock, by the station.'

'What, tonight?' I asked disbelievingly.

'Yeah, when else did you think I meant?'

In my heart I knew this wasn't a good idea. Dale was still after me, after all these years, and I knew it shouldn't be encouraged. But then my head told my heart to shut up. I was going into the city tonight, and what better guide than a local surfer with no connection to the university at all? I looked at my watch and calculated quickly.

'Okay,' I said. 'Nine. By the station.'

'Cool,' said Dale and hung up.

I wandered back into the kitchen, feeling dazed and disorientated, adrenaline pumping through my veins. I wolfed down the piece of bread I'd buttered and gulped the still boiling hot coffee before walking quickly upstairs for a bath.

I wondered what Dale was doing with his life. Until this afternoon I hadn't seen him for over five years and for all I knew he could have a wife and kids stashed away. As I watched the water splash out I couldn't help thinking about the sea again. It had been amazing at the beach, much better than in the old days, when I just took everything for granted.

My bath was ready so I peeled off my T-shirt and let it fall in a heap on the floor, stepping out of my jeans at the same time and kicking them into the corner. Just as I turned my head I was aware of another trajectory of movement separate from my jeans; a brief retinal image shooting across the bath mat. *Damn*. It was the plastic bag with the pills in it. I should be taking more care of it. I made a mental note to remember to take them with me tonight, since I had a feeling Dale's insight would be useful.

I wished there was some way of telling what they were and how they worked. I knew enough about Ecstasy to know that it was unlikely to kill you, even if you took a lot; and that if you were going to have a reaction to it then just one tablet could do it. But someone had gone to a lot of trouble not just to plant these in Jason's room but to remove the other tablets as well. Whoever it was clearly knew the university or at least someone who did. I'd bumped into them (almost) because they'd had the same idea as me. They knew everyone had mistaken the room, and that this was their last chance to plant something before Jason's parents came and put everyone straight; their last chance to plant something *different*. This made me think there was some-thing special about these tablets though I had no way of knowing what that was. *Yet*. I felt uncomfortable being in possession of them nevertheless and pushed the bag under my dirty clothes, not wanting to look at it while I was in the bath.

An hour later I was standing in front of the wardrobe in my room, wondering what I should wear. There wasn't much choice really: jeans or my little black dress. I didn't have anything in between. I chose jeans in the end because I didn't want Dale to think I'd made too much effort.

I finished getting ready quite quickly and as a finishing touch went back into the bathroom and dabbed some perfume behind my ears.

I kissed Mum goodbye and shouted my farewells to Nat, who was sulking in his room.

'Be careful, darling,' said Mum, as if I was still nineteen.

'I will,' I said, appreciating it nevertheless.

'Are you driving?'

'Oh, yes,' I said. 'And I'll definitely be back tonight.'

I walked out into the slightly foggy night and bumped straight into Sue. Mum seemed to be seeing a lot of her lately but I didn't want to think about that. I got in the car and drove to the city, feeling strange but hopeful about the evening ahead.

As I drove I became aware of a funny rattling noise, as if something was in the boot. I dwelled on some urban myths for a while until I was convinced it was either a man with a machete who had climbed into the car while it was parked or the man with the hook for a hand, clinging on to one of the doors. Then I remembered that it was the box of stuff from Jason's room. I had almost forgotten about it in all the excitement following its discovery and resolved to look through it first thing in the morning, once I had got home from the city.

My mood sobered slightly as a fog came down, enveloping the car in its wet clammy silence. I tried to find some music to lift my mood, but all I could find in the glove box were Blur and Radiohead tapes and some atmospheric classical stuff – none of which could be relied on to cheer me up. It was impossible to see anything outside through the dark and the fog and I jumped at every unexpected noise, as startled as a rabbit being chased by an imaginary fox.

After a while, though, the countryside began merging into the suburbs and I was finally driving on lit streets. I drove around the ring road in good time and by the time I arrived in the city centre it was only half-past eight. I had a while before I had to meet Dale, so I decided to sit in a café and have a coffee to make up for the hastily gulped one at home.

I ordered a double espresso and sat down. The café was

small and impersonal and I felt like a private detective sitting by the window, anonymous but alert, watching the world walk past. It didn't seem to be the kind of place that would attract either students or surfers which meant, fortunately, I could be pretty sure I wouldn't see anyone I knew.

As I drank my coffee I watched the city gear itself up for a big night. I saw girls no older than fifteen walking past on high stilettos, trying to attract the attention of some older boys hanging about at the bus stop. I smiled because the scene brought back pungent memories. I remembered my own first night out in the city with Eugénie, and my first taste of alcohol. I remembered the vodka and oranges and later the Southern Comfort and lemonades – I was so sick after that.

I smoked a cigarette and thought about Stephanie, wondering if she had ever done this; sat alone in an anonymous café and then gone on a complicated non-date with an old flame (or *glimmer*, I decided, in Dale's case). I wondered if she had been in love and with whom. More than anything, I wondered who had murdered her and why. I wished that it wasn't my business but it was because Jason had made it so. I pulled my mobile phone out of my jacket pocket and dialled the number for my voicemail. Nothing.

I wiped my hands on a napkin and went to the toilets to touch up my lipstick. I hated the way that cafés like this always had such inaccessible toilets. In order to get to this one I had to go down two flights of stairs and along a corridor. I could smell the stench from the men's room as I walked past, and for the second time that night imagined some hidden predator lurking in the shadows waiting to pounce on me. I had actually been quite frightened by the whole episode in Jason's room this morning, and now the adrenaline had gone I was left with a directionless, empty fear, free-floating, attaching itself to anything that moved.

I hurried into the Ladies' and fished my lipstick out of my pocket. As I was applying it to my lips I became aware that there was somebody else in the small, dank room with me. I

couldn't hear any noise but I could smell cigarette smoke. I looked around and saw that one of the cubicles was locked. There was no actual smoke, just the smell, and silence loud enough to burst with a pinprick. Someone was hiding in the toilets smoking, though, I knew that for sure. I looked in the mirror one more time and left the room, confident I had just caught a young member of staff on an illicit cigarette break.

I left the café and walked out into the night. In five minutes I was back at the station and there was Dale, waiting for me, carrying a single red rose in his hand.

The head wouldn't stop glaring at the man. It was like some kind of fucked-up tendril-less Medusa glowering from under the sea. Actually, she was virtually under the sea; in a virtual sea of formaldehyde.

The man turned the bell jar (or whatever it was called) around to face away from him.

'Don't do that.'

'Why not? Her eyes annoy me.'

'Well, it won't for much longer, if you just help me get it out . . .'

CHAPTER SIXTEEN

E is for Ennui

<hr/>

The rose that Dale presented me with was of the type sold out of buckets by enterprising men on Friday and Saturday nights. Nevertheless I was touched.

'Thanks,' I said.

'You look amazing,' he said.

'What, in my old jeans?' I said, feeling only mildly flattered. 'I don't think so.' We stood there for a moment, our motionless bodies set against the animation of the city. I still felt weird about going out with him, but not *that* weird. We had been friends for a long time, and I remembered that Eugénie was just about to split up with him when she died. I had never told him that, of course, but it changed things somehow. It meant that I didn't connect him with her. He was just someone I used to know.

'Where would you like to go?' he asked.

'Let's get something to eat, shall we?' I suggested, feeling ravenous all of a sudden. 'And then see where we go from there.'

'Cool.'

We walked through the city streets for ten minutes or so until we came upon a small Italian restaurant that had been there forever.

'Do you want to go in there?' I asked.

'Yeah, sure,' he said, looking suspiciously at the red, white and green canopy hanging over the door.

The restaurant was very full and we were lucky to get a table. I ordered a glass of Chianti and some *Bruschetta al pomodoro* as a starter. Dale ordered a bottle of strong German lager. He looked quite attractive in his dark brown jeans and orange T-shirt, albeit in a rugged way. His straggly blond hair fell in wisps around his ears and his brown eyes looked big and heavy in his suntanned, weatherbeaten face.

'So,' I said, after the waiter brought the drinks to our table, 'what are you doing with yourself these days?'

'Surfing, mainly. I've just got back from Australia.'

'Oh,' I said. 'That must have been interesting.'

'Yeah,' said Dale. 'If you like that sort of thing.'

I lit a cigarette and looked around the restaurant. A party of middle-aged people in the corner seemed to be celebrating a birthday riotously and a group of four young professionals (still in their suits) were in the process of arguing over how to split a bill. Eating out was always like theatre to me; watching everyone perform around me, particularly couples following their scripts which ranged in theme from first date to full-blown romantic, illicit affair to marital breakdown (the most boring, usually consisting of silence). Observing groups, I liked guessing who would pair off with whom at the end of the night and it was this I was doing now with the bill-splitting group, while Dale stared blandly at me.

'Has anyone ever told you your eyes don't match?'

'Yeah, only *all* the time,' I responded, moving my napkin on to my lap as the waiter appeared with our starters. Dale eyed my *Bruschetta* suspiciously as he swigged his lager and toyed with an olive. 'I thought you would have remembered my eyes.'

'Of course,' he said. 'I remembered everything. You're looking good, you know.'

'Thanks,' I said, understanding that this was as exciting as Dale would get with the compliments. Fenn had been much more articulate and convincing, I thought uncharitably and stuck an olive in my mouth with a bit of my bread, not caring if I had oil running down my chin.

I ordered another glass of wine when the plates were taken away, thinking this had better be my last. 'Cheers,' I said, holding it up towards Dale.

'To old friends,' he said.

'To old friends,' I repeated, smiling.

'So how's the university?' he asked.

'Fine,' I said brightly. 'Yeah, it's good, except for, well . . . I suppose you've heard all about the murder and everything?'

'Yep.'

'Don't you think it's a bit odd?'

'I don't really know anything about it.'

'Did you hear about the boy who died from Ecstasy?'

'No.' Dale looked a bit uncomfortable, although I couldn't imagine why. Maybe, like me, he still felt odd about anything to do with drugs. That was the reason I hadn't made many friends at university. While everyone else was out having a 'good' time, I stayed in and studied unable to forget the way that drugs had led to the death of my best friend.

'He was one of my students,' I said. 'I couldn't believe it.'

'Really?'

'Yeah. They found him outside the Blue Dolphin last Tuesday night.'

'Oh, *student night*,' said Dale. 'Indie music, lager a pound a bottle. I didn't think that would have been an E-head's kind of scene.'

'Well, that's the thing,' I said. 'I don't really think he *was* into all that.'

'Mind you,' said Dale, 'some of them try it for a laugh anyway. Maybe it was the first time he'd done it, and he had, you know, a reaction or something.'

'Yeah, maybe,' I said. 'But the papers said he took a lot.'

I was glad we were finally on to the subject that was constantly on my mind but felt this was old ground we were covering. One of the main reasons I'd wanted to be out in the city tonight was to try and find something else, some link that would give all the others meaning or at least move me forward a bit. I wondered what Sherlock Holmes would have done in this situation. Probably paid some small boy to follow the suspect around while he sat there with his pipe, working out in about five minutes the series of words I wasn't having any luck with. That was fine except I had neither a small boy nor a suspect, and clearly none of Holmes's intuition.

'It happened to a mate of mine,' said Dale, breaking into my thoughts.

'What did?'

'He took his first E and dropped down dead an hour later. You never can tell.'

'I'm sorry,' I said.

'Yeah.'

We picked at our food for a while, Dale looking slightly morose and me thinking through my various theories about Jason and poor Stephanie. By the time we left the restaurant Dale was drunk and I was lethargic. It had been a long week, and now tonight was turning into a long night. There was one thing I had to do, though, and I needed to do it next.

'I want to go dancing,' I declared, trying to look more alive than I felt.

'Fine,' said Dale, cheering up. 'I like a good boogie on a Friday night.'

I looked at my watch. It was coming up for eleven.

'Where can we go?' I asked innocently.

'Blue Dolphin?' said Dale, smiling ironically.

'Yes, why not?' I said, smiling back because I'd got what I wanted with minimal effort. I was going to be able to ask some more questions that might help sort out some of the problems in my head. I needed to know what train of thought had led Jason to the Blue Dolphin. He must have gone there deliberately: the club wasn't on the way to anywhere else and was nowhere near the university. Had he gone there to buy or sell drugs? Or had he maybe gone there to find Stephanie's killer?

We walked back to the station car park where I had left the Volvo.

'You should have got the train,' said Dale. 'Then you could have had a drink.'

'No, I'm fine.'

'Seriously,' he said, sidling up behind me as I unlocked the door. 'If you want to stay over, I've got plenty of room.'

'I'm sure you have,' I said, inching away. 'But I like having my car and I don't mind not drinking.'

This was absolutely true. Ever since the moment I'd passed my test, when I was eighteen, I had always taken the car on nights out. It was a pain having to give everyone lifts home from the pub, but I didn't really miss the drinking and there was something really nice about going home sober. Once there, I always had a few glasses of wine in front of the TV and the fire and usually found that to be the best bit of the evening.

'You're a funny girl,' said Dale, and got into the car sighing and shaking his head.

We pulled up outside the Blue Dolphin at about quarter past eleven to find that there was a massive queue outside, but luckily there was a parking space right where I'd parked before going to the hospital. I looked up and down the line of young people outside the club. It was the same scene I had observed on Wednesday, although that seemed like a long time ago now.

'We're not going to get in,' I observed as I locked the car.

'Oh, no?' Dale looked at me and I could see his expression had changed slightly. He looked excited, like a little boy in a sweet shop. 'Come with me.'

He took hold of my hand and led me to the front of the queue. I felt myself blushing slightly as I sensed the hot stares of all the kids standing in line.

'Don't bother trying, mate,' shouted a young looking bloke. 'They won't let you in.'

There were two bouncers on the door. One of them was very big and stocky and stared ahead, unsmiling, through black Ray-Bans. Next to him was a sign saying FULL.

The other bouncer was smaller but looked just as tough. His black bomber jacket was slightly scruffier than the other bloke's and he had a fag in his hand. He looked quite animated while the other one looked like he'd been recently carved from stone.

'All right, Billy?' said Dale jovially.

'All right, *mate*,' said the animated bouncer, slapping him on the back. The stone-statue bouncer looked around and nodded at Dale respectfully. I wondered how he knew these people.

'You know I don't take bribes,' laughed Billy.

'Yeah, right,' said Dale, smiling as he walked past into the club. I couldn't do anything but follow him.

'I suppose since you've got a pretty girl with you . . .' Billy called after us. But I got the impression that nothing the bouncers said would have kept Dale out. Just as I was wondering why that could be he turned and smiled at me and explained.

'I know the owner.'

The club itself was as hot and sticky as the night before a storm. After we passed the bouncers we entered what seemed like a dark tunnel. I could see the walls were decorated in purple velvet and there were silver stars glistening on the ceiling. The whole place was done up to look like the kind of underground cavern anyone can remember conjuring up in childhood dreams and I thought cynically that it was a shame that some people could only access that kind of innocent wonder now through drugs and alcohol; that they had left their real childhoods so far behind them.

The tunnel turned into a wider corridor which led to a flight of stairs going down into a basement. I could feel the bass notes from some house record or other pounding through my body and suddenly felt a whoosh in my head which was uncomfortable and claustrophobic. The sensation reminded me of the only E I'd ever done and I immediately broke out in a slight sweat as a result.

'I thought this used to be a cinema?' I shouted to Dale, starting a normal conversation to try and calm myself down.

'It was,' he said. 'But they've converted the basement since then.'

'Right,' I shouted.

'This is the VIP lounge down here,' laughed Dale. As we entered the large basement area I could see that a number of what would be called an 'older crowd' were down here, sitting around ostentatiously drinking champagne and spirits.

The music had grown louder the closer to the room we got. Now, standing by the bar, my ears were full of stodgy Latin beats, mixed to twice their original speed by a lanky-looking young bloke in a glass DJ's box to the left of the bar. I could hear a girl whispering in my ear. 'Wiggle,' she said. 'Shake and move.' I turned to look at Dale but he was striding over to the DJ box. 'Yeah, yeah,' said the girl. 'I wanna see you move.'

I watched Dale shake hands with the DJ, who slapped him on the back and smiled. I turned away and looked around the room. A few young women were dancing on a small stage, all wearing tiny lycra shorts and bra tops. Suddenly I felt overdressed. The heat was overwhelming down here and when I touched my brow I could feel that I was breaking out in a sweat, which would have been embarrassing except everyone was dripping with it. Except, of course, all the men in the Paul Smith suits sitting at the small heart-shaped tables pretending to be gangsters.

'You can change your mind,' said the girl and I realised that she was part of the records the DJ was spinning. Her light, shrill voice came out of several large speakers around the room. I wondered how old she was; she sounded about eight. The music was moving quickly and as I thought about it the original Latin beats faded into something I recognised from last year's pop charts and the girl's voice became more grown-up.

Being here reminded me of working at the Underground Club and I felt slightly uncomfortable in my new role of customer: I hadn't been in a club like this through choice since I was a teenager. I could see Dale pointing at me and smiling from within the glass box. When he saw me looking at him he immediately grinned and gestured for me to come over, whispering something to the DJ at the same time. He must have thought I was finding this desperately exciting but to be honest I just wanted to be driving my car home, fast, down the country roads with the wind in my hair and Blur or Radiohead on the stereo. I really wasn't into all this stuff at all.

I took off my denim jacket and tied it around my waist, rolling up the sleeves of my jumper and reaching into my pocket for a hair band. As I pulled the towelling band out of my jeans pocket something else came too. It was the plastic bag. Shit. I quickly looked around to see if anyone was watching but they all seemed too wrapped up in themselves. I picked the plastic bag up off the floor and shoved it back in my pocket. I was sweating even more now, and felt relieved when my hair was tied back and out of the way.

I walked over to the DJ's box and through the little door.

'All right?' said the DJ, by way of a greeting.

'Hi,' I said. The DJ winked at Dale in a way I could only describe as obvious and went to select another record from a massive box next to the decks. He looked like a nodding dog, with his floppy hair bouncing up and down with the rise and fall of his head as he bobbed along to his music.

I looked at Dale pointedly.

'Okay,' he said, and placed his hand on my back to steer me out of the little room. 'Later,' he said to the DJ.

I sat down at an empty table and looked up at Dale, who was rummaging in his pocket for some money.

'Can I borrow a tenner?' he asked.

'Sure,' I said, and fished one out of my pocket, taking care not to drop the bag this time.

'I'll give it straight back.'

'Whatever.'

'What do you want from the bar?'

'Oh, Coke's fine.'

'Are you sure? I meant it about staying at mine, you know.'

'Yeah, I know. I'll have Coke anyway, though, please.'

'Fine,' said Dale, walking off moodily towards the bar. I watched him go and then focused on the bar, noticing that there was just one person working behind it; a young dark-haired bloke of about my age who seemed fairly full of himself. As Dale approached him I noticed a very male scene developing which involved some pointing and a little dance. They were obviously well acquainted. I wondered if this was yet another way of trying to impress me and sighed. Dale didn't know me very well at all. Of course the irony was that if he had bothered to find out what did impress me he wouldn't have found it that hard to achieve. I mean: a nice bottle of wine, a film and a walk along the river would have done the trick. I leant back in my seat and looked around the club again but nothing seemed to have changed.

Dale reappeared with the drinks and my ten-pound note, which he gave straight back to me, looking pleased with himself and wearing his smile like a medal.

'The drinks are free,' he said. 'I thought they would be but I don't like to assume, you know.' He grinned at me happily. 'That bloke behind the bar is called Al. If you want anything else, just ask him and he'll get it for you.'

'Aren't you going to sit down?' I asked.

'I've got to go and have a word with someone. Just hang on and I'll be back in a tick.'

I sat there for a while drinking my Coke and wondering how I was going to find out what I wanted to know. This Al seemed like my best bet to start with but I wanted to wait for the bar to clear first. While I waited I lit another cigarette and tried to imagine Fenn in a place like this, which proved somewhat difficult. He wouldn't be seen dead in a provincial nightclub like this, I decided, feeling my heart sting as I thought of him for about the thousandth time this week. If Jason's death was in any way connected with this place then I knew for certain that Fenn couldn't have been part of it. He was too subtle, somehow, too sophisticated. He had been to my *mum* asking about feminist interpretations of heroism, for goodness' sake. No, Fenn was definitely not the man.

Eventually the bar cleared and I walked over, taking my empty glass with me. Al didn't notice me approaching, being more interested, it seemed, in a tall black woman in Lycra dancing wildly by the speakers.

'Fucking mental,' he said, partly to me but mainly to no one in particular as I gave him my glass.

'What?' I said.

'It's a fucking bloke. *Mental*.'

I looked again just in time to see a fake acrylic breast emerge from the dancer's boob-tube.

'So it is,' I said, laughing and instantly being reminded of London. 'I didn't think Devon had come so far.'

'What, backwards?' he said, wrinkling his nose. 'Anyway, what do you want?'

'A Coke if that's all right,' I said, adding: 'I'm with Dale.'

'Oh, right, sorry. Of course.'

I leant on the bar, watching him blush slightly as he filled my glass from a sticky-looking spray nozzle.

'Do you work here every night?' I asked.

'Yep. I'm bar manager down here,' he said proudly.

'I bet you see lots of things, just standing here every night?'

'I see fucking *everything*,' he said proudly, sticking out his chest.

'Are you meant to swear at customers?' I said good-naturedly.

'Oh, what? Sorry.' He blushed again and coughed. 'You're a bit different from the usual sort I get down here.'

'What do you mean?'

'One of the things I've seen, right – you won't believe this – a bloke and some girl I swear he chatted up right at this bar, giving it the business in *that* corner.'

I looked in the direction he was pointing. There was a small alcove right in front of the bar which was hardly private.

'Really?' I said, feigning as much interest as I could.

'Yeah, I saw *bodily fluids* and everything,' he said. 'What a slag. She'd only just met him!'

'Er, yeah,' I said, taking my Coke as Al handed it to me. 'Cheers.'

I stood there for a moment while he fumbled around in the back room, eventually emerging with a cigarette and a red nose.

'Everyone's very smartly dressed in here,' I observed.

'Yeah,' said Al, looking me up and down. 'Dress code. You wouldn't have got in if you hadn't been with Dale.'

'Oh, *thanks*,' I said, looking at my jeans and then smiling at Al, disliking him intensely but needing information from him. 'So you work every night?'

'Yep. You'll find me down here every night except Tuesday.'

'Tuesday?'

'Fucking student night. No point in having the VIP lounge open then so I do the door instead.'

'*Do the door*?' I repeated.

'Yeah. I let people in, search them for drugs, and if they haven't got the right attitude, I kick them in.'

'Nice.'

'Students. *Christ*!' he said, shaking his head. 'They get too much fucking grant or whatever it is. The government should be using the money for something useful, not letting them lay about all the time.'

'Did you notice a bloke come here on Tuesday?' I said.

'Dark shoulder-length hair, Oasis T-shirt. In a mess, smelly . . .'

'Whoah!' said Al, holding up his hands. 'You mean the kid that died, don't you?'

'Yes,' I said. 'What time did you let him in?'

'I didn't. I wouldn't let someone in that looked like that,' said Al disdainfully. 'Not even on student night. I mean, we let them wear jeans on a Tuesday but we don't relax the dress code much more than that. He never came in here.'

'Then what was he doing outside?'

'I dunno.'

'Was he a drug dealer?' I asked, remembering what the police had said and sending Al into fits of mordant laughter.

'You're fucking joking, aren't you?'

'No,' I said. 'I'm just curious.'

'Are you some sort of private detective?'

'No, I'm his teacher.'

'Yeah, right,' said Al, propping himself back up on the bar after his extended bout of laughter. A smartly dressed man with long blond dreadlocks had emerged and was waiting next to me.

'*This* is a drug dealer,' said Al, pointing at him.

'Shut up, you twat,' said the man in a thick mock-cockney accent. 'You want this more fucking *on top* than it already is or what?'

'Chill out, man,' said Al. 'She's with Dale.'

'Oh, right. Sorry, love,' said the man, holding out his hand. 'Pleased to meet you.'

He turned back to Al. 'Give us another bottle, mate, on the tab.'

'Yeah,' said Al. ' 'Course.'

The man left with a bottle of Bollinger and sidled back to his table, around which several girls sat looking underage and awestruck.

'So if you didn't let him in, then how come he ended up dead outside the front doors?' I said, finishing my drink and handing the glass back to Al.

'Fuck knows,' he said. 'Although he was found by the *back* door, you know.'

'Oh,' I said, surprised. 'But what about the picture in the paper?'

'Ambulance can't fit round the back, the road's too small. We carried him out front to get rid of him as soon as possible. Fucking loser. Shame about all the press, though. That's where the picture came from.'

'So had you ever seen him before?'

'No. Never seen him before in my life.'

Al tired of the conversation and started pointedly picking up glasses and taking them out the back where I assumed there must be a sink. I left him to it and went to sit back down, concerned that Dale's 'tick' had now turned into an hour.

Just as I was about to leave the club and drive back to Mawlish, he appeared with a small man who was wearing a black suit and a red turtleneck. His hair was short and his face clean-shaven. Nevertheless I recognised him. It was Dale's little brother, Wesley.

'Long time no see,' I said, standing up to shake his hand.

'What do you think of my club?' he asked.

'What club?'

'This club, stupid,' said Dale. 'Wesley owns it.'

'Oh,' I said, unimpressed. 'It's, um, nice.'

I left straight after that, having found out what I wanted to know, but I still ended up back at Dale's flat following a desperate plea for a lift home followed by a persuasive offer of coffee. Now that I realised how involved he was in the Blue Dolphin, I thought I might as well ask him some questions before I went.

Two cups of instant coffee later I decided I'd better get on with it. Conversation between Dale and me had long since dried up and I knew he would probably be angling to get me into bed soon.

I pulled the bag out of my pocket and waved it at him.

'Do you know what these are?' I asked playfully, as if I did.

'Cool,' said Dale, taking the bag and pulling out a pill. 'Brown biscuits. Did you get them from the university?'

'Why do you ask?'

'Did you?'

'Yes, well, kind of. Why?'

'They manufacture them there,' said Dale. 'That's all.'

'That's *all*?' I said. 'How do you know?'

'Let's not talk about it,' he said hurriedly. 'And don't tell anyone what I just told you. I thought you knew anyway.'

How the hell could I know? I'd only been there for a week.

'So you're into all this stuff, then?' I asked incredulously.

'Of course. I just didn't think it was your cup of tea, otherwise I would have done a couple tonight.'

I grinned weakly and got up from the sofa. I wanted to shout at him, to say: *Of course it's not my bloody cup of tea. Don't you remember that drugs killed your girlfriend?*

'I'm going to make some more coffee,' I said instead. 'Do you want one?'

'Yeah, cheers,' said Dale without looking up.

I stood in the kitchen, waiting for the kettle to boil, wondering where it had all gone so wrong for Dale. I knew that drugs were part of the whole surfing thing but they never had been for us, all those years ago, and certainly not after that awful night when only Dale and I remained standing disbelieving and cold in the rain. I remembered the way he used to say that people who did 'all that' were stupid. But he was a completely different man now, and I had to say I didn't like him very much. That made me sad. He had been quite a good friend once.

I brought the coffee back and sat down, flicking mindlessly through a magazine while Dale poked around in another room. As soon as he came back I would have to start making my excuses. I still couldn't believe that he was into drugs.

'Lily?' said Dale, in a slightly broken voice, coming through from the bedroom.

'Yes,' I said, still looking at the magazine.

'Did you do one of those pills tonight?'

'No,' I said, turning a page. 'Like you said, it's not really my cup of tea.'

'Shit,' said Dale. I looked up at him and saw he was breaking out in a sweat. He lit a cigarette and puffed on it furiously.

'Are you okay?' I asked.

'I don't feel so good,' he said, shaking his head. 'I reckon they're moody Es you've got there.'

'You didn't take one, did you?'

'Yeah, well, about three. Why?'

Dale looked up, but it was clear he couldn't see me properly. I could see his pupils dilating as he tried and failed to focus on objects in the room. I put my hand on his arm soothingly.

'Okay,' I said. 'How do you feel?'

'Shit,' said Dale bitterly. 'What do you think?'

'Describe it to me.'

'I feel really sick, but not like I could throw up. I'm having head rushes and palpitations and I can hear a ringing in my ears.'

'Okay,' I said again. I reached out for his hand and took it. It was cold and clammy. 'I'll go and get you a glass of water or something.'

Dale looked at me with a blank expression as I went into the kitchen. My heart was beating so fast I thought it was going to burst out of my chest. I couldn't believe what was happening. With shaking hands I fumbled around in the cupboard for a glass but there weren't any there. I turned to the sink and started to wash one up, but I was shaking so much that I dropped it. I watched the shattered fragments explode in the sink and then I started to cry.

I stood there sobbing for a moment and then I remembered that Dale needed me. I grabbed an almost clean mug and filled it with cold water. I dried my eyes on a bit of kitchen roll and walked through to the living room.

I held out the mug to him.

'Soup!' he said. 'I don't want your fucking soup.'

'Dale? Are you all right?'

He turned to face me and I could see that his eyes were red and swollen.

'What did you say?' He tapped his ears as if to dislodge something that was preventing him from hearing me. 'Who are you? Who's Dale?'

I sat with him for a while, watching him become more confused and disorientated. I couldn't remember how much of this would be normal after taking Ecstasy. How weird were drugs supposed to make you feel? Eventually Dale dropped off to sleep on the sofa, breathing slowly and deeply, and although I was trying to be rational I instinctively knew that something was wrong.

It was all looking pretty bad. I looked at the bag of tablets on the floor. My first thought was to flush them all and get out of Dale's flat as quickly as possible. But then I started thinking clearly and decided that the worst thing I could possibly do was to run away. Everybody had seen me with Dale, besides which I'd never been a coward and I certainly wasn't going to repeat the mistake I made with Jason. I couldn't really flush the drugs, either, because I could be throwing away valuable information that might help save Dale's life. I remembered one of the anti-drugs commercials a few years ago that said you should always provide a sample of the drug involved in an overdose if possible.

I looked over at Dale. His breathing had become slower and more laboured. I placed two fingers tentatively on his neck and was surprised to discover a machine-gun pulse. When I found I couldn't wake him, I decided it was time to call an ambulance.

CHAPTER SEVENTEEN

Post Mortem

I sat in the ambulance next to Dale, holding his hand and trying not to get in the way of the paramedics as we drove at breakneck speed to the City Hospital. They slipped what looked like an oxygen mask over his face and asked me what had happened to him.

'I think he took a pill,' I said vaguely.

'What kind of pill?' said a paramedic, more urgently.

'Ecstasy, I think.' I felt in my pockets. 'I found a bag of them in his bedroom.'

I pulled the bag out of my pocket and handed it to the paramedic.

'Good,' he said. 'The doctor will want to see those.'

After that everything happened in a blur. I sat in a waiting room in the hospital while doctors and nurses rushed by me. I imagined they were all trying to save Dale, but I knew the reality was different. This was, after all, Casualty on a Friday night.

I noticed a couple of police uniforms among the blurred figures but didn't think anything of it. I looked at my watch and saw that it was almost four o'clock in the morning. I wasn't going to get any sleep tonight.

'It's Lily Pascale, isn't it?'

The voice came from behind me and I turned immediately to see whose it was.

'PC Williams,' I said.

'Have you been with Dale Carter all evening?' The police constable's voice was stern and hard-edged. I immediately felt scared. Maybe they had found out that I was the one who inadvertently gave Dale the pill.

'Yes,' I said. 'At least, from about nine o'clock. How is he?'

'Not so good, I'm afraid. The doctors are trying to stabilise him, but they're not having much success.'

I put my head in my hands and rubbed my eyes.

'Miss Pascale?' WPC Newman was looking down at me. 'I'm afraid we're going to have to ask you some questions.'

'Why?' I asked. 'Am I under arrest?'

'No, of course not,' said PC Williams. 'We just need you to help us with our enquiries.'

'Okay,' I said. I stood up shakily. 'Do you want me to come now?'

'If you wouldn't mind,' said WPC Newman.

I followed them out to their car and got in. I sat, dazed, in the back seat until we reached the police station.

Ten minutes later I was walking down a corridor with no windows, feeling as if I was going to be sick. All I could see were grey walls and doors to either side of me. The noise of the wind outside was incredible, like being underwater during a hurricane. The funny thing was, it hadn't seemed particularly windy outside. I pulled my jacket closer around me and realised I was cold. I imagined having to spend days or weeks trapped in this semi-subterranean abyss. I hoped the police would let me go soon.

Before long I found myself sitting in an interview room with PC Williams and a detective constable I hadn't met before, DC Nagy. They told me that they wouldn't tape anything I said, for the time being, then asked me to describe what had happened since I'd met Dale at nine o'clock.

I told the police everything that had happened that night up until the moment when I realised Dale had taken the pill at which point I improvised slightly and invented a dramatic search of his bedroom. Just as the police were preparing to take an official statement from me there was a knock at the door. DC Nagy left the room for a few minutes and then returned with a grim look on his face.

'Right,' he said, pausing and looking at me.

'Is he dead?' I asked, my voice turning to a whisper and my heart becoming numb in my chest.

'No,' said DC Nagy. 'The doctors have managed to stabilise him, but he's still very unwell.'

'What happened?' I asked. 'I mean, how can a couple of Ecstasy tablets do that to someone?'

'When they're at least seventy percent Aspirin,' he said, looking at a piece of paper in his hand.

'*Aspirin?*' I said. 'What do you mean?'

'Well, it's a new one on us. We're assuming some dealer's mixing it in with the MDMA before they make it into tablets,' said PC Williams. 'To make it go further.'

'I don't understand,' I said. 'Surely you can't get that much Aspirin in a few little tablets?'

'Apparently you can,' said DC Nagy, still consulting his piece of paper. He looked up at me. 'My mate from pathology was explaining it to me. Apparently you can get quite a few grams in one of those pills.'

'But surely the dealers would know how dangerous they were?'

'Perhaps, but maybe they were only expecting people to take one at a time.'

'Anyway,' I said, 'how do they know that's what it was?'

'Well, forensic haven't got back to us on the pills you took to the hospital yet, but the doctor dealing with Mr Carter was positive that that's what it was.'

'How?'

'Appearance of the stomach apparently. He happened to have had a case involving the same sort of tablets just recently which helped him diagnose what had happened. Of course, lots of people use Aspirin to kill themselves anyway, so the doctors know the signs.'

Recent case, I thought.

'You were Jason Davies's lecturer as well, weren't you?' said PC Williams.

'Yes,' I said.

'So you may not be that surprised to hear this isn't the first time we've seen these poisoned pills.'

'What, you mean Jason . . . ?'

'Oh, yes,' said DC Nagy. 'We got the results from his post-mortem earlier today. Definitely the same tablets. Cause of death: Aspirin overdose. Your mate Dale Carter was lucky he didn't take as much as Jason did.' He coughed and glanced down at the table before looking me straight in the eye. 'So do you know who dealt them the drugs? I mean, you're the obvious link between the two lads.'

'How?' I said. 'That's stupid. It's just a coincidence. I don't know anything.' I really wanted to tell them the truth, but something stopped me. How on earth had I managed to get myself involved in this?

'Okay, calm down,' said PC Williams.

I took a sip from a glass of water they had provided and lit a cigarette. DC Nagy got up and fetched an ashtray from the top of an old filing cabinet and I wondered why they kept that in here. I was fairly sure they didn't file anything in it. Maybe it was so DC Nagy could bang his fist on it after he'd paced the room a few times, as he did now.

'So you're a college lecturer?' he spat.

'Yes,' I said, defensively. 'What's wrong with that?'

'I was just wondering why an intelligent young lady like you felt the need to get mixed up with local gangsters, that's all.'

'What local gangsters?' I asked, flicking some ash into the ashtray. I was determined not to let this bad-cop routine wind me up. I was too tired and spaced out with the night I was having.

'Oh, come on, Lily,' he said. 'Dale Carter's a well-known loser. A complete crook. I suppose you're going to tell me you didn't know his brother owns the Blue Dolphin?'

'No,' I said. 'I mean, no, I'm not going to tell you that, because I did know.'

PC Williams shook his head slightly and looked down at the floor.

'You did know?' said DC Nagy. 'What were you hoping to gain from rekindling this relationship, eh? Free Charlie? A bit of extra spending money? Champagne in the VIP lounge?'

'I don't know what you're talking about,' I said wearily. 'I know Wesley owns the club for sure, but only since Dale told me about *five hours* ago.'

The detective constable sighed.

'Look,' he said. 'We need to find the dealer so we can stop him. I know you're probably protecting someone but if you don't tell us what you know you could be responsible for more deaths. I believe you've got nothing to do with this, but you can see the position we're in, can't you?'

I looked at him, waiting for the punchline.

'You get back to Devon less than two weeks ago. Within a week, we find you were the last person to see a major suspect who then went missing, then one of your students dies, apparently from a simple drug overdose which then turns out to be an *Aspirin* overdose, from a type of pill that so far as we knew then only existed in Jason's dead body. Then we find you in hospital with a local thug who's virtually dead with the same symptoms, having taken a pill out of a bag *you* were holding.'

'I found them in his bedroom.'

'But where did he get them? What was the dealer's name?'

'I told you, I don't *know*. I hadn't seen Dale for at least six years before tonight. I wouldn't have a clue who he knows, and certainly not where he gets his drugs.'

'Okay,' said DC Nagy, wiping his brow wearily. 'You're obviously not going to tell us.'

'Maybe that's because I really *don't* know,' I said angrily, so convinced by my routine that I genuinely believed what I was saying.

I got home at eight o'clock in the morning feeling tired, dirty and desperate for a hot drink. Poor Dale. I was so relieved the doctor had saved him: there had been more than enough pointless deaths around here already. I didn't know what I would have done if he'd died. Imagine having something like *that* on my conscience. As it was I sat at the kitchen table limply for ten minutes, drinking a cup of hot milky coffee and stroking my cat, until I couldn't keep my eyes open and went and fell on my bed.

CHAPTER EIGHTEEN

The Box

I woke up at about half-past one the next afternoon, feeling disorientated and strange. I lit a cigarette without leaving my bed and lay there for a while, letting the smoke curl around my head and out of the open window.

Outside the sun was shining and I could hear the faint rustle of leaves and birds singing in the distance. Most of them knew better than to come too near the house for fear of being eaten by one of the cats.

I sighed and stood up. I still had my clothes on from the night before and felt hot, bothered and a bit tearful. I walked into the kitchen and bumped straight into Mum, who seemed to be in a good mood.

'Good morning, darling,' she said.

I grunted.

'How was your night?'

'Not so good.'

'Oh dear,' said Mum. 'What happened?'

'I don't know,' I said in a small voice, putting my head in my hands. 'I don't know what happened.'

'What do you mean?'

'Dale's in Intensive Care. He almost died.'

'*What*?' asked Mum incredulously. 'Lily, what happened?'

'I don't know, but I spent half the night at the police station being questioned,' I said weakly. When I saw the look on her face I sat down on a chair and burst into tears again.

'Oh, my God!' she said, sitting down opposite me. 'Are you all right?'

'Yes, I'm fine.'

'No, you're not. What happened?'

'It was drugs. Apparently there are some local dealers cutting Ecstasy with Aspirin, and Dale took a contaminated tablet.'

'Aspirin?'

'Yes.'

'So what did they want you for?'

'Oh, to see if I knew where he got them, basically.'

'Oh, dear,' said Mum. 'You must feel awful.'

'Yes, I do,' I said, smiling half-heartedly and wiping my face with my sleeve. 'Is there enough hot water for a bath?'

'Yes, I should think so. I only had a shower this morning, and your brother's not here.'

'Where is he?'

'Gone to visit Alwyn.'

'Oh.' I knew that Mum didn't approve of Nat's visits to his father and suspected that was what yesterday's argument had been about. I patted her on the shoulder and went upstairs to the bathroom.

I felt slightly better after my bath, although I still didn't feel great. After I got dressed, Mum fussed around me for a while, making me hot chocolate and chatting to me about nothing in particular. She was easily upset by this sort of thing and I couldn't blame her. I knew she worried about the potential trouble Nat could get in to, and anything involving young men and drugs put her on edge.

I looked at the papers while I drank my hot chocolate. There was a small piece on page ten of the local newspaper about Dale's hospitalisation and a warning to young people not to take local Ecstasy. I looked at it for a while, waiting for the news to sink in and for something to happen, but it didn't.

'Don't worry, Mum,' I said eventually. 'Everything will be all right.'

The man sat at home on Saturday morning, ignoring his wife and reading the paper. He had a headache from the night before but had to recuperate sensibly at home and prepare for tonight.

'We need to talk.'

He could hear her voice in the distance, annoying him. If she knew how important he was she wouldn't dare disturb him with her own feeble concerns.

'I know about —'

'Shut up, will you? I'm trying to read the paper.'

He didn't have time for any of this.

Why couldn't she see how beautiful the world was to him now? It wasn't just the plan, although that would be the most beautiful moment. It was everything that had happened since last spring when, by chance, his life became meaningful again.

He chuckled at the story on page ten. So the poisoned apple had been released into the community. His accomplice was cleverer than he'd thought.

I chatted away to Mum for a while until I felt tired. It was nice to be normal; to be able to act like nothing was going on. But of course it was and I had to make some connections quickly before someone else got hurt. At about three o'clock I went out to my car and retrieved the box from the boot. It was time I had a look at Jason's notebooks.

I decided to take the box out to the garden so I wouldn't be disturbed. I made a cup of coffee and took that as well, along with a blanket to sit on and my cigarettes. I felt the spring sunshine warming the back of my neck as I walked down the stone steps into the sunken part of the garden. For a while I just sat there thinking, watching the sheep in the nearby field walk past, occasionally bleating and jumping over hedges.

Eventually I turned my attention to Jason's box. I pulled out a couple of novels and postcards and looked at those first. The postcards were intended to be humorous and all contained curious in-jokes about drugs and politics. They came from a world I didn't really understand but that I had seen second-hand at university and in the squat where I'd lived. Their overriding message was *Fuck the state*, which had never been a sentiment I subscribed to. Sure, I could be subversive at times and stubborn, like last night in the police station, but I had no desire to live in a society without rules or police and all the things that came with that.

I sighed and looked at the yellowing pieces of card in my hands. One of the postcards must have been quite old; it was a picture of Margaret Thatcher dipping her hand into a young working-class woman's handbag, presumably indicating that the Tories stole from the poor. Another featured several policemen standing in what looked like Parliament Square. An artist had added speech bubbles which said things like *Give us a spliff, officer* and *Don't put tobacco in with your hash, sir, it hurts your throat*. Another featured a man sitting in front of a coffee table which was piled high with white powder. Turning to the woman next to him on the sofa, he was saying, *There's nothing wrong with drugs in moderation, Cynthia*.

The two books seemed to be based around the same themes as the postcards. *The Anarchist's Handbook* included chapters on *Grow your own Tai Weed* and *What to do if you get arrested*. I thought, cynically, that if you didn't grow weed in the first place then you would greatly reduce the chances of getting arrested, but what did I know?

The second book was a novel called *Trip City* by an author I'd never heard of. I read the inside sleeve which told me that a potentially lethal new designer drug, FX, was causing havoc on the streets of London. It didn't look like my sort of thing.

I put the books to one side and lit a cigarette. I couldn't believe I'd been so wrong about Jason. I had always prided myself on being able instinctively to know things about people, and I'd never been wrong in the past. So he *had* been into drugs. I still couldn't quite believe it. I was going to have to go back to the beginning again, I could see that, although my hopes of solving this had now soured. How could I have got it so wrong?

I thought about the way he'd looked last Tuesday, with his red eyes and scruffy clothes. He was paranoid and desperate. Maybe he really had been on drugs of some sort. Maybe the Aspirin was just a mistake, and the bag of drugs some sort of aberration. But they'd been put there deliberately.

I turned back to the box and looked to see what else it contained. There were about ten small notebooks and a loose-leaf pad. Around the bottom of the box, I could feel the shapes of smaller unidentifiable articles. Suddenly wanting to see everything in all its horror, I tipped the box over on to the grass. The notebooks fellout with a thud and I had to shake the box a bit to make everything else follow them.

An array of small objects landed on top of the notebooks. A lighter and a pen, a pair of earrings and some Rizla cigarette papers lay there along with some bits of loose dry tobacco and a small pipe on a chain. More drug paraphernalia.

In amongst the notebooks I noticed a piece of orange paper. I recognised the colour and pulled it out to see if it was what I thought it was. Bizarrely, it was indeed another flyer, exactly the same as the one I had seen in Isobel's dustbin. I put it to one side and opened one of the notebooks. It seemed to be a diary, and the front page was dated this month.

I know it's really sad to keep a diary, but there have been so many incredible things happening lately that I thought I would start another one. I can't believe I've changed so much since coming away to university. It's just like everyone said it would be and more. I am learning so much, not just about literature but also about me.

I am sorry to say that I will not be able to include everything that has happened in this book, because most of it isn't legal: *POLICE, IF YOU FIND THIS THEN DON'T BOTHER READING IT BECAUSE IT WON'T HAVE ANYTHING YOU CAN USE!*

I still feel like shit after yesterday. As I write I am SU on my bed. That's a code, by the way. Ha, ha, you'll never catch me. I am inhaling deeply and thinking, which always makes me feel better. I suppose I should write about what's been happening, but I don't know where to begin.

I'm in love for the first time in my life. F is older than me, but I don't think that matters. We are going to get married, I think, one day. The problem is that it's all a bit dangerous at the moment. Even now, I feel like someone is watching me and listening to my thoughts. That might be all the *though. It makes you paranoid, apparently.

I've been depressed as well, lately. Not badly or anything, just a deep feeling of sadness. I haven't spoken to my family since Christmas. I've been too busy and I don't think they would understand the way that I've changed.

I've got a whole new group of friends recently, which is really nice since it wasn't going so well before. I felt really uncomfortable before, but now I'm in control of loads of things. It all started last Easter, after a trip we all went on to Prague. Everybody thought I wasn't into *but then the accident happened and I haven't looked back since. Now I do it all the time.

We all started doing it, not just me, all over the summer when I got involved in BR. Then in February we almost got caught taking the K from the L to help with our projects. That was an amazing experience, like floating around the room. I hinted at what we'd done and F wasn't cross. 'I hope you've saved some for me . . .'

That night was the first time we made love, and it was amazing. After that it all got a bit weird, though, and now I don't know how to stop it. Well, I don't want to stop it all, but some of the stuff I've heard F saying recently is mad. All those *speeches and parties. I'm not meant to call them that but I don't see why not.*

N is the maddest of them all, but I only thinks so because of what happened. F still all mine, though, thank goodness.

Am I making sense? I don't know. I almost feel like I don't want to write about the important stuff, the stuff that's happened recently, because if I write it down it will become real. I don't want it to become real. I'm going to say something, I just don't know when.

Maybe I'll wait until the next party is over.

The funny thing is that everyone is involved somehow. I had to do some 'business' at the BD a while ago for the CS. F didn't approve. Apparently I was made for higher things. I was required elsewhere, which was lucky because the CS got caught just after that. F was so cross — I'd never seen rage like it. It hurt but I pretended I liked it. I'm crying now just from thinking about it. I wish I understood what was going on.

The page ended there. I turned it over but there was nothing more in that notebook. I shut it and lit a cigarette, flipping the pages absentmindedly, trying to work out the significance of what I'd just read. So Jason *had* been into drugs. How strange. As I played with the book I realised there was something written on the middle pages. I opened it properly and found another page covered in signatures. *Stephanie* then something else, it said, almost illegibly, at least a dozen times.

I dropped the book in shock. This wasn't Jason's diary, it was Stephanie's. In fact, everything in the box must have been hers. I quickly grabbed the other notebooks and flicked through them. Each one was a diary with Stephanie Duncan's name in the front. I looked at the loose-leaf pad and discovered it was Stephanie's lecture notes.

I looked at another of the small notebooks and found a second diary entry, from October 1995: Stephanie's first term at the university.

I'm so lonely and depressed I just want to go home. But I came here to get away from home. Fuck. I really thought I'd made a friend, but Jason isn't my friend. He's a pervert. But who can I tell? Even as I'm writing this I know he'll probably break in and read it — well, if you are, Jason, LEAVE ME ALONE.

I've found him in here three times now, playing that CD, lying in my bed and even wearing my knickers. He's never touched me but he wants to. Everywhere I go he seems to be there, watching . . . stalking. Why won't he just leave me alone?

None of this really made sense. But one thing was for sure: I had been right about Jason. He wasn't into drugs, it was Stephanie who was. All Jason had been into was Stephanie herself; obsessed and out of control, he had obviously been watching and following her.

I could see now what must have happened on the night of her death. He had followed her as usual, and then seen something dreadful. That explained the urine stain on his trousers – evidence of one of the physical reactions to fear. So he had seen the murder, as he'd said, then run back, stumbling and getting mud on his clothes and shoes, and that tear on his T-shirt. He'd run back to the Halls to find all the other students off at the party that Fenn had talked about – the one Stephanie was meant to have been at. He got into her room (which it seemed he was fairly accomplished at already) and removed her stuff then sat with it in his room, at some point vomiting from the shock of what had happened. He had known who killed Stephanie all right, I was sure of that now, and here was some evidence to prove it. Here in this box was *the information*, the secrets Jason had wanted to tell someone. I would have to decipher the codes myself, of course, but I knew I was going to find the truth.

CHAPTER NINETEEN

Riddle Me This

———⟫⊙⊙⊙⟪———

Stephanie's code was harder to break than I'd thought it would be. Some things were obvious, like the fact that she was having a relationship with someone called F. I wondered what the F stood for. The obvious but painful *Fenn* came to mind immediately but I willed it away. Instead I tried to think of students with names like Frank or Francis but there didn't seem to be any. She'd said he was older, but that didn't help very much (except to further suggest Fenn). I wondered whose surname it was that she had written down as her own. It certainly wasn't *Duncan* and, thankfully it seemed too long to be *Baker*, but I couldn't make out what it could be. It must be the surname of the mysterious F, but who was he? These were all questions which had to be answered.

I read the short entry in Stephanie's last diary several times but still couldn't make any sense of it. Something sinister had definitely been going on, but she had encoded all the characters pretty well and it was impossible to work out who else was involved. Who, or what was the CS, and who was N?

I felt sure that if I could find out who F was, in particular, then things would look much clearer. I wished Stephanie had been more explicit and smiled wryly as I looked at her little note to the police. I wondered if they would have more luck than me with the diary.

I doubted they had ever seen it. I was aware that they had looked at everything in her room but it was clear that Jason had removed all this stuff before they got to it. He had been concealing evidence and now so was I. The problem was, I couldn't give it to the police without telling them how I had got hold of it. If I said I'd been in Jason's room, I would be in all kinds of trouble.

I wondered why he hadn't told the police what he knew. I remembered that he had been afraid, when I spoke to him, that 'they' would know if he did. I thought about giving the diaries to the police anonymously, but then thought better of it. The problem was I didn't know who was mixed up in it all and what they already knew. Stephanie had said that it was 'everybody' and that scared me. Look what had happened to Jason when he tried to get involved.

I was going to have to solve this on my own and thought maybe I would have more luck if I treated the whole thing like a crossword puzzle. The crossword that I did on a Sunday always used the same codes. You had to learn them by following the thought process of the person who set them, week by week. For example, the word 'worker' in the clue always meant that the letters *a n t* would be in the answer. If any words were followed by any synonym for jumbled – like mixed up, turned around and so on – that meant the answer was an anagram of the previous words.

Taking all this into account, I decided that the only way I was going to decipher Stephanie's code was to try to unravel her mind. I lit a cigarette and settled down to read the rest of her diaries.

Stephanie Duncan had been complex character, full of contradictions and anomalies. Her diaries reflected the thoughts of a painfully shy young woman who could never quite fit in but was desperately trying to. The earliest notebook was dated 1992 which would have made her about fourteen. Glued to the inside cover was a badly lit photo booth shot with the caption 'Me'. I could see why Jason had fallen for her. Her eyes were a dusky brown and her olive skin was smooth and slightly freckled. Her high cheekbones added to her prettiness and made her look older than she was, and more sophisticated. The contents of the diaries confirmed my suspicions that this had got her into trouble on more than one occasion.

Stephanie lost her virginity when she was fifteen, to a twenty-three-year old lad from her home town. Apparently he mistook her for an eighteen year old and she hadn't had the heart, or the inclination, to set him straight. They did it up against a wall behind the local youth club. In her diary Stephanie described in painful detail the way he had hurt her, and the way that all his friends had switched their car headlamps on to get a better look.

When she was sixteen Stephanie became quite promiscuous and slept with most of the boys at her sixth-form college. According to her diary she had been in love with every single one of them but they had rejected her, presumably because she appeared too eager. I got the distinct impression this had been the story of her life. Stephanie would have done anything to be accepted and have real friends and a loving boyfriend.

The fifth notebook found a now sixteen-year-old Stephanie desperately trying to come to terms with herself and those around her. The first half of the book had lots of cuttings from magazines stuck in it, mainly articles with titles like *How to Be More Popular*, and *How to Make Him Love You*. After each cutting Stephanie had written things like, *I must try harder*, and, *If only I could follow all this advice my life wouldn't be so crap*.

She appeared to have been an only child, with a sick mother and a cold, distant father. One entry in particular made me feel there was a lot going on between the lines of Stephanie's life that she only hinted at among the mundane daily entries of the diaries.

I got home from college today to find Dad watching children's TV again. He looked at me and started crying. I couldn't handle it so I ran off upstairs to get changed. I turned around and he was there in the doorway. He looked me up and down and then hurried out.

I followed him downstairs and asked if he was going to visit Mum in hospital today.

'Why?' he asked.

'Because I want to come with you,' I said. 'I never get to see her.'

He looked at me as if there was something wrong with me and walked out into the garden, shaking his head sadly.

'What's wrong with Mum?' I asked, but he didn't answer me. He just walked to the end of the garden and started messing around with his stupid roses. I wanted to cry, but I couldn't. I wish I knew when she was coming home.

It was textbook stuff, really. Stephanie was lonely and felt misunderstood in every area of her life. I imagined that her family had been distant rather than really sinister, otherwise why would her parents have put up the reward? Nevertheless, I wasn't surprised that she had got into drugs.

In fact I was surprised it hadn't happened much earlier. I suspected this was because Stephanie had been so bright. She had her A level results glued on to a page of her diary and it was clear that she'd had a lot going for her; she'd got three As.

And then she ended up at the university and it all went wrong. I didn't really get any idea how this happened, though, because there were only two entries made in the one and a half years she had been there.

It was starting to get cloudy out in the garden, and I felt a spot of rain on my cheek. Not wanting any of the diaries to get wet, I quickly gathered them up and put them back in the box. Just as I was putting the last of the stuff back in, a strong breeze grabbed my hair, tangled it and made it fly around everywhere. I pushed it out of my face just in time to see the orange flyer whirled away by the wind and blown across the lawn.

I jumped up and ran after it, slipping slightly on the grass as I went, and managed to grab it just before it fell in the stream. I read it again as I walked back to collect the rest of the stuff. There were a couple of variations on this copy of the flyer which I hadn't expected to see. It had a phone number written in red pen on the front, which presumably was the number one was meant to 'call on the night', and Stephanie seemed to have corrected several words and spellings. The other odd thing was that she had highlighted the time of the gathering, as if she hadn't wanted to forget. I looked at the date on the top of the flyer before I stuck it back in the box. 26 April. That was today.

I looked at my watch and saw it was coming up for six o'clock. I hadn't realised I had been in the garden for so long. As I walked into the house, I could see that Mum was on her way out.

'I'm going to collect Nat from the station,' she said. 'I won't be long.'

'Okay.'

I walked into the kitchen and put the kettle on. Outside the sky was growing dark as rain fell heavily and clouds drew themselves close around the house. I walked over to the kitchen window and shut it, partly to stop the stuff on the windowsill getting wet but mainly to drown out the *pitter-patter* noise. I had enjoyed the sound of the rain coming down yesterday, but this evening I wasn't so sure. I felt vulnerable, as if everything was out to get me, and I didn't like it.

There was something deeply unsettling about reading the details of someone's life in their diaries in the full knowledge they were destined to end up a headless corpse. Poor Stephanie. It seemed so sad she had never managed to get her life together before everything went so drastically wrong.

The wind started to pick up, and I could see the trajectory of the rain shifting with each gust, first beating at the door and then shifting to the driveway outside. There were other noises too: a tap, tap, tap noise and a scratching at one of the windows. The evening had suddenly grown cold and I shivered and went to my room to fetch a cardigan.

It was dark there which meant I could see clearly outside. For a few moments I watched the silvery outlines of the raindrops, transfixed by a fantasy that I was on a film-set and somebody was pouring the rain from buckets and watering cans. Something crashed outside and I jumped, not realising how hypnotised I had been by the spectacle of the rain. I thought I saw the silhouette of a figure move past the window. I grabbed the cardigan and walked quickly out of the room. Instinctively, I went to the back door and turned the key with trembling hands, imagining the horror of someone pushing it open before I had the chance to lock it properly.

Once the door was secure I breathed heavily with relief, still sweating slightly and shaking with nerves. This was one unpleasant side-effect of specialising in crime and horror fiction, I thought.

I thought back to all the horror and crime stories I'd read for my MA but tried not to let their details get inside my head. Little by little though they came: the monster that liked to feed on raw human flesh, and the small bespectacled man who could find his way into any house then lie there in the victim's bed, waiting patiently for the moment when he would suck out their brains with a straw.

I told myself to stop it and got a mug out of the cupboard and put it down on the work surface. I was still twitching at every noise and twisting around every couple of minutes to check that no one was standing behind me with a meat cleaver. *You locked the door*, I said to myself. *Yes, but what if they were already inside the house?* replied a voice in my head.

The phone started to ring.

Without meaning to, I immediately thought of the classic horror story . . .

Ring ring

In which the babysitter answers the phone . . .

Ring ring

To find a man saying he's watching her . . .
Ring ring
And he's calling from inside the house.

'Hello?'
' 'Allo?'
'*Henri*,' I said, letting out a sigh of relief. It was my father.
'Lily? What are you doing there? What's wrong?'
'Nothing,' I said. 'I'm fine.'
'You sound out of breath.'
'I ran for the phone, that's all.'
'Ah. So what are you doing in Devon? I have been tele-phoning your flat for days but Anthony just says you are out. I assume you've split up. Why didn't you call and tell me?'
'I'm sorry, Papa, I've had a lot on my mind. Will you forgive me?' I smiled as I said that. I was no longer afraid now that Henri was on the phone. I didn't feel so alone.
'I suppose so. Are you now living in Devon?'
'For the time being,' I said. 'I'm teaching at the university.'
'I see.' He sighed. 'Maybe I will come and visit you there.'
'That would be lovely,' I said. 'Actually, Papa, there was something I wanted to ask you.'
'Not another loan?'
'Just until I get paid. Please?'
'Of course I will help you out, Lily, but you must start trying to look after yourself a bit better.'
'I'm not that bad, it's just that Anthony –'
'I know. I'm being unfair as usual. Is your account number still the same?'
'Yes.'
'I will make a transfer tomorrow.'
'Thanks.'
'Anyway, I have to go now,' he said. I could hear the sound of another person breathing in the background then a muffled noise, like a giggle. 'I will speak to you soon, *chérie*. Tell your mother I called.'
'*Au revoir*, Henri,' I said.

'*Au 'voir.*'

I went back to making my coffee. I didn't feel scared at all anymore, which was good. I couldn't work out how I had given myself such a fright. Mind you, I'd had a bit of a shock last night and hadn't eaten anything very much today. It was a recipe for disaster really. Knowing I had to eat something, but feeling sick at the thought, I cut a couple of slices of bread and made a marmalade sandwich.

I took my coffee and sandwich through to the living room and switched on the TV for company. The rain seemed to be dying down and it sounded more peaceful outside. I looked at my watch and saw that it was almost seven o'clock. I thought about the 'gathering' that was supposedly going to happen tonight and wondered why it had been so important to Stephanie.

After I finished my sandwich, my head, which had felt a bit fuzzy all day, started to clear. I lit a cigarette and wandered through to my room. I took the flyer out of the box and walked back to the living room with it, not knowing whether I should call the number or not. I knew it was probably dangerous to get involved any further but had a feeling that I was on the verge of discovering something significant. If Isobel and Stephanie knew about the gathering then it was likely a lot of other people did. I felt almost certain that F would be there, along with the CS, whatever that was. It all linked together somehow and tonight could be my best chance to find out how.

I picked up the phone and dialled the first few digits of the number. I could feel my heart beating in my chest and suddenly had an urge to cough. I replaced the receiver and cleared my throat, lit another cigarette and tried to pull myself together. Tentatively, I dialled the number again, determined not to back out this time.

'*The phone's ringing.*'
  '*Why don't you pick it up, then?*'
  '*Because it will be for you. I'm sick of talking to those stupid —*'

He slapped her around the face and watched her fall to the ground, dazed and confused. She looked up at him with pleading eyes but he turned and looked away. It was her fault. If only she wouldn't nag so much. Christ! He could understand why judges let people off for murdering their wives. Stupid bitch.

He walked across the hallway and picked up the telephone receiver.

'Hello?' said a man's voice, curt, annoyed and slightly familiar, like someone I once knew. I wondered if I had the wrong number.

'Hello?' I tried to make my voice sound different: younger and more stupid.

'Yes?'

'I'm calling for the venue details,' I said.

'You are?'

Shit. I hadn't expected him to ask who I was. I said the first name that came into my head.

'Hélène.'

'Hélène?'

'Duval,' I said, introducing a French lilt to my voice. I figured that if Stephanie had a flyer then maybe other people at the university did too.

'Ah, the delightful Hélène. I'm glad you're coming. It's not far from where we had the last one, actually. Do you remember Salten?'

'Er, yes,' I said, not knowing what the hell he was talking about.

'Turn right at the Eagle pub and then follow the road down to the bridge. Have you got that?'

'Yes.'

'Take the next left and continue until you go over another bridge, across a river this time. Just after the bridge you will see a very sharp turning on the right. Try not to miss it. Take that and follow the track for about four hundred yards. You will come to a derelict farm and then you will be able to see the car park.'

'Thanks,' I said. 'I think I've got that.'

'Good, we'll look forward to seeing you there.'

The phone went dead.

I sat around for a while, listening to my own heartbeat and watching the hill out of the window. After a few minutes I saw what I'd expected to see, the kaleidoscopic quiver of orange lights dancing.

Five minutes later I heard a car pull up outside. It was Mum, of course, back from the station. A few seconds later I heard the rattling of the door handle as she and Nat tried to get in.

I ran over to unlock it.

'Goodness,' said Mum, wiping her feet on the mat. 'It's wet out there. Why did you have the door locked?'

'I wanted to be careful.'

'Of what? We're out in the middle of nowhere here. Nothing ever happens.'

'All the same,' I said, 'I think you should keep the door locked tonight.'

'Okay, darling, if it will make you happy.'

I was glad she didn't ask me why, because I wouldn't have known quite how to explain it all to her.

'Hi, Lily,' said Nat. 'I'm sorry to hear about . . . you know.'

'That's all right,' I said. 'I'm a bit shaken, but I'll be all right and it looks like Dale will be fine. How was Alwyn?'

'Mad,' said Nat. 'Did I tell you about the low-frequency noise scandal up there?'

'No,' I said, smiling. 'But you can tell me tomorrow. I'm a bit too tired to be able to concentrate on Alwyn's mad science at the moment.'

I made hot drinks for everyone and started getting ready for the night ahead. I changed my jeans and put on a warm but trendy-looking roll neck and denim jacket. I made sure I had the directions in my pocket and a small torch, just in case. I took my mobile phone, although I knew it would be useless in an emergency, and put it in my jacket's inside pocket. I gulped down my coffee and then I was ready to go.

CHAPTER TWENTY

Repetitive Beats

I got into the car and switched on the engine. Instead of the Volvo's usual purr I heard a series of misfirings and shuddering noises before the car eventually sprang to life. I would have to get that seen to, I decided. It didn't worry me particularly, though. The car had never broken down.

I moved the gear stick into first and pulled out of the driveway. A couple of minutes later I was speeding over the hill and out of the village, on my way to God knows where. As usual, I hadn't bothered to find a tape to listen to before starting my journey, so the next few minutes involved a desperate scrabble around the back seat with one hand, while trying to maintain control of the car with the other.

I touched something papery and book-like and drew it into the front of the car to see what it was. It was the paperback Isobel had given me. I'd forgotten about that. I threw it back on to the seat and scrabbled around a bit more until I located the new Blur album, just right for a late-evening drive to the moors.

As I drove I thought about what I'd learned last night. I still didn't know who had planted those drugs in Jason's room, but I definitely knew that someone wanted to make his death look like an accident, which suggested to me it had actually been deliberate. If Jason had seen the murder, then the murderer would have a good reason – but that led me back to the big question: who on earth could that be?

And it didn't look as though the police were having much more luck with their scientific method. They had now DNA tested all the students to no effect and were halfway through the staff. What if they all came out negative? What would that say about poor Fenn? I wished he would just come back and get himself tested.

As I thought about it I started asking myself what I would do if he did suddenly reappear and clear his name. I certainly wouldn't be able to give up my investigation now and ditch all the clues I had gathered, and I had a responsibility to make sure the information didn't just get lost because I was trying to protect myself from what the police might say if they found out how I'd got hold of it. If the entries in those diaries, and the last words spoken by Jason were going to help catch Stephanie's killer then I had to be the one to make it happen. I had taken the diaries and the riddle and now I had to face up to my responsibilities. I was good with words. They had to start making sense soon.

In the meantime, though, I was going to an illegal rave, and felt apprehensive but intrigued. What would it be like? I had checked the map before I left and found that Salten was about sixty miles away from Mawlish, right on the edge of the moors. After driving for about half an hour I was able to take a turnoff for a main road and enjoyed the sensation of speed and emptiness. As a contrast with the hedgerows and walled roads of the South Hams the change of scene was welcome and refreshing. I opened the window and accelerated, enjoying the feel of the wind as it blew through my hair.

After a while I looked at my petrol gauge and saw it was almost on red, so I stopped at the next garage to fill up.

I pulled in and parked next to the only available pump. The garage was busy and seemed to be mostly full of young people on their way to major towns and cities to spend Saturday night getting drunk and collapsing in the gutter. I wondered if some of them were on their way to Salten.

Once I was inside the garage, I found myself queuing behind PC Williams, who took one look at me and did an immediate double take.

'It's Lily Pascale, isn't it?' he said.

'Yes,' I said, blushing slightly. PC Williams appeared to be off-duty and looked quite good in blue jeans and a checked shirt. 'Hi, PC Williams. How are you?'

'Very well, actually. And you can lose the PC. It's Jake while I'm off duty.'

'Right,' I said, smiling.

'So where are you off to?' he asked.

'I'm visiting my grandmother,' I said, wincing at my bad attempt at a lie.

'What a lucky lady,' he said.

The queue had diminished as we were chatting and thankfully it was now Jake's turn at the till. He paid for his petrol and bought a packet of chewing gum. He winked at me as he walked past.

'Don't do anything I wouldn't do,' he said, laughing at his own joke as he went out of the door.

I arrived in Salten after a short while and pulled the directions out of my pocket, following the instructions until I came to the bridge over the river. Apparently there was a road on the right just after the bridge but I couldn't see one. All there seemed to be was a dusty farm track covered with rocks and stones of various sizes. Fearing for my car's tyres I proceeded carefully down the track, feeling sure I had gone the wrong way.

I drove for ten minutes or so, wondering why I couldn't hear music or see any lights yet. Just as I was on the point of turning back I noticed a car coming up behind me. After a couple more minutes I could see there were cars in front of me as well. A short distance later I passed the disused farm that the voice on the phone had mentioned and knew that I was going the right way. Everyone was parking on a field to the left of the track and it seemed that the gathering was happening just off to the right, on the edge of some woodland.

I was surprised I couldn't hear loud house music, just the eerily distant sound of bongo drums and what sounded like chanting. I could see smoke from a bonfire and the silhouettes of a few people gathered around it. I parked the car and walked towards the smoke and noise, wondering how close to the moors this was.

I looked at the car park and calculated there must be at least two hundred people here. As I walked closer to the edge of the forest, I could see that there were a number of small marquees placed near the bonfire which were bursting with people, several of whom seemed to be leaving the tents and walking into the woods, dancing as they went.

I decided it was best to stay as anonymous as possible, since I didn't know what kind of people I was going to find here. Just as I was about to duck behind a tree and watch for a while from a distance I felt a hand fall on my shoulder.

'Nancy?' said a German voice. 'It can't be you.'

I turned around and saw Hans standing there, alone, looking just as he had when I had seen him in the service station. In fact, on closer inspection he didn't even appear to have changed his clothes. He was breathing quickly, as if he'd been running.

'Hello, Hans,' I said, smiling not just at him but at the irony and unforeseen usefulness of the trick I'd played at the service station. 'Are you having a good time?'

'I have only just arrived,' he said, slightly breathlessly. 'What are you doing here? Did you get an invitation?'

'Invitation?' I said, slightly confused.

'Yes.' Hans nodded furiously and produced an orange flyer. 'Invitation.'

So they hadn't been flyers at all. That explained why the voice on the phone had asked for my name.

'Oh, yes,' I said. 'I got one of those.'

'Come,' said Hans. 'Let's go join the party.'

He led the way towards the bonfire and as we drew closer I was relieved to see that the faces here were unfamiliar to me. In contrast with my fantasy world, this appeared to be a harmless party, more like a festival than a rave. I could see now why it was called a gathering.

'Who are all these people?' I asked Hans.

'You do not know them?' he asked incredulously. 'You are a member of Beyond Reason, are you not?'

'Of course I am,' I lied. 'I just don't know who all these people are, that's all.'

'Is this your first unconvention?' he asked patronisingly. I nodded.

'Isn't this a good word?' he asked. '*Unconvention*. Dell has explained this to me. It's like a convention, only it's unconventional. Good, no?'

'Yes,' I agreed, none the wiser.

I followed him towards the bonfire. Now that I was closer to the action I had a chance to drink it all in. Over on the right were two food stalls and in between them a barbecue was burning furiously. Over to the left were entrances to the several large tents I had noticed earlier. Now that I was closer I could pick up faint smells here and there: incense, pot pourri, dope, fried onions and a few others that I couldn't place. In front of me, between the tents and the food stalls, was the massive bonfire which a couple of men were poking with sticks.

'Come, let's get something to eat,' said Hans.

'Is that a barbecue?' I asked, pointing to the stall on my right. The cold spring air had made me hungry and I felt like I could murder a hot dog.

'Yes,' said Hans. 'Vegetarian, of course.'

'Of course,' I said, hiding my disappointment.

'We will eat,' he said. 'And then I will introduce you to some people.'

'Thanks,' I said, following him to the stall. 'Where's Dell?'

'With Freddy Future,' said Hans wistfully. 'All the young girls love to be around Freddy.'

I was just about to ask him what he was talking about when I stopped myself. I had already made him a bit suspicious with all my questions so I decided to keep my mouth shut until I'd worked out what was going on. I asked the woman behind the wooden table for a hot dog and she placed a grey thing into a bun and gave it to me. She was middle-aged and dressed in sixties-style psychedelic clothes. I thanked her for the hot dog, but she just stared off into the distance.

'Have you met him?' asked Hans.

'Who?' I said.

'Freddy Future.'

'Oh, briefly.'

'You will meet him properly soon,' said Hans. 'He's going to start speaking in a moment. In fact, most of the interesting people are probably securing their places in the tent right now.'

I looked at my watch and saw it was almost ten o'clock.

'Come on,' said Hans. 'We can't miss the start.'

I took a bite from my hot dog and followed him towards the tents.

CHAPTER TWENTY-ONE

Full of Sound and Fury

We walked across a patch of grass to the furthest of the four tents. Inside, the atmosphere was heavy with anticipation and most people were talking in excited whispers. Almost every person we passed greeted Hans with a hello or a handshake and a promise to chat *after the talk*.

I wondered what was so important about this talk. Who was Freddy Future and why did he have such a ridiculous name? I suspected he must be either the leader of the group or at least one of its most prominent members. In any case, everybody seemed to want to hear what he had to say.

I followed Hans to the front of the audience that was gathering in the tent and sat down cross-legged on the floor next to Dell and a gaggle of girls. In front of us was a temporary-looking stage made out of orange boxes and planks of wood. I wondered what was going to take place on it.

'Hi, Dell,' I said. She looked at me blankly.

'Say hello to Nancy,' said Hans.

'I'm flying,' said Dell, and started giggling inanely.

I ignored her and took the opportunity to look around the tent. There must have been over one hundred and fifty people packed in there, all waiting for Freddy Future. I wondered who they styled themselves on, since there seemed to be an air of homogeneity about all the men, women and the few children. They all wore loose-fitting clothes, mainly in shades of orange, and I noticed I was the only person wearing jeans. A lot of the women seemed to have bright red hair and there were almost no blondes. The red in their hair must be henna, I thought, and realised that this group was probably very much in favour of using only natural substances.

Ironic, I thought, remembering the chemical diagram on the invitation. So it was okay for drugs to be synthesised but nothing else. Interesting. Just as I was about to ask Hans about that, the fairy lights hanging in the tent were dimmed, and a single light was shone randomly on to the makeshift stage.

I waited for somebody to come and step on to it, intrigued by the idea of Freddy Future and wanting to see the man behind the myth, but it didn't happen. Instead, the spotlight gradually focused on a single object on the stage which I hadn't noticed before: an amplifier. Surely this Freddy Future wasn't going to speak through that? How very *Wizard of Oz*.

'I am Freddy Future,' said a man's voice through the amplifier. He paused and immediately everybody started clapping and whooping. I tried not to laugh at the spectacle before me and instead struggled to work out where I'd heard that voice before.

'I am disembodied before you,' boomed the amplifier. 'I have no corpus, no corporeality to stop me. This is the future.'

I looked at the amplifier and wondered what on earth was going to come from it next.

'This is what I have come to England for,' hissed Hans.

'Shhh,' I said, responding to the annoyed looks we were receiving.

I turned back to face the amplifier as the voice began once more.

'Imagine paradise. Imagine heaven. Try and imagine, if you can, the most wonderful fantasy you have ever had and multiply it by one hundred. Think about the most powerful orgasm you have had and the best joke you have ever been told. Multiply these by a thousand and add them to your previous total. What you have then is perfect happiness and fulfilment. I am here to tell you that this state of joy is not an unnatural state. This is the future of life.

'This is not beyond reason, but for most of us this world I am trying to describe goes beyond our imaginations. Our most powerful fantasies do not, I'm afraid, do the future justice. But believe, people, what I will describe for you on behalf of myself and the other Acumen. Biology has things in store for us that are beyond our wildest dreams but are yet there, hanging like fruits from the trees for us to reach out and touch.

'Life on this planet is due to become inconceivably good, and we are gathered here today to talk about the process of quickening the effects. We want nirvana today, not tomorrow. *Now*!'

Everyone cheered at this point and I could hear Freddy Future clearing his throat. I shivered. What the hell was this? Some kind of cult? I didn't know. All I did know was that he was suggesting something which sounded particularly sinister to me. I looked across at Hans, who had a look of rapt concentration on his face. He was clapping and nodding. Dell appeared to be in a state of ecstasy, and I noticed with some horror that she had tears running down her face.

I was suddenly overcome with fear and wanted to get out as quickly as possible. The atmosphere created by the people around me was obsessive and oppressive. Freddy Future was like a hypnotist and I became fearful that if he had duped all these people then maybe he could get into my head as well. I looked behind me and saw that the entrance to the tent was blocked with people, all gazing in awe at the amplifier. It would be hard to leave without attracting a lot of attention so I decided I must sit it out for the time being, breathing deeply and realising it was unlikely much harm would come to me just from sitting here, especially if I didn't let myself believe anything Freddy Future was saying. I couldn't wait for the speech to finish, though. I didn't like these people, and I certainly didn't have any time for this madman's *predictions*. He began to speak again.

'The human species is set to encounter miracles in its future, dictated by nature and its allies. In the next fifty years we will colonise space and time. We will discover new life forms and work out how to imitate the beauty of their states of consciousness. Within one hundred years we will have reached a state of uncorporeality. We will leave our bodies behind as we move into a state of pure consciousness and satisfaction. We will become the pleasure tissue that we seek today. Our minds will be angelic and our desires pure. This is the future.

'But today we will think about the present. The science of the present can be overwhelming and yet it leads us into areas of enlightened consciousness that we all know and enjoy. We must become shamen in our explorations. Only by using the right combinations will we be able to leave ourselves and enter bliss. Some of us are already experiencing the beginnings of this.

'Michael Faraday once said that "Nothing is too wonderful to be true" and in the chemicals we have been given as the legacy of the angels we will discover the truth in this statement. Not many of us here are scientists but we understand the importance of organic matter. Carbon and hydrogen are the most pure substances in the periodic table and we combine them to create joy. We will continue the work of Bhagwan Rajneesh here in Britain and learn to find everlasting happiness . . .'

I let Freddy Future's voice continue in the back of my brain as I tried to understand the implications of what he'd been saying. It had become clear to me that I was sitting in the middle of a group of guinea pigs, all ready to try out the latest chemical combinations in the interests of science and 'everlasting bliss'. Were these people truly gullible enough to believe all this nonsense?

The voice eventually stopped and everybody in the tent started clapping and cheering wildly again, but this time I noticed that people were getting up and stretching as if they were at the cinema and a film had just finished. I noticed that some of them were kissing each other on the cheeks and hands. Hans nudged me and smiled.

'He is superb, no?'

'Yes,' I agreed, smiling falsely. 'Who is Bhagwan Rajneesh?'

'He is the grandfather of Ecstasy,' said Hans. 'You must know about him. Have you never been to Ibiza?'

'No,' I said honestly. 'I'm not very good at travelling.'

Hans laughed.

'Soon I will introduce you to Freddy Future, but first we will get a special drink.'

We walked out of the tent and back to the food stall. The barbecue stuff had now been put away and instead there were about five large punch bowls on the tables. The atmosphere had turned upbeat since the talk, and although I was still in a hurry to leave, I thought I should see who Freddy Future was first. I remembered that line from Stephanie's diary about the big parties and speeches. Could F be Freddy Future?

I looked around me. The main tent off to my left still had people spilling out of it, most of whom were coming over to get their 'special' drinks. Once they'd got their thin plastic cup of liquid they drifted off elsewhere; a group of people were chanting in the forest, others were conducting readings by the fire where a woman with beads in her hair was giving out leaflets advertising a march against animal cruelty. Closer to me were groups of men in spectacles and chinos, looking as academic as Hans. I assumed these were the 'scientists' to whom Freddy Future had referred in his speech and wondered with a wry smile what they would make of the march against animal cruelty.

Hans moved away from me and started chatting to a young man in animated fashion. They seemed to be talking about someone called MADAM 6. I looked at the bowls of liquid and wondered what was in them. They each had a piece of card stuck on them. The one I was standing near said 2C-B. I wondered what that stood for, and why all these people seemed to feel the need to talk in letters, not words. Elsewhere I could overhear words from people's conversations that sounded like N, CH and IPA. I heard the letters MDMA several times as well. I knew that was the chemical name for Ecstasy and I thought that maybe the letters I was hearing were either part of that or else denoted other drugs.

I wandered off to the other tents, wondering what was going on inside them. The first of the four was full of children and appeared to be some sort of crèche, featuring plenty of play-dough, juggling workshops and face-painting. Over the sound of youthful squeals and high-pitched giggles I heard something different: a heavy bass thump, coming from somewhere off to the right. I left the tent through its flap and wandered round to the entrance to the second one, which seemed more like a marquee, and from which the dull thump seemed to be coming. As I walked in I was instantly hit by the smell of cannabis and the oily acrid smoke it produced which stung my eyes and made me cough. There was dry ice in here too, giving the whole place the spooky appearance of a patch of fog and I had to wait a moment for my eyes to adjust. When they did I was able to see that this was what could be described as the 'youthful element' of Beyond Reason.

A DJ with long black dreadlocks stood by some decks, nodding his head and drawing on a spliff every so often, grinning to a couple of what I assumed must be his mates who were busy rolling joints on the edge of the table. Three or four people were dancing in the centre of the tent, their limp puppet-like bodies moving despite rather than because of the thick reggae beat provided by the DJ. Most other people in here stood around the edges, sucking aimlessly on joints and nodding or shaking their heads like a group of spaced-out diplomats unable to agree on anything anymore.

The only person who appeared to be actively attempting to communicate was the drug dealer I had seen in the Blue Dolphin who walked past me, saying, 'Wicked! Cool party – free drugs,' and slapping me on the shoulder.

Soon I was able to pick out the origin of a deeper, weirder noise than the one emanating from the large skyscraper speakers: a didgeridoo, six feet long and as thick as an elephant's trunk, protruded from one corner of the marquee, at the thin end of which a man sat cross-legged, blowing expertly down it while a group of girls I recognised as Lottie, Mercedes, Lisa and Hélène from the first year stood around marvelling at the spectacle. My head was thick with smoke and I didn't want to be seen by my students so I backtracked out of the tent and was pleased to breathe clean air and feel the chill of the wind on my cheeks when I emerged into the night.

Out of the corner of my eye I spotted someone familiar, a woman dressed in orange robes standing by one of the tables. For a moment I couldn't place her and then I realised: it was Isobel. I looked over my shoulder at Hans and saw he was still chatting away happily.

I walked over to Isobel.

'What are you doing here?' I hissed.

'I'm an honorary member,' she said mischievously. 'Doing research for my next horror book.'

She smiled at me and I laughed.

'Spooky, isn't it?' she said. 'That's my story, if you believe it. Anyway, what are *you* doing here?'

'Nothing,' I said, looking at her seriously. 'Are you really a member?'

'Was,' corrected Isobel. 'I'm actually trying not to be spotted – not that the great Freddy Fuckwit has time to notice anyone apart from himself. I'm doing an investigative piece for a magazine on *cray-zee* cults.'

'Oh,' I said, getting an idea. 'I see.'

'I take it you're gate-crashing?'

'Yes.'

'Let me warn you,' she said. 'You do *not* want to be caught. At least I was once a member. If I'm asked I can say I've got my faith back or something.'

'Nancy!' shouted Hans.

'I'd better go,' I said.

'*Nancy?*' said Isobel incredulously. 'Where the hell did that come from?'

'I can't explain now,' I said. 'You haven't seen me though, all right?'

'Yes,' she said. 'Oh, have you located Fenn yet?'

'No, but I'm still working on it.'

'Nancy!' said Hans, more insistently. 'Come and meet Philip Danes. He is a chemistry student at the university in the city.'

'Hi, Philip,' I said, walking over and offering my hand to the young man next to Hans. I looked back at Isobel just in time to see her wink at me before she slipped off into the crowd. I still didn't trust her, but I was glad to have seen a friendly face here at last.

'Hello, Nancy,' Philip said softly, looking at me as if trying to place me. 'Have I seen you somewhere before?'

'I don't think so.'

'Hans tells me you are a new member. I assume Freddy Future enrolled you?'

'Oh, yes,' I said, smiling as hard as I could. 'It was an honour.'

Hans moved off towards the bowls on the tables and took a cup of orange liquid from one of them.

'Who's Madam 6?' I asked Philip, not knowing what else to say.

'Just another phenethylamine,' he said, grinning. 'I'm always up to my arms in one or other of them. I constructed all these,' he said, gesturing at the cauldrons of liquid.

'What's a phenyl . . . what did you call it?'

'MADAM 6 is not active,' said Philip loudly, with a forced smile. 'I was just telling Hans, it's almost the same combination as MDMA, which you may also know as ADAM. It is intriguing, don't you think, that a small methyl group, something that is not much more than a tiny scratch on the surface of a molecule, can so radically change the action of a compound?'

As he was talking he was unobtrusively but firmly leading me away from the main group into the woods where we couldn't be overheard.

'We gave up after 280 milligrams, you know. A completely different story from that of MADAM 2 and 2C-B or 2CB-2ETO.'

We came to a small shed by a tree. Philip let go of my arm but pushed me roughly inside, scaring me and making me lose my footing.

'Ow!' I said, rubbing my arm. I turned to see him standing in the dim light, watching me.

'You're not actually a member of Beyond Reason, are you?' he said.

'No,' I admitted. 'I'm a journalist.'

I blushed slightly at the lie. My mind was working quickly and I decided that being a journalist sounded better than admitting to being an amateur sleuth. It wasn't exactly an original idea though and I found myself wondering whether Isobel was in fact what *she* had seemed.

'Then I would suggest you leave now before someone other than me realises and you're exposed to danger.'

'Danger?'

'Yes.' He was almost hissing now. 'They look harmless, and most of them are, but they don't like being infiltrated.'

'I'm not infilt –'

'That's not how they'll see it, I can assure you of that,' said Philip grimly. 'I've seen what they've done to other journalists who've come sniffing around. Listen to me, Nancy, I've been around a bit longer than you and I can guarantee I have also seen a lot more.'

'I understand,' I said.

I had been looking at him while he spoke and trying to

work out what sort of man he really was. I thought it was weird that he said he'd been around longer than me. As far as I could make out, he was only about twenty-three. His skin was young-looking but his eyes seemed old and tired, probably from prolonged exposure to all the chemicals he made. If he hadn't done so many drugs he could have been extremely attractive. As it was he had the rugged charisma that came from the *been there, seen it, done it* world he inhabited.

Philip looked at me intently.

'Are you doing a story on all this?'

'Yes,' I said. 'I'm just gathering information at the moment.'

'Are you doing interviews? I mean, have you set anything up yet?'

'I'll be doing some as soon as I work out whose story I'm going to tell. I haven't spoken in depth to anyone yet.'

'I'll be interviewed if you want,' he said. 'But not here. I've got some stuff I'd like to get off my chest.'

'Okay,' I said, surprised not just by Philip's attitude but by the fear in his eyes. 'Will you be able to talk about Beyond Reason?'

'Oh, yes. Among other things. This whole scene is more sinister than you think.'

'I can see that,' I said, noticing that he raised his eyebrows when I spoke, clearly thinking I probably couldn't see much beyond the bohemian exterior of the group. But then he didn't know what I knew.

'When?' I asked.

'Monday night,' said Philip, looking over his shoulder anxiously as the sound of voices and singing started to draw closer.

'Where?'

'You know the Eagle pub that you passed in Salten?'

'Yes.'

'Eight o'clock,' he said, talking urgently and looking at me hard. 'And you won't be able to mention my name in your story, okay?'

'That's no problem,' I said, following him out of the shed.

'Shit,' said Philip abruptly, stopping by some bushes. 'There's Freddy Future. You'd better go before he sees us and wants to know who the fuck you are.'

My heart started hammering in my chest. I hadn't been that frightened before, but something in Philip's voice had ripped through me like broken glass. I ducked behind a bush and stood completely still.

'Thanks,' I whispered as he turned away from me.

I watched him walk away and then looked around to try and catch a glimpse of Freddy Future. I could see a crowd gathering over by the bonfire and there, on top of a platform carried by six young women, sat a man in an orange robe, holding one fist in the air. I could see all the group members regarding him in awe. As he turned to face the people by the trees, I got a clear look at him. It was Professor Valentine.

CHAPTER TWENTY TWO

Tepee in California

***

I looked at him for a few moments, unable to believe my eyes. So it had been his voice coming through the amplifier and probably his voice on the telephone as well. Seeing him benevolently surveying his followers, I couldn't help feeling nauseous. Sick with confusion and disgust, I turned on my heel and ran across the field and dirt track, back to my car.

I unlocked it hurriedly and got in, slamming and locking the door behind me. With shaking hands I started the engine and drove away, only looking back once to check I hadn't been followed.

I didn't relax until I was safely back within the anonymity of main roads and roundabouts that severed my link with the gathering. I hated drugs, but I detested cults of any description even more. Beyond Reason seemed to involve both, and I didn't like it at all. I thought about it as I drove along and realised that there were strong connections between the people in both worlds, drugs and cults. They were all trying to escape, and in the case of Beyond Reason it made sense that people would choose to follow someone who gave them not just the hope of nirvana, but also the chemicals to reach it with.

It made sense that Stephanie would have been involved with people like this. It would have given her a chance to finally belong to something, to have a purpose and a supportive community. But at what cost? I felt a shiver run down my spine as I realised that I could have been standing less than fifty yards away from the murderer, or at least the murderer's friends, while I was in the tent listening to Freddy Future – most probably F from the diaries.

If this was the case, I wondered what the Professor's actual role had been in Stephanie's life; whether he had just been a fantasy, a genuine lover or worse. I knew he attracted many women, both in his real and his Freddy Future persona. I wondered briefly if Stephanie had been killed by a love rival, someone else wanting all of the Professor's attention, but in that case why would that person have kept her severed head? I supposed the head could have been disposed of by now, but if so it hadn't been found. Someone must really have hated her to do that. I had to find out who.

I was suddenly seeing everyone in a new light. Could it have been Isobel, jealous and bitter, or some ex-boyfriend, desperate for revenge? Maybe Stephanie had been hanging out with more serious drug dealers like the dreadlocked man from the Blue Dolphin. Whoever it was, I knew I was getting closer, although I sensed I might have to go quite a bit further to reach the real heart of the mystery.

One thing was for sure, though: the cult had infiltrated the university Literature Department. The first years were clearly almost all members – which explained their bizarre death-fantasies. The Professor's 'project' seemed clearer now as well. He was obviously recruiting for his cult at the same time as he recruited for the degree course, and I doubted that all the foreign students were there solely to impress the accounts department; I assumed they were actually there to provide links all over the world. The Professor's real project was much bigger than the one Isobel had talked of. It was totalitarian and sinister, and I needed to know what part Stephanie had played in it.

I looked at the clock on the dashboard. It was almost three o'clock in the morning. I thought about all the losers and dreamers back at the gathering, searching for their nirvana.

They were probably completely off their heads by now on whatever it was that Philip had concocted. I couldn't believe they thought they were going to change the world, as if they were somehow different from any other drug users.

I yawned and rubbed my eyes as I drove, thinking muddled and frightening thoughts. I wondered what Fenn was doing now, and whether he would appreciate what I was doing. Although I realised now I wasn't doing it just for him. Whoever was responsible for all this had killed one of my students and indirectly threatened one of my oldest friends as well. Even if Fenn turned up tomorrow (as I wished he would), I would carry on with my investigation. I was so close now that there was no possibility of going back. I didn't know who to trust or whether the murderer had been at the gathering, watching and plotting to get rid of me. I had to find them first: and quickly.

I turned over the tape in the cassette player and pressed Play, beginning to feel better as the opening strains of 'On Your Own' tore through the speakers and drowned out all the thoughts in my head. I felt for the volume and pushed it up, pressing harder on the accelerator as I did so.

I reached Mawlish just after half-past four and fell into bed as soon as I got into the house. I slept until three o'clock in the afternoon on Sunday, when I woke with the worst headache I had ever had in my life, fuelled by a voice repeating my name. I opened my eyes and saw that someone was speaking to me.

'Lily?'

'Go away.'

'Lily?'

'What?'

'I've brought you some coffee.'

Nat walked into the room and put a mug next to my bed.

'Could you pass me a cigarette?' I asked.

'Sure.' He picked up a blue packet from the windowsill, looked in it but there weren't any left.

'Try my pocket,' I said, pointing at the denim jacket on the floor.

Nat picked it up and looked in each of the pockets until he found a half-full pack of filterless Gitanes.

'Here,' he said, giving them to me. 'What's this?'

'What?' I looked up and saw he was holding the orange invitation in his hand.

'Did you go to this?' he asked.

'Why?'

'You were out all night. You didn't go to this, did you?'

'Why?'

'Did you go or not?'

'Yes.'

'God, Lily, don't you know about this lot? They're mental.'

'Yeah, I know that now.'

'*Shit.*' Nat looked at the piece of paper with a concerned expression on his face. 'I told Beth not to go to this. I didn't know you had an invitation as well.'

'Was she invited?'

'Yes. All her class were. Apparently it was part of some research project, *out of body* or something. Their tutor knows someone who's in it apparently.'

'Why did you tell her not to go?'

'Well, it's drugs, isn't it? You can tell from the flyer that it's a bit dodgy.'

I drew on my cigarette and watched Nat leave the room, wondering why he'd brought me coffee. I made myself get up soon after that and ran a bath, wanting to scrub away the lingering smell of dope, onions and smoke from the night before.

Nat usually saw his girlfriend on a Sunday, but there was no sign of her today.

'Where's Beth?' I asked him when I came down after my bath.

'Working on an assignment,' he said ruefully. 'She's

going on some kind of field trip this week and she's got to prepare or something.'

'Field trip?'

'Yeah, with that stupid Professor.'

'I didn't know anything about that.'

'Yeah,' said Nat. 'She only heard about it the other day, that's why she's working on a Sunday. That's why she missed your class as well, actually.'

Ever since they were about fifteen, Nat and Beth had structured their lives so they could spend every available moment together. Beth's family home was over half an hour away and before either of them learnt to drive, the logistics of their relationship was difficult. Both my mum and Beth's, Mrs Wilkinson, had relented quite early on the 'overnight' issue and as far as I knew Nat and Beth had been sleeping together for over four years. Interestingly, these circumstances had conspired to make them both into highly effective students. They had to manage their time well during the week, or they knew it would be impossible to see each other at weekends. This was why I was surprised not to see Beth's graceful figure swanning around the house today.

Nat looked despondent and wandered up to his room to play his guitar. I sat down at the kitchen table and read the papers for a while and tried to work out some of the crossword. I suspected someone new had set it this week because none of the clues seemed to make sense to me.

I heard a pitiful squeak from outside and then the clatter of the cat-flap as Maude scurried in carrying something in her mouth. It was another vole, prone with shock but definitely alive. It sprang into action the moment she dropped it on the floor and ran under the fridge.

Squeak.

'Have you lost it, Maude?' I said, sighing as I realised I was going to have to retrieve the vole from under the fridge. Mum was terrified of small mouse-like creatures and Nat was no good with that kind of thing either.

Squeak.

The only thing I didn't like about Maude was the way she seemed to enjoy torturing little animals before eventually killing them. I blamed myself really, since she had been spoiled with far too many toy mice when she was a kitten. When the creature was dead it would become a toy to her; its limp fur-covered corpse being thrown in the air and its reanimated body chased all over again with renewed delight.

While it was still alive, though, I felt I had a responsibility towards it. I put down the crossword and sighed. I picked Maude up and felt her wiry body arch as she realised she was being taken away from her prey. I took her through to the living room and dropped her on the rug in front of the fire.

'Stay there,' I said and walked out, shutting the door behind me.

The next task was more difficult, but after about ten minutes chasing the vole around the kitchen I eventually caught it by its tail and took it out to the garden, where I gave it a five minute head-start before I reluctantly let Maude out of the living room.

I looked at the crossword again for a while but just couldn't understand it today. Eventually Nat emerged from upstairs, still looking bored.

'Do you want a game of chess?' he asked.

'God, you must be bored,' I said.

'Please,' said Nat, pouting comically. 'I'm so lonely.'

'Okay, go and get it then.'

He skipped off and I cleared the kitchen table. I hadn't seen Mum all day and wondered where she was. Nat's junk was everywhere and I knew if she'd been here she would have made him tidy it up.

He returned with the chess board and almost all the pieces.

'Can you make the others out of tin foil or something?' he begged.

'Yes,' I said patiently. 'As long as you make the coffee.'

Nat put the kettle on and while I was fiddling around

making pawns out of tin foil I realised this was how a normal day was supposed to be. I needed more days like this and hoped that my adventure would end soon. I had come to Devon to try to get my life back together in peace and quiet but as usual nothing had gone as planned.

I considered telling Nat what I was doing then thought better of it. If I told him, I would have to include the information that students were involved and he might not like to hear that. I also knew he would attempt to stop me doing what I was doing. For someone so much younger than me, Nat did a very convincing job of acting like an elder brother. We were a close family, despite our odd structure, and I knew that he felt protective towards all of us.

'Where's Mum?' I asked instead.

'She's been out since last night.'

'Where?' I asked, my heart skipping a beat.

'With *Sue*,' said Nat, stressing the word. 'She rang at about nine and Mum drove straight over.'

'Why?'

'Why do you think?' said Nat. 'Sue's always having some crisis or other.'

'Has Mum phoned today?'

'Oh yes, this morning, just to say she was okay. She said she'll be back this evening.'

'Oh,' I said, feeling my heart slow back down to normal. I hadn't realised how anxious everything was making me.

'Your move,' said Nat. 'Unless you don't want to be white.'

I sighed and moved a pawn forward, not really thinking about which one it was or what I was going to do next. Nat checkmated me in four moves.

'Now, what did we learn from that experience?' he said afterwards, taunting me.

'Shut up and make the coffee.'

'Only if you do a card trick for me. You haven't done one for ages. Do that detective one.'

'The Seven Detectives?'

'Yeah, whatever it's called. Please?'

'Okay,' I said. 'Do you know where the cards are?'

'In the drawer, I think.'

I found the cards while Nat finished making the coffee. I was distracted all the time thinking that Fenn might call. The phone was silent though, and for a moment I toyed with the idea that it was broken or off the hook. *He's got no reason to phone*, I told myself sensibly, but I still listened as I shuffled the cards and tried to remember the trick.

I started by removing four kings from the deck, showing them to Nat and putting them to one side.

'I love this,' he said. 'You must teach me.'

'Shhh,' I said. 'Now, this is the story of the Seven Detectives.'

I shuffled the cards a bit and fanned them out in front of Nat.

'Select a card,' I said. Nat took one, looking serious. 'Don't show it to me. Just look at it, remember it, and place it face down on the top of the deck.'

He put the card on top of the deck and watched while I stacked the cards on the table.

'Cut the cards,' I said, and watched while Nat did as he was asked.

'Right,' I said. 'The card you chose was the murderer.'

'Oooh,' said Nat without irony. I smiled resignedly. My life seemed to revolve around one theme at the moment.

'And these kings,' I said, 'are the detectives who are going to find the murderer.'

With a few deft movements I inserted the kings into the deck and left them sticking out. I explained to Nat that they were looking in those places for the murderer. Surprised at how much I could remember of this trick I picked up the deck almost without thinking and hit it against the table. Three more cards popped out and I showed them to Nat, explaining that these were suspects who were helping the detectives. I hit the deck against the table twice more at which point Nat's card, the *murderer*, popped out.

'Wow,' he said. 'That's amazing.'

'Thank you. But no more, I'm tired.'

'Oh, I forgot to tell you,' said Nat. 'Some bloke rang for you earlier. Ken or something.'

'Ken Lamb?' I said, remembering my old university friend who hadn't called for ages.

'No, it wasn't Ken's voice. It wasn't Ken, anyway, it was a funny name . . .'

'*Fenn?*' I said, feeling my voice rise and break. 'Was it Fenn?'

'Calm down,' said Nat. 'I think so. Fenn. Yeah, that was it.'

'*Shit!*' I said. 'Did he say when he was going to ring back?'

'Sorry,' said Nat. 'He didn't leave a message.'

'Shit,' I said again. 'If he phones again, can you take his number?'

'Sure,' said Nat defensively. I realised I had been shouting. 'What's the big deal, anyway?'

'Nothing,' I said.

We had some more coffee and waited for Mum to return, which she did at about seven o'clock. I was so tired I went to sleep almost immediately after she came in, and dreamt all night about being stalked in the back garden by a man in an orange robe.

CHAPTER TWENTY THREE

Mercedes Bends

I arrived at the Eagle the next evening with over an hour to spare, thinking it would be a good idea to hang around in the car and wait to check Philip hadn't been followed. I had often been accused of being overcautious but I thought it a sensible precaution, particularly now when it looked as if there might be real danger in store for me.

I parked the car just over the bridge under a tree in a mini car park which was loosely connected with the pub. I had bought a bottle of mineral water at the garage and some cigarettes, so for a while I just sat there smoking and drinking water, listening to the birds saying goodnight in the tree above my head.

At about half-past seven I started getting bored. I looked around vaguely in the car for a newspaper, kind of knowing there wouldn't be one there. In fact the only thing I could find to read was Isobel's novel. I picked it up and looked at it with the same attitude that one has when picking up *Readers' Digest* magazines in doctors' surgeries.

The book was called *Broken Mirror* and seemed to be about two brothers, one good and one evil. This theme was introduced by the blurb on the back and then confirmed by the image on the front of the book: a well-lit, happy-looking man dancing in the shadow of an identical figure, whose posture suggested despair and torment.

I flicked to the first page and began reading, quickly

becoming absorbed by the story. I marked a passage on page five as something that would be useful to use with students to help them understand metaphor. The brothers, Iain and Nick, were six and five respectively at this point and on a visit to the moors with their aunt. As they walked the boys became interested in a spider which had caught a fly in its web.

Nick stood still on the little mound of earth he'd created, watching the sun glisten on the dewy web as the large spider scuttled towards the helpless insect caught in its trap.

Iain craned his neck, straining to see, until Aunt Sylvia picked him up and held him there, right next to the web, where he watched the fly, or more specifically its legs, tremble with fear as it tried to escape.

'Poor fly,' said Iain. 'Why can't it just fly away? It is called a FLY after all.'

'It's stuck,' said Aunt Sylvia. 'In the sticky web.'

'Look!' yelped Nick, excitedly. 'The spider's coming closer.'

'Yuk,' said Iain. 'What's it going to do?'

'Eat it,' said Nick triumphantly. 'Eat it all up. Isn't that right, Auntie?'

'Yes,' she said wearily, pushing a strand of hair away from her face.

'Does the fly know it's trapped?' asked Iain.

'Of course it does!' shouted Nick. 'It's terrified, look!'

'I don't know,' said Aunt Sylvia thoughtfully, responding to Iain. 'That's a very good question.'

Later, at dinner with friends, she used the examples of the spider and the fly to talk about her nephews, who were growing further apart every day. Spiders were terrifying and full of mystique, she said; flies were commonplace and banal.

Nick was a spider, she was sure of that. And little Iain . . . she didn't know. He was older but less wise; more experienced but less demanding. He was thoughtful and quiet – and frequently overlooked in favour of his gregarious brother. He was a fly and she hoped he would soon fly away before he became entangled in his brother's web.

I threw my cigarette out of the window and sighed. It was ten to eight and still no sign of Philip or anyone else. I was still quite gripped by the book so I flicked forward to the boys' teenage years to find Iain ill with chickenpox and Nick beginning to discover his sexuality through an affair with the children's nanny. I read a few more random sections from the book, wondering what could happen that would be horrific enough to categorise it as horror (would Nick really eat Iain?) until I saw a blue Alfa Romeo pull up outside the pub. It was Philip.

I gave it a few minutes then took my notebook and Dictaphone from the glove compartment and checked my voicemail (nothing) before stepping out of the car. The evening sun was still bright and I squinted slightly as I looked up at it. My heart was beating heavily when I approached the doors of the pub, but I stepped inside nevertheless, hoping a cool drink would calm me down.

The smell of old beer and pipe tobacco hit me immediately I entered. Inside the pub it was dank and dark, and it took a few minutes for my eyes to adjust to the lack of light. I walked over to the bar without looking around and asked for a Budweiser.

'Sorry,' said the old woman behind the bar. 'We don't do bottled beer here.'

I could only just hear the last part of her sentence, because all of a sudden the jukebox flared into life and the opening strains of 'Hotel California' began, rather too loudly for my liking, to seep out of the speakers on either side of the bar.

'I'll have a half of whatever lager you've got then, please.'

'A half?' said the woman, slightly incredulously. She shook her head and walked across to the sink at the other end of the bar and removed a slightly grubby half-pint glass from it. As she walked back I could hear that she was singing, although her words didn't seem to be the same as those in the song.

I was eventually handed a glass of suspiciously cloudy yellow liquid before walking through the empty pub and over to a window table to join Philip, who was sitting looking pointedly at his watch.

'Sorry I'm a few minutes late,' I said. 'The traffic was a bit, you know . . .'

'Yeah,' he said, tilting his head towards me. 'I got stuck behind a tractor. Bloody rural communities.'

He smiled and looked around the pub.

'Sorry about the venue,' he said. 'It was the only place I could think of where we wouldn't run into anybody.'

'I think we can be fairly sure of that,' I said, smiling.

For a few minutes we sat in silence, lighting cigarettes and taking tentative sips of the warm lager we both seemed to be drinking. As the last notes of 'Hotel California' died away I looked at Philip.

'Do you mind if I record the interview?'

'I'm not sure yet. You didn't say which newspaper you worked for.'

'The *Guardian*,' I said, blurting out the first newspaper that came into my head. 'I'm doing an investigative piece for their Weekend section.'

'Right,' said Philip, shifting in his seat slightly.

'You are okay about this, aren't you?'

'Yep.' He looked me straight in the eye. 'Fire away.'

'Okay,' I said. 'Could you tell me a little bit about what you do?'

'I make drugs,' he said simply.

'What sort of drugs?'

'Mainly phenethylamines. Organic drugs.'

'I thought "organic" meant natural. Isn't the stuff you make synthetic?'

'It depends on how you look at it. I mean, organic is just a chemistry term meaning "made of hydrogen and carbon". So the drugs are organic in their chemical composition, which makes them "natural" in the generally accepted use of the word, but they don't occur naturally in the world, so I suppose they are somewhere in between.'

'How did you get involved in doing that?' I asked, lighting a cigarette and taking a sip of my beer. Philip looked up and stared at me for a second, as if seeing me for the first time. He sighed and started talking in a faraway voice, as if I wasn't there.

'It all began when a group of us started thinking about trying to synthesise MDMA. I was doing a degree in organic chemistry, so I was messing around making various compounds all the time. In the third year I palled up with a couple of other lads and we started planning: reading up on syntheses, finding equipment and buying materials. We knew what we were doing because of our lab experience and although it's meant to be dangerous, we weren't really worried. All of us enjoyed doing E at the weekends and stuff, and it was a case of why not do it when we know we can?'

'How did you do it?' I asked, genuinely interested. 'Did it work?'

'Oh, yeah, it worked,' Philip smiled distantly. 'After a fashion.'

'Go on.'

'We decided to use the college labs. I know that sounds a bit stupid, but the Science Department at the university is stuck up on the top floor of the main block, and for some reason no one ever goes there except science students. I worked on the top floor where only third years and postgrads are allowed. Our lecturers didn't want to know what was going on, if you know what I mean. They tend to turn a blind eye to everything really, up there.

'The difficult thing was getting the main precursors – that is, the main chemicals we needed. Some of the stuff you use is pretty commonplace and we could find it in our own stores at the university, but stuff like Safrole had to be bought from dodgy blokes we contacted out of the back of magazines. We couldn't find everything we wanted in Britain, but there was no way we were going to risk importing stuff. In the end we resorted to making some precursors ourselves.'

'Did it cost you much?' I asked.

'Five grand,' said Philip. 'The idea was that we were going to sell it and make ourselves a fortune, so we looked on it as an investment.'

He looked slightly regretful at this point and I had the feeling that things hadn't worked out exactly as planned.

'Did you make a fortune?'

'Not exactly,' said Philip, smiling ruefully. He downed the last of his beer and looked at me expectantly.

'Do you want another drink?' I said.

'Yeah. Lager. Half, please.'

I went over to the bar and asked for two more halves of lager. I'd better make this my last unless I wanted to be stranded in Salten for the night, I decided, as I thought over what Philip had already told me. I was going to have to ask him about Beyond Reason and Stephanie soon, but for the time being I was quite fascinated by the story he was telling me. I wondered why more chemistry students didn't get into all of this. Then, I thought wryly, they probably did, I just didn't know about it.

I picked up the two halves of lager and walked back over to the table.

'Where were we?' I asked, lighting a cigarette and looking at my notes. 'Oh, yes. So how did you actually make the stuff?'

'First of all we read *PIHKAL* by Alexander Shulgin and some other basic texts that we got over the Internet. The problem was that a lot of small but vital pieces of information had been left out of all the accounts of syntheses that we had. Luckily we were all chemistry students, so we didn't fuck it up too badly. We did have one big explosion, though, but we blamed that on first-year students.'

'God,' I said. 'So what happened next?'

'After about two weeks' continuous work we had made a kilo. It was hell, really. Most of the fumes that come off when you make that stuff are not pleasant, and we only had one fume cupboard in the whole university. We fucked up the Ritter reaction as well, which wasn't fun.'

'What's the Ritter reaction?'

'It doesn't matter,' said Philip. 'Just a chemical reaction. Sulphuric acid dripping off the ceiling sort of thing. I've got a permanent cough from all the vapours and stuff.'

'Ouch,' I said, making notes. I looked up at him. 'So what happened when you sold it?'

'That was a joke. When we were planning everything we'd imagined selling it off a kilo at a time but then we heard this story about some students in Liverpool who'd done pretty much the same thing as we had. Apparently when they were looking around for buyers they got a knock on their door one night. When they opened it they found a load of blokes with machine guns offering to take it off their hands for nothing. We didn't want that to happen to us so we changed the plan radically. We decided to sell it off in small quantities, locally, in case we aroused suspicion. For a while last year we were supplying the whole university, but then we got busted.'

'Busted?' This must have been what Nat had been talking about. I made a mental note to remember to ask him exactly where he'd got his information. I feared for him being over in the Science Department and thought I should probably tell him to be a bit more careful in the light of all this.

'Yep.'

'What happened?'

'Our Head of Science, Dr Coombes, walked in one day and asked us what we thought we were doing using his labs to make class-A drugs. We were shitting ourselves but he was actually really cool. He said the only mistake we'd made was to synthesise MDMA. After all, he said, why make the only phenethylamine that's illegal? I could see his point. That was when I started experimenting with all the other phenethylamines. There are so many of them. I've synthesised over one hundred different kinds in the interests of science.'

'In the interests of science?' I repeated, looking at him suspiciously. I imagined that science was only a sub-plot in this chemical fantasy.

'Yeah. Do you remember when I was talking about MADAM 6?'

'Yeah.'

Philip sighed wistfully.

'Number 98. 2,N-Dimethyl-4,5-methylenedioxy-A. What a disappointment.'

'I can imagine,' I said, not really knowing what he was talking about.

'Not active. It's amazing how many of them aren't.'

'How many are there?'

'A hundred and seventy-nine at my last count, but people are always making more.' Philip looked at me intently. 'I know you think that it's all just drugs, but for me it's much more about the chemistry. I don't expect you to believe that, but I've grown to love their names and their reactions; their diagrams. Everything about them. Look at this.'

He rolled up his sleeve and showed me a red and yellow tattoo.

'That's BEATRICE, number 11. Not many hits but a beautiful structure. I know them all: BOB, DON, IRIS . . .'

'Do they all have people's names?'

'No, only a few of them. Most of them are just letters and numbers.'

I could see another small tattoo next to the BEATRICE one. It was crude and the letters BR were spelled out in Indian ink. Beyond Reason.

'So how did you get into Beyond Reason?'

'Dr Coombes used to run it. In those days it was just a drug club, really. It was in his interests that I continue making the chemicals in the university labs, but the payoff was that he wanted me to take part in the group, as one of its "leading scientists". I wasn't particularly interested in synthesising large quantities of phenethylamines I had already made, though, I just wanted to carry on tinkering with the chemicals and seeing what new stuff I could discover. But when I applied to do my MSc last year, Dr Coombes made it quite clear what I would have to do in order to be accepted.'

'Why didn't you go somewhere else?'

'Two reasons. First of all, I was addicted to the bloody stuff by that stage and I needed somewhere to carry on making it. Secondly, I was told in no uncertain terms that I wouldn't get a reference if I left. Can you see why I'm talking to you now? I want all this out in the open. I just can't put my name to it.'

'So were you there from the beginning of Beyond Reason?'

'Yeah, long before Freddy Future and all his weirdos got involved.'

'When was that?'

'Last summer some time. The group wasn't even called Beyond Reason then, it was just a scientific thing really. Of course, now it's a fully blown cult and I just want to get out.'

'I can see that,' I said. 'So why did Val – um, Freddy Future get involved? I mean he seems a bit too old to be hanging around with teenagers doing drugs and everything.'

'The story is that he was in Europe last Easter on a trip to Prague with some students when some local hooligan slipped him an E – which he loved. He bought a batch of Doves there and took them all over a week and came back converted: *loved up*, I think they call it. By the summer he'd got together with Dr Coombes and told him about an idea he'd had for a group and Beyond Reason was born.'

'So he's only been into the whole drug scene for about a year?'

'Yep.'

'And am I right in thinking he was involved with some of the young women in the group?'

'Absolutely. Why else would anyone want to be a cult leader?' said Philip, sneering slightly.

'I don't know,' I said, thinking, *Drugs, power and money maybe*. I made some more notes then asked Philip, 'Did you know Stephanie Duncan?'

'Whoah!' He put up his hands as if to tell me to back off. 'I didn't have anything to do with that.'

'With what?'

'I don't know what went on, but she *lost it* completely. I only knew her because she used to deal for Mike and Paul every so often.'

'Mike and Paul?'

'Yeah, the mates I synthesised the E with originally.'

'Did they murder her?'

'No, of course not! Don't be fucking stupid. They've been in the States for almost a month.'

'So how did she get involved with them?'

'They caught her taking Ketamine from one of our supply cupboards. We all thought it was pretty funny really, literature students breaking into our labs and all that. Mike took quite a fancy to Stephanie, though, and teased her, saying he'd grass her up if she didn't go out with him. She ended up doing some of the deals in the city for us, just before we got busted.'

'Was she deeply involved in Beyond Reason?'

'Yes. She was like the secretary or whatever, helping with administrative stuff. You know, designing leaflets and fundraising.'

'And having it off with Freddy Future?' I prompted.

'Without a doubt,' said Philip, grinning.

'I see,' I said, realising that her additions to the flyer must actually have been last-minute amendments that never got as far as the printer's.

'So what's dangerous about Beyond Reason?' I asked.

'Nothing, really. I think I over-reacted on Saturday night. Sorry about that.' He drank the last of his beer. 'That prat Hans was going on and on about some new breakthrough in my area in the States and it was really winding me up.'

'What do you mean?'

'You probably won't understand.'

'Try me,' I said, fascinated by all the scientific details. 'I have got a couple of GCSEs, you know.'

'Okay,' said Philip, smiling. 'The latest thing that everyone's into is trying to synthesise serotonin and some of its receptors, particularly 5-HT2.'

'What's that?'

'Have you heard of Prozac?'

'Yes, of course.'

'Well, Prozac, which is Fluoxetine, is the closest synthesis that anybody has ever got. You must have heard of serotonin. It's the chemical in your brain that makes you happy, or at least that's the simplistic description you get to read in magazines. Anyway, if you could synthesise serotonin and its 5-HT receptors you would instantly become a multi-millionaire. Did you know that there's a ten-billion-dollar market for those kinds of drugs in the US alone?'

'Bloody hell.'

Somewhere in the distance the record on the jukebox changed.

'Have you seen *Raiders of the Lost Ark*?' asked Philip.

'Yes,' I said, smiling.

'Well, no one gives a fuck about arks or covenants any more. Everyone's looking for the new wonder drug.'

I let this information sink in while I lit another cigarette.

'Are you?'

'Of course.'

'Are you getting there?'

'Not really. University research is an uphill struggle. We don't get very far because our methods are traditional and we can't get the resources.'

'What do you mean?'

Philip sighed.

'We can't get human brains for our experiments. Well, I suppose you could if you work for one of the pharmaceutical giants, but not if you're just a lowly postgrad in a provincial university.'

'Do you work by yourself?'

'No. Theoretically I'm research assistant to Dr Coombes, but all he's interested in are the phenethylamines. There's a more senior student working on a similar project to me, though, so we occasionally pool research.'

'Good,' I said, tiring of the subject even though in other circumstances I would have found it fascinating. It didn't look like I was going to get anything else about Beyond Reason so I downed the last of my beer and looked at my watch while Philip did the same.

'Thanks for all this,' I said. 'I won't use your real name.'

'Great,' he said, standing up. 'It feels good to get it all off my chest actually. Even my mother doesn't know what I do. Sad, isn't it?'

'I'm sure you'll do the right thing eventually,' I said, inwardly cursing myself for sounding sanctimonious. 'Anyway, thanks again.'

'Don't mention it,' he said, and walked out of the pub.

CHAPTER TWENTY FOUR

An Axe for the Frozen Sea

The drive home was uneventful. By the time I arrived it was almost midnight and I was dead tired. I couldn't believe I had to teach tomorrow and had no idea which class I was doing, let alone what I was going to teach them.

Before I went to bed I made some hot chocolate and sat in front of the TV with it for a while, trying to calm my mind and stop all the activity within it. I was making connections too fast and needed a good night's sleep in order to make any real sense of what I had learnt from Philip. I had worked out some more of Stephanie's codes, though. K was obviously Ketamine and L was lab. It was a fair guess that CS stood for chemistry students.

Eventually, though, my brain fogged and I became engrossed in some late-night sci-fi series about utopias, with all the letters from the diaries and the drugs floating around in my head like an endless impenetrable acronym. I had another crack at Jason's riddle as well, but it made no sense at all. Maybe he didn't want anyone to make sense of it, I thought. With my mind still cluttered and my stomach turning, I eventually got into bed at just after half-past one and fell asleep with Maude licking my neck.

The house was in darkness when the young man returned home, except for a little lamp in the corner of one room, illuminating all the papers surrounding it and casting a muted orange glow over the squiggled symbols written on them with the usual green pen. These were the documents he was not supposed to see and they were shielded now by a deft hand gathering them up as he walked to the facing chair and sat down on the edge of it.

'I'm leaving,' he said nervously. 'I've had enough. I'm not just leaving you, I'm leaving the university, the city. This is going to ruin me.'

'Where will you go?'

'My mum's. Do you know, I thought about her for the first time in ages tonight? It took some journalist I've never met before to remind me that I've got a life beyond you, beyond THIS.'

'Mmm-hmm.'

'Do you care that I'm leaving?'

'What journalist?'

'Did you hear me?'

'Yes, yes. Who was the journalist?'

'Nancy something. Christ,' he said, rubbing his hand over his damp brow. 'What does it matter? Look, I know things haven't been so great lately – you obviously want your own life, so here you are. It's yours. I'm off. And I don't care about your secrets anymore.'

'Have you been tested yet?'

'What do you mean "tested"?'

'The police. They were in the department today. Doing the staff.'

'Yeah, I gave them some hair or something. Why the hell are you asking about that? I'M LEAVING YOU, for God's sake.'

The two people stood there in silence for a few moments and then the doorbell went, startling both of them. It was late – well after midnight. Who could it be? A quick glance through the peephole soon answered the question.

'It's the police.'

'What do they want?'

'How should I know?'

'What have you done this time?'

'Nothing. Shall I let them in or what?'

'Yeah, whatever.'
And then they arrested the young man for murder.

I woke up in the morning to discover I had no clean clothes and that we had run out of washing powder. I didn't have to be at the university for several hours but I wanted to get there early so I could prepare before my class started at three. I drank my hot chocolate and ate some bread, thinking about the events of the past few days but, frustratingly, still unable to form any conclusions.

I looked at the national paper for a while. There was a crisis in the monarchy of some sort and trouble brewing again in the Middle East. It was funny the way the world just carried on turning, oblivious to its minor crises and simmering evils. There was a science supplement in the paper which I would normally have ignored but today I flicked through it with some interest.

Most of it seemed to be about computers, the Internet and the future of business. From the way Philip had been talking last night I had almost expected to see features on the search for the new serotonin or something but there was no mention of it. I supposed it would be news only when someone discovered something worth writing about. It fascinated me, though, the idea that happiness could not only be quantifiable in milligrams but possibly synthesised in a test tube. I shuddered slightly at the thought and turned to the local paper to look at the horoscopes instead.

Mine told me that if I opened my mind a bit more I could discover something interesting today. 'Sometimes your thoughts are behind the times,' it said. I rolled my eyes and lit a cigarette.

That reminded me of a line I had read a few months ago in a feature in a Sunday supplement, about how the public weren't ready for new advances in science. If I remembered correctly the debate had been about whether it was morally acceptable for doctors to take eggs from aborted foetuses and use them in IVF treatments. I liked to think that I was quite liberal and open-minded but the idea made me feel sick. Imagine growing up, leading a normal life, and then finding out that your grandmother had aborted your mother; that your mother had never really existed. The identity crisis would be unbelievable. I remembered that the article had said that the public were too reactionary to accept that kind of thing and I thanked God for that.

I looked at my watch and saw that it was almost ten o'clock. Wanting to leave by twelve at the very latest, I slipped on the clothes I had been wearing last night and drove to the village shop for washing powder and another packet of cigarettes.

Half an hour later the washing was on and I was bored. I sat in front of the television mindlessly, watching morning TV and listening to the steady whirr of the machine and the *clunk clunk* of my clothes falling around inside it. I hadn't seen either Mum or Nat and assumed they had left before I got up.

While I sat there I tried again to put together all the things I knew but, like the wrong pieces in a jigsaw puzzle, they just wouldn't go. I couldn't believe that within so much information there could be so few conclusions. As a private detective I made a very good literature lecturer, I thought. Still not wanting to be beaten, I grabbed a piece of paper and wrote Jason's words on it, repeating again what I'd been doing all week: writing the words in a line, a circle, and finally jumbling their letters up like an anagram and trying to make sense of them that way. Today I thought I saw something familiar in the words that hadn't been there before but the idea was just an ethereal trace, like the memory of a dream. As soon as it came it was gone, leaving me frustrated and with the beginnings of a head-ache. I screwed up the piece of paper and flung it across the room, angry with the words for not just making sense by themselves.

There must have been some clue at the gathering, since Stephanie had been such a big part of it. I thought about all the students in the first year, the drug dealer from the Blue Dolphin, even Isobel. They had all been there and presumably played some part in the group, and therefore in Stephanie's life too. The Professor was a dark horse but although I was having all kinds of uncharitable thoughts about him now that didn't mean he had actually done anything – or nothing I could prove anyway. He was the leader of a nasty cult but that was it, as far as I could tell at the moment. I got the feeling that if I could come up with one more fact it might join all the others together. But I didn't know what it was or where to start looking for it.

I sat there for a while with my legs pulled up under me, mindlessly plaiting a section of my hair and listening partly to Richard and Judy and partly to the tumble drier. They broke for commercials and I wandered off to make some coffee, returning just in time for the lead item on the news: someone had been arrested for Stephanie's murder. Oh my God. It was Philip Danes.

How the hell could that be? All at once I wanted to jump for joy because it put Fenn in the clear but then I checked myself. Philip wasn't guilty, was he? Surely he wouldn't have spoken to a journalist if he had been. So the DNA had matched? Big deal. People acted like DNA was infallible but mistakes could be made with it, just like anything else. There was no way Philip had done it. He might have been set up, which I wouldn't imagine to be too difficult in a chemistry department. But innocuous, conscience-sticken Philip raping and murdering someone? No.

An hour later I was ready to leave for work, having ironed my clothes and got dressed even more quickly than I'd planned, every movement driven by the speed of my thoughts: breakneck, *Silverstone*. I still wasn't getting anywhere (like going endlessly around a racetrack) but that didn't stop me. I was going to pull out all the stops to reach a conclusion today.

I arrived at the university in good time and drove through

the wrought-iron gates with no obstructions. The yellow police tape was still flapping in the distance off by the woods and there was still activity there, although it seemed less frenetic.

I unlocked my office and dumped my bag and books in there, sitting for a while just thinking before heading off down the corridor to go back downstairs and over to the Halls of Residence, to begin attempting to recreate what I knew of Jason's penultimate journey, to see if I could get any idea of what he'd seen that had driven him mad.

The sun was just beginning to break through the clouds as I walked, feeling the squelch of wet grass under my feet as I went. It must have rained again last night. I stopped when I reached the big locked doors I had entered with Steve's help last week and turned one hundred and eighty degrees to look back the way I'd come. As I did, I became aware of what a good spot this was to observe the comings and goings of the Samuel Beckett Building. Jason's room, too, situated as it was just above me on the third floor and facing outwards, would have made an excellent vantage point. And if he had been stalking Stephanie, and if she had indeed been going back into the Samuel Beckett Building late on the night she died, then it would have been possible for him to observe almost everything, just standing here.

Any normal person could walk from the front doors of the Halls to the doors of the Samuel Beckett Building in about three minutes; cutting across the green, crossing the small internal road next to the exit gate and walking straight across the car park to the door. A stalker could do the journey more ponderously and remain unobserved by cutting around behind the trees next to the Halls and then, I discovered, following the route myself, going through the entrance to the sports hall and up some stairs to a bizarrely psychedelic tunnel leading above the sports hall to the library.

I had discovered this odd piece of architecture by chance

last week; stumbling on it when I was lost and feeling as though I'd fallen into the most kitschly unbelievable sixties film. The tunnel could be seen from the ground, but you wouldn't know what it was from there. Inside it seemed like an orange and brown intestine, dark, small and cold, the light and air from outside entering the yellow-tinted plastic windows and casting a pallid glow throughout the whole thing. Last week I had walked through it quickly, interested but frightened, not knowing where I was or where I would end up when I came out the other end. Had I accidentally entered a workmen's entrance, I'd thought, somewhere embarrassingly remote and terrifyingly unknown? Thinking irrationally as one does when lost, I'd even wondered if I would ever get out. When I saw the library at the end of the tunnel I was relieved but didn't go to it, following instead a turning off to the right, along a corridor holding engineering offices and down a small flight of stairs to an exit by the caretakers' offices. Once out in the fresh air it had seemed like fun up there and I'd remembered a story I had been absorbed by as a child, about two children squeezing through a tunnel into a barley sugar factory.

This time I stopped by a small plastic concave window and looked out, able to see all that was going on between the Halls and the Samuel Beckett Building, yellowed and slightly distorted but visible nevertheless. Had Jason stood here, I wondered, shivering. Had he seen where Stephanie went after leaving the building? I took the same corridor this time as I had the last, running down the stairs and emerging breathless, trying to blink away the orange dots imprinted behind my eyes, as though a polka-dot ra-ra skirt had been imprinted on my mind. I didn't know where Jason would have gone next. Into the woods probably, following Stephanie. If only there was some way of knowing where the killer had sprung from.

Feeling again as though I was simultaneously staring the answer in the face and standing a million miles from it, I sighed and walked back over to the Samuel Beckett Building to get to my register and have a few moments in my office to prepare my class.

'Good morning, *Miss* Pascale,' came a voice from behind me as I strode purposefully towards the stairwell, holding the flimsy piece of grey cardboard in my hand. 'Did we have a nice weekend?'

'Yes, thank you, Professor,' I said, turning to face him. 'And you?'

'Remarkable, yes, quite wonderful. I was away with my wife.'

'That's nice,' I said, trying to keep the sarcasm from my voice. I looked at the Professor in his jeans and shirt and remembered how sinister he had looked in his orange robes. My heart started beating wildly and erratically when I thought about his double life. He seemed in a very good mood considering his chief scientist had just been arrested for murder. Maybe he didn't know yet.

The Professor looked me up and down, and coughed.

'I hear you're going on a field trip,' I said, to fill the silence.

'Yes, that's right,' he said, looking confused. 'With the first years.'

'Not during my class, I hope?'

'No, of course not. We're going this afternoon actually. Now, if you'll excuse me?'

He turned and walked back down the corridor, muttering something about a mini-bus. I walked up the three flights of stairs to my classroom, my head still heavy with nonsensical information; all the thoughts and ideas about the murder lying disordered within it, like a bundle of loose firewood with no rope to hold it together.

Cress was in the classroom before me, reading quietly by the window which was open. Outside the air was crisp and fresh; the sky now clear, bright and cloudless. What a contrast with last week, when this classroom had been dark and oppressive and the TV crew had frightened us all. I remembered Jason coming here too. What had he been looking for?

'Hi, Lily,' said Cress, putting her book down and smiling at me warmly.

'Hello,' I said, dropping my files on the table.

And then it hit me, like an electric shock. The rest came more slowly like the brightest sunrise following the most deathly black night. I had my missing piece. Now I just had to get rid of the students.

They all trooped in as usual, except today there was a general hush and a lot more of them, now the strike was over. In place of the original atmosphere of shock and warped excitement was a feeling of closure and catharsis, as if the whole university had let out a collective breath it had been holding for the last two weeks. They had caught the murderer, the Student Union had got the go-ahead for its lights and the strike and the terror were over. Except I knew it wasn't as simple as that.

I took the register quickly, remembering to call neither Jason's nor Stephanie's name.

'What are we doing today, Lily?' asked Heather, sounding excited.

'Are *we* going on a field trip?' asked Eddie. 'We never got to do that when we were first years.'

'Not today,' I said, thinking quickly. 'Today you're going to start project work.'

'Project work?' said Blake. 'That's a new one.'

'How can we do a project when we haven't even been taught anything?' called Kerry from the back of the room.

'Come on,' I said impatiently, not having time for this. 'You did have a lecturer before I came here.'

'What, creepy Isobel?' said Ash.

'Nick, don't *hurt* me,' screamed Blake in mock horror.

'I see you're familiar with *Broken Mirror*, then?' I said, trying not to smile while they all laughed.

'Shhh,' said Cress, being very grown-up

'Okay,' I said. 'Settle down.'

I wracked my brains for something they could do a project on. I didn't want them to do writing projects really, because I had them doing that in their other class. Mind you, I didn't really care what they did, so long as they were out of my hair for the rest of the afternoon.

'Right,' I said. 'You are going to work in pairs for this assignment.'

Everyone started whispering and nudging each other like schoolchildren, trying to organise their partnerships.

'You can do that in a minute,' I said. 'Just listen for a moment, okay?'

I made up a project off the top of my head, totally disregarding the lesson I'd just planned. The class filed out slowly, chatting and gossiping as they went while I tried to look calm, waving them goodbye cheerily. When the last of them had gone I looked at my watch. It was half-past three. I had to be quick.

I walked out of the classroom and down the hall, tracing Jason's steps from last week, and indeed my own when I had been trying to find him. This time, though, I didn't stop outside the Professor's door as I had done then; I used my key and walked straight in, checking in the main office next door to see that no one was looking but striding author-itatively nevertheless, looking as if I was supposed to be there.

Holding the masterkey in my shaking hand, I walked the length of the small room, vaguely examining the surfaces, my eyes resting on objects for only a split second as they searched, sorted and rejected. I stopped by the desk for a moment, refusing to feel beaten. This had to be the room. Then the key fell, shaken out of my hand by the agitated pounding of my heart, and I reached down to pick it up from behind one of the legs of the Professor's desk where it had fallen. The small, almost unnoticeable smear of blood on the leg confirmed what I had suspected. The key was not the only thing to have fallen in this spot.

From my crouched position on the floor I had only to lower my head slightly then look upwards. From here – but from no other point in the room – the words were clear. *Train, London, Murders, Psycho, Mirror, Pendulum*: the warped and distorted glimpses of the book titles in the glass cabinet above hovering transcendentally, taunting me with the simplicity of their meaning. *Trainspotting, London Fields, Murders in the Rue Morgue, American Psycho, Broken Mirror* and *Foucault's Pendulum*. All titles from literature reading lists stacked on top of one another in such a way that from this position and angle only the first word of their title could be seen. The last three books were, of course, upside down.

So Jason's riddle had not been that at all, or at least he hadn't intended it as one. His last words were just that: the last words he had ever seen; his last memory forever engraved on his mind from the moment he lay slumped here almost under the desk.

It was Cress's book that had provided the final link. I'd never noticed what it was until today; just that she was reading it all the time. There was an exact replica of it up on the shelf, though: *Foucault's Pendulum*, the light and the shadows distorting its appearance from here so the word *Foucault's* was missing. I could have kicked myself there and then for not noticing it sooner but didn't have time for self-recrimination. I had to see if any of the other pieces was here.

As I pulled myself up from the floor and combed the room again, objects I had rejected before became invested with a new meaning and with unforeseen attachments to others. There was the large bust of Dickens, now standing serenely by the computer but, judging by the whiteness of a small patch of paint on the greying window-sill, having recently been moved from there. Why? Because Jason had been hit with something to shut him up?

All at once the rest came. I transported myself back to last Tuesday, after Jason left the third floor. He came down here and waited for Valentine, finding him only after I'd left to get help. Then Jason accused the Professor of something terrible, loudly and vociferously. He panicked. It was past five o'clock and the secretaries had gone home, but out of the window he could see me coming back. Having to act quickly, he grabbed the bust from the window-sill and struck Jason with it, watching as he fell under the desk. Then what? Valentine wanted to make it look like an accident. He needed to kill the boy. What could he use? Ecstasy, of course. With his big salary and new lifestyle he had plenty of that.

Pacing in Valentine's office putting all this together, it was easy to understand the mistakes everyone had made about what had happened to Jason. We were all thinking from the perspective of someone from our own generation, someone who knew about drugs. Naïve Professor Valentine, having only discovered the rave scene a year previously, must have thought he could create an 'accidental' death with an overdose of E, which he then gave Jason . . . until somebody told him differently and he had to change his plans.

Scanning the room then as I was doing now he would have seen as clearly as I could the thing that would do it. A large bottle of Aspirin sat by the computer in a little pot full of staples and paperclips – small, white and innocuous, until I examined it and found it almost empty. Suddenly the scene in Jason's room made sense. The original Es and the Aspirin had been there to imply that the whole cause of death had originated from Jason himself, if the police had been there to check. But then the ingredients, which in themselves suggested suicide – some Ecstasy combined with a deliberate overdose of Aspirin – had been added together to form a whole: a contaminated pill – a terrible accident. Why accident rather than suicide? So no one would look for a note? The Professor didn't know what Jason had written in those six days in his room, or what he had been saying. People listen to suicide victims but not to teenagers who go out to have a good time but end up dead from drug overdoses. People commit suicide for a *reason*. Accidents just happen.

Somebody had been there to help the Professor with all of

this and I was able to work out that this person was definitely a scientist (since they'd made the pills) and was probably based here. That matched up with one of the strange things that Fenn had said about the night Stephanie died. He'd said that a phone call came through to the Professor's room late that night and I'd wondered at the time how that could be possible, since the switchboard closed at five. But if it had been an internal call there wouldn't have been a problem. And there was already a link between the Literature and Science Departments through Beyond Reason anyway.

I grabbed the University Directory from the windowsill and flicked through to the Chemistry Department section. There were several names there I recognised: Dr Coombes, Philip Danes, and then about twenty names down the list one that rang a bell though not in this context: Nadia, or more specifically *Nadia Raven*, PhD student and part-time lecturer. Was this the sister Isobel had talked of and, it seemed, written about? It made sense. Nadia Raven was the sister who had undermined Isobel all her life and finally stolen her boyfriend from under her nose at her own birthday party.

So the Professor must have been in league with Nadia Raven, the evil younger sister disguised in *Broken Mirror* as Nick. Together they had killed Jason and covered up his death. It had to have been the Professor who'd visited the hospital just before me and also he who had switched the tablets in Jason's room.

I left the room in a daze, still thinking at a thousand miles an hour. So Jason must have seen the *Professor* with Stephanie that night. Finally it all made sense. Fenn seeing Stephanie come back into the building, for example. That was because she was meeting the Professor for their usual rendezvous in his office. Except on that night they hadn't stayed there, I knew that much.

CHAPTER TWENTY FIVE

Videodrome

I decided against ringing Isobel since I wasn't sure whether in this case blood would in fact run thicker than water. Instead I decided to see what I could find out by myself.

After thinking for a few moments I left the Samuel Beckett Building and lit a cigarette, shading my eyes from the sun and walking briskly across the car park over to the main block. I decided that the main office was the best place to start so I went there first and asked to see details of science postgraduates.

'Do you want the postgrad prospectus?' asked the secretary.

'I don't think so,' I said. 'I want to see details of the scientific research currently in progress, if possible.'

'Oh, I see,' said the woman. 'I'll go and see what we've got.'

She returned after a while with a surprisingly glossy document which she handed to me with a smile.

'Will this do? It's last year's, I'm afraid, but the new one hasn't been finalised yet.'

'That's fine,' I said, looking at the document in my hand. It seemed to be a publicity brochure, featuring science students posing in their labs. 'Is it all right for me to take it away?'

'Oh, yes, we've got hundreds. They were commissioned by the Chancellor last year to go out to businesses, to try to persuade them to sponsor students in their research. I'd almost forgotten about them. You'll probably find all the details you want in there.'

'Thanks again,' I said.

I walked away from the desk and down the long central corridor in the main building. I wanted to get back over to my office to try and put some more of this together, but there was something else I needed to get hold of first, if I was to convince anyone (including myself) of my theory about what had happened last Tuesday night and therefore the one before as well.

At the end of the corridor I turned right, expecting the post room to be down the hallway on the left. Instead I found the Student Union shop. How stupid of me. I must have got the block the wrong way round.

Eventually I ended up where I had intended to be, at the caretakers' offices. As usual they were all standing around drinking tea, but with slightly more urgency today since they all seemed to be preparing to go to lunch.

I rang the bell and waited to be noticed. The same man I'd seen last time walked over but didn't appear to recognise me.

'Can I help you, love?'

'Yes, I hope so,' I said. 'I lecture over in the Samuel Beckett Building and I was wondering who keeps the security video tapes for the gate next to the Samuel Beckett car park.'

'That would be Trev,' said the man at the desk. 'He does all of that. Go through and see him if you want.'

'Thanks,' I said. The caretaker lifted up part of the front counter and led me into the caretakers' office and through a door at the back of the little room into a passageway which I worked out must be behind the post room.

'Down there on the right, love,' said the caretaker. 'He should be in there, at least, I haven't seen him leave.'

'Thanks,' I said.

I knocked on the brown institutional door and heard a

faint 'Come in'. I opened the door slowly and looked into the room. A small fair man was sitting with his back to the door, surrounded by television screens. All at once I could see what was going on around the entire university; the car parks, the tennis courts and even the bar had cameras fixed firmly on them. The pictures were animated in a way that would suggest the cameras moved from side to side, recording everything, missing almost nothing. I suspected I would get a headache if I looked at these relentless side-to-side images for too long.

I had thought about the cameras up in the tunnel and then just now on my way over here, feeling I was being watched by red flashing eyes in the corners of all the doorways and at the entrances to all the car parks. I thought it ironic that the police had probably taken tapes of Tuesday two weeks ago when Stephanie had been murdered, and found nothing, when if they had taken *last* Tuesday's all the evidence I was hoping to discover would probably be there. I wasn't sure how I could get Trevor to let me see videos of last week, and I wasn't even sure if the tapes would still exist, but it had to be worth a try. I wanted to find out if I could see what Jason had seen, and I wanted to see if he had left the university with anyone last Tuesday evening. He must have left at some point in order to get to the Blue Dolphin and I needed to see how this had happened and with whom he had left.

I took a deep breath and smiled at Trevor, who swivelled around on his chair to get a better look at me.

'Hello,' he said jovially.

'Hi. I, um, lecture over in the Samuel Beckett Building and I was wondering if I could see the tapes for the exit gate from last Tuesday,' I said innocently. 'From about five o'clock.'

'What for?' asked Trevor good-naturedly, giving me the impression he would give me the tapes eventually but that he was in the mood for a chat. Great.

'Just a media project, you know. *Body language*,' I said, improvising quickly.

'Why that day in particular?' he asked, interested in the way only a technician could be, looking at me with a *speak to me, I'm fascinated to know what you arty types do* expression that I didn't have time for right now.

'We were watching from the window,' I continued, talking quickly. 'And the students made some observations. I wanted to see the tape so we could compare what they saw with what actually happened.'

'Oh,' said Trevor, laughing suspiciously. 'And you get paid for this?'

'It's a bit complicated,' I said, shifting from one foot to the other in my desperation to get the tape and go.

'It should be all right,' he said. 'It's a good job you asked me now because I was just about to delete it. Pull up a pew and I'll just go and get it.'

Trevor disappeared into what looked like a cupboard off to the right and I sat down, doing what I was told but balancing on the edge of the chair uncomfortably, wanting to be on my way. Now I was sitting in front of all the screens I was truly daunted by the scale of surveillance that went on at the university. I was more daunted by what I was discovering, though. The information I had terrified me. I just wanted to consolidate it and hand it all over to the police as soon as possible.

Trevor came back into the room and handed me a carrier bag.

'It's in there,' he said, winking and sitting back down on his chair. 'You're not meant to have it, so be discreet.'

'Oh yes.'

I watched as he flicked a couple of buttons to reveal yet more scenes on the screens in front of us. I could see what looked like a drinking competition going on in the bar, and two members of staff kissing in the car park, presumably thinking no one was looking. I blushed slightly and looked away, feeling like a Peeping Tom. I looked at the brochure in my hand. Trevor's eyes followed my gaze.

'All the bright sparks in that,' he said.

'Yes. I suppose you get to see what they do all the time in here?'

'What, the science lot? You must be joking. No one knows what goes on up there. Secret research, apparently. All we have is cameras on the stairs, you know, to see who goes up and down. We only look at them if there's been a theft, but it never really happens. In fact, I don't think the Head of Science has ever reported anything to us.'

'That's lucky,' I said conversationally, trying not to show how uncomfortable I felt.

'Anyway,' said Trevor, turning to say goodbye at last, 'glad to be able to help. But you'll either have to return or replace the video. Stock checks, you know.'

'Yes, of course,' I said, almost stumbling in my haste to get out. 'Thanks.'

'No problem,' he said. 'See you again.'

'Yeah, 'bye.'

I shut the door behind me and gasped for air like a fish caught on a line, walking as fast as I could back down past the caretakers' offices and out of a side door. Without looking behind me I broke into a run and didn't stop until I reached the door to the Samuel Beckett Building.

I walked past Professor Valentine's room as quickly as I could, knowing he wasn't inside but nevertheless scared he might suddenly jump out on me. With my heart beating consistently at about 150 b.p.m. I ran into the stairwell and up the stairs to my office, unlocked the door and fell inside, my chest heaving with exhaustion and relief. I put the bag down on the table and looked at my watch. It was almost quarter past four and I was going to have to move quickly. The Professor was stuck in his 'silly' meeting for another forty-five minutes only.

CHAPTER TWENTY SIX

Dark and Stormy Night

Once I had pulled myself together, I picked up the video and the brochure, put them in a bag and walked up the two remaining flights of stairs to the Media Centre.

The wife was desperate. Desperate enough to go through his things. Oh, yes, she knew where he kept all his fucking secrets. The pills hadn't been working so she took two more. And then some gin, to get her in the mood.

He was so bloody secretive. Such a bastard. She didn't know why she had married him. In those days she had been something else and he was just beginning. Now he was something and she was the empty vapour that just wafted around him: annoying, cloying, clinging.

She knew about his silly little group. Oh, yes, she knew about that. They were harmless. But there was more. She might be drunk and she might be stupid but she knew when something was being concealed from her.

The books were all there, in their usual places. The fairy stories and myths and legends. Children's books mainly. There was the pornography too, hidden behind the books, but that wasn't what she was looking for.

The key to the bureau was behind the magazines in a little box full of old yellow Valium. She took it out and turned the key in the lock, waiting for the little click that meant she was in. The click

came, and then a waterfall of wood crashing on to wood as the
curved cover came down.

She hacked the rest of the drawers open with a hammer. Keys
were too subtle, somehow. She was looking for the address of that
woman, the new one, but instead she found a video.

I found the room I wanted but it was locked. I tried the
handle of the room next door; no good. All the viewing
rooms were locked. I ran down to the secretary's office on
the ground floor and rang the little bell. They had so many
bells here, and I couldn't see the point of them. Eventually a
woman came out.

'Can I help you, dear?'

'Yes,' I said, breathlessly. 'How do I get into the viewing
rooms up in the Media Centre?'

'Well, you'll have to ask George about that, I'm afraid.'

'Where do I find him?'

'He should be up there, dear.' The secretary looked at me
hard, as if trying to remember my name or something. I had
never seen her before so I couldn't work out why. 'You are a
student, aren't you?'

'No, I'm staff.'

'Oh, why didn't you say?' She smiled at me warmly.
'You're new, aren't you? Hang on and I'll go and get you
one of the keys.'

She hurried off and returned a few moments later with a
small bunch of keys.

'I take it there's been no word from Fenn Baker?' I asked.

'Shhh,' said the secretary conspiratorially. 'The students
think he's ill. Anyway, no. Although it seems as if he's got
no reason to hide now, has he? Silly boy.'

She handed me the keys.

'The names of the rooms are on them.'

I ran up the stairs and back into the Media Centre through
some massive heavy doors which were usually kept locked
with a keypad, just as Sue had described. There were four
viewing rooms altogether and I chose the one furthest away

from the door; the only one without a little glass window. I unlocked the door and shut it behind me to find myself enclosed in total blackness. I switched on the light and realised there were no windows in the room, just a small TV set and video, both bolted to the table on which they sat. I flicked the catch on the door to lock myself in, vaguely hoping I wouldn't have any kind of medical emergency, and switched on the equipment.

I took the video out of its case and inserted it in the machine. I sat down on the little director's chair and pressed Play. The tape was at the end, so while I waited for it to rewind itself I picked up the brochure and started to flick through it.

She put the video in the recorder and pressed Play. Nothing happened for a long time so she fetched some more gin. Eventually the tape ended. Stupid cow, she'd forgotten to rewind it.

She laughed at that. Silly, forgetful woman, that's what people would say. She smiled to herself as the clear liquid dribbled down the side of the glass and on to the sofa. There was a click somewhere in the background and the tape was ready.

Nadia Raven turned out to be a rising star of the university's Science Department. Her double-page spread eclipsed the other students' half-page entries. A long biography explained she had studied medicine at Oxford and then gone on to specialise in pharmacology at postgraduate level. There was a half-page picture of Nadia in her lab coat standing by some test tubes, smiling. Her dark hair was all scraped back into a top knot which emphasised her striking features and high cheekbones. Her big blue eyes looked out at me from the page: harsh, luminescent, almost scornful. She was the more beautiful of the two sisters but there was an edge to her good looks that Isobel didn't have. Bitterness or (was I imagining it?) maybe *evil*.

Nadia's research project wasn't outlined until the last two paragraphs of the page. Although what I read didn't surprise me in the light of my meeting with Philip, it still caused me to draw in my breath sharply. My heart started to take up its fast rhythm again as I read the words one more time. *Serotonin: practical applications and the future.*

I realised that my previous problem had been one of approach. I'd never stopped to consider why anyone would remove the head of a murder victim. But as Philip had said, research students couldn't get real human brains to experiment on. So *that* was it. But even now there were dozens of questions to answer. I was jolted roughly out of my thoughts by the loud click of the video coming to a halt after rewinding. I shut the brochure and pressed the Play button, thinking that some of the answers might be on this tape. Slowly and jerkily, the badly lit frames of last Tuesday evening started to unfold before me, shifting across their 180-degree horizontal plane.

The time at the beginning of the tape was 17.00 hours, according to a little strip of computerised numerals at the bottom right-hand corner of the screen. I thought back to that time last Tuesday. Where was I when the video was shot? I remembered that my class with the second years would just have finished. This was then confirmed by the sight of Heather and Cress, then Kerry, Blake, Ash and the others walking out of the doors, giggling and chatting.

As the numbers tumbled around I watched the building, knowing I was at that moment having my tête-à-tête with Jason. I fast forwarded until the display said 17.15. I could see the outlines of two figures walking across the green. The woman was holding out her arms and the man kept making her stop. I remembered seeing the same image out of the window last week, although from a slightly different angle. The next thing I saw was myself leaving the building and walking purposefully out of the frame towards the main block.

The exit gate was between the Samuel Beckett Building and the Halls of Residence but the camera was placed in such a way that both the main door to the Samuel Beckett

Building and the college green in front of the Halls were in frame. I wondered where the camera was; the view it gave was similar to the one from the tunnel but *lower*, not taking in the space beyond the gate and the right-hand wall of the Samuel Beckett Building. That could only mean that it was up high on the wall of the sports hall which stood perpendicular to the gates, facing them.

There didn't seem to be any sign of movement around the door so I fast forwarded the tape five minutes. I watched the events speed up and almost smiled at the comical way that the couple now sped across the grass. I focused on the door to the Samuel Beckett Building and waited.

The couple slowed down as I pressed the button to resume the Play mode. They kissed briefly and separated before one of them walked towards the entrance to the Samuel Beckett Building and the other carried on past the sports hall in the same direction as I had gone. As the man walked across the car park I got a look at his face. It was Valentine. I rewound the tape slightly, wondering who he had been walking with and stopped it at the point just before the couple kissed.

I peered into the TV screen and moved the tape backwards a few frames then pressed Play again. Almost as if she knew she was being filmed, the woman smiled into the camera for a split second before turning back to Valentine. I repeated the rewind, stop, play process several times before I was sure. With my heart beating and my head becoming hot, I verified the identity of the woman on the tape by turning to check the picture of her in the brochure.

Nadia Raven looked different on the video, with her hair down and her lab coat off, but the features and eyes were the same. I left the tape running and watched the goodbye scene one more time. I assumed that Nadia was walking back to the science labs over in the main block. Valentine seemed to shout something to her as she walked away but I couldn't make out what it was.

My eyes were displaced from their focus by a small movement on the screen in front of me. It was the scene

I had been waiting to see: Jason was leaving the building. I watched him walk out slowly and look around, frightened and paranoid, just as he had been when I had seen him.

He walked towards Professor Valentine and stopped. Jason said something to the Professor that I couldn't lip-read and the Professor said something back. The two stood there for a moment staring at each other and then the Professor said something else.

Jason turned to go back into the Samuel Beckett Building and the Professor turned away from him and walked across the car park in front of the building, taking out his car keys as he went. I watched him look around, as if to check whether or not he had been followed before taking something out of the glove box and putting it carefully in his pocket. He shut and locked his car door, and then stood next to it for a moment. He looked straight up at the camera, like Nadia had, but he didn't smile. Instead he mouthed something to himself, unlocked his car again and got in.

The next thing he did was drive the car around the corner of the Samuel Beckett Building, down its right-hand side and out of range of the camera. That was the last I saw of the Professor until he walked around the corner and entered the building about three minutes later. Ten minutes after that I saw myself walk back in. I remembered being spooked and thinking I was the only person left in the block apart from Jason. But Professor Valentine had definitely been inside. I remembered that note I had read on his door. *Nadia called*.

At 17.47 I saw myself leave again, having given up on Jason. The sick feeling in my stomach returned when I realised that in order to leave the building I must have walked past the Professor's office in which Jason had been almost comatose on the floor. I watched the tape avidly to try and get a picture of what happened next but for half an hour nothing much happened. Cars left the university in a steady stream via the gate and I saw students walking across the lawn and going into the Halls of Residence, presumably to get ready for the evening ahead.

Eventually a caretaker came and locked the Samuel Beckett Building. Ten minutes later I saw Valentine driving his car away from where he'd parked it. He was alone.

I rewound the tape and watched again. Jason definitely hadn't left the building. There was no way he could have got out after Valentine left without setting off the alarm. This led me to ask myself an important question. How, indeed, did Valentine get out of the building without using the main doors?

Knowing I couldn't get that information from the tape, I unlocked the door to the viewing room and walked quickly out of the Media Centre and down the stairs, going out of the building and around to the far side where Valentine had parked his car. There was a fire exit there. He must have parked his car just outside it, knowing the cameras would not pick him up. I thought about the tape; about the mysterious object in Valentine's pocket and the exit via the side door. Jason *had* left the university in Valentine's car, I realised. In the boot.

The wood was dark and looked like a jungle. 'It's a jungle out there.' The woman was drunk. She laughed as she thought about the jungle. What were they going to do? Fuck in the bushes?

The girl was carrying the video camera so the woman couldn't see her. Little bitch, show your face. Which bitch was which? I, N or S. Maybe there were others she didn't know about. She took another swig from the bottle of gin. Glasses were no good; they just spilled.

She could hear the girl's voice, though, talking to the husband. 'Why do we have to film this?' he kept asking.

The girl's replies were evasive. 'Shut up and keep walking. You can take the camera if you want.'

It was a dark and stormy night and the woman's husband was in the wood with a crisp-voiced girl.

'It's so we can't stitch each other up,' she said finally.

I lit a cigarette and stood by the exit door, breathing quickly and recapping everything I now knew. So Valentine had bundled Jason's body into his car and driven around for a while, presumably wondering where he should dump it. The Blue Dolphin seemed like a logical choice, and all the stuff Al had told me now made sense. Jason hadn't *gone* to the Blue Dolphin – he had been dumped there, out the back where no one would see it happen. Valentine, not knowing much about the club scene, must have thought that all the young people inside would be in as much of a mess as Jason. But one of his big mistakes had been to assume that people would think the boy had just left the club and collapsed out there. I had known for a while that this hadn't been the case but now, along with all the other pieces of the puzzle, the information was in the right place to make sense.

Now I knew exactly what had happened to Jason, I had to find out what had gone on with Stephanie. I turned and walked back into the building, to go my office and use the phone.

The man pointed at the ground, or to be more accurate at the body on the ground.

'You haven't fucked her?' asked the girl.

'Just like we said,' said the man, the murderer-husband.

The girl took a soggy piece of rubber from a plastic bag and showed it to the man then gave him the stick.

'Do what you've got to do.' She looked away as he turned it into a piece of incriminating evidence.

'Whose did you use?'

'You'll find out when they arrest him.'

The woman fast-forwarded at this point; the dialogue wasn't very interesting. She stopped when she got to her favourite part, the part with the saw. She took another swig from the bottle and watched it again.

CHAPTER TWENTY SEVEN

Dreams of Virtue and Fame

My stomach turned as I walked up the stairs, wishing I could tell someone what I knew but understanding that for the moment all the seemingly trivial pieces of information I had made sense only to me.

A few calls to Directory Enquiries provided the number I wanted and without wasting any more time I picked up the receiver of the heavy institutional phone and dialled tentatively, hoping my gut feeling was correct and that I wasn't going to embarrass myself too much. The phone number was for the archive section of the Oxford local newspaper and my rationale for phoning it was this: I needed to know why Nadia had come here. I guessed there had been a crisis at Oxford, but I needed to know what it was. There had to have been some trouble – why leave such a prestigious post otherwise? Here she was in a provincial university, living in the same town as her sister. Something must have happened, and judging by the scale on which Nadia appeared to be messing up now, I suspected it may have been something big enough to hit at least the local news.

'Archive,' said a friendly, high-pitched woman's voice.

'Hello,' I said. 'I'm not sure exactly what I'm looking for but . . .'

'Do you know the year?' she asked efficiently.

'Last year,' I said. 'I think.'

'Is it a particular issue you're looking for or coverage on a story?'

'Story,' I said. 'Something on a scandal in the university?'

The woman giggled. 'There's plenty of that in most editions,' she said. 'Can you be more specific?'

'Science,' I said. 'Research students?'

'Well, there's the Nadia Raven story,' she said thoughtfully. 'That was last year.'

'Yes! That's it,' I said excitedly. The woman's tone remained serious.

'Are you local?'

'No,' I said, thinking, *This is it!* and wondering why she was asking these questions.

'You probably won't have heard the story then. Her lawyer put an injunction on when the nationals tried to snap it up.'

'So what happened?'

'This is rumour, okay?'

'Yeah, whatever.'

'She had to leave the department after speculation that she had been involved in unethical research.'

'What kind of "unethical research"?' I asked, feeling my heart pound deeper and faster in my chest.

'Use your imagination,' said the woman. 'It was abroad, and involved people and experimentation. I can't tell you more than that, I'm afraid.'

'Oh,' I said, disappointed.

'You could try the university,' she said. 'They might be more helpful.'

I spent the next ten minutes phoning around the Science Departments at Oxford, being met with secrecy, scorn and unhelpfulness as soon as I mentioned the name Nadia Raven. But when I used a different approach and rang the Registry to get details of what her research project had been I struck gold. They only had to say three words and I had enough to work out what she was playing at.

There was only one piece of information missing now,

and one last clue to find. It was almost quarter to five which meant I had just over ten minutes before the Professor finished his meeting. I needed to get back into his office and check something I'd missed the first time, and I had to do it now, before he came back.

I couldn't believe I hadn't explored the Professor's computer the first time round. The massive dirty-white PC was the focal point of the room and I anticipated that it would hold all sorts of useful information which, no doubt, I wouldn't have time to read. I only needed to find one thing, though, to see if my suspicious were correct.

Nadia's Oxford crisis had confirmed three things for me: she was ambitious, unscrupulous, and didn't care what she did to people. She had sucked in the Professor somehow, intending him to be a part of her research. She had managed to get rid of her sister, who was too curious, and Stephanie, who knew too much and on whose head she could experiment. What could she have told the Professor to make him go along with the whole plan? I had an idea about what she would need from him, but what would she offer him in return? Not sex, he was getting that from Stephanie and Isobel. What then? What would the Professor value more highly than sex and be prepared to kill for? It had to be something to do with the druggy dream that he'd articulated at the gathering. But what?

Valentine had organised his hard drive into a complex system of folders within folders. Most were work-oriented but I homed in on the one marked *Private* which opened to display a number of files. Most were DTP documents with the letters BR in the title. I assumed these must be flyers for Beyond Reason that Stephanie had helped design. The word-processing files looked more interesting and had titles like: *Flying, Up Again*, and *DeadAlive*. I double clicked on the title of one of them but it didn't open. Instead a small dialogue box appeared with a soft bleep, asking for a password.

I sat there for a few seconds wondering whether I should abandon this but, being me and loving puzzles, I had to give it a try. And the fact that all these files were password-protected must mean I was on the right track.

If only I knew the password.

Thinking logically, I quickly entered the first word that came into my head: *Stephanie*, which led to the bleep again and the words *Access Denied*. I tried *Nadia* then *Beyond Reason*. *Password Must Be One Word Only*, I read.

Then followed all the drug words I thought someone like Valentine might use: *e; ecstasy; high; pill; pleasure*. Nothing. Then all the key words from Beyond Reason that I could remember: *nirvana; future; leader; orange*; and *Freddy* and then *Future*. Still nothing.

I thought about Valentine's liaison with Nadia and her research and, thinking creatively, entered the word *serotonin*. I really thought I had it, but again nothing.

I sat back and sighed, knowing I would have to get out of here really soon. It was silly to have tried really – I didn't know enough about Valentine to be able to second-guess his password. For all I knew it could be the name of the first dog he'd owned or his mother's maiden name. But then I thought about what I actually did know about this man. Thinking, laterally and moving away from my own ideas about what he was and what he thought, I let my mind drift towards the following question: What does Professor Valentine value more than anything else in the world? Answer: *Himself*.

In the password box I entered the word *Valentine* and hit the carriage return. The box disappeared and the file started to open. Bingo! I'd done it.

Unfortunately the contents of the file didn't warrant the effort I'd put into opening it. It was a short story, presumably written while the Professor was off his head on drugs, dated 29 April last year and practically unreadable. I closed it and scanned the rest of the files until I found one called *Digesting Pure Pleasure*, dated 17 October 1996. It was another short story, more coherent than the first one and featuring a rather perverted sex scene which led into the following piece of dialogue.

> *– I want it so much.*
> *– Yes.*
> *– Will you help me get it?*
> *– Oh, yes. I'm surprised I never thought of the idea myself.*
> *– It's got to be the best feeling in the world, hasn't it? Real serotonin. Better than any synthetic drug.*

And then I knew. Leaving the office and breaking into a run, I left the building and got over to the main block as fast as I could. On my way I passed the Professor hurrying towards the Samuel Beckett Building, past the yellow university mini-bus into which the first-year students were already climbing, but I didn't pay much attention to these details. I needed to get up to the science labs to see if my terrible suspicion was correct.

CHAPTER TWENTY EIGHT

When the Curtain Comes Down

I could have walked back into my office and called the police. The problem was, I still didn't have any real evidence, and certainly nothing to rival the conclusive DNA test results that the police were so pleased with. So I was going to have to continue finding the last pieces myself and had a feeling the biggest piece of evidence would be found somewhere around the labs.

I saw the camera watching me as I walked up the stairs to the Science Department and shivered, wondering what comings and goings it had recorded over the last year and what sinister motives lay behind them.

The department covered three floors of the main block and each year was assigned a floor for lectures, seminars and lab work. Nadia Raven's office was the last on the right on the top floor, down a hallway marked 'Third year and Postgraduate Only'.

I took my time walking down the hallway, using the opportunity to look at everything. As I went through the two sets of heavy double doors I noticed their keypad locks. They were the same as the ones in the Media Centre and, as you would expect, were not locked during the day. I supposed that gave another level of security to the unfilmed areas up here. Whenever Dr Coombes wanted to stop people wandering around all he would have to do was flip the latches on the doors.

I looked at the silver and white labs to either side of me as I walked down the corridor and could see why research students wanted to come here. I didn't know much about science but I knew that resources were scarce in universities everywhere. It must have been a pleasant surprise for Nadia, I thought, when she had to leave Oxford in such a hurry, to find something like this so near her sister.

The pristine whiteness around me was comforting until I realised that I hadn't seen another human being on this floor so far. I looked at my watch. It was past five o'clock and as the video had shown, this was when everyone left to go home. Although it was clear Nadia was staying late. As I approached her door I could hear the phone ringing inside and then a crisp voice, cold and impatient. I stood still and listened, only moving away from the door and into a lab opposite to hide once it was clear the conversation was nearing a conclusion.

'*Yes?*'

'*It's me. I'm just about to go.*'

'*I'll put everything you need in the back of the bus if you just give me a minute.*'

'*Good.*'

'*Remember to use the two girls you told me about – the normal ones. I don't want anything to go wrong. We won't get another chance, you know.*'

'*Is it really going to work?*'

'*I hope so. It had better.*'

'*I've waited a long time for this.*'

'*Me too. See you soon.*'

The woman gathered up the syringes and the glass bottles and put them in the opaque bag. She opened her door and walked out, making sure to close it firmly behind her. There was no one about but you couldn't be too careful. Especially now.

She wondered how her ex was doing with the police. It had been a shame he didn't have an alibi for that night he'd walked to the woods looking for her, and that the stick they'd used had been one he'd touched, without even knowing, one night when he was asleep.

I waited until Nadia entered the stairwell at the end of the long corridor then used my key to slip into her room, almost jumping out of my skin when I heard the door slam behind me, heavy on its springed hinges. I tried to stop feeling so frightened but it was difficult. I knew that if anything happened to me up here then no one would find out about it until it was much too late.

I stood with my back to the door, trying to focus on Nadia's office, knowing I had to search it before she came back. The small room was filled with books and journals, most of which stood on the shelves lining the wall to my left. Below the shelves was Nadia's desk, covered with bits of paper and chemical diagrams which surrounded a large university computer. The wall to my right was made of glass and I could see through to a small lab which seemed connected to this room but not to any of the others. Although I was sure it couldn't have been intended as Nadia's private laboratory, I suspected she used it as such. There was a door connecting with it in the far right-hand corner of the room, at the end of the glass wall.

There was an end-of-term feeling about the office; the bin was full of screwed up pieces of paper and the surfaces looked as if they had recently been tidied. A suitcase in the corner aroused my suspicions and a quick flick through the top drawer of Nadia's desk confirmed them. A huge pile of cash lay there, ready no doubt for when she would eventually disappear without trace. My eyes scanned the room and I saw that the wall straight in front of me was lined with two sets of dark wooden cupboards. Between them was what seemed to be a work bench, which was also made out of dark wood and had a little sink set into it. For some reason this part of the room reminded me of my school lab rather more than anything else up here had done. I remembered finding hideous things in cupboards there and starting an anti disection campaign in the school after that. I smiled when I remembered how naïve I'd been, thinking I would change the world.

One of the brown cupboards was padlocked. I shivered as I looked at it. Was that the place I would find it? There was only one way to find out.

I opened the cupboard next to the one that was padlocked and discovered what I'd thought I would. The partitions were only held in place with four screws. I remembered helping Anthony with his mum's DIY fitted kitchen and hating every minute of it. I was glad I'd helped out now, though, because it only took me two minutes to unscrew the partition with a one pence piece.

The light was too bad for me to see what was in the next cupboard, but I could almost make out the outline of a large container. I reached in and felt that it must be glass. Not wanting to see what was inside, but also realising that this was why I was here, I pulled the glass jar slowly towards me.

The accomplice placed the items in the back of the mini-bus and walked quickly back up the stairs, not wanting to leave her office deserted for too long. All the incriminating evidence was rather too close for comfort today, because tonight she would get to see whether her experiment would work.

She still couldn't believe she had sucked him in so well. A lot of it was to do with the way she sucked, of course. All she needed to do was find out what someone's dream was and then exploit it. So she had set him up. Stupid bastard. If he'd known anything at all about science he should have been able to work it out. Or maybe not. Did he really think she was doing all this to give him his nirvana? All she needed was the remaining data from her big experiment. And for that she needed a human test. Did he really think she could extract serotonin from a load of teenagers? What a prat! He was going to die, just like the others, but at least she would know what the side effects were. Lab rats were only viable up to a point. She preferred using real rats, though: rats like Valentine – sad Freddy Fuckwit.

The accomplice, or rather the instigator, walked the last few feet to her office suspiciously. There was noise in there; a tapping – a telephone conversation.

Nadia flung open the door and there was the girl with the curly hair and blue and green eyes, looking just the way Philip had described the mysterious journalist.

Bitch!

I had expected to see Stephanie's face glaring out at me, but of course why would Nadia have kept the entire head? Instead there was a brain, too big to belong to an animal and, judging by its secret location, almost definitely Stephanie's. Various holes in the tissue and bits of tube lying around in the cupboard suggested it had indeed been experimented on.

I picked up the phone to call the police but didn't get very far. I had only just begun talking to the switchboard operator when the door burst open and in flew Nadia, red-faced, angry, and looking *murderous*.

She threw herself at me and grabbed me by the hair, pulling it hard and shrieking obscenities into my ear.

'You fucking bitch! You slag!' she shrilled, digging her nails into my head as she tore out my hair by its roots.

'Get *off*!' I shouted, panicking and attempting to wriggle away from her increasingly painful grasp. She grabbed my chin, pushing her face closer to mine as increasingly foul language tumbled out of her cerise lips. I found this scared me more than anything else and trembled inside, my whole body becoming cold as she dug her nails into my cheek and tried to poke at my eyes. I tried desperately – almost hysterically – to pull away but found I couldn't move. She had my face covered with one hand and my hair in the other. We were tangled up in each other, she with the upper hand and I flailing miserably, unable to get free.

Then I snapped.

I had never been the fighting type and therefore had no practice at all in any of these manoeuvres. The only time I had ever hit anyone was when I was eleven; a boy had been taunting a friend in the school playground, calling her vile racist names, and I snapped then as I did now, running after him and hitting him in the face, breaking his nose and his pride. Now as then I was suddenly and inexplicably taken over by a strength and ferocity I would have sworn I didn't have in me. Not knowing what to do, but finding my limbs moving independently from my brain, I elbowed Nadia hard in the stomach with my left arm, barely noticing the large gash she left in my cheek as she fell backwards and doubled up in pain.

Full of adrenaline, I launched myself at her, driving her further back from the workbench until she was almost pressed up against the door. My slight disbelieving pause at this moment almost became my downfall as she straightened up and grabbed my right arm which I had lifted in order to try and grab the lapels of her lab coat. Automatically my left hand closed into a fist and swung backwards, gathering momentum as it changed direction and hit her full in the face, hard.

I gasped as I saw her fall, lips crumpled and swollen, blood gushing from her nose. I'd never realised that I knew how to punch someone.

She lay on the floor and looked up at me angrily.

'What fucking paper are you from?' she screeched, clutching at her bleeding face in disbelief. She looked small on the floor: in fact she *was* small, a slighter, more sparrow-like woman than I'd seen on the tape, and from here it was easy to see that she'd have difficulty matching me in a fight.

I grabbed some tissues from the desk and handed them to her, pushing her back down with my foot when she tried to sit up.

'Stay there,' I said shakily.

'I'm not going to do anything, *Nancy*,' she said, pronouncing my alias sarcastically but lying back down nevertheless.

'Look, I know everything,' I said. 'I know what you did to Stephanie and I know what you did to Jason. I even know *why* you did it.'

'Yeah, right,' she said sulkily.

'What was it this time?' I asked. 'Don't tell me – an *anti-depressant*, am I right?' The look on her face told me that I was so I continued.

'Synthesised serotonin,' I mused. 'A multi-billion dollar market. Or so your friend was telling me. Philip *was* your friend, wasn't he? Or maybe more than a friend. A friend who slept with you. I bet that was convenient when you needed to get hold of somebody else's sperm. Such a shame he's now been charged with murder.

'So let's see if I've got this right. You leave Oxford in a blaze of publicity. We both know why. Then you run away to your sister's and get a job at the local university. You give up on your old research and think about new projects. What could make you a billionaire? The new Prozac – not just a miracle cure for desperate depressives but a lifestyle enhancer. But you had two problems, didn't you?'

Nadia looked at me sullenly, her swollen lip hanging open as if she couldn't believe what she was hearing.

'I'll tell you what they were,' I said. 'You needed to get at some real serotonin to study and you needed a real brain to experiment on. It was nice of poor Stephanie to solve both those problems for you, wasn't it? And so convenient. I bet she was always in the way, hanging around the Professor like a puppy all the time, filling his head with all sorts of ideas. There was only one idea you were interested in, though.

'Let's see. You met Valentine on Isobel's birthday, on the sixteenth of October last year. He told you about Beyond Reason and some of his hopes and dreams. I bet you couldn't believe your luck. You slept with him that night and cooked up this idea which he thought was his. What was it? Oh, yes. You were going to make the Professor a miracle drug, weren't you? Better than Ecstasy; better than anything Philip could conjure up in his lab. I'm assuming that what you were really going to do was inject him with some mega-dose of your anti-depressant, to see what it did to him, am I right? And then, let's see . . . Suitcase. Money. You were planning to kill him as well, weren't you? Or maybe your drug would do that all by itself. Then you were going to disappear.'

As I spoke Nadia's face grew more thunderous and bloody as she scrubbed at it with the pink powdery tissues, but there was something else that got me thinking: a twinkle in her eye and the briefest glance at the clock behind me. As I had been talking a phrase I'd heard her use on the phone earlier resonated uncomfortably in my head. *Remember to use the two girls you told me about –; the normal ones. I don't want anything to go wrong. We won't get another chance, you know.* The field trip . . . *Shit!*

That was the bit I hadn't worked out. The Professor was taking those students, or at least two of them, off to certain death. Suddenly it all became clear. Nadia hadn't corrected me when I'd talked about the experiments on Stephanie's brain (as if she would) but I'd missed the whole purpose of it. It wasn't just experimentation: it was *practice*. Practice for something Valentine was going to attempt with two other students later on. There was something that needed to be taken from their brains that Nadia was going to use as a final ingredient in her magic potion. The notion was so implausible I almost rejected it, but the mad malevolent expression in her eyes just before she averted them to the clock confirmed what I thought.

So I looked up at the clock too, following Nadia's eyes. At that instant she pulled herself up, grabbed a heavy stapler from the desk and hit me on the side of the head with it. The time when I'd glanced at the clock was quarter to six.

When I came round it was five past.

Everything came back to me in an instant. Nadia, the field trip. Where the hell was it and where had she gone? I noticed that the suitcase was now missing and when I looked in the drawer, so was the money. I picked up the phone to call the police but nothing happened. Naida had taken the phone cable with her when she went.

I approached the door as quickly as I could, feeling my head pound with every step I took. An uncomfortably sticky wet patch of something had collected in the creases of my neck when I had been out cold on the floor. I reached up to touch it and almost passed out when it turned out to be congealed blood. My head swam as I wondered, irrationally, whether she'd slit my throat and I hadn't noticed (like a film I once saw) but then I remembered my gashed cheek, still wet and oozing fresh blood, which I wiped from my fingers on to my jeans.

I took the door handle in my hand and pressed firmly downwards, feeling a formidable resistance as it refused to move anywhere at all, indicating it was locked from the outside. No problem, I thought, and reached for my master key. But there was no keyhole on this side of the door. I was trapped.

Or at least that was what Nadia had intended. Thinking quickly, and still holding the key, I walked over to the glass lab door in the corner of her office and tried that instead, quickly punching in the keycode 002512 to free the second latch. The door opened heavily as I pushed it and I ran through into the shiny white lab, almost slipping on the polished tiles in my haste to get out of the main door to the corridor, where I was met with three more keypad locks before I reached the stairwell.

I knew where the Professor was, on the field trip. I just didn't know where the hell I'd find it. I knew where Nadia was as well: anywhere else in the world. There would have been no point in killing me – she'd just locked me up to give herself time to get away. She had been clever and cut her losses. But the Professor wouldn't know that. I'd heard her on the phone talking about talking him some equipment. There were no prizes for guessing what he was going to do with that.

I ended up standing breathlessly at the bottom of the stairs, wondering where I should go next. I had to find the field trip. One of the 'normal' students was bound to be

Beth and I knew now that she was in terrible danger. I didn't have time to hang around and tell anyone here what I suspected (as if they'd believe me) so I ran across the car park to my car and opened the door, slamming it hard and locking myself in. I picked up my mobile and switched it on. All it said was *NO SGL*. I considered jumping out of the car and running up to my office but knew there wasn't enough time. I started the engine and drove out of the university without looking back.

I stopped at the first phone box I found and scrabbled around in the car looking for the right change. I dialled Mum's number. My brother answered.

'Nat,' I said urgently. 'Do you know where Beth's gone?'

'She's on that field trip,' he said. 'What's wrong? What's happened?'

'Nat, she's in danger. Do you know where the field trip is?'

'No. What's going on?'

'Are you sure you don't know? It's really important.'

'It might be in one of her folders,' said Nat. 'She left a pile of them here yesterday with her diary and stuff. I'll go and have a look.'

'Hurry up,' I said, gasping for breath. I felt in my pocket and found a packet of cigarettes. My hands were shaking almost too much to light one, but I just about managed it. I waited a few moments, looking round all the time in case Nadia turned up, then Nat came back on.

'Lily?'

'Yes?'

'It's the moors somewhere, I think. She's written something about it in her diary, but it doesn't say exactly.' He paused and I could hear him breathing quickly. 'She was telling me about it the other day, I just wasn't listening.'

'Is it anywhere near a place called Salten?' I asked, thinking quickly. What better place to commit a double murder than down that lonely track?

'It rings a bell,' said Nat slowly. 'Yes! It was somewhere near Salten. What's going on?'

'Don't worry,' I said. 'Thanks.'

I picked up the phone to call the police this time and then I got back in the car and started to drive.

CHAPTER TWENTY NINE

And the Circus is Through

---

*The man drove the mini-bus, oblivious to the chattering and noise
in the passenger seats behind him. Someone was skinning up on the
back seats, trying to hide what they were doing. He didn't see why.
Surely everybody knew how young and . . . what was that new
word . . . Hip? Yes, how young and hip he was.*

*The students were excited and apprehensive about the field trip
– the ones who were here that was. Two were missing, Zoe and
Jay. Never mind, it was probably a good thing really. Those two
always caused trouble.*

*The students were in fact more curious than anything about the
whole 'field trip' thing. Why were they going so far away? The
Professor had said it was a creative writing exercise (why weren't
they doing it with that new teacher?) which they'd had to prepare
for like mad. They were supposed to bring three pieces of writing to
read out, but now it looked, to Beth at least, as though this was just
going to be one long, boring party.*

*She turned to her companion, in her opinion the only other
'normal' person on the mini-bus, and smiled.*

'Are you all right, Bron?'

'Yeah.'

*'Why haven't you been coming to classes recently? Are you
okay?'*

*'You might as well know,' said Bronwyn. 'Everyone's going to
soon.'*

'What?' hissed Beth excitedly.

'*I'm pregnant,*' *said Bronwyn.* '*And you'll never guess who the father is.*'

'*Jay?*' *asked Beth, not realising that it wasn't a game; that she wasn't supposed to guess. Bronwyn's face became pale. She'd been having a 'secret' affair with Zoe's boyfriend for months now, and wasn't aware that Beth knew anything about it.*

'*No, actually,*' *she said. And then she said something she knew would get a reaction; she just hadn't anticipated quite how far-reaching the implications would to be.*

An hour later the mini-bus trundled over the small bridge then wound its way unsteadily down the narrow farm track. The plan went smoothly – or as smoothly as he could have hoped.

The two girls sat chatting by a tree, separate from the others, not drinking the wine or smoking the spliffs. The man thought his students must think he was so cool, sitting there with them, taking joints from them and just being so with it. As he had anticipated it wasn't long before they were all high on something or other. What was it they kept saying – 'I'm off my head'? Whatever. Then he sent them off in twos, to the moors, ostensibly to see what kind of writing would emerge from being lost, cold and wet in the middle of the night.

'*This was such an amazing idea,*' *said Lottie, as she wound her way through the woods with Hélène and Lisa. They were supposed to be in twos, but Lisa had ditched Richie Lettuce because he kept trying to get off with her, and had gone with her best friends instead.*

Richie thought the whole thing was a bit tame, really. And the Professor, he was so sad, trying to be like his students; taking drugs and saying all those ridiculous things. Even Richie, whose first language was Spanish, knew that English expressions like 'with it' just weren't cool. Bored, lonely and abandoned, he turned back towards the clearing with the intention of walking down the lonely track to Salten to get to the pub in time for the football (if they had satellite, which he thought unlikely in this rural vacuum). How funny that would be: all the others lost, cold and lonely on the moors, but Richie Lettuce warm, comfortable and pissed down the pub.

★   ★   ★

I drove as fast as I could, and badly by my usual standards, overtaking on bends, and breaking the speed limit by an embarrassing amount. I didn't care. I just had to get there in time. The police were on their way, but I suspected they were some distance behind me. I just had to get there.

All the pairs left to go off on to the moors except one.

'Could you stay behind for a moment, please?' he had said.

Beth and Bronwyn looked at one another. What could they have done to get into trouble? They were the hardest working members of the class and not usually singled out for attention.

'I've got a different project for you two,' said the Professor, smiling nicely. 'Since you're both a bit beyond all the stuff the others are doing.'

The two girls looked at each other, flattered, and giggled a bit, suddenly liking this man more than they had done in the past.

'So what do you want us to do,' asked one of them, the Professor couldn't remember her name.

'Well,' he said, leading them through the bushes and past some trees, 'you won't get wet and cold like the others, that's for sure.'

He laughed and so did they.

Small, brown and dingy, the shed stood behind some undergrowth and was almost impossible to see from the track or the main clearing. Its location was perfect, and the Professor had fitted two metal loops, one on the doorframe and one on the door itself, in order that a padlock could be used to secure the girls inside.

'So,' he said, once they reached the shed, 'You're going to be locked in here.'

One of the girls shivered.

'Not really locked?' said the other one.

'No,' he laughed. 'Just in your imagination. It will be a psychological lock.'

The girls were relieved. He held the door open for them as they walked in.

'It's warm in here,' said Beth, surprised.

'Yes, I even supplied a heater,' said the Professor, smiling.

Or at least the heater had been supplied, along with the other important items, by Nadia Raven. They had argued over what the cause of death for the two girls should be. Nadia had insisted that just leaving them to die from carbon monoxide fumes – supposedly from the faulty heater but in fact from the cylinder she'd stolen from the labs – would be sufficient. The gas was odourless, she'd said, and would provide the required unconsciousness in under an hour. Since death would follow two hours later, she saw no reason not to leave it at that.

The Professor had suggested instead that once the girls were unconscious he could administer some of the poisoned Aspirin and Ecstasy mixture. He pointed out that now the drug was, as it were, doing the rounds, it wouldn't look so suspicious if they took some and died. In the end they decided on a compromise: the gas to make them unconscious; the pills to kill them.

And then the elaborate bit – the excuse. He would say that he had sent all the students off to the moors, but these two naughty girls must have stayed behind without his realising and taken Ecstasy in the shed. He was even going to organise a dawn search for them when they didn't come back. Before then he would have removed the heater, the cylinder and the padlock – and, of course, part of their brains. And the minute prick of a needle would never show up in a post-mortem, he was sure of that, although Nadia didn't seem to care one way or the other. Valentine's only problem was getting back to the university to test the drug, and then somehow making it back here for the students in the morning.

He couldn't understand what Nadia's problem was. It was almost as though she didn't care about these important arrangements. When he'd suggested the Ecstasy instead of the poisoning she'd been positively blasé: not like a scientist at all.

Of course as far as Nadia was concerned, sitting on the train to London, he could leave their bloody heads on the village railings for everyone to see. She was long gone, and nobody would find her for a very long time.

The Volvo flew over the small bridge and skidded dramatically as I turned right on to the small farm track, almost running into a dark figure walking down the middle of it. I hit the brakes and felt the wheels lock dangerously, sending the car careering towards the figure who calmly stepped out of the way as I drove into a tree.

'Are you all right?' asked the boy, as I stepped out of the car. It was Richie Lettuce from the first year. He took one look at my face, which was still covered in blood, and at my wild-eyed appearance and gasped. I nodded my head and pulled a face. Crashing the car had not been part of my dramatic rescue plan.

'Are you sure?'

'Yes,' I said, quickly. 'Help me move the car. The police will need to get down here.'

'The police?' he asked, raising his eyebrows and smiling. 'Not a drug raid, I hope?'

'No,' I said, becoming exasperated. 'It's a bit more serious than that. Just help me move the car and I'll tell you on the way.'

'On the way where?' He moved reluctantly towards the back of the car. I didn't respond. Instead I hopped into the driver's seat and released the handbrake, steering hurriedly around the tree, shouting out for Richie to stop pushing once the car was clear. Then I clambered out and ran back to the road, shouting for him to follow.

'I might need you to help,' I called, starting to run as quickly as I could towards the clearing where the gathering had been held; not being able to see too well in the darkness, but using sound to make sure I kept on the hard crunchy track and off the soft squelchy grass. Leaving the car off the lane was a good idea, I thought, and it at least gave me the advantage of surprise. I just wished I'd brought a torch.

Richie caught up with me eventually and we both slowed to a halt in the clearing where the gathering had taken place. My eyes had adjusted to the dark now.

'Where are they all?' I asked, looking around the empty clearing, seeing nothing and hearing silence.

'On the moors,' said Richie. 'Except the Professor.'

'Where is he now?' I asked, breathless and desperate. I

couldn't be too late: that was too awful to contemplate.

'How should I know? What *is* going on?'

'What about Beth and Bronwyn?' I asked, ignoring the question. 'Where did they go?'

'Last I saw they were by that tree over there,' he said, pointing to the spot where the barbecue had been situated on Saturday night. 'They stayed behind to talk to the Professor about something, but I suppose they're *lost, cold and alone* on the moors now, just like everyone else.'

I must have looked confused because Richie explained.

'It's a creative writing exercise,' he said. 'A bit stupid, if you ask me. That's why I was going to the pub.'

'I see,' I said, eyes darting everywhere as I struggled to make sense of this.

How *clever*, I realised slowly, as it came to me. I bet that had been one of Nadia's ideas: send most of the students on to the moors but keep two behind . . . But where would they be? Suddenly I remembered the way Philip had dragged me away from the others on Saturday night, behind the bushes and then into that weird shed. That had to be where it was going on. I ran over to it, with Richie following close behind.

When I got there it was instantly clear what was going on. I saw the new padlock hanging from a new link which had been recently screwed to the doorframe, and through the partially open door I could just make out a shape moving around inside.

I hit the door hard with my hand, sending it flying open, shattering some glass bottles and startling the Professor, who straightened up and turned to face me. He was wearing gloves and what seemed to be a dust mask and holding a bag of big brown pills in his hand. In the corner were Beth and Bronwyn, unconscious but still breathing, lying limply next to a small table on which further scientific equipment was arrayed: syringes and a couple of petri dishes and more glass bottles. Although I'd been expecting to find something like this, I was absolutely shocked.

'Oh, fuck,' said Richie shakily as I took a step into the shed and pressed past the Professor, who just stood frozen, his mouth open in disbelief. I bent down and took the girls' pulses. They were both weak, but still evident. Through my horror and dread I felt the excessive heat in the shed and wiped my brow which was growing stickier and clammier with every second.

'What the fuck have you done to them?' asked Richie, still standing in the doorway, as shocked as Valentine and not being much use.

'Don't worry about that,' I said. 'We've got to get them out of here. They're being poisoned by the fumes.' I looked at the Professor and raised my voice. 'Can you tell me what it is and how long they've been in here?'

He didn't answer me, but my question seemed to galvanise him into action. He lunged towards me, grabbing one of the syringes from the table as he did so.

He fell on me, pushing me down on the ground; keeping me in place with his knee, which he jammed into my chest. I flinched as I felt something prick my arm.

'Shit!' I said, hardly able to breathe from the weight on my chest.

Richie sprang into action at this point and grabbed Valentine by the neck.

'I wouldn't do that if I were you,' said the Professor. 'Unless you want . . .'

And then I noticed the syringe sticking out of my arm; a needle with nothing in it. Potentially dangerous, except . . .

'Ignore him!' I shouted to Richie, feeling my head begin to swim. We had to get Beth and Bronwyn out of here. 'Pull him off me.'

'But the syringe!' said Richie, sweating and hyperventilating behind Valentine's taut body.

'Don't worry about that,' I shouted impatiently, using my free hand to grab Valentine by the balls. I dug my nails in and twisted, hard, making him fall back and lose his grip on me at which point Richie was able to pull him off and, clearly not being the fighting type, punch him rather ineptly a few times before they both fell just beyond the door outside the shed. The Professor fought back halfheartedly but I got the impression that now it was so obviously *over*, he didn't care what happened. Nadia had chosen her accomplice well, I thought. All he cared about was his dream.

My head was starting to swim from the fumes, odourless but definitely there, giving me a headache and making it hard for me to breathe. Once the weight of Valentine had gone I was left with the syringe dangling loosely and painfully, but not in any way *dangerously*, from my arm. Luckily he had made two big mistakes when he stuck the needle in me. If he had, as I assumed, been intending to inject me with air then it would have helped if he'd pulled the plunger up first and actually struck a vein. I withdrew the harmless but painful needle slowly and got to my feet, noticing a thin trickle of blood running down my arm. I threw the syringe down on the floor, noticing my vision was starting to go.

It must be carbon monoxide in here, I worked out, noticing the by now blurred old heater and the cylinder under the table. If it was having an effect on me after such a short time then I didn't want to imagine what it had done to Beth and Bronwyn.

I got hold of Bronwyn first by her legs and started dragging her towards the door. Summoning up strength I didn't know I had, I gathered her limp body into my arms and carried her outside where I laid her carefully on the ground. Then I did the same thing with Beth, while Richie kept the Professor busy with some nasty kicks to his shins.

'Did you give them anything?' I asked Valentine urgently, gesturing at the tablets he was still holding in his hand. He shook his head and I looked away from him in disgust. I considered telling him about Nadia then I decided he didn't deserve to know.

I put Beth and Bronwyn in the recovery position and sat

watching them for a while, checking their pulses every so often, hoping with all my heart that they were going to be all right.

When the police and the ambulance finally arrived I was so exhausted I could barely move.

CHAPTER THIRTY

Picnic

———❦———

The early-May sun shone high in the sky. I listened carefully to the moment of silence as everyone watched Mum walk down the stairs into the garden to join us. As soon as she had sat down, everyone focused their attention on me again.

'So how did you manage to carry them both?' asked Nat, looking at me wide-eyed. 'You must have been shitting yourself.'

'Well, I wouldn't put it quite like that,' I said, smiling and pouring more champagne for everyone. 'I don't know really. It's funny that when something's a matter of life and death, you seem to get all this strength from nowhere. I'm just so glad I got there in time – which was all thanks to Sue, of course.'

'*Moi*?' said Sue, laughing. 'How did you work that out?'

'Well, you did give me the master key – the *key*, you could say, to the whole thing.'

'Boom-boom,' said Nat, reaching across me to grab a cream cake from the plate Mum had brought out.

'You should have phoned the police long before it got to that,' said Mum, smiling at me reproachfully. 'I mean, we're all glad you're a hero and everything but . . . just promise me you won't do anything like that again?'

'You sound like the mum at the end of the Famous Five books,' said Nat, laughing.

'Shut up,' she said, hitting him with a cushion.

' "And we would have done it as well, if it hadn't been for you meddling kids," ' said Nat, pretending to be a *Scooby Doo* villain and receiving another swift hit with the cushion. 'Ow!'

'The famous who?' said Henri. He had come to visit, encouraged by the idea that his daughter was a local hero.

'Never mind,' I said. 'They're just making fun of me.'

'I think you were very brave,' said Beth. 'I dread to think what would have happened if . . .'

'Don't then,' said Nat, putting his arm around her protectively.

'What happened when you called the police?' asked Sue.

'Well,' I said, smiling at Jake Williams who was sitting on the other side of the picnic mat, 'first of all I had to convince them to come.'

'The problem was,' said Jake, 'Nadia and the Professor had planted Philip Danes's DNA at the scene. I shan't go into the details, but it was very convincing.'

'Yuk,' said Beth, grimacing.

'We thought we had the right guy,' Jake said. 'Luckily Lily was particularly insistent.' He laughed and did an impression of me. '*I've seen Stephanie's brain!*'

'So you believed her then?' asked Nat.

'We couldn't afford not to.'

'So what happened then?' asked Sue.

'Well, some of the team went straight to the university labs and I went with the others over to Salten,' said Jake.

'It was lucky I'd seen PC Williams – sorry, *Jake* – at the petrol station that night, since I was able to just give them directions from there. It's all a bit remote if you don't know it, which was precisely why the Professor chose it.'

'I live quite near there so I knew where she meant,' said Jake, helping himself to another cake and a cup of tea.

'You should join the police,' said Beth, who still had a bad cough from the carbon monoxide poisoning. She had only been kept in hospital overnight, but Bronwyn had suffered a bad concussion and some complications with her pregnancy and had been kept in for a week. It was by her bedside that

I'd eventually found Fenn, trying to get to grips with his new role of father-to-be.

'Don't bother trying to convince her,' said Jake. 'I've already tried.'

'I want to carry on teaching for a while,' I said. 'I mean, they haven't exactly got many literature lecturers at the university now.'

'So what exactly was Valentine going to do with us?' asked Beth.

'He was going to suck your brains out,' said Nat. 'With a straw.'

'Don't be disgusting,' said Mum. 'He wasn't, was he?'

'Well, not quite like that . . . but kind of,' I said. 'You see, once he and Nadia had worked out how to extract whatever bit it was she actually wanted from Stephanie's brain, they knew it would be easy to do the same thing to Beth and Bronwyn.'

'Would it have killed them?' asked Sue.

'Oh, yes,' I said, watching Beth shiver at the thought.

'I have never heard such a thing in all my years in medicine,' said Henri. 'This is entirely ridiculous and stupid.'

'Well,' I said, 'that was the point. I mean only someone like Valentine would have believed something like that to be possible. God knows what Nadia was actually getting him to extract.'

'She sounds like an absolute nutcase,' said Mum. 'How on earth did she ever persuade him to go along with it?'

'By making him think it was his idea,' I said. 'She did it very cleverly as well, I'll have to give her that.'

'So what were the three words they told you?' said Beth. 'You know, at Oxford.'

'*Curing male impotence*,' I said, laughing. 'Yet another way of making loads of money – and one with so many people desperate enough to have it tested on them. It didn't take much to work out that Nadia Raven wanted to make herself a millionaire by trading on other people's insecurities.'

'And bodily fluids, from the sound of it,' said Nat. 'How was she going to get away with that? I mean, if she'd found that her antidepressant thingy worked, wouldn't she have had to keep on killing people to get her magic ingredient?'

'No,' I said, looking to Henri for confirmation. 'I assume she would have cultivated it in rats or something.'

He nodded.

'How come you know so much about science?' asked Jake. 'I mean, all that stuff with the syringe and everything. It was a hell of a gamble to take.'

'I know a few basics,' I said, laughing. 'I'm no expert, but I suppose I've always been fascinated by all the equations and symbols and everything. The stuff with the syringe was just common sense, really. I mean, if there's no air in the thing, someone's hardly likely to be able to inject you with it.'

'It was very clever of you, though,' said Mum. 'I think I would have just been frozen with fear.'

'Doesn't fear drive you to action or something?' said Sue.

'It depends what type of person you are in the first place,' said Henri.

'So when's the court case?' asked Mum. 'I heard it would be soon.'

'Yes,' said Jake. 'I can't tell you very much, but we've more or less completed our enquiries so it'll be ASAP really.'

'I thought you would have had enough evidence by now, with the video and everything,' I said.

'The police move in mysterious ways,' he said, smiling.

'What video is this?' asked Henri.

'They filmed themselves cutting Stephanie's head off,' said Nat.

'That is seriously disgusting,' said Beth, visibly shivering.

'Why did they do this?' asked Henri, looking slightly bewildered. 'They must have known that it would be evidence.'

'That's why they did it,' I said. 'So that neither could drop the other in it. The plan was that if one went down, they could take the other with them.'

'Except Nadia knew she was disappearing anyway, right?' said Beth.

'Exactly,' I said. 'She must have known that the trail would lead to Valentine eventually. The whole thing with Philip's DNA was just a way of stalling the inquiry and the video was to stop Valentine grassing her up. She was safe, since she knew she would be gone by the time any important discoveries were made. And she was right.'

'Doesn't Isobel know where she is?' asked Nat.

'Oh, no,' I said. 'I mean, they'd never got on, and after Nadia stole Isobel's boyfriend and drove him to murder . . . She's just disowned her now, I think.'

'And it was the wife who had the video?' asked Sue, pouring herself another glass of champagne.

'Yes,' I said. 'She was looking for the address of one of Valentine's girlfriends and found it hidden in one of his drawers apparently.'

'Where is she now?' asked Mum.

'She was sectioned, wasn't she?' asked Sue.

'I think so,' I said, lighting a cigarette. I looked at Jake. 'Will she be giving evidence?'

'No,' he said. 'She's completely mad.'

'Well, who wouldn't be, married to that?' said Beth. 'I always knew he was a freak.'

'And you found her actually watching the video?' asked Nat.

'Yep,' said Jake. 'Over and over again.'

'I can't believe she didn't just call the police,' said Mum. 'Silly woman.'

'I think she might have been a bit too gone by that stage.'

'What about Nadia?' asked Nat. 'You really haven't any idea where she went?'

'Still searching, I'm afraid,' said Jake.

I looked at all my friends and family sitting on the picnic rug. I was pleased they were so proud of me. In fact, I hadn't stopped grinning since the press conference, when the Chief

Superintendent had thanked me by name. At last I felt I had done something worthwhile. It was too late for Stephanie and Jason of course, but as a result of everything I'd found out the Blue Dolphin had been closed down and Wesley and Dr Coombes were each facing separate charges of conspiracy to supply class-A drugs. It seemed that Coombes hadn't followed his own advice and had been making MDMA on college premises for some time. He then passed it on to Wesley who organised distribution via his club.

The Vice Chancellor made me acting Head of Literature, which made me simultaneously pleased and frightened. I tried to reinstate Isobel, but she was too involved in her new book or something. Fenn would be staying, of course, although I hadn't worked out how to get around the situation between him and Bronwyn, professionally or personally. Dale had made a full recovery, although I hadn't yet received another invitation for 'coffee'.

'Did Isobel know anything about what they were up to?' asked Sue, breaking into my thoughts.

'Not really,' I said. 'I mean, she gave me that book deliberately but only because she was bitter about what her sister had done to her. She wrote the book just after Nadia got chucked out of Oxford. She knew her sister was evil, I just don't think she realised how much.'

'So what happened at the end of the book?' asked Nat. 'I only got as far as page fifteen.'

Everybody laughed; he wasn't particularly known for his interest in literature.

'Nick kills Iain,' I said. 'Because of a woman.'

'Aha!' said several people at once, making the rest of us laugh.

'What are you going to do with the money, Lily?' asked Beth. I had been awarded £50,000 at the press conference, although the cheque was still sitting on my chest of drawers.

'I don't know,' I said. 'I'm going to go and see Mr and Mrs Duncan on Monday to discuss it with them. I don't want to accept the whole lot, I'd rather see some of it go to charity or something, if they really want to give it away.'

Jake said his goodbyes after a while and made me promise to ask him first if I needed any help in future. Sue said goodbye at the same time and walked up the path after him, trying to get a lift to the station. Nat and Beth went walking hand in hand down to the stream at the bottom of the garden and I helped Mum and Henri pick up all the cups, glasses and plates.

I watched them walk up the stairs together, chatting away, and stood still for a moment, just looking at the flowers in the garden. I heard a squeak behind me and then I felt Maude brushing around my legs, telling me she wanted food. I put down the stuff I was holding and picked her up.

'Look,' I said to her, pointing. 'There is the sky and the trees and the sea.' She squeaked and dropped out of my arms just before I could point out my favourite sight, the silhouettes of cows on the horizon.

I laughed and walked inside.

Epilogue

I stood at Eugénie's grave for almost an hour, telling her about everything that had happened, not having to censor it. I told her how frightened I had been and how frightened I still was: about the nightmares I sometimes had about that day in April.

She was the only one I could tell about Fenn. I had felt so euphoric when I walked up to him in the hospital. *Isn't it nice*, I'd thought, *that he's come to visit his old tutee?* I was so pleased to see him (the first time since his disappearance!) that I almost kissed him until I realised he was holding Bronwyn's hand. Then I didn't know what I felt. Shocked, betrayed, *stupid*. I was polite to her and asked how she was without catching Fenn's eye. Then I left.

Outside the graveyard I got into the cab that was waiting for me. Since the car was a virtual write-off I was going to have to wait a while until it was fixed, so I was relying on public transport (and cabs) to get me everywhere. Today was important: I was meeting Fenn to talk properly and get his side of the story.

I arrived at the tearooms at exactly four and walked in slowly, expecting him to still be on his way. Instead I found him there early, already drinking a cappuccino and smoking. He looked up at me and smiled.

'Thanks for coming, Lily,' he said. 'You look wonderful as usual.'

I smiled without meaning to and sat down. A waiter came over immediately and I ordered a double espresso.

'So,' I said, pulling out a cigarette and lighting it, 'you look tired.'

'Yes.' Fenn raised one eyebrow. 'The problems of life.'

'I heard.'

'It was an accident,' he said. 'A bloody stupid accident. I'm sorry.'

'Sorry?' I said. 'Why are you saying sorry to me? It's your life. You don't owe me anything, I don't *think*.'

'What do you mean?'

'That night we went out and I stayed at your friend's. We didn't . . . did we?'

Fenn laughed.

'You mean you don't know?'

I laughed as well and from nowhere our spark reignited.

'No,' I said.

'I hope I'd be more memorable than that,' he said. 'But to put your mind at ease, we got home, you collapsed on the bed and started snoring – daintily. I pulled the covers over you and left you a note. That was that. The next day I was on my way to Scotland.'

The waiter brought my coffee over and I took a sip from it, waiting for the information to sink in. So we hadn't even kissed.

'Scotland,' I said. 'So that's where you went.'

'To my sister's,' said Fenn sheepishly. 'I know it was cowardly and unprofessional, but it was such a shock.'

'Yes. I still can't believe it myself. What were you thinking of?' I didn't mean to show Fenn that I cared but as well as being a betrayed friend I was now also his head of department.

'What can I tell you? It was that horrendous Christmas party when the first years spiked the vodka with some bloody drug or other. I can't remember very much of it, to be honest, but when I woke up in her bed the next morning, Bronwyn was very clear about what had happened. I was just bloody irresponsible, and now I'm facing up to the consequences.'

'Yes,' I said.

'I did try to call you once, but you weren't in.'

'Well, I was busy,' I said. 'Spending all my time trying to clear your name.'

I looked down at my fingernails, embarrassed that I still cared.

'I didn't know,' said Fenn. 'I'm really sorry. I just got a bit of a fright. I didn't know about the DNA tests or anything. I never got the memo.'

'I don't mean to come on strong,' I said. 'I do understand why you went away. I just . . .' I sighed, not knowing how to get the words out, or what they should be.

'I know,' he said gently. 'I felt it too.'

He took a sip of his coffee and I did the same. We both lit cigarettes and sat in silence for a while.

'Well, I suppose none of that matters anymore,' I said. 'Now that you're doing the honourable thing.' He and Bronwyn were getting married in the summer, much to the disapproval of everyone else – including me. Bronwyn was delighted though, according to Beth, although I had the feeling there was a bit more to all this than met the eye.

'God,' said Fenn. 'The *honourable thing*. Do you think I'm mad?'

'No,' I said. 'I think you're honourable.'

'Did you say *horrible*?'

'No,' I said, laughing. '*Honourable*, you fool.'

'Really?'

'Yes. I suppose you would have to be a bloody hero, wouldn't you?'

'I suppose so,' he said sadly.

'As long as we're still friends?'

'The very best sort. And I think I'm going to need a friend.'

'I'll always be there,' I said. 'No matter what you do.'

Fenn smiled broadly and so did I, both of us knowing that the story wasn't quite over. But for the time being we could pretend it was, and so we sat drinking coffee and smoking for a while, chatting about nothing in particular, until the café shut and we said goodbye and went home.